You Were Always Mine

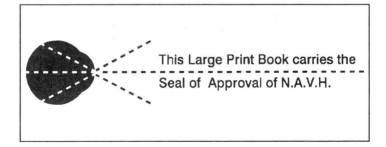

This Large Print Book carries the
Seal of Approval of N.A.V.H.

YOU WERE ALWAYS MINE

NICOLE BAART

THORNDIKE PRESS
A part of Gale, a Cengage Company

GALE
A Cengage Company

Farmington Hills, Mich • San Francisco • New York • Waterville, Maine
Meriden, Conn • Mason, Ohio • Chicago

LIBRARY OF CONGRESS CIP DATA ON FILE.
CATALOGUING IN PUBLICATION FOR THIS BOOK
IS AVAILABLE FROM THE LIBRARY OF CONGRESS

ISBN-13: 978-1-4328-6372-2 (hardcover)

Published in 2019 by arrangement with Atria Books, an imprint of Simon & Schuster, Inc.

Printed in the United States of America
1 2 3 4 5 6 7 23 22 21 20 19

This one is for my boys.

"You never really understand a person until you consider things from his point of view . . . Until you climb inside of his skin and walk around in it."

Harper Lee,
To Kill a Mockingbird

BEFORE

He was in over his head.

Coming here was a terrible mistake, and he regretted it so much he could feel remorse curdling like sour milk in his stomach. It made him nauseous, unsettled, and all at once he knew that he would vomit.

His palms slipped on the steering wheel as he veered off the highway and pulled onto a gravel road. Rocks hissed and popped beneath his tires, spraying a cloud of dust into the spiderweb of branches that arched overhead. He was going way too fast, and only realized it when he felt the give of the soft shoulder. It dragged the car toward the ditch, catching the tires and tugging so hard he could feel himself losing control.

Brakes, an unholy screech of rubber and metal and earth, and then, the back of his vehicle whipped toward a leaning oak tree and hit it square. The sound of the crash was dull and elemental, flesh on flesh instead of shattering glass or terrified screams. He barely uttered a sigh, but the impact made him bite his tongue clean through, and when he finally freed himself from the seat belt and wrenched open the door, he leaned over and threw up blood and bile and not much else.

He couldn't remember the last time he'd eaten. He couldn't remember why he had thought this was a good idea or what he'd hoped to gain from digging deeper. Oh, God. Now he was so far down he feared he'd never be able to climb his way up and out.

What had he done?

He passed the back of his hand over his mouth and reached around for the box of tissues that he kept in the armrest. But this wasn't his Grand Cherokee. It was a trade-in, or rather, a car that he had bought on the side of the road from some guy outside of Mankato. He wasn't even a dealer, just a farmer with a few vehicles parked at the end of his drive. The farmer gave him a rusting LeSabre and two thousand dollars in crumpled cash. Mostly fifties and twenties, the wad was so thick he had to split it into two stacks — one for each pocket. Even so, it was less than the Jeep was worth, but neither of them were in the mood to haggle.

It seemed like a fair enough trade at the time, but suddenly the car felt dirty and foreign, as unfamiliar as a stranger's bed. The odor of stale cigarettes lingered in the upholstery, and he realized he might vomit again.

He threw himself from the car, leaving the lights on and the engine running, and trying to avoid the mess he had already made in the pale dirt. The air was cold and sharp. Instantly sobering. He gulped a few ragged breaths, his chest heaving against the dress shirt he had picked up at a secondhand store. It was too tight, the frayed tie even more so, and he lifted a shaking hand to loosen the knot, undo a button.

The crisp autumn breeze, the way it slid cool fingers against his neck, began to steady him. A warm trickle made him raise his hand to his forehead and his palm came away hot and sticky. He realized with a start that he was bleeding. Had he hit his head on the steering wheel? The windshield? It didn't matter. The wound wasn't serious. He wasn't about to die from a head injury.

What now? The question was insistent, ever present, the dependable drum of his heartbeat in his ears. *What now? What now? What now?* It was the question he had been asking himself for months, and answering it had brought him here.

And he had no idea where he was.

A gravel road. A beat-up car. He had intentionally left everything of value in the safe at the run-down motel where he had rented a room on the second floor. There was nothing in his pockets save a single scrap of paper. And that was hollow comfort at best.

When he finally climbed back into the car and tried to put it in reverse, the transmission sputtered and clunked and refused to shift. He didn't know much about cars, but it didn't take a genius to guess that the axle was cracked. Spitting a curse, he thought of his cell phone tucked carefully away back in the room. There was nothing for him to do but turn off the car and walk for help.

A farmhouse? A nearby town? He could hit the highway and hitchhike, but now that the vehicle was quiet and the gravel road dark, the October night pressed in heavy and assured him that nothing could be done without drawing attention. He was bloodied, reeking of vomit, strange. He felt it coming off him like an odor, the sense that he was not who he was supposed to be. That everything about this night was wrong.

But as he was about to strike off in the direction of the nearest farm, headlights swung down the gravel road. Because the terrain was so wooded and the night so still, he hadn't paid attention to the faraway traffic of the blacktop less than a mile away. It streaked past at a distance, a blur of light and motion that seemed more like shooting stars in a distant galaxy than vehicles filled with people. Laughing, listening to the radio, dozing. They were as disconnected from him as the silver crescent moon that hung askance above the trees.

Still, he straightened his tie. Smiled. When the headlights touched his face, he was sheepish and apologetic, his mouth quirked charmingly and arms outstretched.

"Hey," he said as the car slowed down and the passenger-side window made its steady descent. He couldn't see the driver, so he took a careful, measured step and bent to peer inside. "I was in a bit of an accident and —"

He couldn't stop himself from recoiling, from shuddering as if the person in the driver's seat was an apparition, so freakish and grotesque he had no choice but to flinch in shock. But that was ridiculous. Flesh and blood. Nothing more. He took a breath, forced a smile. "What are you doing here?"

The moment the words were out of his

mouth, he knew the answer.

In some ways, he had known all along.

5554403686

CHAPTER 1

Mariah K.
24, Caucasian, GED
Short blond hair, blue eyes, average height
  and weight. Soft-spoken but articulate.
Little to no family support.
MAN/DEL CS, 36m, 16w

The kitchen was cold, the air flat and vacant. Lonely. Jessica shivered as she clung to the doorframe with one hand and bent to slide on her shoes, kitten heels in a leopard print that struck a dissonant chord in the stillness of the hollow room. *Coffee.* That's what was missing. Jess puffed a frustrated breath through her nose. Of course she had forgotten to make coffee.

Jess straightened up and crossed the kitchen at a determined clip, her shoes clicking a confident rhythm that left little room for remorse. But it was there.

Sometimes she missed him so much it ached.

For the fifteen years of their marriage, Evan had made the coffee. Every night, while Jess was smoothing night cream on her face and brushing her teeth with the baking soda toothpaste she preferred, he was grinding beans. Such a simple thing to do, and the little measuring scoop made the recipe foolproof, but nobody could brew a pot of coffee like Evan could. He set the timer for seven o'clock so that when Jessica walked downstairs in the slanting, early light, the house was fragrant and welcoming.

"Get a grip," Jessica whispered, flicking on the fixture above the sink and lifting the tin of Folgers from the cupboard. She didn't have time these days for grinding whole, gourmet beans, but the hit of caffeine was nonnegotiable.

While she measured the grinds and filled the carafe with water, Jess reminded herself again of all the reasons she had kicked him out. It was a daily ritual. Sometimes hourly.

Evan Chamberlain was a workaholic. Before he moved out, he had become an absent husband and father who was more committed to his caseload than his wife and boys. He was distracted and selfish, obsessed with the lives of his patients. Addicted to his phone. Evan stayed at work late and forgot her birthday and had become a roommate instead of a lover and friend. When he was home, he slept. And snored. Loudly.

In the end, Jess didn't have a choice. But in moments like these, when the house raised goose bumps along her arms, she missed him so much she felt scraped out, hollow.

"Are there any muffins left?"

Jess pivoted to find her thirteen-year-old son framed in the double-wide archway that opened onto the dining room. Beyond the harvest table she could see the welcoming arrangement of her creamy linen couches, the sweeping open staircase, the oversized front door hung with a rustic olive wreath. But Jessica wasn't admiring the view or the artful rearranging the interior designers had recently overcharged her for. She only had eyes for Max. He was rumpled and bleary-eyed, his mop of blond hair sticking up in every direction. She almost told him he was overdue for a haircut, but she bit back the comment and smiled instead. It didn't take much to set Max off these days. "Good morning, handsome."

He grunted.

"Breakfast before shower?" Jess asked, her tone wafer light. No response. Her smile crumbled away. "The muffins are gone, but there might be a blueberry scone in the breadbasket. Would you like me to scramble some eggs for you?"

"Nah."

"You love scrambled eggs. With cheese?"

"*I* want scrambled eggs." A voice from the hallway preceded the entrance of Jessica's baby — though he was hardly a baby anymore. Gabe padded into the kitchen in bare feet and football pajama pants that Jess realized were at least a size too small — the hems barely grazed his ankles. Gabe yawned noisily, shuffling across the linoleum floor with his eyes squinted almost shut. He reached for Jess and wrapped his arms around her, burying his face in her stomach. "Eggs with lots of cheese," he murmured against her. "That's my favorite."

Jess tried not to visibly melt at his touch. Max had accused her for years of playing favorites, but it was hard not to bask in Gabe's generous spirit. He was a lover, an encourager who was liberal with his affection and his laughter. These days, if Jess wanted to hug her firstborn, she had to steal it while he was sleeping. And even then she risked waking him up and making him furious at the weight of her hand on his forehead.

"Good morning, honey." Jess squeezed her youngest close. He had recently hit a growth spurt, and his head fit snugly against the curve below her rib cage, just above the soft spot that would have been his home for nine months had he grown in her womb instead of in her heart. Though that wasn't quite true. Gabe didn't exactly "grow in her heart" like the poem on the front cover of his baby album proclaimed. He appeared there overnight, an explosion of unexpected emotion that overtook her in the moment that Evan sat her down and said, "So, there's this boy . . ."

Gabe was a mushroom cloud, a force of nature, a big bang that defied every theory she had once thought to be true. He was a complete stranger and wholly her son.

"Eggs it is," Jess said, raking her fingers through his dark hair. He was, in so many ways, the opposite of his brother. "You too, Max? There's plenty of time."

"I'm good." He pushed back from the counter where he had been leaning and palmed an apple as he headed out of the room.

"That's it? You have to eat more than just an apple."

"I'll eat at school."

"Doughnuts," Jess muttered, remembering that she still hadn't written an email to the superintendent suggesting that maybe it wasn't the best idea to let the cheerleaders sell doughnuts before school.

"Why aren't there doughnuts at *my* school?" Gabe wondered, rubbing his face against her stomach and crumpling the sheer fabric of her blouse. It would be wrinkled for the rest of the day. Jess extracted herself carefully and kissed the top of his head. He smelled of coconut shampoo and shea butter and sleep, her favorite combination.

"Because doughnuts aren't good for you."

"Are eggs?"

"Yes." Jess grabbed the frying pan from the cupboard while Gabe went to riffle through the refrigerator for the egg carton. "On the bottom shelf," she told him. "Behind the yogurt. Be careful."

He brought the eggs to her attentively, eyes fixed and serious as he balanced the cardboard in small hands that still bore the chubbiness of his toddler years. In some ways, Jess wished that he would never change, that he could remain as innocent and sweet as the little boy who still believed that someday he could marry his mommy. But beneath that fragile yearning was the hope that life would get better with time.

That Gabe would grow out of all the things his doctors and therapists rather cavalierly chalked up to minor developmental delays. Some days, Jess would give almost anything to fast-forward to a time when Gabe's differences would be relegated to the past, a mere footnote in his personal history that she could smile tenderly about in retrospect. *Remember when . . . ?*

"Thank you," Jess said, giving him a genuine smile. "Why don't you put the orange juice on the table, too?" And then she was turning on the burner and cracking eggs and breaking the sunny yolks with the side of a spatula. She was so lost in her own thoughts she didn't even hear the phone ring until Gabe was answering it. "Manners!" she reminded him as she spun from the stove. "Remember, we say: 'Hello, this is the Chamberlains . . .'"

But Gabe was already chattering away, talking about eggs and orange juice and an upcoming kindergarten field trip to the fire station.

"Give it here." Jess motioned for the phone, and when Gabe didn't cough it up, she leaned over and pulled it from his hand.

"Hey!" he shouted.

"This is Jessica Chamberlain." She pressed a finger to her lips for Gabe's benefit, and shouldered the headset as she ran the spatula beneath the bubbling eggs.

"Is this 555-440-3686?"

"I suppose you'd know." Jess laughed, an edge sharpening her voice. What kind of telemarketer rang at seven in the morning? "You're the one who dialed it." She lifted a hand to the phone and would have switched it off without saying good-bye, when the man on the other end of the line stopped her with a word.

"Deputy Mullen, Mrs. Chamberlain. I hope I'm not catching you at a bad time."

Jess had frozen at the title "deputy," and the scent of browning butter and crisping eggs thawed her enough to give the spatula a final flick. She switched off the burner and grabbed a plate, sliding Gabe's breakfast onto it without the added benefit of melted cheese. He noticed.

"Mom! I wanted —"

She cut him off with a fluttering of fingers against his lips, but he was complaining loudly even as she hurried to the laundry room and pulled the pocket door shut behind her.

"Is this a bad time?" Deputy Mullen asked.

"No," Jess said, holding the door shut against Gabe. He was trying to slide it open, to chastise her for forgetting the cheddar that she had promised. "We're just getting ready for school. But, actually, Max isn't here right now. He's in the shower and —"

"Max?"

"Max," she echoed, and then realized belatedly by the tone of his voice that he had absolutely no idea who Max was. Jess didn't know whether to be relieved or alarmed. Relieved, she decided, and glided open the door to find some cheese for Gabe's eggs. He was banging away and wouldn't quit until he got what he wanted.

Thank God the phone call wasn't about Max. Thank God this had nothing to do with what had happened last weekend. "I'm sorry," she said, waving her hand as if this Deputy Mullen could see it. "We actually *are* a bit busy this morning."

"I'll only take a minute of your time. I'm with the Scott County Sheriff's Department and I'm calling because we have a couple of questions for you."

"Scott County?" Jess had located the shredded cheddar in the meat drawer and was sprinkling some on Gabe's eggs.

"Near Minneapolis, ma'am. And you're in . . . ?"

"Iowa," Jess said slowly. She paused with one hand on her hip as Gabe finally, blessedly, dug into his eggs. He hummed contentedly. "Who did you say you were again?"

"Deputy Mike Mullen. I'm calling because it seems there has been an accident, and we're wondering if you might be able to help us out."

"An accident? What kind of accident?"

"We'll get to that in a moment. May I ask you a few questions?"

"Okay." Jess drew out the word as she sank onto the bench of the breakfast nook across from Gabe. He was happy now that there was cheese on his eggs, oblivious to the fact that his mom was growing more tense by the second.

"Is your husband around this morning?"

Jess felt her skin prickle. This Deputy Mullen had done his homework. He knew the Chamberlains were at the other end of the phone number he had dialed. He knew the number was registered to Evan and Jessica. "No. No, he's not here." The words stuck in her throat, but she forced herself to say them anyway. "We're separated."

"And where does he live?"

"Across town. I'm not sure how this is relevant."

"Could you describe him for me, please?"

Jess sighed. "Evan's tall, medium build. Brown hair, brown eyes."

"Any distinguishing characteristics or birthmarks?"

All at once, the line of his questioning hit her. Jess's heart thudded painfully in her chest and she sat up straight, her gaze wide and panicked as she watched her son forking eggs into his mouth. He was blissfully unaware. Jess got up and walked into the dining room on the balls of her feet, as if the tap of her heels might alert her baby to the fact that a cop was asking some pretty terrifying questions.

"No." The word was barely a whisper. She tried again. "Evan has a scar from an appendectomy when he was a kid, but I suppose that's not unusual. You need to tell me what's going on here."

"There's been an accident," Deputy Mullen said again. "A body was discovered yesterday afternoon on public hunting land —"

"A body?"

"Middle-aged man, gray hair, one hundred and sixty-eight pounds. No . . ." He paused. A shuffle of papers, a word muffled with his hand over the mouthpiece of the phone. Then: "No identification."

Jess began shaking her head the second she heard "gray hair." Evan was forty-one, but his hair was a dark mahogany color that she had admired from the moment she laid eyes on him nearly twenty years ago. Even after all this time it was thick and glossy, not a streak of gray in it. And he had perfect eyesight — well, almost. He wore drugstore reading glasses at night sometimes when he was in the middle of a chapter and she wanted to sleep. He had left them in the nightstand next to his side of the bed when he moved out, and she had never bothered to return them. Not because she was malicious, but because she liked the way they looked sitting cross-legged beneath the desk lamp. The slender X of the tortoiseshell stems was homey, comforting. They seemed to say: *Be back soon.*

But Jess didn't say any of this. "It's not him," she breathed, and was surprised at the tears that had sprung to her eyes, the sudden quiver in her voice. "It's not Evan. It can't be. He's six foot two and a hundred and ninety pounds. What made you think it might be him?"

"I think we're getting a bit ahead of ourselves, Mrs. Chamberlain."

"Oh." She sagged a little and found herself leaning against the edge of the dining room table. It was such a relief she wondered how she had stood at all as these horrifying possibilities unfurled like ghosts in the air around her. "Why are you calling me?"

"We found your number written on a piece of paper in the victim's pocket."

"*This* number? You mean this phone number?" Jess shook her head. "But we don't even use our landline. We only have it for emergencies — for the boys or baby-sitters to use. It's not even listed."

"We're exploring every lead, Mrs. Chamberlain," Deputy Mullen said. "This is just one of them. Thank you for your help."

"I'm not sure I was very helpful."

"Could I take down your cell phone number in case we have any follow-up questions?"

Jess rattled it off without hesitation, eager to hang up and leave such an unsettling conversation behind her. Deputy Mullen would never call again — there would be no reason to. It was ridiculous to think that the Chamberlains' home phone number had been written on a piece of paper in a stranger's pocket. In a *dead man's* pocket. "Maybe it's a code," she wondered out loud. "A password or a combination or something."

"Possibly. Thanks again for your time."

"Of course." Jess couldn't keep the relief out of her voice. But when she turned off the phone, it shook in her hand.

"Who was that?" Max stood at the bottom of the stairs, his damp hair the color of sand and his blue eyes narrowed. Her landlocked surfer boy. She wanted to tuck a piece of that long hair behind his ear, but Max was looking at her as if he already didn't trust what she was going to say. He was wearing an old shirt of his dad's, a fading maroon T that proclaimed Gryffindor the quidditch champs. Jess had made fun of Evan for buying it, accusing him of being too old to pull it off, but it looked great on Max. Jess fought the urge to smooth it across his shoulders.

"No one you know," she said truthfully. She was already forgetting about the call, filing it away someplace where she would never have to think about it again. What a morbid way to start the day.

Max eyed her skeptically. The set of his jaw was tough, but it was difficult for him to ask: "Was that about . . . ?"

He couldn't finish. Didn't have to. "No," Jess said quickly. "Principal Vonk told me that they wouldn't press charges if you do your part. Tomorrow morning —"

"Yeah." Max cut her off abruptly and swung his backpack onto his shoulder. She hadn't even realized he was carrying it.

"Are you leaving already? Gabe is finishing up breakfast. I'll help him throw some clothes on and we can all go together."

"No thanks."

"Don't you want a ride?"

Max was already swinging open the front door. "I'll walk," he said without turning around. "Bye."

"Max?"

But he was already gone.

June 2012

I don't know how to address this letter. But I know exactly what I want to say, so I'll skip the formalities and get right to it.

I know we agreed to a closed adoption, and I need you to understand right off that I have no desire to change my mind now. And yet, I can't walk away from this without at least setting the record straight. I'm not who you likely think I am, some tragic character who was coerced into a decision that I will forever regret. I was nineteen years old when I found out I was pregnant, happy and independent and working through a bachelor's degree in political science. I was not (nor have I ever been) a drug

29

addict or alcoholic; I was not raped or abused or neglected. And I knew, even as I stared at the pregnancy test in the bathroom of my college dorm room, that I would never abort my baby. I also knew that I couldn't parent the child growing inside me.

I decided not to keep my son because I want more for him than I can provide. And I want more for me. I can't see myself as a baby mommy, diaper bag slung over my shoulder and spit-up stains on my shirt. I want a career in law, an apartment downtown, drinks at the corner pub after a long day at the office. That's no life for a kid. Every child deserves a family, and I want that for my boy. A home that sometimes smells of fresh-baked chocolate chip cookies and bedtime bubble baths with a yellow rubber ducky. A daddy and a backyard and Saturday morning cartoons. Siblings. I can't provide any of that. Not now. But you can.

Love him well. Take him to a Twins game every summer and buy him a hot dog and a big bag of popcorn with extra butter. One year, be sure to wrap a brand-new bicycle and stick it crooked beneath the Christmas tree. Play board games and have a standing family movie night and always, always show him that you love him to the moon and back. And tell him that his birth mom was smart and strong and that she loved him so much she gave him the sort of life he deserved.

Thank you for telling him the truth.

LaShonna Tate

(and yes, this is my real name — just in case he'd like to find me someday)

CHAPTER 2

Jordyn B.
31, African American, BEd
Natural hair, brown eyes, short, thin. Funny,
* well educated, dog lover.*
Sister involved.
AA/DW, 40m, 32w

"Have a good day!" Jess twisted around as Gabe clicked off his seat belt. "Give Mommy a kiss before you go. And don't forget that Daddy is picking you up after school tonight."

Gabe launched himself over the back of the seat and took Jess's face in both of his hands. He kissed her full on the lips and then pressed the tip of his nose to hers for just a second. "I want Daddy to come home."

"You get to go swimming tonight," Jess said, trying to distract him. "Remember? Daddy takes you swimming on Friday nights."

"Max doesn't want to go."

"Well, Max can get over it."

"Maybe Dad will take us to McDonald's before the pool. I want a Superman Happy Meal." Gabe slid across the backseat and wrenched open the car door, letting in a cold blast of late October air. Jess shivered, grateful for the knit stocking cap that she had crammed onto his head in the moment before they left the house. "Bye, Mom! Love you!"

"Love you too, buddy! Be good! I'll see you Sunday!" But the slam of the door cut off her final words.

Jess watched through the window as Gabe ran across the sidewalk. The bell hadn't rung yet, and the kids of Auburn Elementary were gathered in front of the school, talking and laughing and playing little games to stay warm. Freeze tag and a series of elaborate hand songs that involved clapping and shouting. One little girl threw her arms up in the air and almost knocked over Gabe as he wove through the crowd.

A short, friendly honk reminded Jess that she had paused in the drop-off lane for just a second longer than necessary, but she continued to stare at the clusters of kids as she let her foot off the brake and slowly eased forward. Gabe didn't join a group.

33

He never did. He just beetled straight for the doors and stood expectantly, fingers twisted through his backpack straps and face lifted toward the clock that would strike eight in less than two minutes and let him in.

Jess wished for the hundredth time that Max was still at the elementary campus instead of ensconced in the middle school. He could be moody, but he was protective of his little brother. Sadly, he rarely got the chance to lend Gabe the protection and exclusivity of his eighth-grade star wide receiver wings. The middle school and high school were attached, but Max's entrance was on the other side of the block from the elementary school, and he was no doubt already leaning against his locker, eating a jelly-filled doughnut. His favorite. Maybe if Jess bought doughnuts for breakfast he'd sit in the kitchen and eat with them instead of disappearing as quickly as possible. Maybe he'd let her drop him off and spend just a couple of minutes waiting with Gabe so he didn't have to stand surrounded by people but utterly alone.

The sprawling, combined high school and middle school building faced the elementary campus across a private road and a wide parking lot. With a population of just over ten thousand, Auburn was hardly a bustling metropolis, but the public school system was large and well funded. The elementary building was brand-new, and so was the huge parking lot where Jess took the last space marked "staff." She was later than usual, but sat in her car a few seconds longer to check on Evan.

Instinct caused her to pull up his name in her contacts and tap the little phone icon. Deputy Mullen's unnerving call still rippled like static against her skin and she longed to hear Evan's voice. But his number only rang once before Jess quickly hit end. Of course he was fine. He was at work right now, his personal cell phone replaced by the clinic phones that all the staff used. And really, a phone call would send a different type of message altogether. Jess didn't have time to consider every possible scenario — the things that Evan might read into a voice mail, her choice of words, the tone she used — so she texted instead: *Don't forget to pick up the kids after school. Gabe is looking forward to swimming. And McDonald's. Max-code black.*

Jess smiled a little in spite of herself. Max had always been a solemn boy, serious and intellectual and unimpressed by frivolity. The Chamberlains were used to it. But when Max was in a truly dark mood, they had learned it was best to give him a wide berth. He was only seven when Evan instituted the Maxwell Chamberlain alert system. Code black was the highest level warning. Steer clear.

Classes began at the high school at eight thirty sharp, but Jess's first period was free. She used the time to grade a couple of reading responses and assign roles to her tenth-grade students for act 1, scene 5 of *Romeo and Juliet.* The party scene. They pretended to hate the play, but she knew they secretly loved it. And though they'd rather die than admit they enjoyed acting it out, it was by far the easiest way to help them understand exactly what was happening as the play unfolded. She had a navy cape for Romeo and a pair of ivory angel's wings for Juliet; Mercutio wore a dark purple hat with a ratty-looking peacock feather sticking out of it and Tybalt a leather scabbard with a cardboard-and-tinfoil sword. Ridiculous, and intentionally so, for the less her students took themselves seriously, the more they fell under the spell of the play. When they watched the Baz Luhrmann movie at the end of the unit, even some of the boys would inevitably blink back tears. It happened every year.

"Are you still doing that?"

Jess looked up, Juliet's angel wings in one hand and a piece of Scotch tape crumpling over on itself in the other. The fine, gauzy fabric had torn a bit, and since she didn't sew, tape was the best she could do. "What do you mean?" Jess managed a crooked grin as Meredith Bailey, her best friend, walked into the classroom. It wasn't uncommon to see Meredith at school — she washed dishes at least once a month and volunteered when the guidance counselor needed an extra hand.

"The whole *Romeo and Juliet* thing. My kids hated acting that out in your class."

Jess laughed. "Did not. I distinctly remember Jayden made a very convincing Paris. 'O, I am slain! If thou be merciful, Open the tomb, lay me with Juliet.' "

"Do you have the whole thing memorized?" Meredith's nose crinkled as if she had tasted something sour.

"Almost. What are you doing here? Are you on dish duty today?"

Meredith held up an accordion file. "Jayden forgot her research notes for her senior paper. I'm being the dutiful mother."

"Nicely done. You get an A for the day." Jess bobbed her chin to motion Meredith over. "Can you help me with this a minute?

Apparently I can't hold the fabric together and tape it at the same time."

Meredith huffed at the inconvenience, but she was smiling. "Are we still on for tonight?" she asked, lifting a new piece of tape from the dispenser and sealing the tiny hole.

"Of course. Wine, chick flick, yoga pants. No kids." Jess tried to make their girls' night in sound exciting, but the words felt lifeless on her tongue. She knew that Meredith was trying to be a good friend, that she wanted to be supportive of the new reality that Jess found herself living, but they were both fumbling along. Jess was hardly a swinging single, and neither of them knew how to act like their lives weren't completely dictated by their spouses and children. Never mind that Meredith's kids were older. Amanda had graduated last year and was attending Iowa State, and Jayden was a senior at Auburn, but weekend nights were still family time. Auburn football games just for the fun of it, or, at the very least, some time alone with Meredith's husband, Todd. But Jess was too desolate to let her conscience suggest they call off their plans. When the bell finally rang on Friday afternoons, there was only one word that described the emotion that raked bony fingers across her broken heart: forsaken.

Never mind that Jess was the one who had suggested she and Evan take a break.

"A classic?" Meredith asked. "Or do you want to try something new?"

"I don't care. I have a bottle of sauvignon blanc chilling and I'll make some guacamole."

"Don't." Meredith ran her hands down her sides, smoothing her curves with a wry twist on her full lips. "I'm on a preholiday diet."

"Sounds like fun."

"Don't be mean. I eat my emotions; you starve yours."

It was true. Jess had lost interest in food when Evan finally packed his bags and rented a town house on the other side of Auburn. Actually, she had lost her appetite long before that. But her thinness wasn't lovely. It was angular, sharp. Her cheekbones were high and keen in her face, her skin too pale. Even her bra size had withered to a barely B-cup. Jess would have loved an extra ten pounds. But she didn't say that to Meredith.

"How's it going?"

"I think we've got it," Jess said, holding up the wings so she could see them better.

"That's not what I meant."

"I know." Jess slipped the elastic loop that

held the wings together over a hook beside her whiteboard. She sighed. "I'm fine, Meredith."

But her friend wasn't buying it. "When's the last time you talked?"

"We text a lot. But I haven't seen him for . . ." Jess had to think about it. "Two weeks?"

"Two weeks!" Meredith's eyes widened behind her trendy cat's-eye glasses. They were oversized and robin's-egg blue, a look that would have been ridiculous on Jessica but that seemed tailor-made for Meredith. "I thought you were working on things. What happened to counseling?"

"We've been busy." Jess glanced at her watch, flustered by the turn that the conversation had taken and aware that she would have students pouring through her door in minutes. It had been closer to three weeks since she had seen Evan last. They had fought when he dropped off the boys on a Sunday night nearly a month ago, and he'd been tactfully avoiding a front-door meet and greet ever since. Evan picked the boys up from school on Friday and brought them home after supper on Sunday. Jess wasn't sure if she liked the arrangement or hated it. But she wasn't about to admit that to Meredith. "It's not a big deal. We're working it out."

"Hard to work things out if you don't see each other." Meredith sounded hurt, as if the slow dissolution of Jess and Evan's marriage was personally wounding. And it probably was. Meredith had been the Chamberlains' social worker when they adopted Gabe, and she loved him with a passion usually reserved for family. Both Max and Gabe called Meredith auntie. Of course, it was probably against some code of ethics that Meredith became personally involved with the Chamberlains, but their friendship was inevitable. Jessica knew it the moment Meredith rang their doorbell with her elbow and spilled the contents of a fat file folder all over their front porch. She had laughed at herself as Jess scrambled to collect the papers, a cell phone in one hand and a mug of cold coffee in the other. The mug was stamped: CLASSY, SASSY, & A BIT SMART ASSY. Meredith was all that and then some. She smelled just like she looked: bright and citrusy, with an undercurrent of spice. Black pepper.

"It's complicated." Jess fussed unnecessarily with the tattered costumes, her back to Meredith.

"And I'm worried."

Jess sighed and turned to give Meredith

41

her full attention for a minute. They had been mistaken for sisters before, though it seemed obvious to Jess that their similarities were superficial. Both she and Meredith had shoulder-length blond hair and blue eyes, but that was about all they had in common. Jess was petite and forgettable, while Meredith wouldn't have been seen without a wild splash of color or something that sparkled cheerfully. Even now, with her gaze sad and the corners of her mouth turned down in disappointment, Meredith shimmered. "I'm doing the best that I can," Jess said, and she meant it in more ways than one.

"I know you are." Meredith pulled her into a hug, the accordion file squished between them.

The bell rang and Meredith pulled away. "I've got to get this to Jayden," she said, waving the file. "And you've got class. See you tonight, okay?"

Jess nodded and gave the hem of her cardigan a steadying tug. "I'm looking forward to it."

"Me too." Meredith shot her one last meaningful look and let herself out of the room, high-fiving everyone she passed as the first of Jess's English 10 students began to file in. Jess took a deep breath and donned her upbeat teacher persona as surely as if she were putting on a costume herself. Her students couldn't see it, but she had her own special armor and it fit her very well. Jess even managed a genuine grin as the kids groaned when they saw who she had assigned certain roles.

"You'll make the perfect Juliet for our scene today," Jess assured the shyest girl in her class when she realized her name was written on the board beside the initials *JC*. Leaning over to whisper in the girl's ear, she added: "If you smile, they'll never guess you're scared."

It was something she told herself every single day.

There was no reason for Jessica to hurry home after school. Nobody was waiting for her, eager for a snack and a listening ear. The Chamberlains didn't even have a pet, and Jess found herself wishing for one on the long weekends when the abandoned rooms were filled with echoes and silence. Even a fish would make the empty house feel more like a home. Maybe she would run past the pet store tomorrow and grab a goldfish or two. Gabe would be ecstatic when Evan dropped the boys off on Sunday night. She suspected even Max would be pleased.

Jess's arrangement with Evan wasn't legal or anything, and they had existed amicably for almost six months of separation without the situation devolving into something ugly or final. They were merely treading water, going to counseling when it worked, and existing with minimal drama when it didn't. Jess knew that Evan was waiting for her to *do* something — to say something or issue an ultimatum that would force them to confront the issue at hand — but she couldn't bring herself to give him the satisfaction. She wanted an apology, plain and simple. An admittance of wrongdoing. A lightning bolt of understanding that would help him grasp that it was all the things that he didn't say that were making her heart break.

Once, before she asked him to move out, Jess kept track of how long Evan could go without touching her. He hugged the boys, ruffled their hair, or put a hand on Max's shoulder when he was helping him with homework. But Evan orbited Jess. He cared about her, Jess knew that, but somehow they had fallen out of love and into something that felt a lot like a business partnership. They checked things off their to-do lists, co-parented, worked hard at their respective jobs. Nothing more. There was a red pen in the organizer beside the family calendar, and one day Jess grabbed it and put a tiny dot in the corner of the square that marked the date. Ten squares bore a microscopic dot before Jess couldn't stand it anymore. She caught Evan in the kitchen one morning, hugged him from behind, and pressed her cheek against his back as she held him tight. It was all she could do not to sob when he patted her hands and asked, "Now, what's this all about?" *I love you,* she wanted to say. *And I'm afraid you've forgotten to love me back.*

Maybe it would have been easier to just keep going on as if everything were fine. They could be roommates and partners, parent their children together, nothing more, nothing less. But Jess wanted more than that. Did that make her selfish? Greedy? She felt herself melt a little, her heart turning liquid with lament, but she steeled herself before she could fall to pieces. No. She deserved passion, devotion, love. Everybody did.

Jess was putting a stack of papers for weekend grading into her messenger bag when the phone on her desk rang. It was unusual for anyone to still be in the school building so late on a Friday afternoon, and

Jess reached for the handset with a snag of irritation. "Hello, you've reached Mrs. Chamberlain's room."

"Hey, Jessica. Carol from the elementary school here. The secondary office rang me through."

"Hi, Carol." Jess buckled her bag shut and slipped the strap over her shoulder, then absently busied herself by straightening the things on her desk. "What can I do for you?"

"Well, I've got Max and Gabe here with me. We can't seem to get ahold of Mr. Chamberlain. Max says he was supposed to pick them up in front of school this afternoon?"

"That was the plan," Jess said, fishing in the front pocket of her bag for her cell phone. It was dark, and when she opened the lock screen with her thumbprint, there were no missed texts or calls. "I'll try him," Jess said. "Tell the boys to stay put."

"Of course. We can't let them go without a parent or guardian."

"Tell them I'm on my way. I'll wait with them or I can bring them over to Evan's, if need be."

"Will do, Jessica. We'll see you soon."

A burr of frustration lodged itself in her chest as Jess hung up the phone and hurried out of her room. It wasn't like Evan to forget something as important as picking up his boys after school. In fact, he had gone through the trouble of rearranging his schedule at the medical clinic so that he could take off early on Friday afternoons and spend extra time with them. But maybe this was the beginning of the end. Maybe Evan was tiring of the limbo that they were caught in and he was ready for something to happen — even if it was something as irrevocable as divorce.

Jess keyed in his number as she walked to her car, holding the neck of her sweater closed against a cold breeze that had blown down from the north. She had forgotten her coat in the classroom, but she didn't feel like running back for it. There was snow in the forecast, and with the frosty edge in the air, Jess could believe it. She swung into the driver's seat and groped for her keys, her breath making lacy patterns in the still car.

Evan's phone rang four times and then went straight to voice mail. She didn't leave a message.

Auburn Family Medicine was still in her contacts, and Jess hit the call icon with more than a little trepidation. She and Evan were more or less on cordial terms, but she couldn't say the same about her relationship with his nurse, Caitlyn Wilson. In fact,

Cate was one of the biggest reasons she had kicked Evan out of the house all those months ago. He swore that nothing had ever or would ever happen between him and the pretty redhead who worked long hours with him, but he had come home smelling of perfume on more than one occasion. Their counselor said Jess had to make a conscious, intentional choice to trust Evan, to believe that he was telling the truth, but there was a tiny part of her that just couldn't quite do it.

"Hello, Auburn Family Medicine. How may I help you?"

It wasn't Caitlyn on the other end of the line, but that wasn't surprising. The nurses only answered the phone if the secretary was busy and they had a free hand. More often than not it rang through to an automated answering system. Jess held the phone a little tighter and angled the heater vent so that the paltry warmth would blow directly on her as she trembled in the chilly air. "It's Jessica Chamberlain. Dr. Chamberlain's wife?" She didn't mean to make it sound like a question, but the tacit understanding that their relationship was complicated only made her feel more flustered. "Is Evan with a patient right now? I need to speak with him."

"I'm sorry, Mrs. Chamberlain, but Dr. C. isn't here. He hasn't been in since Wednesday."

"Excuse me?" Jess's head spun. "What about Cate? Can I speak to Cate, please?"

"She's not here either. Should I take a message?"

Jessica hung up.

She sat in the car, hands choking the steering wheel as she stared out the windshield at the long shadows of the late afternoon. Evan was gone. Caitlyn was gone.

It could only mean one thing.

Jess felt a surge of adrenaline. It burned like lava in her chest and all the way to her fingertips, which she realized were trembling where they clutched the wheel. She forced herself to release her death grip and shook out her hands until they were hot with blood flow.

Of course, she thought to herself. *Of course.*

"It's not what you think," she said, trying to convince herself that she was being paranoid. But deep in her heart she believed it was true. If Evan and Caitlyn were both gone, it only made sense that they were gone together.

June 2013

Dear LaShonna,

It's crazy to think that it has been a year since you wrote your letter and over a year since Gabe was born. In case you don't already know, that's what we named him: Gabriel Allen. Maybe if we would have known that your surname was Tate, we would have worked that into his name, but he's our Gabe now and we would never want to change that.

I called our caseworker and was told that we get to set the rules about how this plays out. When we signed on for a closed adoption, we knew that we would be in the dark about how you received information (if you received any at all), but I didn't really expect you to write. I can't tell you what it meant to me to read your note and learn just a bit about who you are. I would like to stay in contact if you are open to the idea.

Gabe is an incredible little boy. I'm enclosing a picture of him in the baby swing in our backyard. At thirteen months he crawls all over the house and keeps us hopping. He isn't walking yet, but he pulls up on everything, and he babbles nonstop. He has a big brother who he adores, and a stuffed blue elephant that he must have within arms' reach at all times. We could not possibly love him more. And yes, I give him bubble baths with rubber duckies (we have four) and my wife bakes the most delicious chocolate chip cookies I've ever tasted. Gabe agrees.

Jessica took some time off work to stay home with Gabriel, and her twelve-week maternity leave turned into a year. Gabe is a wonder, and Jess is happy being a full-time mom right now, so I'm not sure if she'll go back to teaching or not. And of course you know that I am a family practitioner. I suppose you could say that Gabe is in good hands. Max, our other son, is in first grade and loves all things football and Harry Potter. I've read him the first book but will wait until he's older to read more.

I guess that's it for now. I realize you chose our family, so you know some things about us, but since you were so forthcoming with your name, I want you to know that we are the Chamberlains.

However, please don't try to contact us directly or reach out thinking that we want to change the status of our adoption. We don't. I'm sure you can understand that my wife is happy with the way things are right now, and we wouldn't want to upset the balance of our home or life. Maybe someday. For now, thank you.

Evan Chamberlain

CHAPTER 3

Elena M.
22, Latina, HS diploma
Long dreads, brown eyes, tall, broad
  shouldered. Nonverbal, recovering addict.
Family uninvolved.
UPF, 43m, 21w

Max was sullen as they pulled into line at the McDonald's drive-through. He sat in the front seat with his arms crossed over his chest and his face angled toward the passenger window, away from Jessica. She could see him scowling in the inky reflection.

"You want a Big Mac?" Jess asked for the second time. He hadn't answered the first.

"I want a Happy Meal with nuggets!" Gabe called from his booster seat in the back.

"I know that, honey. I need to know what *Max* wants."

"Fine." The word was barely audible, but

Jess didn't have time to demand manners. It was her turn to shout their order into the microphone.

When she had passed out the food and Gabe was contentedly flying a plastic Superman around the backseat while ignoring his chicken nuggets, Jess tried again. "I know you wanted Dad to pick you up tonight." She handed Max the straw that had dropped into her lap when the paper bags were passed through the window.

He grunted noncommittally. But Jess could tell that he was hurt, cut to the bone that Evan had so carelessly abandoned his sons. Granted, it was one afternoon. One slip in the almost twenty-five weeks that he had been a weekend father. All the same, she felt a surge of anger, a groundswell that carried with it all the pain and confusion and rejection that she had been harboring through the long months of their separation. She seemed to have been saving it for such a time as this.

"I don't know where he is," Jess said between gritted teeth, "but when I get ahold of him, I'm going to —"

"Mom." The sharp bite of that one word pulled her up short. Max was looking at her, finally, and the shock in his eyes wasn't the reaction she was hoping for. Was he con-

demning her?

"I'm mad, okay? I'm allowed to be mad."

"This is all your fault," Max muttered, turning his back toward her yet again. "If you hadn't kicked him out —"

"My fault? *My* fault?" Jess could hardly believe her ears. "What in the world makes you think that this is *my* fault? I didn't call up your father and tell him to forget to pick you up today. I didn't abandon my family and stop showing up for my own life and —" She broke off, suddenly struck by the fact that this was the last thing her thirteen-year-old son needed to hear. What could be more emotionally scarring than enduring a bitter tirade from his dejected mother? No matter how entitled she was to be livid. She had been strong and stable since the moment she sat down across from Evan and said the words: "I think we need a break." But Jess was human. She was allowed to be broken, too. She just wasn't allowed to flaunt that brokenness in front of her kids.

"I'm sorry," Jess whispered. "I shouldn't have said those things."

Max ripped the paper off his straw and stuck it into his drink.

"We'll get to the bottom of this," she went on. "I'm sure there's a reasonable explanation."

But when Jess drove past Evan's town house, the windows were dark, heavy with drapes that had been pulled across the glass as if it were the dead of winter. Evan was not at work, not at home. And he wasn't answering her texts or phone calls.

Mexico. The thought came unbidden as she pulled into the driveway of their renovated bungalow. They had bought it together only six weeks before Max was born, and Jess had painted his nursery on the second floor a cool, pistachio green even as she ignored the contractions that were coming more and more frequently. It was no-VOC, low-odor paint that the cashier at Home Depot assured her was safe for use during pregnancy. But Jess breathed shallowly anyway and powered through, leaning with her hands on her knees when the tightening around her abdomen threatened to snap her back in two. She was determined to finish the task before she let Evan take her to the hospital.

Jess did, and with plenty of time to spare, because the contractions turned out to be prodromal labor and she didn't end up delivering Maxwell Thomas until ten days later. By that time she was a wreck in every possible way. There was a rib out of place and she hadn't slept in days, but she had managed to also paint the dining room a deep, whale blue and apply fresh grout to the heirloom subway tile backsplash in the kitchen.

"When he's old enough to stay with your parents, I'm taking you to Mexico," Evan had said, crawling carefully onto the hospital bed beside her. She didn't tell him that the movement hurt, that *everything* hurt, because she was so grateful to just be held.

"Cabo San Lucas. We'll go scuba diving."

"I don't think I want to go scuba diving."

"We'll lie on the beach and drink margaritas."

"Perfect."

They had never gone on a honeymoon because medical school bills were already piling up, but though they regularly promised each other that they would right that particular wrong, they never did make it to Mexico. Instead, life got in the way. Not that Jessica minded. She loved their charming home with the black spindle rocking chairs on the front porch. She loved watching her boys toss a football in the front yard or ride their scooters up and down the sidewalk of their tree-lined neighborhood. But Evan brought up Mexico from time to time. Just the two of them, *away,* bright skies and turquoise waters and sun-kissed skin. He had wanted it more than she did, and so it never happened.

He had taken *her* there. Jess was sure of it. Evan had whisked Caitlyn Wilson to Cabo San Lucas. They were probably snorkeling together right now.

"Take your garbage out of the car," Jess snapped as she turned off the car and stepped out.

"My nuggets fell on the floor," Gabe told her matter-of-factly. He was already skipping past her toward the house, Superman held high overhead.

Jess would have called after him, but it was easier to just pick up the mess herself. Her throat felt tight, choked as she knelt on the concrete garage floor and leaned into the backseat so that she could scrape soggy french fries and fake-looking chicken nuggets into the Happy Meal box that Gabe had abandoned. It was nearly impossible to breathe around the disappointment that was welling up inside, threatening to drown her.

"Don't forget your garbage, Max!" Jess croaked from the cavern that was the backseat, but the only response she heard was the slam of the door to the house. She was alone in the freezing garage with the remnants of a pathetic supper strewn in the car around her. And yes, a quick peek over the seat told her that Max's bag, cup of Pow-erade, and Big Mac wrapper were still lit-tering the floor where he had sat.

She could have cried. She could have sunk to the ground, put her head in her hands and wept. Jessica Chamberlain wasn't much of a crier, unless you counted the way that she teared up at every life insurance and telephone company commercial. When it came to the real stuff, the big life events that would render most people a sobbing puddle, Jess held it together. Someone had to do it. Someone had to be brave. It wasn't so much a conscious choice for her as it was a part of who she was. But now her son was mad at her, that precocious little boy who used to talk with a lisp and crawl into her bed in the middle of the night because he wanted to feel his mama's arms tucked tight around him. Max was so angry he could barely look at her. Gabe was strug-gling in school and Jessica wasn't sure who she was anymore, and Evan had defied her hopes and expectations and she was on the verge of a divorce.

Why wouldn't he fight for her?

He was in Mexico with another woman.

Jessica squeezed her eyes shut for just a moment, then she pushed herself up and dutifully threw the garbage she had collected into the bin by the door. She gathered Max's remnants, too, and shouldered the backpack that he had left on the ground just outside the car. Apparently it was her job to pick up the pieces.

When headlights swung into the driveway, Jess paused with her hand on the door. Evan? But it was a sedan, not her estranged husband's SUV. Jess's stepmom drove a VW Beetle in a blinding pearl white and her father a sexy little Audi A4. Meredith wasn't supposed to show up for a couple of hours yet. Jess had no idea who had just pulled up to her house.

She left Max's backpack on the step by the door and walked slowly out of the garage to stand in the glare of the lights. It wasn't truly black yet outside, but the sun was long gone and she couldn't see past the opaque windshield to the interior beyond. The headlights flicked off as the engine went silent.

"May I help you with something?" Jess asked, watching an unfamiliar man step out of the unremarkable four-door sedan.

"Mrs. Chamberlain?"

"Yes," she said, and felt the first drop of alarm hit her veins like a drug.

"Deputy Mullen with the Scott County Sheriff's Department." He held out his right arm as he walked toward her, and when she tentatively did the same, he enveloped her fingers in both of his hands. Jess was sure he was trying to be friendly, but his grip made her feel trapped, panicky. "We spoke this morning."

"I remember. Can you please tell me what this is about?"

The corner of his mouth pulled up in a mournful half smile. "Is there somewhere we can sit down? Somewhere private?"

"My boys are in the house," Jess said, her mouth suddenly so dry she could hardly form the words. She knew what was coming, or was beginning to guess at it, and there were warning bells going off in her head that made it difficult to focus, to breathe.

Deputy Mullen let go of her hand and ran his knuckles over the salt-and-pepper stubble that was growing on his chin. He looked like the kind of man who could shave once in the morning and again at night, but that didn't detract from his wholesome appearance. A full head of neatly trimmed hair and a slightly rounded belly straining over the waistband of his dark-wash jeans made him look like someone's young grandpa, the kind of person who would take his grandkids fishing and hunting and make them struggle to keep up with him. In some quiet corner of her mind Jess noted his plaid shirt and leather bomber jacket and wondered what kind of deputy dressed so casually, but he didn't give her time to contemplate such things.

"Is there someone you could call? A family member or friend who lives nearby?"

And there it was: the truth hovering in the air between them. A specter so ominous, so immediately terrifying, Jess felt her legs buckle beneath her.

"Whoa," Deputy Mullen said, catching her by the elbow for just a moment. "Let's get you inside, shall we?"

"No." Jess shook her head almost violently. "No. I told you, my boys are in there. Why are you here, Deputy Mullen?"

"Please, there has to be somewhere we can go. Someone you would like to call."

"There isn't." Anger was forming like a crust over her fear, and Jess found herself welcoming each sharp, jagged edge. "You need to say whatever you came here to say, Deputy Mullen, and you need to do it now."

He sighed heavily and put his hands on his hips, looking over his shoulder to the car he had parked in the driveway, as if help might emerge from the passenger seat. But there was no one there. It was just the two of them in the dimly lit garage.

Jess could feel herself separating from the situation, floating away from her body and the moment, distancing herself from the words that he was about to say that would surely change her life forever.

"Is it Evan? The body you found?"

The deputy looked her full in the eye, pressed the palms of his thick hands together, and quickly, compassionately said: "I'm sorry to tell you this, Mrs. Chamberlain, but we believe your husband died in a hunting accident."

"No," she said, the sound somewhere between a harsh laugh and a growl. Everything inside of her screamed: *impossible.* "No, that's not true. It can't be. Evan doesn't hunt. And why would he be in Minnesota? That doesn't make any sense."

"We believe that —"

"You said he had gray hair," Jess interrupted, details of their conversation coming back to her as she strained away from his hateful words. She was shaking her head, the whip of her hair lashing her cold cheeks as if in punishment. "You said that the man you found had gray hair and was a hundred and sixty-eight pounds."

"That's true, Mrs. Chamberlain. But I'm afraid we're pretty confident about our identification." Deputy Mullen reached out and put a heavy, anchoring hand on Jessica's shoulder. "I'm so sorry, but we believe the body we found is Evan's."

June 2014

Happy anniversary.

Or something like that. Two years. Our boy (do you care if I call him that?) will be two years old by now (twenty-six months and four days at the writing of this letter). Is he talking? And walking? I read in a book that by two years old most children have 50 words and may have the coordination to pedal a tricycle. Does he kick a ball? Scribble? Have you cut his hair? I like it long like it was in the photo you sent me. And that's exactly how I picture him, though a little taller and more narrow in the face. I think about him all the time.

I would love some more pictures and I'm eager for an update. Overeager, maybe, as I have thought many times about just picking up the phone and giving you a call. I know you work at Auburn Family Medicine and that is where I would contact you. So Jessica never has to know. Talking could be our little secret.

Sorry. That sounds terrible, doesn't it? I swear I'm not a stalker and the last thing I want to do is disrupt your life. Gabe is happy, I believe that, and I have no regrets. But sometimes I would just like to hear about his day, you know? What did he do? Does he like peas? (I hate them.) Is he athletic? (I played varsity soccer for three years in high school and went to college on scholarship.) Of course, I know a two-year-old can't be athletic per se, but I think you know what I mean.

In case he ever asks, you can tell Gabe that his birth mom did what she always said she would do. I graduated in May summa cum laude and am working this summer as an intern at a law firm in downtown St. Paul. I'm not going on in my education right now but have my fingers crossed for a position as a law clerk. I have a mind for details and a perverse love of research that may have something to do with the fact that I consider books to be better friends than people.

Speaking of books, I'm enclosing a copy of *To Kill a Mockingbird.* I know Gabe is only two, but if you honor only one of my requests may it be this one: read him this book. Someday, when he's older. When it will mean something to him. This particular copy is the one that my dad gave me when I was in sixth grade. I can't say I fully understood it at that age, but I loved Scout like a sister. I hope Gabe will too.

Thank you.
LaShonna

CHAPTER 4

Josephine (JoJo) V.
43, Latina, 2 years of high school
Short bob (pink highlights), brown eyes,
  short. Queen Bee, mother figure, 4 kids.
Family doesn't know.
PROST, 75m, 29w pp

Jessica leaned her forehead against the window and let her eyes go soft and unfocused as the car hurtled down the highway. Her father — the formidable Henry Lancaster, retired attorney in little Auburn, Iowa — was in the driver's seat, glaring through the windshield as if he could smooth the path before them with the ferocity of his gaze. Jess didn't have to look to know that he was gripping the steering wheel at ten and two. His seat belt was carefully fastened, his mirrors adjusted to the perfect angle for his long torso. Henry was meticulous in everything from the careful part in his silver hair to the sharp crease in his dry-cleaned trousers. His argyle socks always matched the handkerchief he kept in his pocket, and that, too, was neatly pressed and immaculate.

The only indication that this nighttime drive was extraordinary was the fact that Henry was speeding. A good ten miles over the speed limit, or more. Jessica could feel the momentum in her chest, in the way that her stomach seemed wrapped around her spine. But maybe she was just being hollowed out by fear.

Evan wasn't dead. Jess knew that. She knew it deep down in a place where she believed there was still a connection between herself and the man she had once called her home. Weren't they one? Wasn't their bond immutable, eternal? So what if they were separated, if promises had been broken and the covenant between them severed the day he walked out their front door.

But of course Jess was being idealistic. She was a hopeless romantic, Evan a clear-headed realist. She wondered if he had ever really felt the one-in-a-million love-for-the-ages that she had experienced with him. When she met Evan, love unfurled like a tender, winged thing. It had been a birth of sorts, a burgeoning that made her whole life seem both significant and just a little out of control. Evan's love had been much more pragmatic, even in the beginning when they were still breathless with desire for each other. He could always turn it off, be practical. Not Jess. Never Jess.

"I can't get enough of you," she had told Evan once, straddling his lap while he sat at his desk and pored over a book that was so big it was almost comical.

He laughed, indulgent, and strung a line of kisses along her collarbone until she shivered. She wound her arms around his neck and pulled him close. Jess wasn't done, not by a long shot, but Evan gave her one last squeeze and eased her off unceremoniously. "I have a lot of work to do," he said, keeping one hand on her waist until she was untangled, her feet beneath her. His expression was a study in regret, but Jess could feel the sense of obligation pulled tight beneath his skin. She admired his dedication, his discipline. She just hadn't realized at the time that there was little room for her in the shadow of his devotion.

"We're just over ten miles away," Henry said into the stillness of his Audi A4. It was built like a jet and so quiet that the sound of her father's voice startled Jess. She turned toward him and the thought raced through her mind: *I married my father.* They were so similar, so grounded and cool. Jess bristled at her father's tacit need for control when she was a teenager, but when Evan walked into her world and started straightening every crooked edge, it felt so right. It felt like home.

At first, Evan confined himself to things just within reach. They would be curled on the couch in her apartment, and when Jess got up for a drink, he would stack the magazines on her coffee table and then fan them so that she could reach for exactly the one she wanted. Pillows were arranged, water stains on the fading wood of her secondhand furniture smudged out with the damp edge of his thumb. Once she caught him in the act, but instead of being sheepish, Evan licked his thumb and rubbed out the ring with a series of enthusiastic squeaks. "Admit it," he said. "You need me."

And right now, her father was just what Jessica needed. She reached for him, grazing her fingers across the taut seam of his navy blazer.

The night was black, the sky cast-iron. It was hard and cold and jealous, swallowing up the glow of their headlights so that they had to squint at the dark road. At some point, they had passed from prairie to forest, and the starless sky above them had filled with the shadows of twisted branches. They were bare and peculiar, gnarled fingertips that seemed to reach for them. But when Jess turned her attention to the gloom, they were nothing more than wood and wind, hollow with the echo of silence.

"When we get there, I want you to wait in the lobby." The tone of Henry's voice brooked no argument, and just like that Jess's warm feelings toward her father chilled.

"I'm a grown woman, Dad. You can't tell me what to do."

"You don't want to do this." Henry cut his chin to the left: *no.* One sharp, definitive movement. When Jess had been a teenager, it was more than enough to set her straight. But she wasn't sixteen anymore.

"He said —"

"Deputy Mullen said that I could make the identification," he interrupted before she could go on. "I've done this before, Jessica. I've been there when family members had to identify a loved one. It's not like the TV shows, but it's still not something you can ever forget."

"It's not Evan."

"You don't know that."

"I *do,*" she said, but even as she spat the

71

words, Jess realized that she had absolutely nothing to pin her hope on. What if she was wrong?

"We can turn around. Both of us. I'll tell Deputy Mullen that we want them to use dental records or fingerprints."

"He said this was the easiest way. The quickest way." Jess whispered, "I have to do this."

"No," Henry sighed, softening. "No, you don't."

Jessica realized for the first time that though he was starched and seemingly flawless, her father had a hint of five o'clock shadow peppering the length of his jaw. His tortoiseshell glasses were slipping down the bridge of his nose, and while she watched, he stifled a yawn by grinding his teeth until a vein in his neck popped. This wasn't easy for him, either.

Henry and Anna, Jessica's stepmother — though she rarely thought of her father's recent bride as such — had raced over after Jess's frantic phone call. Anna was already in a pair of yoga pants and a flowing sweater with multicolored tassels, clearly ready for a weekend night at home and maybe a bottle of wine. Henry, on the other hand, had dressed intentionally in one of his "casual drinks with a client" outfits that Jess remembered from her youth. He looked professional but tired, and she felt guilty for judging him so harshly.

"Let's do it together," she said.

He didn't say anything, and Jessica took it as a good sign. A sign that he would let her have her way without much of a fight. How could he not?

The parking lot of the medical center was drawn with stark shadows from the cold, practical lamps that lined the curbs. They were ugly, bulbous things, and as Jessica stepped out of the car she realized they hummed. It was an unkind sound, electrical and somehow menacing, and when her father crossed in front of the car and took her by the elbow, she did not shrug him off.

"Can I offer you a bottle of water?" Deputy Mullen asked as he watched them approach the sidewalk where he stood. He had arrived only moments before they pulled up, and he waited for them now with his hands tucked deep inside his pockets. His jeans bulged around his fists, and his shoulders were rounded against the chilly Minnesota breeze. "It's a long drive. Coffee? Tea?"

"No," Jess said, but she didn't sound very convincing. She cleared her throat and tried again. "I'm not thirsty."

The truth was, she wasn't anything. Not hot or cold or anxious or calm. Her legs should have been stiff from the drive, her right knee (the one that she had injured playing volleyball in high school) aching from inactivity. But Jessica was numb. Head to toe unfeeling. Her father could sense it and moved his arm to wrap around her shoulders.

"We're fine," Henry said for both of them. "We'd like to get this over with."

The deputy led them inside the building, past the reception desk and down a long hallway into a waiting room that seemed poised for bad news. Four chairs in a circle, a small round table with pamphlets about the effects of chemotherapy and the importance of a living will and heart disease in women. A kaleidoscope of diagnoses that seemed distant and impossible to Jess. The kinds of things that happened to people in movies. But her reality was even more incomprehensible.

"Don't we get to —"

Henry squeezed Jessica's shoulder to cut her off and eased her into one of the waiting-room chairs with the weight of his hand. She didn't have it in her to fight back. Instead, she perched on the end of the slippery gray seat obediently. Waiting.

"How confident are you that we're about to identify my son-in-law?" Henry stood over Jess, his fingers light at the base of her neck as he surveyed Deputy Mullen.

The deputy paused for just a moment. "Confident. He'd be a John Doe without the number we found in his pocket. But there were ten digits, and calling them was our first step."

"I told you this morning that Evan doesn't match your description." Jessica laced her fingers together in her lap and squeezed. "The numbers could be a combination or an IP address."

"We have to follow every lead," Deputy Mullen explained patiently. "We ran finger-prints, of course, but nothing popped. So we found your husband on social media, and when we realized the resemblance was strong in spite of your skepticism, we pulled as much information as we could on Evan Chamberlain. Cell phone location records and credit card activity place him in the area recently. And repeatedly over the course of the last six months."

"But those are private records."

Henry shook his head, a wrinkle deepening between his eyes, and said to Jessica: "They're not."

"When you said that you were estranged,"

Deputy Mullen addressed Jess, "we also called Auburn Family Medicine. Evan hasn't been at work all week."

"He hasn't?"

"Look, Mr. Lancaster, Mrs. Chamberlain, you wouldn't be here if we didn't believe that we've positively identified our accident victim." Deputy Mullen spread his hands in front of him. In apology or supplication, Jessica couldn't tell.

"So what now?" she whispered.

"I'm going to bring in Sarah Ellens, our grief counselor. She'll explain how the identification takes place."

They fit perfectly around the coffee table, the four of them. Jessica was hemmed in by her father on one side and Deputy Mullen on the other, though he referred to himself as Mike and asked that they call the young woman who joined them Sarah. She seemed too innocent for the job, barely out of high school with long brown hair that fell in a curtain down her narrow back, and lipstick in a ripe shade of plum. But Jessica had become a poor judge of age, and when Sarah spoke, it was with a still maturity that turned a key inside Jessica's heart. Something opened and a piece of her fell loose.

"I'm going to pass you a clipboard," Sarah was saying. "There is a photograph facedown on it. You may turn over the picture whenever you feel ready, but let me first tell you what you're going to see. It's a photo of a face. The eyes are closed and the head is resting on a blue sheet. I want you to know that you'll see a wound above his left eye. It's about two inches long. It did not cause his death."

Jessica's eyes blurred with stars and she realized that she had stopped breathing. She tried to swallow a little gulp of air, a furtive, secret breath that wouldn't alert everyone to the fact that she was suffocating.

"Take a moment," Sarah said, reaching across the coffee table. She wrapped her small hand around Jessica's and held it. "Take all the time that you need."

But Jessica was already pulling away. "I'm ready."

The clipboard was wooden with a silver clasp that looked like it was original to the hospital. Jessica studied it and the back of the eight-by-ten Kodak photo paper until her father reached to take it from her. "Jessica, please."

"No," she said, and carefully slid the sheet from under the clip. She turned it over.

The man in the picture had wiry gray hair and thick brown eyebrows that didn't match. A straight, slender nose. A neatly trimmed goatee that was brown shot through with gray — though this gray was lighter, whiter, than the color of his gunmetal hair. He was a study in contradictions: harsh cheekbones but a starburst of laugh lines. Tiny, happy wrinkles around a mouth that was tight-lipped. Smooth forehead torn by a jagged cut. It would have required stitches if warm blood still pumped in his veins.

Jessica wanted to say: "It's not him." She could feel the words on her tongue, lavish and warm, hopeful.

But there was a silver pleat in the skin by his ear, a tiny zipper that only Jessica would notice. She had caused the scar herself in their first year of marriage when school debt was piling up and Evan insisted that she should learn how to cut his hair so they could cross that one expense off their budget. Unfortunately, Jess proved to be incompetent with scissors, and the clippers they borrowed from a friend was more of a weapon than a tool. She caught the tender fold of skin in front of his ear in the serrated teeth of the personal clipper, and the blood that beaded there caused her to burst into tears. Evan laughed.

"I'll survive," he told her, leaning in to kiss her even as he pressed a tissue to the blood that pearled on his cheek. "A flesh wound, nothing more."

"I'm so sorry," Jessica whispered. Then and now.

June 2015

Dear LaShonna,

Three is joy. And mess and noise and utter chaos. Gabe never stops moving — except when gripped with the sudden, often inexplicably timed need to sleep. He has landed face-first in his macaroni and cheese, and Jessica once found him suspended between the coffee table and the couch. He was out cold. How is that possible? Of course, if we try to move him to his crib (he hasn't made the switch to a toddler bed yet — we'd like to contain him a little longer for obvious reasons), he wakes up instantly. Gabe doesn't believe in naps, eating his vegetables, or hugs and kisses. "I big boy," he tells us. But when we can catch him, he forgets that he's newly autonomous and snuggles into our arms like a battery recharging. Then he wiggles and squirms until we set him down. And he's off. Again.

Gabe lights up our home. He's bright and beautiful and I can't imagine our world without him in it. That's why it feels increasingly wrong to me that you don't know all that he is and all he is becoming.

I don't think I can do this anymore. A sealed letter once a year is not enough to contain all that I have to say. All that I think you should know. Gabe is perfect to us, but he hasn't met several of his three-year-old milestones. Of course, he's newly three. And strong willed. Gabe gave us a fresh perspective on the concept of the "terrible twos," and he has shown no signs of leaving that particular stage behind now that he is officially a year older.

We're not concerned, not really, but Gabe's language has been slow to develop, and he is indifferent to learning things like colors and numbers and even animals. We don't have a dog, but our neighbors do, and Gabe insists it's a cat. (In his defense, it's the most pathetic excuse for a dog I've ever seen.)

Do you want to know these things?

Should I whitewash the hard stuff? Like the fact that Gabe broke his arm last fall when he tumbled from the top of the slide in our backyard. We've had that swing set since Max was a toddler, but it was ascribed a different threat level when Gabe learned to climb the ladder. He was fine, of course. I gave him a red cast because Marshall is his favorite puppy on *PAW Patrol.* And Jessica watches him even more closely now than she always has. Sometimes I think her life consists of tracking his every move.

I don't know what else to write. I suppose I could keep a journal for you, a daily record of what Gabe did and ate, what he said or didn't say. Or we could put more letters in the file. Once a month, maybe, instead of this strange, annual pattern we've developed. If you're ready, so am I. You won't get this letter for months (more?), but when you do, and if you want to, you know how to find me.

Evan

CHAPTER 5

Emery V.D.
20, Caucasian, HS diploma
Light brown hair, strawberry highlights, green
  eyes. Homecoming queen.
Disowned.
CAG, 26m, 11m pp

The day was too beautiful for a funeral, and somehow the way the sun warmed the top of her head made Jessica want to rend her clothes. She knew exactly what it would feel like to snag the fabric of her charcoal dress between her fingers and rip. The satisfying sound as the seams tore, threads snapping and popping as she ruined the knock-off cashmere. And what would she do then? Stand there in her black slip in front of her friends and family? Would she sob, beat her chest, scream? Jess wanted to, and it was those wicked thoughts, those wild, unmanageable urges that kept her eyes dry and her feet stepping surely forward. Down the sidewalk in front of the church and past the parking lot to the place where the hearse marked Evan's grave. Jessica held herself together because she was terrified of what would happen if she let go, even for a moment.

Gabriel's hand was impossibly tiny and cold in her own, and Jessica gave it a little squeeze. He didn't squeeze back, but she didn't expect him to. Gabe didn't really understand what was going on. And she was grateful for that one small grace. On any other Saturday, her son would be reveling in this picture-perfect October day, this brilliant afternoon that seemed staged for a Thanksgiving commercial. He would be wearing short sleeves, careening through the backyard with the neighbor kids as their noses began to water and their cheeks blushed pink. The warmth of the sun was deceptive, the fact that Jessica could just make out the mist of her breath in the bright autumn air evidence that it was barely fifty degrees. Lovely, still. And crisp with the scent of fallen leaves and the hint of woodsmoke.

Entirely inappropriate for the task at hand.

"You okay?" Jessica whispered to Max. He flanked her other side but refused to hold her hand. The suit was new, bought by Anna because Jess couldn't bring herself to shop for her son's funeral outfit. It fit him well and made his shoulders look startlingly broad, as if slipping on the coat had transformed him from a boy into a man. An instant, irreversible metamorphosis. In some ways Jessica supposed it was. Max would never be the same. None of them would.

"Max?" she glanced at him in profile, slowing her steps so that she wouldn't stick the willowy heels of her shoes into a sidewalk crack. It wouldn't take much. The pumps had been a ridiculous choice and she wondered what had possessed her to put them on in the first place. Shock, probably. The detached feeling that made it seem as if she were looking at the world from behind frosted glass. "You okay, hon?"

He didn't flinch or nod or acknowledge her in any way. It was like Jessica didn't exist.

Apparently grief and anger were secret lovers, because Jess tipped into blind rage so quickly it left her teetering. Gabe tugged her hand, pulling her gently toward him even as she longed to break away. She wanted to take Max by the chin and force him to look at her. To see the misery that was written there so clearly and know that they shared this ache. It was too heavy to bear, the weight of the whole messed-up world against her chest, and Max's rejection only made it worse.

"Me too," she whispered harshly, because it was all she could bring herself to say. *I feel this too. He wasn't just your dad; he was my husband. My lover. My best friend.* But of course she didn't say those things. Her oldest son flicked his eyes in her direction and looked quickly away. Instead of wiping the tear that had suddenly spilled down his cheek, he lifted his shoulder and erased the evidence with the sleeve of his new coat.

Sweet man-child. She adored him even when she was furious with him. Sometimes she wished that she could set aside this soul-deep affection, this love that bordered on worship. But he was her flesh and blood, even when he ignored her or refused to listen. Even when he intentionally hurt her. It would be easier to stay angry at him, but nothing was ever easy where her children were concerned. Jessica waged war every day: for their safety and well-being, for their hearts and minds.

Jess brushed away her own unwelcome tears and reached for Max's arm, holding it just above the elbow as if he had offered it to her like a gentleman. He didn't pull away.

They had discussed what the pastor would

say. In meetings over the last few days Jessica had sat in the deep leather sofa in his office, her arm rubbing against her father's because the cushions sagged and she had no choice. And because she was drowning beneath the implications of all that had happened, and swallowed by the couch that seemed intent on consuming her whole, Jess let her father make all the decisions. No open casket. Memorial service followed by internment instead of the other way around. Pastor William would read Psalm 23.

She remembered little to nothing about the memorial service, though the waxy fragrance of the candles still lingered in her hair. And now here she was, standing on a square of artificial turf with the sleek, black casket laid out before her. There was an enormous spray of roses arranged on the lid, and as she watched, her gaze hazy and uncertain, Jess saw Max reach out and take one. Yes, they were supposed to have a rose each, but she couldn't recall why.

"Mama?" Gabe asked. So she nodded and he leaned forward to pluck a rose in each hand. He offered one to her.

They were thornless flowers, denuded of their barbs, and Jessica ran her thumb along the smooth stem as people filled the space behind her. Everyone had walked from the church, through the parking lot and between the gates of the cemetery that were forever open. If she would have turned around, she would have seen her father and Anna close enough to touch, and beside them, Evan's father in his wheelchair. Bradford Chamberlain had lost himself to Alzheimer's years ago, and he didn't know why he was here, even though they had told him no less than a dozen times. He was sad without knowing why, his heart remembering the gravity and significance of a funeral, even as his mind refused to understand.

"I'm so glad you're here," Jessica had whispered when Bradford arrived at the memorial hours before. He was flanked by an aide, a young man with a tender half smile and teddy-bear-brown hair that was an inch or two too long. It gave him the appearance of a mournful puppy, and Jess had to resist the urge to comfort them both. "Evan loved you so much."

"Who?" Bradford said. It was an innocent question, and her father-in-law patted her hand and smiled sweetly as he asked it. Her heart splintered.

But now Jess was tightly buttoned, each shattered piece pulled tight and held close so she could manage her brokenness with the same efficiency she employed in every other aspect of her life. Jessica didn't have the luxury of weeping over her father-in-law or quietly fuming about the distance between herself and Max. She couldn't even cry the way that she wanted to, loud and keening, wracked with sobs that were dragged from her very core. Her grief had to be muzzled, maintained.

Pastor William took his place on the other side of the polished casket and gave Jess a little nod. It was sympathetic but firm. A question. Now?

No, not now. Not ever. But Jessica didn't have a choice in the matter. She nodded back.

He didn't say much. There was a Bible passage and a prayer, but Jessica couldn't focus because her heart kept time with the countdown clock. Five minutes? Four? Soon Pastor William would say "amen" and then it would all be over. Her life as she knew it arrested before she had a chance to make everything right. To put the pieces back together.

Jessica knew when it was done because the hush of the crowd expanded like dough until she feared she would suffocate. There was a moment of total silence, not the swish of fabric or a single sigh, and then the world exhaled, and slowly, slowly those who had gathered to say good-bye began to move.

"I'm so sorry," someone said, touching her elbow and giving Gabe's hair a tousle. It was Dr. Murphy, from the clinic. They hadn't been close. He was new.

What was she supposed to say? It's okay?

There were more, a growing tide of people who blew their noses into soggy tissues and clasped Jess and her boys to their chests.

"Mom?" Gabe called, his voice hitching in indication of the level of his distress. It was too much for him. He had been touched by strangers, shushed and ignored for hours. Now Jess could almost see the switch flip as Gabe crumpled. *Not a tantrum. Not now.* But it was too late. Gabe was crying, screaming, really, and arching his back against the cold ground as if the earth carried a charge and he was being electrocuted. The book on her nightstand said that Jess was supposed to hold him through it, speak gently and lovingly until the fit of rage passed. But she didn't want to hold him. She wanted to spank him.

"We'll take him," Henry said quietly as he crouched down to wrestle his flailing grandson. Jess felt a rush of gratitude that was quickly tempered by guilt. She should be on her knees, comforting her son. Too late. Her father had scooped up all fifty-five pounds of shrieking little boy and was carrying him in the direction of the parking lot. Gabe's arms and legs thrashed, and his screams only intensified at the injustice of being so unceremoniously hauled away. But Henry knew what he was doing. He knew how to calm his grandson.

"It'll be okay," Anna said, putting a hand on Jessica's arm. "Don't you worry about a thing. I have a pot of potato soup on the stove. Come over when you're done here."

"Sure," Jess managed. "Fine. We'll meet you at the house later."

"Max can come with us if he'd like. Max?"

Jessica felt her teenage son's absence in the sudden chill. He was already weaving through the crowd, making his way to the parking lot and his grandfather's car. She shivered.

"You can all spend the night — I have the guest room ready for you." Anna didn't give her a chance to protest but gave Jess one last hug, then turned and melted into the sea of dark-clothed mourners.

Jess didn't want to spend the night at her father's house, and she certainly didn't want her sons to. She wanted her own bed, and the warm weight of Gabe beside her in the place where Evan used to sleep. Gabe had taken to sleeping in Jess's king-sized bed when Evan moved out for good, and because she loved his company she had never discouraged him. She should have; Jess knew that now. But it was too late. Instead of going to sleep in his own bed, Gabe crawled into hers every night as if it had been his all along. But she loved his mussed hair, the sound of his breath in the middle of the night when she couldn't sleep. He whistled when he inhaled, and she even loved that.

She could say no, Jess decided as she accepted a stiff hug from yet another one of Evan's coworkers. A nurse this time, Evelyn, whom Jessica had always liked simply because she had a laugh like bells ringing.

"Here." Jess felt someone slide the rose she was clinging to out of her hand. She hadn't realized that she was still holding it. "Let me take that for you." Meredith cradled the head of the flower, preserving it for the vase where it was supposed to serve as a tender reminder of this moment, this day. Jess wouldn't keep it. She knew that now. She'd drop it in the garbage the first chance she had.

But her best friend didn't need to know that. "Thank you," Jess said, leaning into the arm that Meredith had thrown around her. To anyone looking on, it seemed like a warm half hug, but Jess could feel the protection in it, the unspoken promise that Meredith was here to run interference. Jess could have wept into the scratchy fabric of her friend's funky tweed coat. There was something about Meredith's bosomy embrace that reminded Jess of her mother. But as quickly as she felt a pang for her mom, Jess squelched it. To think about Betsy Lancaster was to tip off the edge into an abyss.

"You saw Gabe's meltdown?"

"Honey, everybody saw his meltdown." But Meredith smiled to soften the blow. "It's expected, Jess. If I were you, I'd be the one screaming on the ground."

Later, when everyone who wanted to offer their condolences had filed past the place where Jessica stood rooted to the ground, Meredith gave her a fortifying squeeze. She hadn't moved from Jessica's side as coworkers, friends, and acquaintances pressed their sympathy into the new widow like a brand. Jess felt like she would carry the scars of this day forever, and she ran her hands up and down her arms, longing for a way to erase the evidence from her skin, her bones.

"This is a nightmare," she said, and didn't realize that she had spoken aloud until Meredith linked arms with her and tugged in the direction of the parking lot.

"I'm taking you home."

"I don't want to —"

"Not my home," Meredith clarified, clearly understanding the root of Jessica's reluctance. "Your home. Todd already left with the kids."

"Amanda came?"

"Of course she came. You talked to her before the service, remember?"

Jessica didn't, not really. And when she stumbled a little, her heel sinking into a divot on the brown grass, Meredith held her tighter and powered through, half carrying Jess along on a wave of willpower and friendship.

"It's probably good that everything blurred together," Meredith said. "These things are never pleasant. Let's get you home."

Jess was silent, compliant, as Meredith buckled her seat belt, drove the scant miles to the Chamberlains' home, and then ushered her into the entryway. It was late afternoon, but the sun was already mostly gone, and Jess trembled in the darkness. Once she started, she couldn't stop.

"You poor thing." Meredith hurried Jess over to the couch and wrapped a blanket around her shoulders. She gave her a hard hug, all blustery and fierce, and deposited Jess against the pillows as if she were a child. "I had intended to draw a bath, but I think you need a few minutes."

Jessica just nodded, teeth chattering.

"Give me your feet," Meredith demanded, sinking onto the coffee table as she reached for Jessica's legs. She slipped off the offensive shoes and gave the arches of Jess's feet a quick rub. "Better? I mean, I know nothing is better, but does that help, even a little?"

Jess wasn't used to seeing her friend so ruffled, so uncertain. Meredith was warm but uncompromising, the kind of woman who made decisions and did not regret them for a second — even if they proved to be problematic. Her heart was huge, but her confidence equally so, and it was alarming to see her flustered.

"Yes," Jess told her. "That's better. I'm better. See? I'm not shaking anymore." But she was, a little.

"Liar."

"I should check on Gabe."

"He's fine. Your dad would have called if he needed you."

Jess closed her eyes. The truth was, she didn't want to know how her boys were doing.

"Tea?" Meredith asked.

That made Jessica bark out a humorless laugh. "Are you kidding? Whiskey, neat. I think there's some Tennessee Honey in the liquor cabinet."

"Good girl." Meredith hopped up, flicking lights on as she went, and returned a few minutes later with two stemless wineglasses. They were nearly half-full, a double shot for sure, but Jessica accepted the drink gratefully. She sipped and felt the alcohol burn the back of her throat. A moment later there was the hint of sweetness on her tongue.

"What just happened?" Jess asked.

Meredith sank onto the couch beside her friend and put her feet up on the coffee table. She wiggled her toes in black tights so that her feet looked webbed. "I don't know, Jess."

"It was rhetorical."

"I know."

"I can't believe it," Jess said, and was surprised by a howl that caught in her chest. It came out a whimper. "I'm a widow. I'm thirty-six years old and I'm a widow."

Meredith, for once, was speechless.

"I have to go through his apartment. Get rid of all his things. There's no one else to do it." Panic began to rise like steam.

"Give yourself some time."

"What am I going to do?"

"I don't think you have to do anything right now," Meredith said slowly. As if she were talking to someone hard of hearing. Or crazy.

Jessica gave her a sidelong glance. She was angry, she decided. Downright pissed off. "Of course I have to *do* something."

"You need to take care of yourself and your boys," Meredith said. She tucked a strand of hair behind her ear and leaned forward to try and catch Jess's gaze. "This is going to take time, Jess. Give yourself a little grace."

But Jessica wasn't paying attention. "Evan is gone," she whispered, her throat nearly too raw to speak at all. "All I can keep thinking about is how he can't be. I mean, *he can't be.* Like, it doesn't make any sense. Evan wasn't a hunter. He didn't know anyone in central Minnesota. There has to be some mistake."

Jess hiccupped around a sob and sloshed a few drops of whiskey on the front of her dress.

"There's no mistake, hon." Meredith patted her arm, but Jessica shook it off.

"You know what I keep thinking?" Jess asked. "What keeps me up at night? That it wasn't an accident. What if it wasn't an accident?"

Meredith stood abruptly and took Jess's drink from her. She set it on the coffee table, where it immediately made a ring. "Look at me," she said, bending so that they were eye-to-eye, so that Jessica had no choice but to look at her. "I'm so sorry — more sorry than I could ever begin to express — but Evan is dead. He was killed in a hunting accident and we buried him today. It's awful, I know, but you have to accept it."

Jessica shuddered. "But I don't want to."

"Honey, you don't have a choice."

July 2016

Dear LaShonna,

I've been waiting for an email notification from Promise alerting me to the fact that you have sent another letter. It never comes. Maybe you took me seriously when I wrote "I can't do this anymore." Of course, I was employing hyperbole. Of course I can keep doing this. And I will. As long as you want to know about Gabe, I will continue to write you letters. And if you tell me to cease and desist, I'll do that, too. It's your call.

First the good. Gabe is hilarious and adorable. He loves to dance and play outside and copy everything his older brother does. "I'm a big boy!" is his favorite declaration, and he makes sure that everyone around him knows it. He's completely obsessed with soccer right now — probably because it doesn't take too much coordination to run around booting a big ball. This kid is amazing. A walking, talking miracle. I'm enclosing a picture of him at his preschool graduation. They let the kids wear caps and gowns — which Gabe thought was the greatest thing since Jess introduced him to Nutella. After kindergarten round-up it was decided that Gabe was not quite ready for kindergarten next year, so he'll be attending TK (transitional kindergarten). Thankfully he's thrilled about that, too. Word on the street is TK takes the best field trips.

Now for the hard stuff. Although Gabe lags behind his peers in some areas, it is my professional opinion that his developmental delays are just a part of who he is. I refuse to call kids slow, and Gabe certainly isn't that. He's lightning quick in some areas and easily distracted in others. Jessica would like to have him tested. It's something that we fundamentally disagree on. I don't believe it's healthy to label children, especially at such a young age when development can be so different — and still healthy — depending on the unique characteristics of each individual. Right now we are taking it a day at a time and trying to learn Gabe's needs. He craves routine and dislikes disruptions. He loves to make noise but can't process it when the sound is not originating from him. He likes to play near other children but not necessarily with them. And don't even think about encouraging him to try a new food. He's firmly in the chicken nuggets, macaroni and cheese, and crackers camp. We'll work on it. Someday.

I hope that all is well with you and I hope that I hear from you again. Or, if your life has taken a different turn and you are no longer interested in writing, I respect your decision. Unless you tell me otherwise, I will assume that this chapter in your life has closed. Thank you for letting me have a glimpse of who you are.

Regards,
Evan

PS — Exchanging letters is such an archaic way of communicating. I hope this isn't overstepping some invisible boundary, but if you would rather take this conversation to the digital age, my email address is: echamberlain@comnet .com.

Chapter 6

Patricia K.
37, African American, GED
Cropped hair, brown eyes, chunky glasses.
Husband, son at home (11).
CF/TM, 20m, 18m pp

The autopsy report came in a nondescript brown envelope less than two weeks after the funeral. Jess was on bereavement leave, thirteen days in, but the boys had returned to school. "Continuity, connection, care," the family counselor had told her, ticking off his fingers one by one as he listed her sons' needs in this strange and terrible season. "Give them time and space to talk and grieve, but try to keep their lives as normal as possible."

Normal. Jess felt certain that nothing would ever be normal again, but she nodded as if she understood, and asked the boys if they were ready to go back to school. They were. She wasn't.

When she padded outside on stockinged feet to get the mail that day, Jessica hadn't showered and was still wearing the yoga pants she had snagged off her bedroom floor that morning. She vaguely remembered a flimsy inclination to go for a jog, a brief hope that maybe this would be the day things would turn around. But after she dropped the boys off at school, Jess sank into the corner of the couch, legs curled beneath her, and stared at the wall while her mug of coffee went cold in her hands.

The sound of the mailman on her porch roused her.

A Pizza Hut flyer, a slim stack of bills, and then, an envelope from the Scott County Coroner's Office.

Jess called Deputy Mullen.

"You said it would take a month or more," she said when he answered the phone.

"Jessica?"

"Yes." She rubbed her forehead and realized that her hair was limp and greasy. "Sorry, this is Jess Chamberlain. I thought, you know, caller ID."

"Your name came up," Mullen told her. "Just making sure. You okay?"

"The coroner's report came today."

He sucked in a breath. "They were supposed to call me before they sent it. I'm sorry you weren't warned." He sounded genuinely concerned.

"I thought you said it would be weeks."

"We expedited the process a bit."

Jess sensed a moment of hesitation. "I don't understand. Why?"

Mullen didn't sigh, but he was quiet for longer than Jess would have liked. Weighing his options, measuring what he was going to say. Finally he offered, "We had some questions about Evan's wounds, among other things."

"What other things? What's that supposed to mean?" Jess didn't realize she was pacing until she clipped her toe on the edge of the coffee table. She bit her lip to stop from crying out.

"It's nothing, Jessica. Really. The autopsy came back just as we suspected. We had some unanswered questions about why Evan was where he was that night. We still do. As you already know, he didn't have any identification on him and we didn't find his car until the next day. But everything checked out."

Jess wasn't sure she was hearing him right. "Are you telling me you thought that maybe Evan's death wasn't an accident?"

"We're just covering all our bases, Jessica. It's our job," Deputy Mullen said calmly.

"And Evan died of wounds from a single round of buckshot to the back. That's what the autopsy says. The simplest answer is usually the right one, and after all the interviews, we have no reason to suspect foul play."

They had been through this all before. The difference between manslaughter and homicide. No one mentioned murder (first or second degree), but Jess was the daughter of an attorney — she wasn't naive. Still, all of it was unfathomable in regard to Evan. Quiet, unobtrusive, hardworking Evan. He was steady and kind, and just a little nerdy, but that was one of the things she found attractive about him. He was handsome in a distracted, "aw, shucks" kind of way, the resident small-town doctor who Jessica was sure made the stay-at-home moms' hearts pitter-patter just a bit. He was a safe crush, and she knew exactly what they were thinking: "Maybe *I* can get him to sit up and take notice." Jess had once thought the same thing.

"I'm sorry to say, it happens all the time," Mullen told her. "Roughly a thousand people are injured in hunting accidents every year, and approximately ten percent of those are fatalities."

"In the middle of the night?"

"Time of death was between eight and ten p.m.," Deputy Mullen reminded her. "Not all that late."

"But I told you that Evan wasn't a hunter."

"We never suggested he was hunting. He had just been in a car accident, Mrs. Chamberlain. Maybe he was walking to find help. Or he was confused. Evan had a significant laceration on his head and there was blood on the windshield of the LeSabre, as well as vomit on the ground beside the car. If he had a head injury and wasn't thinking clearly, he could have easily missed the public hunting ground signs."

"I know," Jess whispered. The fact that the car had been in an accident helped them identify it as Evan's. It wasn't his SUV, but the blood on the windshield was a match. "But he was miles from his car . . ."

"Not that far as the crow flies," Deputy Mullen said. "It's just under a mile and a half on foot from where his car was found to where his body was found."

The conversation was starting to feel circular. They had gone over this again and again, but Jess needed to hear him explain it one more time. "What makes you think his death was an accident?"

Deputy Mullen was nothing if not patient.

"The DNR issues two hundred permits on a lottery-based system for that area, and the season for hunting with a statewide firearm license is short. Evan was killed on the third day of the season with legal hunting ammo. If his death was intentional, whoever killed him knew an awful lot about deer hunting season in Minnesota."

Jess's chin dropped to her chest. She knew what was coming next. She had asked the questions a dozen different times in just as many ways. Was there another hunter nearby? Did any neighbors hear the shot? How could someone mistake her husband for a deer? Or, why would someone blindly shoot into the darkness on a moonless night?

"We're tracking down every single license holder," Deputy Mullen reminded her kindly. "This isn't a closed case. Accident or not, we are still looking for the person who killed your husband. Somebody knows something. It will come out."

It had rained that night, the night that Evan was shot. And it wasn't until late the following afternoon that a local resident — fifty-nine-year-old Wendy Anderson — discovered his body while she was bow hunting with her pair of Irish setters. They found his body before she did, and by the time she caught up they had trampled the area as they sniffed and nudged and whined for her to hurry and investigate their morbid find.

Dogs and wind and rain that coated the ground in a thin coat of ice that melted by midday hampered the investigation significantly, but even if the conditions had been perfect, Mullen explained that the deck was stacked against them. The firearm season for deer was short, and the woods were crawling with hunters hoping to get their buck. In central Minnesota, shotguns with single-slug shells were permitted for eight days, and the Tri-Ball 12-gauge buckshot that ended Evan's life was consistent with the ammunition any number of hunters used. The ground was crisscrossed with boot prints and cigarette butts and spent shells. Finding evidence from one specific discharge was a nearly impossible task.

"Someone took one last shot in the dark," Deputy Mullen said. But he didn't sound very convincing.

After Jess hung up, she went to her bedroom and put the envelope from the coroner's office in the drawer of her night table. She couldn't read it, not yet, but the knowledge that it was there rumbled beneath her skin like distant thunder. Because she wanted to scratch, to drag her fingers across her arms and legs and stomach, Jess turned on the shower and scrubbed her hair instead. It felt good, the hot water, the rising steam, and she stayed beneath the spray until she felt raw. Scoured clean.

Jess slipped a fresh shirt off a hanger in her closet and then put on a pair of jeans. How long since she had worn real clothes? At least, something other than yoga pants and soft T-shirts that espoused mantras like *Exhale* and *Namaste.* Clearly it had been a while, because her jeans hung off her hips and her fingers fumbled over the buttons on her shirt.

But she was dressed. And that was something. She ran a brush through her damp hair and pulled it into a neat knot at the base of her neck. No makeup. Jess couldn't be bothered.

She was up, off the couch for the first time in days, and because she had forward momentum, Jess decided to keep moving. The grocery store for sure. People had been bringing food, but her boys weren't interested in chicken and broccoli casseroles or eggplant lasagna. Jess knew what her kids wanted and it was comfort food. Brown Sugar Cinnamon Pop-Tarts and cheddar popcorn for Max, anything baked and frosted for Gabe. Cinnamon rolls, usually, but he would accept boxes of doughnuts, Little Debbie snacks, anything nutritionally bankrupt and bursting with empty calories. Jess could do that.

Because they worried about her and checked in every day — sometimes multiple times a day — Jess forced herself to text Meredith, her father, and Anna before she pulled out of the driveway. She didn't want to, but reaching out was like putting a little deposit in the bank. *See? I'm okay. I'm going to be okay.* On days when she couldn't bring herself to get out of bed, she could point back to that one time she got groceries.

I'm out, she wrote. *Groceries.*

The flurry of replies kept her parked for longer than she would have liked, and the more they congratulated her, the more they chimed in, the less she wanted to leave. There was an indent on the couch that was exactly her shape and size, and it called to Jessica like a lover. It was comfortable, safe, the only place in the entire house where she could sit and relieve just a bit of the pressure that threatened to crush her heart. Arms curled in close, legs tucked sideways beneath her. Head resting on the back of the couch or the arm if need be. For some reason she could breathe there, just a little, and for a measure of time every day it was enough.

Good girl, her father texted. Then: *Time to move on. No guilt.*

No guilt. What a joke. Jess knew that she was the only one to blame for what happened to Evan. If he were with her, if they were still a family, he would have been beside her on their sofa that night. They liked to watch *Parks and Recreation,* even the first season, which nearly everyone agreed could be skipped right over as if it had never happened at all. Maybe they would have shared a bag of microwave popcorn, Evan's favorite, their hands brushing against each other as they reached for greasy handfuls. Surely even that, the tentative, unfamiliar way they touched in their final months together, was better than Evan's body cold in the ground.

Jessica felt a tremor shake her from head to toe. If she didn't leave now, she never would. She tossed the phone into her purse and put the car in reverse, texts be damned. She had done more than her part.

The big Hy-Vee close to school was where Jessica usually got her groceries, but she would run into people that she knew there. Like the cashier with the peasant braids who knew her by name and who always joked about all the bunches of bananas in Jess's cart. "Got a couple monkeys at home?" she asked without fail. Jess would smile and nod. "You know I do." And the aisles were littered with moms from the school who timed their shopping to coincide with the final bell and the perfect position in the pickup lane. No, Jess couldn't go there.

Instead, she pulled into the parking lot of the Food Court, a mom-and-pop store that was a quarter of the size of Hy-Vee but conveniently located on the opposite side of town. Jess was convinced it stayed in business thanks to milk, bread, and eggs alone, but it contained all that she needed for her first real outing since Evan's funeral. Sure, she had brought the kids to school, stopped by her father's house to sign some papers, and even ventured into her own classroom late one evening so she could gather up her books and lesson plans, a few stacks of grading, and the novel that her English 10 class would start right before Christmas. *The Book Thief.* She'd had to make a presentation to the school board to get permission to teach a book narrated by Death. Now she wished she hadn't bothered.

And Jessica wished that she had gone online and ordered grocery delivery instead of venturing out into the harsh, noisy world.

Too late now. The wind was stiff, the air

crisp and set to shatter, so she pulled the cuffs of her sleeves over her palms and pushed the cart quickly through the cold aisles. Three bunches of bananas (Gabe had at least two a day), a loaf of bread, a gallon of 1 percent milk. Then a box of chocolate doughnuts and a clamshell from the local bakery with an oversized cinnamon roll. SunnyD and Dr Pepper and a family-sized bag of Doritos. Jess was grateful that the store was all but empty and no one was around to see her make such horrific nutritional choices for her family.

Her phone rang while she was checking out, and Jess ignored it. But when it started to trill again (the twinkle ringtone that Gabe had chosen when she first upgraded to an iPhone), she dug in her purse to see who was being so insistent. Caller ID told her it was Auburn Elementary.

"Hello?" Jess said, pressing the phone between her cheek and shoulder as she rooted in her purse for her wallet. The cashier was waiting for her to insert her credit card.

"Hi, Jessica. Nurse Amy here."

Jess's stomach cartwheeled as every worst-case scenario skittered through her mind. A fall on the playground, an accident in PE, a fight.

But Amy knew the drill and continued before Jess could truly panic. "I've got Gabe in my office complaining about a sore throat. He's got a bit of a fever, too."

"I'm on my way," Jess said, scrawling her signature on the electronic pad. She nodded at the cashier and accepted her bags, lining them up on her arms so that she could carry them all in one trip.

She wasn't happy that her son was sick, but it felt good to have a purpose, something that she *had* to do. Gabe needed her, and the click into full-fledged Mama Bear mode hitched just a little before Jess gave herself over to the task at hand. He'd need ginger ale, but she could buy that from the vending machine outside the pharmacy where she would pick up numbing throat spray and a tin of cherry throat lozenges. And maybe it wouldn't be a bad idea to have him looked at.

Jess jerked to a full stop in front of the trunk of her car. Her children had never, not once, seen a doctor other than their father. At least, not for the basic stuff. He often checked them out at home, lifting his stethoscope from the ratty backpack that he lugged back and forth to the office every day. If the situation was really serious, Jess would just show up at the clinic and he'd squeeze them in, usually in his private office or the back hallway or even the break room if the examination rooms were filled with other patients. His verdict was almost always the same, the prescription doled out with a kiss to the forehead: one bear hug from Dad, an afternoon of snuggles from Mom, plenty of liquids, and rest. Besides Max's emergency appendectomy at the age of eleven, the Chamberlain boys had never experienced an illness beyond the seasonal flu or the occasional ear infection.

No, Jessica decided. She could not take her boys there. Not yet. Maybe not ever. There was another medical office in town, bigger and fancier and connected to the hospital. She had never been there because Evan's community health clinic needed patients with good insurance to cover the ones who didn't have any. Jess had always been proud of her husband's generosity, of his commitment to providing quality, afford-able health care to anyone and everyone — especially those who society tried to over-look. But now? She knew that even people with the best of intentions made the worst kind of mistakes. And she couldn't face Cate. Thankfully Evan's nurse hadn't shown up at the funeral. Or, if she had, Jess hadn't seen her. And Jess had no desire to see her now. Gabe would have to tough it out. Ginger ale and rest would have to be enough.

But by the time she had him signed out at the school office and bundled into the backseat of her car, he was shivering uncontrollably and had more than a bit of a fever.

"You're burning up, buddy," Jess said, putting the car into drive. Her lips were still warm from pressing a kiss to his temple. She had found over the years that she could measure a temperature nearly as accurately as a thermometer — 102 degrees, she guessed.

"I don't feel so good," Gabe said weakly. His eyes were glassy when she caught his gaze in the rearview mirror.

Jess didn't have a choice, not really. "I know. We're going to take care of that, okay? I'm taking you to the doctor."

Strep throat, Jess was sure of it. She had battled it more than once in the years that she had been a teacher. Teaching was a hazardous profession, and after her first miscarriage she had seemed prone to every infection that crept through her classroom. She knew what a sore throat and a sudden, high fever meant. Strep every time.

At Urgent Care, a heavyset woman with rust-colored curls photocopied Jessica's insurance card and handed over a clipboard with a new-patient questionnaire. It felt strange to fill out information that had been a given for so many years. Patient history, known allergies, and past surgeries (none) were all things that Evan had known by heart, and Jess realized she had taken the simplicity of their medical care for granted.

But besides the fatherly kiss at the end of the appointment, the minutes Gabe spent with the unfamiliar Dr. Zhu were really no different than Evan's exams. Jess was right; a rapid strep test confirmed the infection, and as she accepted the prescription for antibiotics, she felt a burst of gratitude that her son was in the throes of a fever dream. He was so out of it she was sure that he didn't have the emotional capacity to feel wounded by the fact that it wasn't his daddy who stuck the giant Q-tip down his throat for a swab.

"Come on, baby." Gabe was sitting on her lap, head lolling back against her shoulder, and Jess turned him around gently so she could carry him to the car.

"I'm sure he can walk," Dr. Zhu said, and although she couldn't see his face, she was certain that he rolled his eyes at her. Gabe was a big boy, taller and broader than most kids his age, and people expected him to act as old as he looked. But he was only six, still her baby — and a child who had to deal with more than his fair share of obstacles.

"I'm sure I can carry him," Jess snapped back, and left the office without a backward glance, the prescription crumpled in her sweaty hand.

Jess brought the prescription to a new pharmacy instead of the Walgreens where the pharmacists knew her by name. While they filled the prescription, Jess carried Gabe around the store, a surgical mask firmly over his mouth and nose so that he wouldn't infect anyone else. His cheeks were blazing beneath the blue paper, the red so high and alarming there was no doubt that he was seriously sick. But what else could she do? He couldn't stay in the car while she gathered children's ibuprofen, throat lozenges, and Vicks VapoRub.

She gave him the first dose of ibuprofen and the pink, bubblegum-flavored amoxicillin in the car. Gabe hardly knew what was going on, and she had to hold the bottle of cold 7UP to his lips and coax him to drink, then wipe the evidence of the fluorescent medicine from the corners of his mouth.

"We're going home, honey," she whispered, resting her cheek against his hot forehead for just a moment. "I'll make you a bed on the couch and you can watch *PAW Patrol* for the rest of the day."

Jess was late to pick up Max, and as she pulled up to the school she worried that he had left without her. Walked home or caught a ride with someone or simply disappeared. He seemed to want to these days. But she was relieved to see that he was lounging against one of the stone pillars at the entrance to the middle school, thumbing through his phone even though Jess knew that there was nothing for him to look at. He didn't have a data plan and could only access the internet when Wi-Fi was available. The school Wi-Fi was on lockdown.

"I'm so sorry I'm late," Jess said when he wrenched open the passenger door. "I got called to school because Gabe is sick." She motioned toward the backseat, but Max didn't bother to look.

"Strep," she said. "It's really contagious. How are you feeling?"

"Fine," Max said. He took the earbuds that were hanging around his neck and fit them into his ears. A second later she heard the fast beat of a song that sounded explosive, angry.

They drove home in near silence, though the song that Max was listening to thrummed in the still air of the car and

Gabe whimpered occasionally. Both sounds made Jess's skin crawl.

At home Max disappeared into his room and Gabe waited in the armchair while Jess riffled through the linen closet for a set of sheets. Her mother had turned the couch into a bed when Jessica was a child, and now she did the same thing for her children when they were sick. Fitted sheet tucked tight around the cushions, flat sheet on top. A bed pillow with a crisp, cool pillowcase and a water bottle with ice at the ready on the floor. The TV was nearby, and so was Mom, because the hub of the house — the kitchen — was only steps away. It was comfort and proximity and everything Gabe needed to feel better. Well, almost everything. The patina of grief that made every surface in the house seem slick with loss made Jess squeeze her eyes shut for just a second. It was a relief to have something to do, a purpose to fulfill, but she was breathing heavy, winded from the effort of holding the pieces of her broken heart still.

Jess cupped her face in her hands so she could gather herself. Then she hobbled on her knees to the place where Gabe was waiting in the chair. "Hey, how're you holding up?" She wanted to pull her baby onto her lap and hold him until his fever broke, but she knew from experience that his skin was alive, every nerve ending awake and tingling in pain. "I'm almost done here. Do you want a bath before I settle you on the couch?"

Gabe shook his head, his shoulders trembling.

Jess reached to touch him but thought better of it. Instead, she stood to shake out the fitted sheet. But when she went to slip it over the cushions, something stopped her. The corner of the couch, the place that she had claimed as her own, was not as it should be. A gray throw pillow, the one with the plush lambswool cover, was on the floor, partially hidden beneath the coffee table. She had been clutching it against her stomach only hours before, hadn't she? Between the arm of the couch and her body? She had left it crumpled there, against the whorl of the elaborate stitching — she was sure of it.

Something dangerous, mercurial rippled through the air. Her house felt *different.* Jess spun a slow circle, taking in everything from the clock on the mantel to the heavy curtains that were still drawn over the tall windows flanking her front door. Everything was as it should be, except that it wasn't.

The hang of one of the curtains was off; it

was caught on a lip in the hardwood floor, tented forward as if someone had peeled it back to look at the driveway. Jess hadn't done that. And the picture beside the half wall that bordered the staircase was crooked. Just a bit. Not enough to make her blame Max and his broad, oblivious shoulders. He routinely bumped into her and kept right on walking as if he didn't register the contact. She wondered if he even noticed.

But she did. Jess noticed everything as she hurried around the house, fingers flying over shelves and her dining room table and the little desk in the kitchen where she kept her mail. The drawer that stuck open had come off its slider again, and it was wedged at an angle, the right side lifted like a cocked hip. Jess knew that drawer. She hadn't left it askew in years.

For just a moment, Jess's vision blurred. Her house swam out of focus and then just as quickly snapped back to hi-res. Everything was just a little bit wrong.

Someone had been in her house.

LaShonna Tate
RE: Hello
To: echamberlain@comnet.com

February 4, 2018

Dear Evan,

I know this email must come as a bit of a shock. I didn't intend to write to you ever again, but circumstances both out of my control and fully my fault have landed me in an awful situation. I really don't have anyone to talk to about this. I know it's crazy that I'm contacting you, but if you're open to meeting with me (in person) I have something to ask you.

You owe me nothing and I don't expect you to respond. But it's a shot I have to take. Thank you for loving Gabe so well. It means more to me than you will ever know.

Sincerely,
LaShonna

Evan Chamberlain
RE: Hello
To: lashonna.tate@fastnet.com
February 5, 2018

Hello, LaShonna.
It's so good to hear from you. I wasn't sure that I ever would again.

I'm sorry to hear that you're in an awful situation. I'm not sure what I can do to help, but if you think that it would be beneficial to meet, I am open to the possibility. Should I contact Promise and make sure that a face-to-face meeting is not in breach of our contract?

Regards,
Evan

LaShonna Tate
RE: Hello
To: echamberlain@comnet.com
February 5, 2018

Please don't contact Promise. There is nothing illegal about us talking, I swear. Would it work to meet halfway? Mankato is in between Auburn and the Twin Cities. I know it's a bit of a drive for you. We could meet at the Starbucks near the campus of MSU. Wednesday morning? Ten?

LaShonna

Evan Chamberlain
RE: Hello
To: lashonna.tate@fastnet.com

February 5, 2018

Yes. That works. See you then.

Evan

CHAPTER 7

Susana L.
30, Caucasian, working on GED
Long, dark hair. Recently dyed. Nail biter.
Boyfriend consented.
H&R, MANSL, 51m, 1yr pp

"Jess, seriously. I need you to sit down."

A beat of silence, and then the sound of a door closing harder than Jessica intended it to.

"You're not sitting."

"No," Jess hissed into the phone. "I'm going through every square inch of my house. Wouldn't you?"

Meredith sighed on the other end of the line. "Honey, I love you, but you really need to calm down for a minute."

"I'm perfectly calm."

"You're a train wreck. You're probably scaring the kids."

"Max is in his room with the music turned up to deafening, and Gabe is sleeping on the couch. He's sick."

"Really?"

"Strep throat," Jess confirmed as she riffled through the closet in the spare room. The Chamberlains' winter coats were lined up on their hangers, looking innocent and maybe a little put out that she was disturbing their slumber. As far as she could tell, there was no evidence that someone had been in the spare closet. But then, it had been months since she had looked inside.

"I'm coming over," Meredith said.

"No, don't." Jessica shut the bifold closet door, not bothering to muffle the bang. "I'm fine."

"You're clearly *not* fine. Do you really think someone was in your house?"

It was Jessica's turn to sigh. She paused in the hallway with her hand on her hip. "Yes," she said after a moment. "Yes, I do. I can't explain it, Mer, but everything is different. Little things, you know?"

"You're going through a really difficult time," Meredith said carefully. "Maybe things have slipped a bit and you just haven't noticed."

Jess was already shaking her head, even though Meredith couldn't see it. "I'm not crazy."

"Oh, honey. I never said you were. Stay

put. I'm coming."

The phone line went flat before Jessica could protest. She had said that she didn't want Meredith to come, but now the thought of having her friend in the quiet house — bustling around, filling up space, helping her catalog the infinitesimal differences that she couldn't quite put her finger on — was comforting.

Jess put her phone in the back pocket of her jeans and consulted the palm-sized notebook that she had been carrying around. The stub of a pencil was tucked in its spirals and she poked it out with her pinky, then flipped the notebook open. Evan had turned her into a fastidious note taker in the years that they had been married, and now she could hardly function without a detailed to-do list. She cataloged everything from recipes she wanted to try to home repairs that would require Evan's attention. A honey-do list of sorts that she never presented to him because Evan was not much of a handyman. Now she never could.

Jess swallowed tears and shook her head to scatter unwanted thoughts. She turned her full attention to the notebook. On the very first page she had written a list that spanned just a few lines. She'd scrawled:

- pillow on floor
- curtain askew
- picture crooked
- junk drawer off its rollers
- bathroom cupboard ajar
- bed mussed

It was a ridiculous list, and as she stared at it she knew exactly why Meredith was so worried. Everything she had written down was circumstantial at best, paranoid at worst. Was she coming unhinged? Had her conversation with Deputy Mullen unsettled her more than she realized? Of course her bed was messy. She hadn't made it in days. Longer? What in the world made her think that she could remember the exact way the comforter had fallen when she crawled out of bed that morning?

Jess threw the notebook on the dresser in the spare room and turned off the lights as she left. Meredith was right. No one had been in her house. There was no motive, no reason. Nothing was gone. They didn't have a private bank account in the Cayman Islands or anything really of interest. And what little jewelry she had was exactly where it was supposed to be on the wire tree in her en suite. Most of her pieces were cheap, clothing-store necklaces that she had bought to match a specific outfit, but she had a real gold chain with a strand of three small pearls and a pair of diamond earrings that she wore on special occasions. They were all present and accounted for.

"You're losing it," she told herself. "Get it together."

But as she descended the stairs to check on Gabe, Jessica couldn't shake the feeling that something was off. Her blood hissed in her veins, a primal warning that everything was not as it should be.

Jess felt like someone was watching her.

"Hey, baby," Jess forced herself to say as she came around the side of the couch. She wrapped the cardigan she had thrown on tight across her chest and knelt next to Gabe. As she laid her hand on his pink cheek, she asked, "How are you feeling?"

"Okay," he croaked. His eyes were trained on the television, yet another episode of *PAW Patrol.* Jessica recorded them on the DVR and then played them back ad nauseam to Gabe's never-ending delight. He sounded terrible, but it was obvious that the ibuprofen had done its job. His fever had broken, though Jess guessed it still hovered around one hundred degrees.

"How's the throat?"

Gabe just shook his head. His eyes were

dark pools, the pupils dilated wide in the dim light of the living room.

"How about a little drink?" Jess lifted the water bottle to his lips and he complied, taking a couple of tiny sips through the plastic straw before turning his head and looking past her pointedly. She got the message loud and clear.

Gabe was sick, but he was certainly going to be okay. He could still watch TV, and Jess guessed that if pressed, he could also rouse himself enough to play Mario Kart. She pulled the blanket up to his shoulders and dropped a kiss on the top of his head. His curls were damp with sweat and he smelled slightly medicinal, of VapoRub and fevered skin.

"I miss Dad," Gabe mumbled.

Jess wasn't sure that she had heard him right. His words were muffled and she was convinced his attention was on the TV. But when she pulled back to look at his face, there were tears leaking out of his glassy eyes. He sniffed a little and winced at the pain Jess knew it caused in his throat.

"Oh, honey." Jess cupped his cheek, her tears coming just as quickly as his. She hadn't realized they were still so close to the surface. "Me too. I miss him too."

"When's he coming back?"

The question was a splash of ice water. Chilling. Jess tried to swallow, but her mouth was dry as a desert. "Gabe, we talked about this, remember?"

But his attention was already gone. Eyes trained on the TV, expression slack. There were crooked trails on his cheeks, evidence that he had been crying only a moment ago, and Jess smoothed them away with her thumb.

"I love you, Gabriel," she whispered.

In the kitchen, Jess blew her nose and ran her wrists under cold water. It was bracing, clarifying, and she could almost convince herself that her exchange with Gabe was wholly the result of his illness. But she knew that wasn't true. They had a long road ahead of them, and they were only a few steps into their journey. Jess was already weary.

Max had been in his room since they arrived home over an hour earlier, but that wasn't entirely unusual. Jess decided she would start on something for supper, maybe homemade biscuits and some chicken breasts from the freezer, and if she was lucky, the scent of cooking would lure him out.

With a start, Jess remembered the groceries in the trunk of her car. She had forgotten all about them in the fuss surrounding Gabe's illness and their dramatic homecoming.

Jess gathered the plastic bags quickly, leaving the garage door up because her hands were full and she couldn't reach the button. As she deposited two armloads on the kitchen counter, she heard the door click open.

"Hello?" Meredith called. She must have pulled up seconds after Jess left the garage.

"In the kitchen!"

But Meredith ignored her. "Oh, buddy . . ." Jess could hear her best friend huff as she bent to undo her shoes, then the steady pad of her feet across the living room floor.

"How are you doing, kiddo?"

Jess put away the groceries while Meredith loved on Gabe, tucking and retucking his blanket and making him laugh in spite of himself because he was swaddled tighter than a sausage in its casing.

"Auntie Meredith," he barked, his throat clearly straining to form the words, "I can't move!"

"Good," she said. "You shouldn't move. Too much moving is bad for your health."

"But you and mom go on walks."

"That's different. We're old. You're young

and vulnerable. You need to stay safe and protected and warm. Your mom and I are going to talk about making a sling for you so she can carry you around on her back."

"No!" Jess smiled at the horror in Gabe's cry.

"Oh yes. Complete with Bubble Wrap and a helmet. No head injuries on our watch."

"Auntie Meredith . . ."

"You heard me."

Jess could just make out the smack of a quick kiss, and then Meredith was coming into the kitchen, arms outstretched. Putting down the box of Little Debbie Nutty Bars she was holding, Jess walked right into her friend's embrace.

"You're going to give him nightmares," Jess scolded. "The poor kid is borderline claustrophobic to begin with."

"He needed to laugh." Meredith gave Jess an extra-hard squeeze and then pulled back and held her at arm's length. "Hey, you don't look as bad as I thought you would."

"I showered today, I'll have you know."

"Good for you." Meredith's eyes softened. "But what's this about someone breaking into your house?"

Jess shrugged off Meredith's hands and grabbed the box of snacks. Sticking it into a random cupboard she said, "Nothing. It's nothing."

"It's not nothing. You were really upset when you called." Meredith leaned against the counter with her palms hooked over the edge. "Want to talk about it?"

"Not really."

"I do."

Jess sighed and turned to face her friend. Meredith was still wearing her work clothes, a pair of brocade pants that hugged her curves in all the right places and a blouse in lipstick red. She looked so pretty, so professional and put together and *sane,* Jess could have cried. "I'm a little stressed," she managed.

"You don't say." Meredith gave her a long look, then took her by the wrist and led her to the breakfast nook. They sat on opposite sides of the painted plank table, their hands between them as if they needed the physical proximity. "You have every right in the world to be coming apart, Jess. I would be. But I don't want you to start blurring the lines of reality. Know what I mean?"

Jess felt a stab of irritation. Whether the evidence she uncovered was real or not, the truth was that *something* felt off. Evan was all about cold, hard facts, but he had also taught her that intuition was an incredibly powerful tool. Once, when Max was a baby,

Evan woke in the middle of the night and sat straight up in bed. "Something's wrong," he said, and threw back the covers. Before Jess had a chance to rub the sleep from her eyes, Evan was back with Max cradled in his arms. Even at a distance Jess knew something wasn't right. Her bright, happy nine-month-old was limp in his dad's embrace, one fat hand open to the ceiling, fingers curled as if he were reaching for something but didn't have the strength to grasp it.

"What?" Jess croaked, lacking the ability to form a coherent thought.

"Influenza?" Evan guessed. "Quick onset, high fever. He's burning up."

"I didn't hear him crying."

"He wasn't."

"Then . . ."

"Sixth sense," Evan said, pressing his lips to Max's hot forehead. His kiss left a white crescent on the pink flush of his son's damp skin.

Jess's sixth sense was clamoring for attention now.

"Nobody would have to break into my house," Jess said. "I don't lock the doors when I'm gone during the day. Neither do you."

"Okay, but you thought someone came in

while you were gone? Why?"

That was the million-dollar question, wasn't it? "I don't know, Mer. That's what I'd like to find out."

Meredith pulled her glasses off and delicately rubbed the bridge of her nose. Jess could picture her friend doing exactly that in difficult interviews, or while she was facilitating a meeting between birth mothers and adoptive parents. It was exactly the same move she used on the Chamberlains when they were in the process of bringing Gabe home, and Jess knew that it meant one thing: Meredith's patience was thin. "What evidence do you have, Jess? What makes you think that someone has been in your home?"

Jessica thought of the list she had made and left on the dresser in the spare room. "I don't have any evidence. Just a hunch."

"Sweetie, you're not a private detective."

She had never claimed to be one. All at once Jessica wished that Meredith had never come at all. Her friend could be so calculating sometimes, almost masculine in her need to fix everything. Jess had just wanted someone to listen, but she realized now that Meredith was not going to be that person. She drew her hands into her lap, where she wrung her fingers.

"I'd like to talk about something else."

Meredith narrowed her eyes, assessing. "You sure you're okay with this? You don't think anyone has been in your house?"

"What in the world would they be looking for?"

Meredith smiled a little. "It's good to see you up and about," she said, abruptly changing the conversation. Then, "You've lost weight. Let me make you supper."

"I've got chicken thawing," Jess said, but it was a lie. She had intended to take some out of the freezer but she hadn't gotten around to it. "In fact, I'd better get started."

"I'll help. Pour you a glass of wine?"

"I shouldn't," Jess said. She had just started taking antianxiety meds and Meredith knew that. She was less than two weeks in and feeling worse instead of better. All Jess had to do was give her friend a pointed look and nod her head in the direction of the sink where the little amber bottle of pills sat in wait on the windowsill.

"Oh."

Meredith seemed sad, like she knew she had said or done something wrong, so Jess got up and gave her a one-armed hug. It was a conciliatory gesture, but her heart wasn't really in it. "Thank you for putting up with me. I know that I haven't exactly been myself lately."

"How did you end up comforting me?" Meredith laughed a little. "I came here to comfort you."

"Maybe this is exactly what I need."

"What?"

"For people to stop treating me with kid gloves."

After Meredith left, Jessica did take chicken out of the freezer. Deciding soup was the way to go, she threw the breasts in a stockpot with a few cans of chicken broth and some thyme. Normally she would finely chop carrots, celery, and onion, then sauté them in butter with a couple of healthy pinches of sea salt. But she couldn't be bothered today. She dumped a bag of frozen vegetables into the pot and decided to call it good. Jess was starting to feel fuzzy around the edges, tired and heavy limbed, as if her outing had been a marathon instead of a handful of errands that she could have done in her sleep only weeks ago.

Maybe she could join Gabe on the couch, close her eyes for a few moments.

"Mom," Gabe croaked when she came into the living room. "Can I have some sugar toast? I'm hungry."

"Baby, I just put soup on. Toast won't feel good on your throat."

"Gatorade?"

"I have 7UP."

Gabe swiveled his head to look over the back of the couch. His lips were dry, his eyes a pair of dark, shiny buttons. He was perkier than he had been all afternoon, but Jess knew it wouldn't last. She could see the fever hiding behind his earnest gaze. "There's a cupcake in my backpack. Can I have that?"

"There's a cupcake in your backpack?"

Gabe jiggled his head on the pillow. It was close enough to a nod. "It was Ella's birthday and I missed her treat because my throat hurt. Mrs. Rosalind let me take it home."

"Let's save it for after chicken noodle soup, okay? I'll get you some 7UP."

Gabe shrugged and turned back to his show. Jessica longed to join him, to cram herself into the space between his warm little body and the back of the couch, but there was a cupcake in her son's backpack. She had found one too many forgotten water bottles toxic with unidentifiable sludge to simply let it go.

Gabe's backpack was hanging on his hook in the entryway, beneath the placard with the chalkboard paint and his artfully written name. Jess had been so proud of the

139

redesigned space, the sleek, black bench and locker-style cubbies. But it had nearly taken an act of God to convince her boys to use the proper hooks, and she often wondered if an old-fashioned closet would have made more sense — though she would've never admitted that to Evan. They had spent a small fortune on the remodel.

Unzipping Gabe's Pokémon backpack, Jess extracted the cupcake. It was in a plastic bag, thank goodness, but the frothy swirl of pink frosting was mashed and melting just a little. It belonged in the garbage can along with the other odds and ends that Jessica found in the dark recesses of the backpack.

A used glow stick, a single sock, and a stack of bent and folded papers that had somehow *not* made it into Gabe's take-home folder. How long had it been since she had riffled through her son's bag? Clearly way too long.

Jessica upended the backpack and sorted through the mess, hanging a sweatshirt on one of Gabe's hooks and making a pile intended for the trash. Rummaging through the detritus, Jess worked quickly and un-emotionally, deciding what to keep and what to toss with little consideration. Until she found something she wasn't expecting.

Wedged in the very bottom, half-hidden beneath a flat panel that was torn and flapped open, Jess's fingers met a dog-eared paperback. It was worn soft, the pages gently waved as if it had once been left out in the rain. When Jess worked it free, she realized she was holding an old copy of *To Kill a Mockingbird.* It was the same edition she had read in high school, a pale lavender cover with a night scene in a framed square. A crow flying, a tree with a knotty hole containing a ball of yarn and a stopwatch instead of an owl. Just holding it in her hands, Jessica could remember the feeling in Mr. Defoe's classroom. The way he stood with one foot propped on a chair, pretending he was indifferent to the many distractions that made it nearly impossible to discuss Harper Lee's legendary book. The titters of the girls at the back of the class, the damp fug that lifted off the boys who had just finished PE and elected to reapply deodorant instead of braving the wall of showers in the locker room.

Jess was fifteen again and listening to Mr. Defoe with her heart in her throat, even if she pretended to be as unaffected as the rest of her tenth-grade classmates.

Where in the world had Gabe gotten this

book? He was in kindergarten, not high school.

Jess stood up and patted herself, wondering if she could fit the paperback in the back pocket of her jeans. But as she looked down she realized she was wearing one of Evan's old cardigans, an oversized sweater with leather buttons and pockets big enough to contain all her secrets. She didn't even remember putting it on. Jess slid the paperback into one of the cardigan's pockets, then gathered up the rest of the garbage.

"Gabe?" she called, coming into the living room with her arms full. "Can I ask you about something?"

But the second she laid eyes on her son she knew. "Mom," he whimpered, his skin gray, tears beginning to leak from the corners of his eyes. "I don't feel so good . . ."

And then Gabe threw up all over his pillow.

February 7, 2018

I met LaShonna Tate this morning. At a Starbucks in Mankato. I'm recording the meeting here for legal purposes. For times and dates, details. Things we discussed.

Jessica doesn't know because she doesn't want to know. I've tried to bring it up with her a couple of times, but she shuts me down. I even asked her what she would do if we found out that Gabe's birth mom had been writing letters, and she acted as if the mere suggestion was obscene. I think her exact words were: I'd burn them.

I've backed myself into a corner.

LaShonna told me that there is going to be another baby. Gabriel is going to have a sister.

CHAPTER 8

Darcie M.
28, Latina, HS diploma
Long hair dyed blond. Quiet (mute?),
  homesick.
Friend knows.
DWLR, 20m pp

The Chamberlains were sick for the rest of the week. Even Max caught the bug, though he only suffered from the stomach flu, while Jessica and Gabe had to contend with strep throat, too. Meredith wanted to sweep in and help, but Jess barred the door and refused to let anyone inside. Not even her father was allowed to cross the threshold. "We're fine," she told everyone, but it was a lie. They were falling apart at the seams. But that particular process had begun months ago. Their slow unraveling was ongoing, not the direct result of a bacterial infection.

"Was it something you ate?" Henry asked

through the safety of the telephone. It was Monday morning and Jess had just dropped the boys off at school. Gabe had been fever-free for over forty-eight hours and they had both kept three solid meals down. Well, solid was a relative term. They managed toast and crackers, a Pop-Tart or two. Jess wasn't in the mood to squabble about nutrition. They had survived. That was enough. Her father continued, "It could have been food poisoning."

Jess thought back to her hurried attempt at chicken noodle soup. After Gabe threw up, she had completely forgotten about supper until she could smell it burning to the bottom of the pot. The stench of burnt chicken was enough to make her nauseous, but she didn't start vomiting until much later that night.

"No, Dad," Jess said. "I didn't poison my kids."

"I wasn't suggesting you did." Henry sounded smug, but he often sounded that way. "Lots of people brought food for you. Who knows what kind of hygiene standards people have? I have friends who don't believe in washing their hands."

"That's disgusting."

"I know."

"Either way, it wasn't food poisoning. We

got sick, fair and square." Jess put the final crease in the towel she was folding and tucked it into her laundry basket.

"Well, I'm glad you're feeling better. Anything I can do for you?" There was a lilt in his voice, the tiniest shift up as he asked the question, and Jessica felt herself soften immediately. He was hurting, too. Her father had loved Evan in his own way, but even more so he loved his daughter, his grandsons.

"We're fine, Dad. Thanks for asking."

Jessica left her phone on the kitchen counter and settled the hamper on her hip. She was supposed to go back to school today, and she would have if they hadn't been waylaid by illness. "One more day," she told Alexa Hastings, the principal at Auburn High School. She was younger than Jess, a hipster former teacher in gray pencil skirts and graphic T-shirts that she dressed up with fitted blazers. Really, she was new and untried. She would have given Jess more time.

It felt good to fill the linen closet with fresh towels. Jess had practically doused the house in bleach and scrubbed down every single door handle with Clorox wipes, but nothing was quite so satisfying as the feel and smell of crisp, white linens. Their sickness was a cleansing of sorts, a scouring that left Jess feeling hollowed out inside. She was purged, empty, as lifeless and starched as the laundry she had just finished. It wasn't necessarily unwelcome, for there was little to grieve in the barren landscape of her heart. Jess was sad, but quietly so.

Her bedroom was stripped bare, sheets still in the washing machine and comforter hanging over the clothesline in the bitter November air. It would smell of frost when she took it inside, bracing and just a little dangerous. A reminder that the world could not be tamed, that soon it would snow. Blanket the world in white.

Jessica deposited her empty hamper on the bench at the foot of her bed and began to put her room back in order. It had been less than a month since Evan had died, but she had amassed what seemed like a lifetime of stuff. She picked up shirts and sweatpants and deposited them in the laundry basket, then stacked books and magazines that well-meaning friends had brought her and that she had never touched. There were a few plates that contained the remains of old food, a half-eaten slice of toast, crackers and cheese that she had taken to bed one night, thinking that she would be able to stomach a few bites. Instead, the crackers went stale and the cheese turned moldy. Jess was ashamed of herself.

Her nightstand drawer was hanging half-open, and when she tried to push it shut with her thigh, she couldn't because something was in the way. A book, its pages spread and curling at the edges. And tucked inside the book, a letter.

Jess sank to the bed and took the paperback in both hands. She barely recalled stuffing it there and didn't remember at all sticking the envelope in the front cover. But here they were: the coroner's letter proclaiming the cause of Evan's death, and *To Kill a Mockingbird,* courtesy of her six-year-old's backpack. She hadn't even asked Gabe about it.

Slipping the letter out of the book unread, Jess put it on the bed beside her. Then she thumbed through the book.

Just inside the front cover was a penciled number: *2.50.* Most likely the price. It was a secondhand book, then, purchased at a used bookstore or maybe a garage sale. There was no name written in the cover, but on the title page she found two words scrawled in blue pen: *LOVE, DAD.*

A gift from Evan to Gabe? Jessica doubted it. Two words were hardly enough to get a real sense of the handwriting, but it didn't seem like Evan's. He wasn't like any doctor she knew, and his handwriting was far from the hen-scratch stereotype. Evan was slow. Thoughtful. Measured and kind. It was reflected in everything he did — including his handwriting. He typically wrote in a slanting cursive hand, the loops even and eloquent somehow, like amateur but heart-felt poetry. This was seven letters, capitals all. Jessica turned it around and then again. She just didn't know.

Because sometimes Evan could behave opposite to everything she knew him to be. Sometimes he became frantic, obsessed. She remembered a few specific patients that had caused him to lose sleep and weight in tandem. He wanted to fix problems and diagnose every ailment and make the world right again. When Evan was buzzing with the need to mend what was broken, he was distracted and forgetful. He left his reading glasses all over the house when he forgot to take them off, and Jessica would find them between the couch cushions, on top of the refrigerator, inexplicably tucked into the mailbox. He also scribbled.

There was no way to know if he had written a note inside this book.

Jess flipped to the back but nothing grabbed her attention. Then she let her thumb graze the pages, fanning them slowly so the page numbers ticked by like an old film. Halfway through, the paper stuttered beneath her careful attention. Jess skipped back, trying to find the spot. Maybe there was something hiding there. An old bookmark that would indicate where the paperback had come from and why it had been hidden in the bottom of her son's backpack.

Nothing. Not even an old receipt marked the spot. But as Jess turned each page individually, she found that one page was torn. Hastily, it seemed, and unevenly. A large chunk of the corner was missing, approximately the size and shape of a business card, though the edges were jagged. It was disappointing, really. The name "Atticus" was cut in half, and three lines were missing a swath of words. Jessica hated it when her students dog-eared pages in their books or wrote obscenities in the margins. It drove her crazy. And this ripped page pained her, but it wasn't so unusual.

Since the book held no mysteries, Jess felt emboldened to reach for the coroner's report. Putting *To Kill a Mockingbird* on the nightstand, Jessica grabbed the fat envelope and tore it open before she could consider what she was doing. Why not? She had nothing to lose.

Roughly a dozen stapled pages contained all the secrets of her husband's death. It was clinical, unemotional, each sheet stamped at the top with *Scott County* and then *Department of Medical Examiner — Coroner.* Really, there wasn't much to see. A series of boxes with seemingly innocuous checks. Yes, he was clothed. His sex was male. A few pages in there was a diagram of the human body documenting every old scar and each new wound. There were three black *X* marks. Neck, shoulder, upper back. Jess already knew that the carotid had been severed. It was over in less than a minute.

Jess took a shaky breath, surprised that she had made it this far, but determined to at least scan the entire report. She knew that she couldn't move on until she had turned the last page. Afterward she could burn it in a memorial or put it in Evan's safe. But really, what was the point of keeping such a horrific piece of literature? She shuddered at the thought of her boys discovering it someday, going through her paperwork when she was old and they had families of their own. It would be like setting a land mine in her home.

No, she'd read it and get rid of it. They all knew what happened.

But Jess paused at the very last page. It

didn't bear the Scott County emblem and only held a few spare lines. *Addendum,* it read. *Evidence collected.* Then: *There was no identification on the body. A scrap of paper was found in the right back pocket of his jeans. It was torn from page 195 of "To Kill a Mockingbird" and contained the following number written in black ink: 5554403686.*

Jess ignored her phone for the rest of the day. She had left it on the kitchen counter and there it stayed, emitting its silent beacon like a homing device. It was almost impossible not to pick it up and ring Deputy Mullen's number. But what would she say? "I think I found the book that the paper in Evan's pocket was ripped from." So what? They were married. Separated, but still. They had contact with each other and shared kids. Things were passed between the family house (the mortgage was in both of their names) and Evan's town house on a weekly, sometimes daily basis. It made perfect sense that if Evan has a scrap of paper in his pocket, it would have come from something that she was at the very least familiar with.

And yet, Jess's world felt off. She couldn't put her finger on it, but the old book with the torn page and the addendum to the autopsy report felt just a measure wrong. A coincidence that was too intentional to be mere serendipity. The air was laced with suggestion, ripe as a plum that was starting to turn, skin firm and flawless — but the flesh beneath was soft and sickly sweet, just a hint rancid.

Jess had to *do* something. She grabbed the magnetic pad of paper that hung on the fridge and jotted a quick list of all the people who knew the Chamberlains left their garage door unlocked during the day. Weeks ago, Deputy Mullen had asked her if Evan had any enemies, but she had scoffed at the question. Evan? Enemies? It was impossible to believe. But she had to start somewhere and she still believed that someone had been in her house.

Max's close friends were first: Trey, Lucas, Bradley, and Colin. They weren't bad boys — Jess genuinely cared for them all — but they could be troublemakers. It was typical teenage trouble — innocent for the most part — but they were a good place to begin. Then came the neighbors. Mr. and Mrs. Henderson, though they were painfully proper and would never dream of entering her house when nobody was home. However, Jake Holmes lived on the other side and he was a definite suspect. He was an older, single man with an obvious chip on his shoulder and an abrasive personality. Jess was a bit afraid of him, and even Evan had avoided Jake after they'd had a run-in about the apples from the Chamberlains' tree that fell onto his property every autumn. Jake had become unhinged. Jess put a fine line underneath his name.

Half a dozen people rounded out the list, including some of Jess's coworkers and a few of Evan's, too. Then there was Trevor Albright, a friend that Evan used to go biking with who was also an avid hunter, and Lane Cameron, who was not only their financial advisor but also Evan's beer drinking buddy.

With a start, Jess realized that there was another name to add to her list. Cody De Jager.

It had been a long time since Jessica had thought about Cody. He was a meth head, an addict in their relatively close-knit community that most people tried to ignore. But when he showed up in Evan's exam room with pneumonia one day, Evan had taken him under his wing. Gabe was just a toddler when Cody began coming to the Chamberlains' house for dinner twice a month on every other Wednesday night. At first, Jess had balked at welcoming a recovering drug addict to their table. But Evan was a fixer. He was insistent that Cody was on the upswing; it would be okay. And it had been. At least for a while. When Cody fell off the wagon, Evan retracted his invitation — and came home with a cut on his cheekbone and the swelling purple flush of a bruise.

"Did he *hit* you?" Jess had asked, incredulous. She snagged an ice pack out of the freezer and wrapped it in a tea towel. Pressing it to the side of Evan's face, she kissed his opposite cheek. Whiskers from his five o'clock shadow tickled her lips.

"No," Evan said, pulling away.

"What do you mean, no?"

But Evan had refused to tell Jess what happened.

She looked at Cody's name on her list and underlined it twice.

Anna texted midafternoon and said that she would pick up the boys from school. *I'm out and about,* her message read. *Can I get anything for you?*

Jess was tempted to text back: *Answers.* Instead she wrote: *A gallon of milk.*

Anna was trying and that was something. She and Henry had only been married for two years, though Jess's mother, Betsy, had been gone for over a decade. Why was it so hard for Jess to accept her dad's new wife? She was a grown woman, steady and mature and really rather accepting, but everything about Anna rubbed her the wrong way. Anna's childish voice grated, and her worn Birkenstock sandals seemed more suited for a wandering hippie. Jess didn't like the layers of bangles Anna wore on her arms or the little Chinese symbol tattoo on the nape of her neck that was just visible beneath the fringe of her stylish silver hair. Anna was quite lovely for her age, quick to smile and generous with her hugs. But she was also a bit ditzy. She often said the wrong thing but didn't have the grace to realize when she had put her foot in her mouth. In short, the new Mrs. Henry Lancaster was nothing like the original. Still, Jess felt like a recalcitrant teenager in the presence of her stepmother, and she could never quite seem to graduate from that small, critical place.

It was the yoga clothes, Jess decided when Anna swept in, batik fabric billowing on a cold breeze of boys and laughter. Well, Gabe was laughing. Both he and Max had a Dairy Queen Blizzard in hand, an enormous cup of ice cream and candy that would ruin dinner completely. Not that a frozen lasagna was anything to get excited about.

"Sorry," Anna said, handing Jessica a gallon of 1 percent milk. "Gabe asked and I couldn't resist."

Jess thought unkindly, *It's because the crystals are interfering with your brain waves.* She was shocked by her own harshness. "Thank you for the milk," she said, turning to the refrigerator and depositing the jug inside. "And for picking the boys up. It saved me a trip."

"No problem," Anna practically sang. "Happy to help."

Jess knew that she was. Her stepmother had been angling for an inroad, hoping for a way to connect with Jessica and the boys. They were the only children and grand-children that Anna had ever had, and she was earnest but bumbling. Henry Lancaster was her first marriage. It showed.

"Would you like a cup of tea?" Jess asked, surprising herself. Maybe she could try too.

Anna's eyebrow quirked, her lips lifting in a mixture of surprise and delight. "I'd love to!" she said. But then, crestfallen: "I can't. I have an appointment with the chiropractor. It's what brought me out this afternoon."

"Next time," Jess said. "Thanks again for bringing the boys home."

"No problem. Happy to do it. I think they appreciated a cheerful face when they hopped in the car!"

Anna bustled over to give Gabe a parting kiss on the head and Jessica was happy that her stepmother couldn't see her roll her eyes. As if Jess wasn't cheerful. Well, maybe she wasn't *cheerful,* per se, but she was their mother and she loved them with all her heart. She was doing her very best. Wasn't that worth something?

And yet, as Anna left in a whirl of glittering earrings (totally inappropriate for a Monday afternoon) and patchouli oil, Jess had to admit that her boys looked more relaxed than they had been in days. Even Max had chosen to sit at the breakfast nook to finish his ice cream instead of retreating to the solace of his bedroom.

"Hey," Jess said, scooting onto the bench beside Gabe. "Let me guess. Mint chocolate chip" — she pointed at Gabe's cup, then Max's — "and cookie dough, no chocolate sauce."

Gabe gave her a long-suffering look. "Mom, I always order mint chip."

"You could have been feeling adventurous today."

"Nope."

Jess opened her mouth for a bite and Gabe spooned it in carefully, then grinned when she pretended to swoon.

"How about you?" Jess said, turning to Max. Her throat was cool from the ice cream and she felt a little lighter. Maybe Anna had been on the right track with sugary treats. "Did I get it?"

Max showed her his empty cup and moved to slide out of the booth. "I guess you'll never know."

"You were right: he had cookie dough!" Gabe shouted. "Grandma ordered it in the drive-through."

"Baby," Max huffed, employing his favorite insult. It made Gabe crazy.

"I'm not a baby!"

"Max!" Jess said, her voice rigid with warning. And then, "Of course you're not a baby, Gabe. You're almost seven." He tried to climb over her to get to Max, but the table was in the way and he gave up, choosing Jess's lap over a fight he wouldn't win. Jess wrapped her arms around his warm weight and nuzzled into his neck for a kiss. He smelled of fresh air and pencil shavings and essence of little boy. She could have stayed curled around him for hours, lost in the innocence of his banter, but she didn't want to miss another opportunity with Max.

"Love you, bug," Jess whispered against Gabe's temple. Then she deposited him on the bench and eased herself out. "Finish your ice cream. I'll be back in a minute."

Already there was no trace of Max. Not in the dining room or in the hall. He was so quick, so stealthy. He stole through the house like a shadow, and sometimes Jessica wondered if her son was disappearing right before her eyes. Fading like dusk, until all that was left was darkness and the tragic sense that something beautiful was gone.

"Max?" she called, starting up the stairs. "Max, honey, I want to talk to you."

Jess heard the sound of his bedroom door closing and raced the final distance so she could turn the handle before he locked it. She caught it just in time, and pushed the door open into Max's shoulder.

"Ouch!" he accused, rubbing his arm as he backed away. Jess knew he wasn't hurt, but it was frustrating that he had something else to blame on her.

"Sorry," Jess said. "I wanted to catch you before you turned on your music."

"What for?" He flopped on his bed, making the springs creak in protest. He stayed there, sprawled out, facedown and tilted away from her until the silence stretched thin and awkward.

Jess knew he was hurting. First his parents separated, and then his father died. It was more than any thirteen-year-old could bear.

And yet, what choice did he have? If wishes were pennies, Jess would be rich from all the secret hopes she had for her son. But the world she longed to give him and the reality they lived were oceans apart.

"I know this is hard," Jess said, sitting down on the edge of the bed. She chanced a touch, just her fingertips on the hem of his jeans. "Want to talk about it?"

"Talk about what?" Max rolled over and brought his arms behind his head. He studied her dispassionately. "We don't have anything to talk about."

She sighed. "Fine. I'll talk. I love you, Max. I'm here for you."

"Sure," he said. Then he reached in his front pocket and extracted a pink square of paper. He tossed it at her.

"What's this?"

"A one-day suspension."

"What?" Jess nearly tore the paper in her haste to unfold it. Of course she recognized the pink half sheet. They used the same ones in the high school. Still, it was hard to believe that this one had her son's name written across the top. "I don't under-stand . . ." But as she said it she caught sight of the note scrawled on the bottom.

Jessica, I'm so sorry, but Max never

showed up for work detail. We've already extended the deadline past the contractual end date. According to the agreement we reached with the police department, this is the next step. He cannot come to school tomorrow and he MUST show up for his community service hours next week.

— Mason

Of course. Jessica raised a hand to her neck and massaged the tight cords of muscles. She had emails in her inbox from Mason Vonk, the middle school principal, but she had intentionally ignored them. Jess had figured they were condolences, well wishes. After Evan's death, she had all but forgotten about the trouble that Max was in.

"I forgot," she said by way of apology.

"Yeah, whatever." Max threw his feet off the side of the bed and shuffled over to his desk. He plopped down in the straight-backed chair, clearly dismissing her.

"Max, I'm so sorry. I feel like this is my fault. I'll call Mr. Vonk first thing in the morning." Jess was warming up, rising to the occasion of fighting for her son. Mama Bear was a role she played well, and she felt her skin tingle at the prospect of being *needed.* "Better yet, I'll stop by his office. Let's leave early tomorrow morning and you can come with me. He'll understand."

"Stop!" Max threw up a hand and gave her a hard look over his shoulder. "So what? I'm suspended for a day."

"But —"

"Let it go. I didn't clean up the graffiti like you promised I would. It's not a big deal."

"It *is* a big deal —"

"I don't care, okay?" Max was yelling now, his voice cracking in a way that reminded Jess he was still a child — no matter how much he looked like a young man. "I don't give a shit about this school! Or Auburn! Or —"

He cut off abruptly, the word sliced from the air between them with the snap of his teeth. But Jess knew it anyway. It was reflected in his eyes.

You. He was going to say: *you.*

LaShonna Tate
RE: We need to talk
To: echamberlain@comnet.com
March 17, 2018

I wasn't entirely honest with you when we talked several weeks ago. Yes, I'm

163

pregnant. Yes, the baby is due in July. And yes, I would still like you and Jessica to consider adopting her.

What I didn't tell you is that I'm going to prison. It's a 16-month sentence for a crime that I didn't commit. At least, not knowingly. Search my name and it'll come up. I've been linked to the embezzlement of a quarter million dollars from a nonprofit organization that works as an advocacy group in downtown St. Paul. There was a "lack of managerial oversight" and it fell in part to me because I filed the reports. Never mind that I was handed fabricated audits from someone I had no reason to doubt. I'm still in shock. My sentence starts next week.

Evan, my baby is going to be born in prison. It's hard for me to get my mind around this. You don't need my whole family history, but it's just me and my mom and she isn't talking to me right now. I don't know if she ever will again.

I don't think I can do this alone. But I can and I will. I just need to know that this baby is going to be taken care of.

Before the sentence was handed down, I actually thought I'd parent this time. I'm older and wiser, all those things you tell yourself when you think your life is about to begin again. I had visions of Gabe meeting his sister someday, of the relationship that they could have. That maybe we could have — all of us, I mean. It's ridiculous, I know, but I believe that family is so much more than blood.

Of course, everything is different now. I can't stand the thought of my child becoming a ward of the state, and I can't ask my mother to help. It would mean the world to me to keep these two together.

Please say yes.

LaShonna

CHAPTER 9

LaShonna T.
25, unknown, BA
Curly, chin-length hair. Gabe's eyes.
I know.
FEL. EMBZ, 16m, 1m pp

There were flowers waiting in Jess's classroom, an autumnal arrangement with sunflowers, orange dahlias, and giant mums that looked like peaches ripe for the picking. Jess knew without reading the card that they were from Meredith. Meredith, whose love language was simply: gifts. Giving and receiving. Jessica had been the beneficiary of her best friend's extravagance for years.

The bouquet was bright and happy, but it didn't do anything to dispel the glum mood in Jess's classroom. It looked as if her substitute had left the kids in charge. Textbooks were at odd angles on the shelves, candy wrappers on the floor. The janitors swept each individual classroom once a week, on Fridays, and the rest of the time the teachers were supposed to keep things neat and tidy. Jess had always been meticulous about her space, barring the door when the bell rang until everyone had done their part to clean up the room. Papers in the recycle bin, garbage in the trash. Desks lined up and chairs tucked underneath. Clearly Mrs. Chamberlain's standards had not been observed in her absence.

Dropping her bag in her old swivel chair, Jess pushed her hair behind her ears with both hands and heaved a sigh. She felt as if she couldn't get quite enough air — her chest was pinched and aching — so she tried again. It was no use.

Jess had left Max at home. She had to go back to school, *had* to, but it drove her crazy to just leave him there. Her skin itched knowing that instead of leaning against his locker, laughing with friends, her son was lounging in bed. At least, that's where he had been when she left less than a half hour ago. Jess had rapped softly on his door, and when he didn't answer, she eased it open. Lights out, covers drawn. The room was quiet, but that didn't mean he wasn't sleeping. Max slept as still and silent as the dead. He always had. When he was an infant, this particular skill cost Jess over a year of good sleep. She was terrified that one day her son would just stop breathing.

Today, she felt like she could.

Sitting on the edge of her desk, Jess picked up the school phone and punched in the numbers of a three-digit extension she knew by heart. Mason picked up on the first ring.

"Jessica," he said, bypassing "Hello" and "How are you?" entirely. Clearly he knew Jess's extension, too. "I'm so sorry."

It was probably unprofessional of Mason to be so transparently sympathetic. When they had powwowed with the police in the middle school conference room a few weeks before, Jess could see that it nearly caused the principal physical pain to confront Max. "He's a good kid," Mason had told her, gripping Jess's arm in his broad hand. He was a nice-enough guy, middle-aged and softening both around the middle and in his disciplinary tactics, but his fingers were a little too insistent, too tight. "He's just going through a hard time right now." As if Jessica didn't know.

She was convinced Max's angst was compounded by the fact that Evan had not made it to that particular disciplinary meeting. Jess had to handle the situation alone, but Max felt like his advocate had abandoned him. Never mind that she was his biggest cheerleader.

"It's okay," Jess said now, pressing her fingers to her collarbone and trying again to catch a breath. "I totally understand. But I need to know: Will this go on his permanent record?"

A beat of silence. "You know that it will. I don't really have a choice."

Jess had hoped for a little preferential treatment in light of everything their family had endured in the last couple of weeks. But that wasn't just unfair, it was foolish. Life went on, even if it felt like hers had come screeching to a halt. "I'm sorry," she said. "I shouldn't have asked."

"I understand. I wish that we could have given him a bit more time, but we agreed to handle the issue off the record and —"

"I know," Jess broke in, silently chastising herself for making Mason so uncomfortable. "And I need you to know how grateful I am that the school decided not to press charges. He'll be there first thing tomorrow morning and every morning thereafter until it's done."

"Thanks, Jessica. I really appreciate your cooperation in this."

When Jess hung up, her hands were shaking. In the chaos of everything that had happened since Max was caught with a small arsenal of spray paint cans in his backpack, bigger issues had taken center stage. But of course nothing ever just went away. And Max's crime remained in brilliant swaths of rainbow graffiti all over the redbrick wall of Auburn's middle school gym.

Really, it was quite pretty, the swirls and angles and angry bolts of color as bright and shocking as modern art. Maybe they would have considered leaving it if it wasn't so clearly, painfully filled with rage.

At least he hadn't painted cuss words.

Jess made it through the morning buoyed by the unexpected mercy of teenagers. They were gentle with her, funny and tender in turns, making her laugh in spite of herself, just when she needed it most. Her mother had questioned her sanity when Jess proclaimed that she wanted to be a high school English teacher, but it was days like these that confirmed she was exactly where she was supposed to be. Jess genuinely cared for her students, but more than that, she took them seriously. They were sensitive and smart and sometimes capable of seeing things that the adults who looked down on them simply couldn't. Jess needed them and they knew it. They rose to the occasion.

When the bell rang for her lunch period, Jess grabbed the granola bar that she had stuffed in her bag and refilled her water bottle in the drinking fountain. She couldn't quite stomach the thought of going into the teacher's lounge and facing all her coworkers. Jess got along with everyone at Auburn High well enough, but this was entirely new territory. Her son was a criminal, her husband dead. She felt like people were watching her, and it was true. They were kind, but they were also secretly grateful that they weren't her. And somehow that hurt worse than knowing that they disdained her. A stroke of luck separated them, nothing more.

In between the middle and high school there was a long hallway with a bank of tall windows. The window ledge was low and wide enough to sit on, and the hall was rarely used. It was one of Jessica's favorite spots in the school. She took her granola bar and water bottle, and found a quiet nook to sit with her back against the glass. The autumn sun glittered and danced furiously off the yellow walls and cream-colored tiles, making the hallway almost too warm in spite of the frosty air outside.

Jess leaned against the cool window and pulled up Safari on her phone. Ignoring her lunch, she settled into her new favorite pastime: scouring the internet for any information she could dig up on the people she had collected on her list. The stack of papers that she needed to grade was growing by the day, but Thanksgiving was coming up. Jess could catch up then. Besides, she was learning so much. So far she had discovered that Cody De Jager had spent a couple of months in jail for a DUI — his third — and Jake Holmes had once been charged with assault. Jess wasn't surprised. She took screenshots of everything she found and filed the pictures in a folder marked "Evan" on her phone.

An incoming text appeared on her screen, bisecting an article about a suspected drug ring in Auburn. Jess had sent Max a few messages throughout the morning, but he had made it clear he wasn't interested in communicating with her. He answered with single-word replies, no capitals and no punctuation.

You up?

yes

Have you had breakfast?

no

Now her phone zinged with an incoming text, and she brightened a little at her son's name in the window. But then she squinted, trying to make out what she was seeing. Max had sent her a picture. It was his hand holding a book. *To Kill a Mockingbird.*

where did u get this

The book had been on her nightstand. What was Max doing in her bedroom? Jess quickly typed a reply.

I found it.

where

Does it matter? What are you doing in my room?

phone chrgr

His phone charger had been acting up. Sometimes it worked and sometimes it didn't power up his phone completely. Still, they had a strict "no screens in bedrooms" rule and Jess's skin prickled at the thought of all the trouble Max could be getting into in her absence. She loved her son more than her own life, but he hadn't exactly proven himself trustworthy in the last several months.

What are you doing? she typed, ignoring the snapshot of the book and his obvious frustration with her.

He didn't reply.

Max?

Make wise choices.

But for the rest of the day he pretended as if Jessica didn't exist at all.

Jess was secretly exasperated when the mother of one of Gabe's friends flagged her down in the parking lot after school. Clearly it had been a mistake to park instead of rolling through the pickup lane, and Jess wished that at the very least she would have stayed in her car rather than choosing to stand on the sidewalk while she waited for Gabe to appear. She wasn't in the mood to talk with anyone. All she wanted to do was gather up her kindergartener and get home — make sure Max was okay.

Too late. "Hi, Jessica," Cara something-or-other called. She extended a tentative hand to touch Jess on the shoulder. At the last moment, she thought better of it and pulled away, crossing her arms awkwardly around a puffy dove-gray coat. Probably a wise choice since Jess couldn't even remember her last name. "I know you've been really busy, and I'm sorry I haven't reached out."

The woman's guilt was almost palpable, rising in the air between them like a whiff of burnt bread. Good intentions, charred. And: *busy?* The euphemism was ridiculously inappropriate. Jess resisted the urge to roll her eyes.

"It's fine, Cara, really. We're doing fine."

The woman's mouth turned down a little, and Jess felt a stab of worry. She had called her by the correct name, right?

"Well, I was wondering if Gabe would like to come and play at our house this afternoon." Cara smoothed the tight, clean lines of her blond ponytail with her palm, even though there wasn't a single hair out of place. "I mean, just a short playdate. I'll bring him back around suppertime."

Any irritation Jess felt melted away. *Yes,* that sounded perfect. Wonderful, in fact. It was exactly the sort of invitation that Jess had always hoped for Gabe. But just as quickly as she warmed to the idea, her blood cooled. Gabe didn't have friends. Not really. Was this a pity invite? Was Cara forcing her kid to play with Gabe against his will?

A chorus of "Mom! Mom!" erupted from the front doors, and Jess looked up in time to see Gabe separate from the pack of kindergarteners emerging from the elementary school. It was impossible to tell if he had shouted to her or if it was one of the dozens of kids racing for the buses or their carpool rides. Either way, Jess was glad for the distraction and raised her arms in welcome as she waited for Gabe to come.

He launched into her embrace, already chattering.

"Mom! Can I go to Sawyer's house today? He has a new LEGO set and he said I could build it with him!"

Jess rubbed her cheek against Gabe's hair and shot Cara a sidelong glance. The other woman was smiling a little, her arm around a boy with white-blond hair and two missing front teeth. One of his incisors was just starting to come in, but Jess had no doubt his lisp was pronounced. Maybe a playdate would be okay.

"Can I? Please, Mom, can I?"

"Okay," Jess said, pressing Gabe's busy little body against her own. He was jumping and wiggling and squirming to get away, but instead of being hurt by his dismissal, Jess had to blink away a sudden tear. It was great to see him so excited about a friend.

"Thanks for the invite." Jess released Gabe and he joined Sawyer, throwing his arm around the small boy's shoulders as they took off in what Jess assumed was the direction of Cara's car. She watched them go. "I really do appreciate it."

"No problem," Cara said, the corner of her mouth dimpling as she, too, looked after the boys. Their small, messy heads were together, their conversation animated, even at a growing distance. "Sawyer's a bit shy, so I'm happy he found someone he wants to spend time with."

Jess nodded, wondering if she should share her concerns with Cara. Would Cara know how to handle Gabe if he grew quiet? Sometimes he could retreat into his own little world, and it was nearly impossible to draw him out. Or should Jess warn that too much stimulation always ended in disaster? The music couldn't be too loud, the television turned up too high. Even strong scents could prove overwhelming to Gabe, garlic and onions sizzling in a pan, heady perfumes sprayed with a heavy hand. But, no, Jess decided. It was okay for Gabe to have a normal playdate. Maybe it would be simply perfect.

The women exchanged cell phone numbers and Jessica didn't pull out of the parking lot until she had received a short message. *Hi, it's Cara Tisdale!*

Tisdale. Of course.

At home, Jess threw her bag on the dining room table and slipped off her shoes. It felt good to wiggle her toes out of the pointy flats, and she would have enjoyed a moment to stretch out her legs, her back, her tired arms if she wasn't so eager to see Max. She suspected he would be hiding in his room, so there was no use calling his name. If she knew her son, he had his headphones on, music blaring.

Jess took the steps two at a time and stopped at Max's door. It was closed and silent as a tomb; she couldn't tell if he was inside or not. Knocking loudly, she waited just a second before turning the handle.

Max was sitting cross-legged on his bed, staring straight at her. He didn't have his headphones on, and it looked as if he had been in that exact position for a while. In his hands he held the book that she had found. Jess couldn't read his expression, but he had obviously been waiting for her.

"Hey," she started, but the atmosphere was leaden, and she faltered to a stop with her bare feet sinking in the carpet. "How was your day today?"

Max ignored her. "Where did you get

this?" He held up the book as carefully as if it were evidence in a court case, and she were on trial.

Jess paused for a beat but couldn't think of a reason not to tell him. It was just a book. "I found it when I was cleaning out Gabe's backpack. It was stuck under the liner at the very bottom."

Max studied her, assessing her words. Jess couldn't tell if he found her lacking or not.

"Honestly, I'm really not sure that it's any of your business," she said, prickling at the haughtiness in his gaze. He always thought he knew better than her. "It's not yours."

"How do you know that?"

"Well," Jess said, "is it? Is it yours?"

"No."

"Do you know whose it is?"

For a split second, Max's tough-boy facade cracked. It was a hairline fracture, but Jess could just glimpse the child beneath. Her Max was in there somewhere, the tow-headed little boy who used to sit on her lap with his head against her chest and tap out her heartbeats with his fingertips. "I can feel your heart, Mama," he used to say. "It's singing to me."

Jess crossed over to the bed and perched on the very end. She didn't touch Max, not even his foot clad in a white sock with a hole starting to unravel at the heel. But she wanted to. She wanted to touch that tender place where his skin peeked through, then curl up beside him and snug her arm around his chest. She wanted him to talk to her, *really* talk to her.

"Is this your book?" Jess wasn't sure why it mattered, but her son was visibly distressed about the paperback. It meant something to him.

"No."

"Do you know whose it is?" she asked again.

Max jerked his chin once — no. But his eyes said yes.

"If you know whose it is, we should probably return it to them. I think it may have some sentimental value. Did you see that there is a note written in the cover?" As soon as the words were out of her mouth Jess realized the significance. That was it. *Love, Dad.* Of course the note would undo him. Maybe Max thought that the book had been a gift, something from Evan that Jess had hidden away. She almost gasped at the misunderstanding.

"Look, Max, I don't think this is Dad's book." Jess couldn't stop herself. She reached out and cupped his ankle, willing him to believe her.

Max had been staring at his lap, but his eyes cut to her now. The look he gave her was fierce, condescending. "I know it's not Dad's book." He jerked his leg away from her touch.

"Really?" Jess couldn't help it that she was hurt. The tears that she had held back all day suddenly rimmed her lashes and came dangerously close to falling. She wished that Max would have even an ounce of sympathy for her when she cried, but he seemed to see it as a sign of weakness. Jess sniffed hard and squared her shoulders. "You don't have to be so mean to me, Max," she said, her voice quavering. "I'm doing the best that I can. I'm doing everything in my power to keep this family afloat. Why do you . . ." But she couldn't say it out loud. *Hate me so much* was simply too painful.

If he was affected by her outburst, he didn't show it. Instead, Max tossed the paperback toward her. "Keep it," he said as if it didn't mean anything at all. As if they hadn't just fought about it.

Jess pushed a groan of frustration between her teeth. "Fine. It's going in the recycle bin. It's damaged anyway." She snatched up the book, stood, and spun on her heel to flee the room. Jess knew that there was more work to be done, that beneath his granite exterior Max was so vulnerable, so hurting. But she didn't know what to do with him when he was like this. It was like he took pleasure in baffling her, in saying and doing everything he could to frustrate and confound her. To cut her.

She needed Evan.

The tears that threatened spilled down both her cheeks, but Jess wiped them hastily away. No time to cry. Not now.

"I wouldn't throw that away if I were you," Max called when she was half out the door. Jess had one foot in the hallway and the other still in Max's room, and for a heartbeat she contemplated pretending that she hadn't heard him at all. But she was the adult; she had to be the bigger person even if it was the last thing she wanted to do.

"Excuse me?" she said, stopping with her back turned to him.

"I said: I wouldn't throw that away if I were you."

Jess decided to play along. "And why not?"

"Because it's Gabe's."

"Gabe can't read this," Jess sighed. "He would have absolutely no idea what to do with a classic novel."

"I think she intended him to have it when he's older," Max said casually. "You know, when it'll mean something to him."

The floor beneath her felt suddenly precarious, soft as sinking sand. Jess's heart stumbled in her chest. Still, she turned. A part of her knew that once she asked the question, she couldn't unhear the answer, but it was inevitable. She had to know. "Who's *she*?"

"Gabe's birth mom. The book is hers."

BirthCentral.com
Babies Born in Prison

As American society continues to turn a blind eye to the epidemic of mass incarceration, a forgotten population of women and children reap the consequences of our shortsightedness. Although there are statistically more men than women in prison, the rate of growth for incarcerated females has outpaced their male counterparts in staggering numbers. And a recent study shows that 60% of women in state prisons have a child at home under the age of 18.

It stands to reason that incarcerated women of a childbearing age will follow national parturition trends. Experts predict that 1 in 25 female inmates are pregnant. What happens to those women? What happens to those babies? The answers may surprise you.

Although some state and federal prisons are progressive in terms of resources and programs for pregnant offenders and their babies, the fact remains that giving birth while in prison is a dismal prospect for all involved. The incarcerated mother has very little control over what happens to her or her baby during and after pregnancy, and because most institutions do not have adequate facilities or funding to house both inmates and their babies, newborns are usually taken into custody by the state, an outside family member, or an adoptive family.

Most mothers who give birth while incarcerated will face obstacles that can have a grave impact on their mental and emotional health. Giving birth while in handcuffs, without the aid and comfort of a family member or friend, and being allowed only 24 hours or less with their new baby are just a few of the possible disadvantages of childbirth during institutionalization. Prison staff are often unequipped to handle the physical and emotional needs of pregnant inmates, and the psychological strain of being separated from their newborns can heighten the risk of postpartum depression.

Granting temporary guardianship to a family member or friend may seem like the best option for women who are nearing the end of their sentence, but for others it's neither reasonable nor wise. Parenting may be a long shot for some incarcerated mothers, and adoption can open a door that previously seemed locked tight. Nobody dreams of having a baby in prison, but for those who are willing to find hope in the midst of despair, there is a path forward. There are several adoption agencies that work with incarcerated women, offering support, educational opportunities, and counseling as mothers-to-be face one of the most difficult decisions of their lives. When parenting is not an option, paving the way for a brighter future is a priceless, selfless gift from a birth mother to her child.

CHAPTER 10

Melisandre A.
34, Caucasian, BA
Oversized plastic-framed glasses. Angry.
Husband involved, consented.
HOM, 3m 2w

Gabe wasn't supposed to be home for at least an hour, and Max refused to say another word, so Jessica did the only thing she knew to do: she grabbed her purse and hopped in the car. At first, she didn't even know where she was going. She just needed to get away. It was cruel what Max had done, mentioning *her* in that way. Jessica knew that people didn't really understand why it was so hard for her to think about Gabe's birth mother, but then, she didn't expect them to. They had no idea what she'd been through.

When they buried Charlie over seven years ago, Jessica's milk had just come in. None of her pants fit because her stomach was still soft, stretched and sagging like dough from the sweet babe who had just spent nine months growing safely inside. In the hours after his birth, while he grew cold and placid as a doll, she wished on every pure and holy thing — and then tried to make deals with the devil. But nothing worked. A couple of days later they still stood over a grave so tiny she could scarcely bear it. She folded her arms over all the things that ached inside, her heart and her empty womb and her very soul, and wept, breasts tingling and warm with milk that would never feed the child she had only held for a few hours.

It broke her. Charlie's death and what felt like the loss of everything good in the world. There was Max, there was always Max, and she loved him too hard in those months, pushing him away by pulling him suffocatingly close. He was being smothered beneath her need. "I'm sorry," she would say, sobbing because she couldn't help herself. She couldn't stop. And Max would wriggle his way out of her embrace, casting her furtive looks that betrayed exactly how he felt. Scared. Her own son was scared of her, terrified by the depth of her grief and the empty space that he couldn't fill. He was only six years old.

Jessica was crying now, too, her hands

strangling the steering wheel as she drove blindly down the streets of her subdivision. Her vision was too blurry for the open road, so she wove slowly down the streets she knew by heart, passing familiar houses and marking each place that held a memory, no matter how small, in her family history. Here was the park where Max used to ride the merry-go-round, begging her to spin him faster and faster. Jess had worried that one day it would be too much, that he would throw up from the centrifugal force. But he never did. And here was the path to the pond where Gabe liked to feed the ducks. She always saved the crusts of bread that she cut from his peanut butter and jelly sandwiches for just such an occasion. Brown wood ducks would flap to the dock, jostling each other for attention, eager for a stale morsel from Gabe's chubby fingers. If they were lucky, a mallard would appear, and Gabe would clap his hands in delight, laughing.

They had a good life, didn't they? It had been. A world bittersweet, dark as chocolate and just as sharp and rich. But Gabe was the heart of it, wasn't he? When Charlie died and the whole earth was broken and jagged and ugly, Gabriel was the unexpected sweet that cut the bitter. Her angel.

Of course, she hadn't always felt that way. Evan came to her, already convinced, when the grass on Charlie's grave was still patchy and sparse. "There's a baby . . ." he said. And Jess had said, just as quickly, no. Never. *I could never do that.*

But Evan held it before her in his gentle way. Bringing it up in conversation, looking so hopeful she could almost believe.

It was a unique situation that caught Evan's attention, an adoption that had fallen through. A tiny baby waiting in a hospital for someone to call him son. Evan had been the attending physician, and he spent long hours in the hospital nursery praying his orphan would find a home. When the boy was three days old, a family was found. Or the paperwork went through or some mysterious legal process was completed. Whatever happened, they descended in a flurry of blue blankets and footie pajamas and plush brown puppies. There was a dad and a mom, a little girl with two matching braids who skipped into the hospital singing. They gathered him up in their arms, sobbing and laughing and rejoicing at a life more precious than gold. One instant he was alone, and the next he was theirs. Forever.

Evan had witnessed a miracle. A father for

the fatherless, a mother to rock him to sleep. It was a mystery, a wonder, the most beautiful thing he had ever seen. And somehow, he convinced Jessica to *try.*

Six months later, Meredith called. "So there's a boy . . ."

Jess could pluck that day from history, crisp and clear as cut glass. The smell of the hospital: bleach and the sweaty, desperate tang of fervent wishes. The way the air shimmered like a dream. It didn't feel real until she peered down into the bassinet and saw him, a comma of hope, the very thing that joy was made of. He fit perfectly in her arms.

Gabe's birth mother wasn't there. Jessica never met her and they were both more than happy to leave it that way. She had never questioned the arrangement. There was never any reason to.

Six years. Jess had spent the last six years of her life loving Gabe with every ounce of her being. Flesh and blood and heart and soul. She knew every square inch of his body, still soft with folds of baby fat, and had wiped every tear that had fallen from his eyes. Jess had kissed bruises and bandaged cuts, cleaned up his vomit and the toilet seat when he forgot to put it up and peed all over it. She had sat through meetings with the special ed teacher and the sensory therapist and the speech pathologist, had tucked him in bed with a weighted blanket and pressed a cool cloth to his forehead when he was overstimulated and couldn't calm down. He was home. He was hers. Why was Max bringing up Gabe's birth mother now?

And why did Max know anything about her in the first place?

Jess didn't even realize where she was going until she turned into the parking lot of the little strip mall on the outskirts of Auburn. It was an attractive building, fronted by stonework pillars and tall windows that glowed in welcome. Of course, the glass was frosted and you couldn't see inside the businesses that were housed there, but the overall effect was of warmth. A dental office in the corner proclaimed pain-free dentistry; a travel agency boasted gorgeous, framed prints of exotic locations; and at the very end was a nondescript sign that said simply: Promise Adoption Agency.

It had been years since Jessica had darkened the doorstep. Back when they were going through their home study process, Meredith came to them, inspecting their house with a well-trained eye and taking careful notes of everything they said. At first

Jessica had felt ridiculously uncomfortable. She chose her words so deliberately she sounded stiff and wooden, nothing like herself. Evan would take her hand underneath the kitchen table and squeeze it in comfort or warning — Jess couldn't tell. But Meredith had a way of breaking down her defenses, and it wasn't long before they were chatting like old friends. Jess wondered sometimes if their friendship was what precipitated Meredith's departure from Promise Adoption. Mixing business and pleasure and all that. Shortly after they had brought Gabe home, Meredith had quit to strike out on her own. Now she was an independent home study provider and adoption consultant, helping to facilitate private adoptions for families who didn't want to go the agency route. She also volunteered at school and was currently providing anchor for Jess's storm-tossed life.

Meredith or no, the Chamberlains' paperwork remained at Promise and always would. Somewhere inside that building was a file marked with their name, thick with all the things they said and did in the days and months leading up to Gabe's adoption. Somehow they were given the official stamp of approval; they were deemed fit to take home their squealing, gorgeous bundle of pure joy. It still baffled Jess. In many ways she felt like the blushing twenty-two-year-old who had blissfully said "I do" so long ago. How was she the adult? Who put her in charge and what were they thinking?

Jess pulled into a parking space across from the front door of Promise and put the car in park. She angled the rearview mirror and surveyed the damage her tears had done. Her smudge-proof mascara had held up, but there were salty trails down her cheeks and she smoothed these away with the palms of her hands. A bit of lip gloss, a finger comb through her hair, and a deep breath. She was ready. Or not ready at all, but what choice did she have?

Turning off the car, Jess pocketed the key and headed toward the office. *Be calm,* she told herself. *Collected.*

When the door chimed at her entrance, the woman at the front desk looked up with a smile already on her face. "Welcome to Promise," she said. "How can I help you?"

The heels of Jess's boots clicked on the wooden floor as she crossed the spacious room. There were plush chairs arranged in semicircles around mahogany coffee tables. Brochures of smiling families. A woven basket filled with toys. On a child-sized picnic table there was a jigsaw puzzle half done, and Jess wondered if it had been staged. It was all so pretty, so perfect.

Including the receptionist. She had periwinkle eyes and cropped chestnut hair that brushed against her apple-pink cheeks. She was probably thirtysomething, but she looked younger than that. Healthy and whole in a way that made Jess put a self-conscious hand to her throat. She quickly pulled it back down.

"Hi," Jess said, trying out a smile. It didn't work. "My name is Jessica Chamberlain. Several years ago Promise facilitated an adoption for us."

"How wonderful!" The receptionist seemed genuinely pleased. She stood and offered Jess her hand. "I'm Samantha. I'm new here, but I love meeting all the families."

Jessica held out her hand and Samantha clasped it in both of her own. Promise did an excellent job of employing the best kind of people: sincere, compassionate, friendly. Samantha was no different, and Jess felt her limbs go dangerously soft. She had made it here on willpower alone, and it wouldn't sustain her if she gave in to a stranger's kindness. Jess squared her shoulders.

"I'm actually here because I need to see our file."

Samantha's smile faded the tiniest bit, but she brightened again almost immediately. She sat down and typed something into her keyboard. "I'm afraid I don't have you scheduled for an appointment, Mrs. Chamberlain."

"Jessica."

"Yes, Jessica," Samantha amended. "Who was your social worker?"

"Meredith Bailey, but she doesn't work here anymore."

A small wrinkle appeared between Samantha's eyes. "I'm not familiar with Ms. Bailey, but I'm sure her cases were assigned to new social workers. Do you remember who took over your file?"

"No." Honestly, Jess had wanted to leave the agency and the entire adoption process behind completely. It wasn't that it had been a bad experience — in fact, it had been very good, healing even. But after everything was finalized and the post-adoption reports had been filed, she wanted to focus on Gabe, to do the hard work of knitting their family together and make up for lost time. In the months she and Evan spent preparing for Gabe, Jess learned that a baby in utero could not only recognize his mother's voice but could identify her smell, too. Babies were born intimately knowing their mothers. Really, the first nine months of Gabe's life had been without her, and she wanted nothing more than to somehow reclaim those days. The nuts and bolts of paperwork and parenting classes were finally behind her. She intended to leave it that way.

"Look," Jess said as Samantha continued to type and squint at her computer screen. "I just want to see my file. It's my file, right?"

Samantha bit her bottom lip. "Well, technically, no. I'm sure you remember that after an adoption is complete, the file is sealed. Why don't we take a look at our calendars and schedule a time for you to come in and talk with one of our social workers? I'm sure Delilah or Anthony would love to connect with you."

"I don't want to see the full file," Jess clarified, struggling to keep her voice even. She put both her hands flat on the countertop to ground herself. "We have a closed adoption. I just want to see the communication file."

Samantha's eyebrows knit together, forming a deep V in her unlined forehead. "We discourage closed adoptions," she said, apparently before she could stop herself.

"I know; it was a unique situation." Jess

was getting flustered. "And I guess it's not technically closed. Semi-open? I forget what it's called. We agreed to leave a file open at Promise for any communication. I just want to know if there has been any. Communication, I mean." Her heart was thundering in her chest, threatening to pound right through her rib cage.

Samantha pushed back her chair and it glided away from Jess and the thick, desperate air that surrounded her. "I'll be back in a minute," she said softly. Samantha rose in one fluid motion and disappeared down a short hallway.

Jess cupped her face in her hands. She was a wreck. What was she thinking, coming here? A quick glance at the giant, decorative clock on the wall told her that it was almost five o'clock. Surely Cara would be dropping off Gabe any minute, and she should be home to greet him, to say thank you to her new acquaintance. Max was responsible enough — he stayed with Gabe when she ran to the grocery store or forgot something at school and had to run back to pick it up — but she had left him in a state, too. Could he be trusted home alone with Gabe? And come to think of it, why had she let Gabe go home with a relative stranger? Auburn was a small town and she trusted the families that she knew, but really, she didn't know the Tisdales. Cara seemed like a nice enough person, but what did Jess really know about her? Nothing.

Dread wrapped a cold fist around her stomach, and Jess turned to go. She'd call. Come back later. She had things to attend to at home and this crazy goose chase was poorly timed at best, foolish at worst. But before she could take a single step, someone called her name.

"Jessica Chamberlain."

Anthony Bartels entered the reception room with a smile and his arms outstretched. He walked around Samantha's high counter and pulled Jess into a hug before she could protest. He smelled of musk and moss, and his embrace was sincere. Gentle. "I am so sorry about Evan," he said, only for her ears.

Jess took a shuddering breath.

"Why don't you join me in my office? I don't have any more appointments this afternoon."

Because it felt so good to have someone else tell her what to do, Jess followed him down a carpeted hallway to the room where she had met Meredith for the first time over seven years ago. Anthony had been working for Promise at that time, too, but he had been new and his office was the smallest of the bunch, crammed in at the very end of the hallway. Clearly he had moved up in the world.

"Thank you," Jess said when she was sitting in a leather chair across from Anthony. There was a small table between them and a glass bowl filled with round, green mints. Meredith had opted for chocolate. But other than that and a different set of framed family photos arranged on his desk, the office was unchanged. "Thanks for seeing me without an appointment."

"Of course," he said. "Anytime. And, Jess, truly, I am so very sorry for your loss."

They had only met Anthony a handful of times, but he seemed genuinely wonderful, and Jess was glad that he was taking her so seriously now. Evan had liked him right away. In fact, Evan had liked him better than Meredith. After their first meeting he had suggested they ask to be put on Anthony's caseload. Jess refused.

"What can I do for you?" Anthony asked. He sat back and templed his fingers together. He had dark hair and black, plastic-framed glasses above a short, neat beard. "Samantha mentioned something about your file?"

"Yes." Jess toyed with the zipper on her

coat, acutely aware that her request was oddly timed. In some ways, it came years too late. And yet, she had just buried her husband. What was she doing at Promise now? Still, she was here. She had made it this far, and a few more minutes away from home wouldn't hurt. Jess pressed on. "I'd like to see the communication file. Is that what it's called?"

"You can call it whatever you like," Anthony said amiably. "We're not picky."

"It was a closed adoption," Jess said, though she felt stupid as soon as the words left her mouth. Clearly he knew that. "We wanted to keep some things private," she tried to clarify, to make him understand why they did what they did. "When it happened, I mean. And Gabe's birth mother felt the same way."

"But you're wondering if she ever wrote."

"We kept that option open. We wanted Gabe to be able to . . ." She stalled. What had they wanted for Gabe? She could hardly remember. The family that they had become seemed so far removed from that strange, unsettling time. "Just, you know, if he ever had questions when he was older."

"That makes perfect sense."

It was easy to talk to Anthony, and Jessica found herself letting her guard down just a bit. "I didn't want to know," she confessed. "I didn't want to know anything about her."

"But now you do?"

Jess thought about the book, the way Max had reacted to it. Could it really have come from Gabe's birth mom? It didn't make sense, and yet her son had been so sure. So angry. About what? "Yes," she said after a few seconds. "I want to see the file. Evan's death put a lot of things into perspective for me."

Anthony nodded as if he understood. "Well, as you already know, the agreement that you reached when Gabe's adoption was finalized stated that any and all communication would flow through Promise. Neither parties wanted direct contact."

He wasn't saying anything that Jess didn't already know, and yet she found herself sitting forward in her chair. "But did she write letters?" Jess asked. "Do you know?" She was gripped with the sudden need to bite her fingernails, a habit that she broke years ago. Instead, she threaded her fingers together and held on tight.

"Yes," Anthony said. His voice was level, his eyes trained on her. "She did."

Jess waited for him to say more. But he didn't. "Can I —" She paused to clear her throat. "Can I see them?"

"They came once a year in sealed envelopes," Anthony told her. He paused. "And once a year Evan came to pick them up."

For a second the room went dark. Jess blinked and then shook her head a little as if she were dislodging an errant thought, something wild and unpredictable. Risky. "Excuse me?" she said, her voice barely above a whisper.

"Are you telling me you didn't know?" Anthony was smooth as glass, professional. Jess knew he had to be dispassionate, but his manner suddenly rubbed her the wrong way.

"Of course I didn't know!" she all but shouted. "I wouldn't be here if I knew."

Anthony said nothing, just leaned forward with his arms on his knees, hands clasped casually between them. Jess knew what he was doing. He was trying to be warm and approachable, to let her know that she could talk to him about whatever had brought her here in the first place. Maybe Evan would have opened up to him, but she couldn't. Suddenly, she didn't trust him at all.

"I'd like to see the file," she said.

"There's nothing in it," Anthony told her. "I checked. The file is empty."

"There are no copies? Records?"

"We don't photocopy private correspondence, Jessica. That would be illegal, not to mention unethical."

Jess bolted up, gripped with the need to be out of his office and away from the cloying scent of spearmint and old books. "Thank you for your time," she said, and moved to hurry past him.

But Anthony was also on his feet, and he stopped her with a hand on her arm. "Jessica," he said, his gaze earnest, just a little sad. "I'm sorry. Maybe Evan didn't tell you about the letters because he was trying to protect you."

She had so many questions. How many letters were there? Did Evan write back? Was there ever a return address on the envelopes? But she swallowed them all and forced herself to say, "I'm sure you're right."

Then she swept out of his office and hurried down the hallway, through the reception area, and out into the cold. The world had gone dark, the sky laced with long, wispy clouds that stretched wide across a pewter sky. Jess wanted to scream at the hidden moon, kick her car, lose it. But there were two boys waiting for her at home. And whether she liked it or not, she was all they had left.

Jess wrenched open the car door and slipped inside, then started the engine and turned the heater on high. She was itching to get home, but she had to do something first. Taking her phone out of her purse, she opened the folder marked "Evan" and found the document she was looking for. It was a list of names, now a dozen long. Tapping carefully, she added Anthony Bartels to the bottom. Jess knew she was being paranoid, but she couldn't help it. Something felt off about Promise.

March 18, 2018

I met LaShonna at the Starbucks in Mankato one last time. She begins her sixteen-month sentence on Monday. She's five months pregnant. I meant to snap a picture of her, but I forgot. This is for Gabe's sake.

LaShonna Tate has dark, curly hair that falls just below her chin. When I saw her this morning, she wore part of it pulled up on the top of her head. It suited her. I don't think she was wearing makeup, or if she did it wasn't much. A little something on her lips, maybe. She has brown eyes and they remind me of Gabe's. Extra wide and long lashed. She wore dark pants — I don't think they were jeans, but I don't remember — and a button-down shirt with pinstripes. She's average weight and height, but somehow none of this adds up to average. She is a very pretty young woman. Mixed race, I think, though I wouldn't dare guess which ones. She looks healthy and put together, but sad. And scared.

I didn't want to forget.

CHAPTER 11

Trinidad U.
24, Native American, 1 yr college
Tall, weight lifter, full sleeve of tattoos (right arm). Born-again Christian.
Cousins know.
CRIM HARASS, 27m, 1yr pp

Jess woke up the boys when it was still dark.

"But it's night, Mama," Gabe complained, rolling over and taking the blankets with him.

"We have to go to school early today," Jess said. She tried to draw him to her, but he was curled into a tight, immovable ball. "We'll stop at the bakery on the way. The doughnuts will still be warm."

That got him moving. He groaned, but he scooted toward her and offered his arms for the sweatshirt Jess was holding. Gabe slept in nothing but his football pajama pants — summer or winter — so dressing him was easy. Not that he needed to be dressed anymore. And yet, Jess held out his joggers and then helped him into his socks, pulling them all the way up to his knees. It was a tangible sort of love.

While Gabe was lacing up his tennis shoes in the entryway, Jess went to knock again on Max's door. He had refused to talk to her when she came home the night before, and his bad mood still hung in the air like grease smoke. Jess could feel it in her hair, against her skin. It made her feel sick and slightly nauseous.

"We gotta go," she said, pushing open his door. Thankfully, Max was fully dressed and putting a notebook into his backpack. He zipped it closed and swung the bag over his shoulder. The motion hit Jess in a tender place. "You ready for this?"

Max turned to her but didn't meet her gaze. "Sure," he grunted. "I've always wanted to be a janitor."

Jess flinched. "Don't forget an extra set of clothes."

"Whatever."

He brushed past her and jogged lightly down the steps, disappearing before Jess had a chance to make sure he had everything he needed.

The head custodian had sent an email outlining what Max would be doing and how he should dress for the job. A scaffold had been set up against the side of the building, and Max would start at the top then work his way down. The school had bought an entire box of a special graffiti remover and sent the bill to Max, and he would spend the next several mornings getting rid of the evidence of his crime. Spray, wait, scrub, pressure wash, repeat. Raincoat recommended, as well as old clothes, warm gloves, and boots. It was wet, messy work, and not much fun in the thirty-degree weather they were currently having. Jess felt a pang of sympathy for her son. Even if his punishment was entirely justified — and much less than he deserved.

They picked up doughnuts at Melly's, a half dozen in a variety of flavors, the entire lot still warm from the oven. It was a small perk of having to get up before the crack of dawn, though Max didn't appreciate it. Jess bought him two raspberry jelly–filled, but he refused them.

"I'll eat 'em!" Gabe said as he reached into the box that sat between them on the backseat and grabbed one of the glazed long johns. Jess's eyes flashed to the rearview mirror and she witnessed the exact moment when he took a big bite and a blob of ruby-red jam spilled out of the end and onto the knee of his gray pants. "Oops!" he said cheerfully, then leaned over to try and lick it off.

"Don't!" Jess said, catching his gaze in the rearview mirror. She was just pulling into the roundabout in front of Auburn Middle School, and could soon put the car in park and clean up Gabe's mess with something more sanitary than his tongue. "Let me get a wet wipe. I think there's one in the glove box. Max —"

Her words were cut off by the slam of the car door. She hadn't even fully stopped moving, but Max was already gone.

Jess sighed heavily as she threw the car in park and rummaged for the plastic pack of wet wipes. She wondered if she should follow him. Could she trust him to go to the janitor's office? They were supposed to meet there at six thirty so Darren could give Max his marching orders. Darren was a nice guy; he'd been the head custodian at the Auburn school district for as long as Jess had worked there. He was quiet and hardworking, and when he had confronted Max about the graffiti, it was done with a gentle disappointment. No shouting or shaming, but Auburn was his castle, and Max had defaced it.

"Should I go after him?" Jess wondered, and didn't realize she had said it out loud until Gabe replied, "He's a big boy, Mom."

"True," she said. "But that doesn't mean I don't worry about him."

Because it didn't make sense for them to go back home, Jess took Gabe to her classroom. He liked to color on her marker boards and play with the costumes. Sometimes he set up the textbooks like dominoes and then giggled as he watched them fall. Jess had a deep affinity for books, but Gabe was happy and that was all that really mattered right now. Her heart was too battered to expend even an ounce of worry on something as trivial as a textbook being toppled. She didn't complain except to say, "Be sure to pick them up when you're done and put them back where you found them."

Jess tried to mark papers and watched the clock, telling herself that it would be overbearing to call the middle school to find out how Max was doing. Was he freezing? Was it hard work? Jess had nothing against hard work, but there was something about the thought of her son out in the cold, dark morning that made her stomach twist painfully. Max's sentence was so public, so glaring. Anyone who came early to school would see him there, scrubbing the wall. Alone.

At seven forty-five Jess decided it would be okay to walk over to the middle school.

She had to deliver Gabe to his kindergarten room, and cutting through the high school meant that they would only have to walk a short distance outside to cross the campus. And it would give her a great excuse to check on Max.

"Get your coat on, babe," she told Gabe. "And don't forget your backpack." Jess slipped her arms into her own coat, and as she did so she felt her pocket buzz with an incoming call. Max?

It was Meredith.

"Hey," Jess said, tucking the phone between her cheek and shoulder so she could button up her coat. She turned to Gabe and helped him with his zipper. "What's up?"

"I know it's a hard morning," Meredith said. "I just wanted to say hi. I've got your back."

Jess felt her shoulders relax the tiniest bit. "I know you do. He's out there right now. At least, he's supposed to be."

"He is. I had to drop Jayden off for basketball practice and I saw him on the scaffold."

"Ugh." Jess felt a burst of righteous indignation. "It's so public. Do they have to make it so public?" She took Gabe by the hand and led him out of her classroom. The halls were still quiet — the doors wouldn't

211

unlock for students until eight. Jess was grateful for a few more minutes of peace.

"He should have spray-painted the baseball backstop or something," Meredith said. "No one ever sees that."

It was true. Auburn didn't exactly have a stellar baseball team. But Jess got the point: Max had done this to himself. He had covered the side of the gym — a tall swath of wall that everyone drove past at least twice a day as they dropped off and picked up their kids — in fifteen-foot arcs of fury and fire. Unless he worked in the middle of the night, there would always be someone who would see him righting his wrongs. And the afternoon and evening would be infinitely worse because people would have time to linger on their way to and from practices and basketball games.

"I hate this for him," Jess said, her voice cracking. She squeezed Gabe's hand tighter until he pulled it out of her grip and skipped ahead down the hallway. "It's not fair. Not so soon after Evan . . ."

"Maybe it'll be a good thing," Meredith said. "Healing."

"I hope so." But Jess didn't feel very confident.

"So," Meredith said, changing the topic. "I hear Gabe had a playdate with Sawyer

Tisdale yesterday afternoon."

"Wow." Jess knew that word traveled quickly in small-town Auburn, but this was a little over the top. "How did you know that?"

"Cara and I have spinning class together. Remember? I've been trying to get you to go for months."

"Oh." Jess remembered, but she absolutely no desire to go to Summit or Crunch or any of the other workouts Meredith frequented. And it bothered her that she had been a topic of conversation at a gym class. What else had they said about her? "What did Cara say?"

"What do you mean?"

"I mean, did she say anything about Gabe? Was he good for her? Did it go okay?"

"Didn't you ask her that yourself?"

Jess paused in front of the set of doors between the middle and high school. She needed her fob to unlock them, and she dug around through the tissues, lip balm, and other odds and ends in her pocket trying to find it. "Well, I would have," she admitted slowly, "but I had to run an errand. I missed her."

"You weren't there when Cara dropped him off?"

Something about the tone of Meredith's

voice made Jess believe that she already knew the answer to her question. Meredith was fishing. "Clearly you already know," Jess said, her warm feelings for her friend frosting over a bit.

Meredith inhaled deeply. "Okay. I do. Why weren't you there, Jess? Where were you?"

Jess thought about her visit to Promise Adoption. A part of her wanted to confess what she had been doing, but something held her back. Meredith already thought she was acting crazy; she didn't need to give her more evidence to support her theory.

"Max was there," Jess said. "He's thirteen, Mer. He can take care of his six-year-old brother for ten minutes while I run to the store." She finally found the fob and held it in front of the electronic pad beside the double doors. The lock popped and Gabe wrenched the door open, then took off running down the hallway ahead of her.

"Cara said she had to ring the doorbell four times."

"It's Gabe's house!" Jess was getting exasperated. "He can walk into it anytime he wants to."

"The door was locked."

It was true. Jess had started locking her doors after it became obvious that someone had been in her house. "Look, I didn't realize it was such a big deal. But if Cara has a problem with how the playdate went, she should talk to *me* about it. She has my number."

"Hey, I didn't mean to upset you," Meredith soothed. "I just wanted you to know it was a little unnerving for Cara."

"Then she should have told me so. We could have worked it out," Jess said. "Look, I gotta go. The bell is going to ring any minute and it's about to get really loud in here."

"See you tonight?" Meredith asked quickly, trying to squeeze her words in before Jessica hung up.

Tonight? Jess racked her brain, trying to come up with any plans they might have made. "I don't know," she said, stalling. "We kind of have a lot on our plate right now."

"You forgot."

"No I didn't. We're just —"

The bell rang over Jess's head, a squawking, tinny scream that signaled the floodgates were about to open. Jess jogged ahead and grabbed the back of Gabe's coat, drawing him against her and away from the wave of preteens that would soon surge through the doors. "I'll call you later," she said, not waiting for a reply. She clicked off her phone and slid it into her pocket.

"I'm going to be late!" Gabe screeched, trying to pull away from her. Jess could feel the tension in his shoulders, his anxiety pulling muscles taut as he strained ahead.

"It's okay, buddy," Jess said. "It's fine. The middle school bell rings before the elementary school bell, remember? We've got —" she jutted her wrist out of the arm of her coat and consulted her watch — "three minutes. That's plenty of time."

Gabe still held himself mannequin-stiff, but he allowed Jess to lead him as she parted the sea of middle schoolers hurrying past. They were going against the current, but they wove through the crowd to the front door and then hurried down the sidewalk toward the elementary school. As they rounded the corner by the flagpole, Jess's gaze snapped to the scaffolding and the thick lines of spray paint that would soon (hopefully) be gone. Max was nowhere to be seen, but the highest corner of graffiti — a sweep of orange that looked like a flame licking up the brick — was smeared and faded. It was working. Sort of.

Jess deposited Gabe inside the elementary school doors just as the first bell rang. "Made it!" she said, smacking his cheek with a quick, comical kiss. At least, she hoped it was funny, lighthearted. His morning had been thrown off and she prayed that he would be able to find center before the rest of his day went careening off its axis. Gabe was shaking his hands a little, ticking his tongue in a *click-click-click* against the roof of his mouth. This was just the beginning, but he was learning to calm himself down before his tension erupted into a full-fledged fit. Jess made a mental note to text his teacher and suggest that the sensory room would be a good idea. Gabe could swing for a few minutes, or run his fingers through the colorful bins of dry rice and beans and water beads. That usually quieted him. She prayed that today it would.

Since Gabe wasn't with her anymore, Jess cut straight through the parking lot and made a beeline for the middle school. She was late. She'd miss a few minutes of first period, and by the time she settled her class down they'd be behind schedule. There was nothing quite so frustrating to Jess as throwing off her lesson plan — each day was already filled to overflowing — but as she retraced her steps through Auburn Middle School, she found that she just didn't care. She had to see Max. *Had* to. Jess was terrified that this experience would be the end of him. It would break him in two.

Max's locker was down a side hallway near

the science classrooms. The lab always gave off the slightly clinical smell of Bunsen burners and formaldehyde, and Jess found herself breathing shallowly through her mouth as she peered over and around students, trying to catch a glimpse of her son.

"Hi, Mrs. Chamberlain," a petite girl with cropped hair called. Jess found her almost instantly. She was wearing leopard-print leggings with a chic black tunic, and though she looked like a teenager, Jess knew she was barely twelve.

"Hi, Avery." Jess smiled a little. It felt fake. "Have you seen Max this morning?"

"Yeah, he was scrubbing the wall before school."

Jess heaved an inward sigh. "I know. Have you seen him recently? I was hoping to catch him before classes start."

"Nope." Avery shrugged. "Sorry. Have a good day, Mrs. Chamberlain!"

Jess watched as the girl all but pranced off down the hallway, clearly oblivious to her distress and unconcerned about all that had happened to the Chamberlain family. Is this what Max had to put up with every day? No wonder he was so angry. The world was moving on without them, already forgetting all that they had lost. Avery had lived down the street from the Chamberlains for most of her life. Her mother had brought a pan of brownies when Evan died. But clearly their pain was already old news.

Max wasn't at his locker and the crowd in the halls was beginning to thin. The final bell would ring in a minute or two and anybody not in their assigned seat would be given a tardy. Three tardies equaled a detention. Jess wondered for a moment what happened to teachers who were late. It had never happened to her before.

She hated giving up, but Max was nowhere to be seen and she didn't have his schedule memorized. There was no way that Jess could find him without peeking her head into each and every classroom. Even in her current state she knew that was utterly out of the question.

But the route back to the high school ran right by a pair of bathrooms, and as Jess rushed past she nearly stumbled right into Max. He was coming out of the boys' restroom, head down and hands thrust deep in the kangaroo pouch of his black hoodie. His blond hair was mussed and flecked with bits of debris, his sweatshirt dusty and damp. Jess pulled up hard and caught his upper arms in her hands to stop herself from bowling him over. He hadn't seen her coming.

"Hey," she said, tugging him close. It wasn't hard to let their momentum press them into a sort of hug, but Max yanked away almost instantly.

"What are you doing here?"

"Looking for you," Jess said, trying not to be hurt by his rejection. "I wanted to ask you how it went this morning. I wanted to see how you're doing."

"Fine," he spat. But he was clearly not fine. Max's eyes were rimmed with pink and the chemical odor of industrial-strength cleaner clung to him.

"You don't look fine."

He just glared at her.

"This is ridiculous," Jess said, something inside of her splintering. She blinked back hot tears. "This is never happening again. You're not doing this."

"Whatever."

Max moved to sweep past her, but Jess caught his arm. "Look at me," she said. "You do not get to just run away from me. I'm so sorry that you had to do this. I won't let it happen again. We'll find another way, okay?"

"It's not a big deal," Max mumbled. He flicked his gaze to hers for just a second; then he stared at his shoes. They, too, were filthy. "Really. It's fine. I don't mind doing it."

"Then what in the world is wrong? What is going on with you?" Jess felt stupid the second the words left her mouth. Max had just lost his father. It was obvious what was wrong with him. And yet, this behavior had started months ago. Long before Evan passed away, Jess had lost her son.

"Is it the book I found?" Jess whispered. It felt dangerous to bring up the book here, in such a public place. Never mind that the halls were empty or that in the moment she paused to take a jagged breath the final bell rang and they were both officially late. "Does this have something to do with Gabe's birth mom?" Her voice gave out on those final two words, but Max was looking at her when she mouthed them. He knew what she said.

"How could it have anything to do with her?" he asked coolly. "She's dead."

And then he pulled out of her grip and disappeared down the hallway, shoulders hunched and chin angled defiantly at the ground.

March 26, 2018

LaShonna turned herself in this morning and will serve a 16-month sentence. The baby is due in July. I don't really know how childbirth is handled in prison, but I guess we'll find out.

It's a day for the record books because I moved out this afternoon. It's been a long time coming, but that didn't make it any easier. I know I've made mistakes. I've kept secrets from Jessica and been self-involved and I'm never as present as I should be. We're both stubborn. But this is on me and I own it. I'll make it up to her, work this out somehow. I love my wife. I love my family. I'm just not sure how to get from here to a place where we can talk openly about Charlie and Gabe and the unexpected way our family has come together. I'm both scared to death and excited about what the future holds.

I've emailed a new adoption agency. I'm not comfortable contacting Promise, even though that's what LaShonna wants. Right now I just want to ask questions. Figure out how this might all play out. I understand her desire to keep Gabe and his sister together, but there's a part of me that wonders if that's just what LaShonna believes she should want. Are there resources for her if she decides to parent? And is there something I can do to support her if she makes that choice? I think she misses Gabe. Well, she doesn't know him, so that's not quite right. I think she longs for him.

CHAPTER 12

BeeBee G.
40, Caucasian, 3 years of HS
Tiny, fierce, opinionated. Short, pink hair.
  Petite build. Neck tattoo.
Family uninvolved.
FRD, 32m, 8m pp

By the end of the day, Jessica understood that the world could keep spinning while it seemed to fall into ruin around her. It was a personal Armageddon, nothing more. Jess was crumbling to dust, but still the bells kept ringing, the kids filed in and out of her class, the clock ticked. Most surprising and unsettling of all? *Jess* ticked. On and on, smiling at all the right spots, answering each question that was asked of her, and pretending that she lived and breathed. It was an elaborate act. She was a ghost, convincing, but empty inside. How could they not know?

Gabe's birth mother was dead.

Jessica believed Max because she knew his tell. Someone had once told him that a liar was easy to spot — the truth was in their eyes. So when Max lied, he stared straight at her, unblinking until Jess was the first to look away. It was unnerving. And in the hallway that morning? He was already looking past her. Moving on as if she didn't matter at all. Max's words were truth, cold and harsh and so very cruel, but they were honest. At least, *he* believed that they were.

But Jess couldn't waste heartache over a woman she didn't know. No, her hands trembled as she packed her bag at the end of the day because *Max* knew. He knew things that he should never have to know, secret things that had been hidden away and carefully guarded until now. When had Evan opened the vault? Max could only know because his father told him. But why would he do that?

A pit opened in her stomach every time she considered how Max could have found out about Gabe's birth mom. The pit was deep and dark and filled with things she couldn't bear to consider. What now?

There was one thing she could do. Hesitantly, Jess added "Gabe's Birth Mom" to her list. Of course, she didn't believe that a dead woman could have killed her husband

and broken into her house, but clearly there was much more to the story than she had first imagined. Who was this woman? What had she known? Why had she died? How? The questions piled, compounded, collected like snow until Jess felt crushed beneath the weight of them.

After school, Jess gathered her boys and hurried home, unconcerned for once about Max's moody silence and Gabe's endless chatter. Usually she encouraged a healthy snack after school, a banana with peanut butter or some cheese and crackers, but when Gabe reached for the candy jar, she told him three pieces, and then sweetened the deal by telling him to take them into the living room.

"By the TV?"

"You may watch a show," she said.

"Now?"

"Sure."

The rule was no media until after supper, and then only half an hour. A single show or a handful of funny cat videos on YouTube. Jess knew she was strict, but she didn't care. She wanted her boys to be well-rounded. Polite and able to carry on a conversation and aware of current events. Evan had agreed with her approach and taught Max how to play chess when he was seven. Often the television never went on at all in the course of a day, and Jess used to love listening to the sound of her boys talking and laughing, the soft *clink* of pawns being moved, forming a cozy soundtrack beneath the hum of their words.

This was new. TV after school. Candy in the living room. Gabe looked at her sideways, as if waiting for the other shoe to drop.

"One show," Jess said, holding up a single finger, a serious slant to her mouth. "Then it goes off."

Gabe looked downright relieved. A grin broke across his face. "One show," he agreed.

Max was in the kitchen, rummaging in the cupboard and coming up empty-handed although the shelves were filled with boxes of every processed food he liked. They were still grieving.

"Come," Jess said, striding into the kitchen and taking him by the elbow.

He tried to shake out of her grip, but she held fast and pulled him past the breakfast nook and through the French doors that led to the porch. They didn't use the porch in the winter — it wasn't insulated — and the cold of the painted cement floor seeped through Jess's socks and nipped at her toes. Their grill, lawn furniture, and hoses were piled up around them, summertime remnants that still held the faint scent of charcoal and cut grass.

"It's freezing out here!" Max complained. "What are you doing?"

"We're talking," Jess said. Her voice trembled with emotion. "Right here, right now. I don't want Gabe to hear us, but I need you to know that we will stand out here and freeze to death if you don't start talking."

"Geez." Max rubbed his neck and looked at her as if she were crazy. Jess didn't care. "Chill, Mom."

"No, I am definitely not going to chill, Max." Jess didn't want to be *that* mom — she didn't want to stand there and shake her finger in Max's face — but she felt herself getting dangerously close to doing exactly that. She wanted to take his chin in her hand and force him to look at her the way that she used to when he was younger and he was being defiant, disrespectful. Jess wanted to grab his shoulders and shake. Instead she took a long breath. When she exhaled, it misted in the air between them.

"I'm serious," Jess said, slightly more calm. "I know you're mad at me, and I have some pretty good guesses why, but this is not the right time to play games. You can be as pissed off as you want to be, but you're going to start talking to me. Right now."

Max gave her a wary look, but it was obvious that she had unnerved him. Good. If that was what it took. "What?" he asked.

"How did you know that book was from Gabe's birth mom?"

"Dad told me."

"When?"

Max crossed his arms against his chest in an effort to look tough, nonchalant. "I don't know. A while ago."

"That's not good enough. Does 'a while ago' mean a month ago or a couple of years ago?"

"One of the last times I saw him." Max's voice cracked and went suddenly rough. He swallowed hard.

"Oh, honey." Jess exhaled hard, her resolve fizzling like a spent flame. What was she doing? But she couldn't give up now. Later. She could deal with this wound later. For now, she had no choice but to push past the pain in her son's eyes. "I'm so sorry. But this is important. Dad never told me about Gabe's birth mom."

"You could have asked." It was barely a whisper.

Jess chose to ignore it. "Were they in contact with each other?"

Max paused a beat. Looked away. He lifted one shoulder and then let it drop again. "No. I don't know. Yeah, maybe."

"I mean, he had the book, right? So she must have given it to him?"

"I guess."

"When?" Jess pressed.

"I don't know."

She shook out her frozen hands and tucked them under her arms. "Come on. Meet me halfway, okay? Did Dad give the book to you? To Gabe?"

Max shook his head. "No. He just showed it to me. That's why I was surprised to see it in your room."

"It was in Gabe's backpack."

"Yeah, you said that."

Jess rubbed her forehead and squeezed her eyes shut, working to make sense of what she was hearing. Everything felt fragmented. Wrong. "Okay. So how do you know that Gabe's birth mom is . . ." She couldn't quite say the word.

"Dead?" Max's eyes were glass-bottle blue, but they were flat and gray as he stared at her.

"Yeah," Jess said quietly.

"Dad told me. He showed me the book and said he was going to give it to Gabe someday. That it was really important because Gabe's birth mom had died."

"When?" Jess whispered.

"I don't know."

"Okay." All the fight went out of her, and Jess was left feeling deflated. She reached out to touch Max and he allowed her hand to rest on his arm. A small grace. "Is there anything else you can tell me? I need to know, Max. I need to know everything I can."

"That's it," he said.

"Do you know her name?"

He shook his head.

"Thank you," Jess said. "Thank you for telling me."

Max bit the corner of his lip, a gesture that made her think of his elementary school years. He used to stick just the tip of his tongue out the side of his mouth when he was concentrating. Forming his letters or adding two plus two or struggling to stay between the lines with his green crayon. Such difficult equations, big-boy problems. If only.

"Can I go?" he asked, and she watched as a shiver trembled through him. Suddenly Jess was shivering too.

"Yes," she said, wrapping her arms around herself. "Of course. But you have to promise me that you'll tell me if you remember something. Anything."

Max nodded, but he was already turning around. She hadn't cracked him, not really, but a tiny fissure would have to do. Jess watched as he turned the handle and stepped through the door, but just over the threshold he stopped. "Mom?"

Jess felt her knees go weak. He hadn't called her "Mom" in a long time. Usually he avoided addressing her at all. "Yes?"

"Do you think this has anything to do with . . ." He paused, then managed: "Dad?"

"No," Jess said instantly. She cut her chin to the right, a definitive, decisive *no.* "Dad died in a terrible accident, Max. And my heart is broken in two. But this is something different, okay?"

He nodded.

"I just need to know," she said. "I need to know what you know."

Max studied the floor, blond hair flopping on his forehead so that Jess had to resist the urge to reach out and smooth it back. "Okay," he said to his feet. But he didn't sound convinced.

Jess understood. She wasn't convinced either.

Are we on for tonight?

The text was waiting on her phone, a subtle reprimand from Meredith. Jess thumbed to her calendar and found it written there: *GNO Mer.*

Girls' Night Out. Her stomach curdled at the thought, but she remembered now. Meredith had convinced her to take just a couple of hours to do some Christmas shopping for the boys. "It'll be good for you," Meredith cajoled. "We'll go on a weeknight, before Thanksgiving. Nobody will be around, the stores won't be busy, it'll be great. Okay, not great, but it'll be good for you to get out. And it's not like you can forgo Christmas. The boys need it." A pregnant pause. "*You* need it."

Christmas shopping was the last thing that Jessica wanted to do (what was wrong with buying everything online?), but it was too late to back out without tipping Meredith off to the fact that she was not doing well.

They had made plans for Todd to come over with a couple of pizzas so that Jess could snag a few hours alone without abandoning her kids. Todd only had daughters and he missed out on all the mess and mayhem of having boys of his own. Back when the Chamberlains and the Baileys used to hang out, grilling together in the backyard or sharing a bottle of wine while the kids watched a movie, Jess would catch Todd looking at her boys almost wistfully. "I don't even have one of these at home," he once said, lobbing a football to Max as the burgers sizzled. Jess wasn't sure if Todd was talking about the football or the boy, but Max was wholly focused on the pass. Of course, he caught it easily and rolled his eyes a little at the older man. He was ten, big enough for a tight pass with a perfect spiral. He threw a laser back at Todd and laughed when it hit him square in the chest and Todd pretended to be bowled over.

Now that same sweet but bumbling man was going to spend an evening with her grieving boys. What in the world made her agree to such madness in the first place? It was Meredith. Always Meredith. She had assured Jessica that it would be amazing. A good break for all of them. Jayden had play practice and Todd would *love* a few hours to watch something sportsy with the boys. "All the sportsing and the balls and the boys . . . And we'll be alone. It'll be good for everyone. A win-win." Jessica said yes simply because it was easier than saying no.

Sure, she texted back, mounting the stairs to put on a touch of lipstick at least. She felt like a ghost, but she didn't need to alarm anyone else by looking like one.

"I'm going out with Meredith for a little while," Jess told Max, leaning into his room with one hand on the doorjamb.

He shrugged.

"Todd's coming over with pizza."

That got him to look up, but just as quickly as his eyes flashed to Jessica's they looked away. "Whatever."

Half an hour later Meredith and Todd swept in on a wave of forced cheer and the aroma of hot pizza. Todd stomped his feet as if there were snow on his shoes, even though it had yet to fall. Then he held high the pizza boxes he was carrying and announced: "Anchovies and veggie delight. Your favorite, right, Gabe?"

"Ew!" Gabe shrieked, wrapping both his hands around his throat as if he might choke. "That's disgusting!"

"It's good for you," Todd said, nodding seriously. His glasses slipped down his nose and it struck Jessica, not for the first time, that he looked a bit like a nutty professor. Tall and thin with dark brown hair and a full beard to match, he liked to wear wool pants and plaid shirts tucked in. He was so different from Meredith it was almost comical, but they seemed to get along well enough. Who could really tell? They didn't fight. At least, not in public. But Mer was all sparkle and glam, while Todd was about as interesting as a spreadsheet. He was friendly, though, and good with kids. Gabe loved him.

"Sausage is my favorite," Gabe said, following Todd into the kitchen and trying to peek inside the square boxes.

"Phew, I guess it's a good thing I got sausage, then." Todd winked as he put the pizza down on the table. "And all the meatiest toppings I could order for Max. Where is he?"

"In his room," Jess said, accepting the hug that Todd offered. He was a master of the quick, one-armed hug, and she was in and out and zipping up her coat mere seconds later. "He'll come down for supper if you ask him. Please ask him. Maybe you can get him to come out of his shell a bit."

Todd nodded. "I'll try."

"And we won't be late. I'll be back to tuck the kids in."

"We *might* not be late," Meredith amended. "We'll see how things are going."

Jess secretly rebuked her friend. She *would* be home. She didn't want to go at all. But she smiled thinly and held her tongue as she slid her arm beneath her hair to free it from the collar of her coat. "Love you, bug," she said, planting a kiss on Gabe's sweet cheek. He threw his arms around her neck and held on.

"I want a *Star Wars* LEGO," he whispered in her ear. "And Max wants a hoverboard."

"Who says I'm Christmas shopping?"

"Auntie Mer did."

Jess gave him one last squeeze and ruffled his hair as she let go. "Be good for Todd."

"He doesn't have to be good for me." Todd laughed. "We plan to get in lots of trouble, right, Gabe?"

Gabe giggled as he lifted the lid of the top pizza box, and Meredith took the opportunity to grab Jessica's hand and lead her toward the door. "See?" Meredith stage-whispered. "They're already having fun. They're going to be just fine."

"It's not them I'm worried about."

"You need this," Meredith said. "It'll be good for you to get out, even if it's just for a few hours."

Auburn didn't have a mall, but there was a small historic downtown lined with quaint shops. A couple of stores catered to a slightly more upscale crowd, but there was also an old-fashioned drugstore that carried everything from over-the-counter cough syrup to toys around the holidays, and a hardware store that specialized in trikes and bikes and scooters. It was a strange hodgepodge of shops, but it was still fun to walk around downtown Auburn during the holidays. The city strung multicolored lights across the street so that the entire road was lit up like Santa's Village, and they even piped Christmas music from speakers on the corners. Best of all, the coffee shop and wine bar on the corner sold hot buttered rum.

"Drink first?" Meredith asked, reading Jessica's mind.

"Sure." Jess dug her hands deep into the pockets of her parka and waited for the warm rush of wonder that usually accompanied her first holiday walk downtown. It didn't come. It wasn't coming, she realized. Not this year. She glanced at her watch and calculated the amount of time it would take to grab a drink at The Humble Bean. Then a bite to eat, shopping . . .

"Stop it." Meredith gave her a sidelong glance and paused in front of the door to the coffee shop. The light from inside cast perfect, buttery squares on the sidewalk, a succession of fat blondies reminiscent of The Humble Bean's most famous dessert. But Meredith wasn't charmed by the magic around them, either. "You're killing me here."

"Sorry," Jess said automatically.

"You don't have to apologize. Maybe I shouldn't have taken you out tonight."

"It's fine," Jess rallied. "I'm fine. This was a good idea. You were right."

"Liar," Meredith said. But she pushed open the door to The Humble Bean and Jess followed.

They both ordered the holiday special, a pair of hot buttered rums, and a charcuterie board with extra olives for Meredith. Jess resolved to try harder, to be more upbeat and fun, but her heart was anchored firmly in some deep, impenetrable place. She was halfway through her drink when she mustered the courage to ask the question that had been nibbling at the corner of her mind all night.

"You work with birth moms, right?" It was hard to even say the words, but she managed. Of course Jess knew that Meredith did exactly that. But she was tiptoeing in, taking the easiest route she knew.

Meredith looked surprised at the turn of conversation. They had been discussing whether or not it was worth it to spend $250 on a hoverboard for Max. "You know that I do."

"I was just wondering about letters."

"Letters?" Meredith seemed genuinely floored. "What do you mean?"

"You know, like the kind of letters birth moms write. For the file, I mean. In adoptions like ours."

Understanding bloomed on Meredith's face. Her lips pulled into a soft, genuine smile as she rolled a thin slice of prosciutto between her fingers. Popping it into her mouth she said, "It makes sense that you would have a lot of questions right now. Are you wondering about Gabe's birth mom?"

Jess wasn't sure why she had opened this particular can of worms, but she couldn't sit here and pretend that her world wasn't unraveling around her. Her suspicions were wild, fanciful things, and they wouldn't be tamed. The question popped out before she could fully contemplate it. She might as well follow it through now.

"Yes," she said. "I have to know, Mer. Did she ever write?" Jess considered telling Meredith what she knew, but in the end she decided it was better to play dumb and see if her friend had any information to offer.

Meredith's smile faded just a bit. "I don't know, Jess. I left Promise right after Gabe's placement. You know that. And Gabe's birth mom wasn't my client. It was kind of an accident that she ended up choosing you at all."

Jess did remember, but she had to ask

anyway. She knew that their profile had been shared with a young woman who wasn't working with Meredith, but once the decision was made she was unwilling to back out. They made it work. And it shouldn't really have mattered since it was a closed adoption and all. But clearly it did matter.

"What's in those letters?" Jess asked, toying with the handle of her glass mug. The caramel-colored liquid inside was still steaming. "What do people typically write?" She took a quick, shallow breath. "Contact information?"

"Oh, nothing like that," Meredith said. She looked uncomfortable. "Are you sure you want to talk about this? We're supposed to be having fun."

"I am having fun."

The corner of Meredith's mouth pulled up doubtfully. "I call bullshit."

Jess shrugged. "I want to know, okay?"

"Fine," Meredith sighed and leaned back, throwing her napkin on the table in defeat. "It's your night. You want to know what's in those letters? The absolute best. It's an art form, really. People know that it's often the only contact they'll ever have with their birth child or the mother of their child. So they work at it for days or weeks, making it as perfect as they possibly can. Every word is scrutinized and the final result often sounds nothing like the person who wrote it."

Jess picked up an olive and then put it back down. "That's kind of awful," she said quietly.

"I don't know if it's *awful*, but it's not necessarily real. It's a bit of a false narrative. A spit-polished version of reality."

Jess digested this without comment. "What do you know about Anthony Bartels?" She hadn't planned to mention him, but all at once she felt bold. Why not? Why the hell not?

Meredith's lips tightened almost imperceptibly. But Jess had known her long enough to spot the tiny wrinkle that creased at the corner of her mouth. "Nice guy," Meredith said lightly.

Liar.

"He makes me nervous," Jess admitted, watching her friend.

Meredith shrugged one shoulder and took a sip of her drink.

So she didn't want to talk about Anthony. Jess wasn't sure what to do with that. It could be because he took Meredith's place when she left Promise, but Jess couldn't shake the feeling that there was more to it than that. The mood around the table had turned sour, pungent as the garlicky tapenade on their rustic board. Jess knew it was her fault.

"I'm sorry," Jess said again, because she was. Always right now, for a dozen different reasons. She was so very sorry for everything.

"You don't have to be," Meredith said. But when Meredith turned away, Jess could have sworn her friend was crying.

CONVERSATION WITH
LASHONNA TATE
(June 1, 2018)

LASHONNA TATE: HEY, IT'S ME.

EVAN: SORRY I COULDN'T TALK YESTERDAY. THANKS FOR TRYING AGAIN.

LASHONNA: WHATEVER. IT'S FINE.

EVAN: HOW ARE YOU DOING? I'VE BEEN THINKING A LOT ABOUT YOU.

LASHONNA: YEAH.

EVAN: YOU FEELING OKAY?

LASHONNA: NOT REALLY.

EVAN: THE LAST MONTH OF PREGNANCY IS SO HARD. YOU SLEEPING OKAY? TAKING CARE OF YOURSELF? IS THERE ANYTHING I CAN DO TO HELP?

LASHONNA: NAH.

EVAN: HAVE YOU HAD A CHANCE TO TALK WITH YOUR MOM?

LASHONNA: NOT YET.

EVAN: BUT YOU'VE MADE YOUR DECISION, RIGHT? YOU WANT TO KEEP THE BABY?

LASHONNA: IT'S ALL I'VE EVER WANTED.

CHAPTER 13

Andrea S.
21, Caucasian, HS diploma
Former goth, black hair, pale skin.
  Homemade tattoos. Scared.
Disowned.
PROST, 60m, 4m 1w

Max worked on cleaning the wall every single morning for the rest of that week and the next. Jessica tried to talk him out of it, tried to convince him that she could meet again with the principal and the local police and help them to understand that their punishment was doing more harm than good, but he wouldn't hear of it. Every morning they got up early, grabbed a breakfast to go, and headed to school an hour earlier than normal. Gabe played in her classroom while Max scrubbed the gymnasium bricks.

On Friday morning Mason Vonk rang Jess's classroom. "You'd better come down here," he said.

"Is something wrong?"

He paused for just a second longer than Jess would have liked.

"Just come."

They raced through the building, Jessica holding Gabe's hand — partly because she wanted him to keep up and partly because she needed something to hold on to. She crushed his small fingers in her own until he cried out and yanked them away. By the time they arrived at the middle school office, Jess was panting and Gabe was shaking out his hand.

"Where's Mason?" Jess asked breathlessly.

The receptionist, a new girl whom Jess barely recognized, pressed her siren-red lips together and gave Jess a cryptic look. Her expression was unreadable. "He's outside."

"With Max?"

The woman just pointed.

They hurried down the hall, through the tall glass doors, and around the side of the building where the evidence of Max's crime had been slowly but surely fading away. But the moment they turned the corner, they met the impenetrable wall of a growing crowd. People were lining the sidewalk, making it impossible to go any farther. Students stood arm to arm, talking and laughing and pointing. Jess quickly scanned the scene and saw several parents, too.

Jessica's heart skidded painfully and she instinctively wrapped her arm around Gabe's shoulders.

"What's going on?" he asked, peering up at her. His eyebrows were scrunched together, his bottom lip caught between his teeth.

Jess didn't answer. "Stick with me," she said, angling her body and pushing through the mob. At first people resisted, but when they turned and realized it was Jessica, they backed against one another and parted the way before her and Gabe. She wanted to ask someone what was going on, why they were grinning at her and whispering, but she was too hurt, too angry. This was exactly what she had been afraid of all along. They had made a spectacle out of her son, and now her broken little family would have to face the disdain, the *ridicule,* of their community. They were judging her, judging her boy, and it tore her heart to shreds.

By the time Jess and Gabe emerged from the crowd that had gathered, Jess was shaking, ready to quit her job and leave Auburn and do whatever it took to put the pieces of her life back together. But the scene that greeted her was not at all what she had expected. For a stunned minute she just stood, trying to make sense of what she was seeing.

The scaffolding had been removed as Max reached the bottom of the graffiti, and standing shoulder to shoulder at the wall were a dozen young men. Their backs were turned, their bodies bent, and as one unit they sprayed and scrubbed and washed away the last of the paint. They laughed as they worked, jostling each other with their elbows and flicking water at one another.

Max stood in the middle of it all. He was smiling, a bemused half grin that took Jess's breath away. He was so handsome. Such a young man. And she had nearly forgotten what it looked like when he smiled. It was everything.

"What is going on here?" Jess whispered to no one in particular.

But she had emerged from the crowd at Mason's side. "They've been here for an hour at least," he said.

"All of these people?"

"No. The audience is a more recent development."

"What are they doing?" Jess breathed.

"They're helping him!" Mason laughed and put his arm around her briefly. It was an affable, almost-embrace. "Has Max told you what's been going on this week?"

Jess shook her head.

"Well, it started with the applause. Some kid — I don't even know who — clapped for Max when he got dropped off one morning." He slid Jess a quick glance and shook his head as if to ward off any suspicion at the nature of the gesture. "It was sincere. He was trying to be encouraging. They all were."

"All?"

"It's been a thing. The last few days, as kids arrive at school, they've been greeting Max with high fives."

"What?" Jess hardly knew what to think. Max hadn't said a word to her.

"He's become a sort of symbol. Of sticking it to the man or something. I don't know." Mason shrugged. "But really, it's grown into such a positive thing. They've all been pulling for Max. And this morning, his last morning, a bunch of kids showed up to help. They've been here almost the entire time."

As Jess watched, Max stepped back and surveyed the wall. There were still faint strokes of color, but nothing the sun and snow and rain wouldn't fade over time. The last of the bright marks had been scrubbed away, and Max stood with his hands on his hips and nodded once.

A cheer erupted from the crowd, and the boys who had stood beside him, who had rolled up their sleeves and gotten dirty with him, gave Max fist bumps.

Gabe was clapping too, and when he looked up to see why Jessica wasn't, he patted her side good-naturedly. "Why are you crying?"

Jess didn't even realize she had been. "I don't know, bug," she said, her voice so unsteady it came out as a squeak. She swept her palms across her cheeks and tried to laugh around the thickness in her throat. "I guess because I'm happy."

"That Max is done?"

"And that so many people wanted to help him."

Gabe nodded sagely. Then he raced to where Max was standing and threw his arms around his brother's waist.

"You've got yourself a good boy there," Mason told her. "These are defining moments, you know?"

Jess knew.

People were already leaving, kids filtering into school and parents getting back in their cars. But Max lingered with his hand on the top of Gabe's head and waited as Jess stepped slowly toward him.

"Hey," she said, faltering a few feet shy. "You didn't tell me about . . ." She waved her hands around, trying to encompass what had just happened. *"This."*

"I didn't know this was going to happen." Max shrugged, but there was a smile playing at the corner of his mouth.

Jess had the feeling there were a lot of things that Max didn't tell her. Still, she wasn't about to ruin the moment. Maybe there was hope for them after all. "It's pretty amazing," she said. "What you've done. And how so many people saw what you were doing and respected you for it."

"I spray-painted the school," Max reminded her, tilting his head as if he couldn't quite believe she was praising him.

"I know. But you handled it so well."

"I also changed the combinations on all the lockers and flooded the bathroom in the teacher's lounge and —"

Jess stopped him by waving her hands in front of his face. "No! No more." She couldn't help it. She erupted in giggles. It felt so good to laugh, to really laugh, that she almost started to cry again.

"You did all that?" Gabe asked. He was staring openmouthed at his big brother. "You're so *bad.*"

"No," Jess said, pressing her fingers to her

lips. She kneeled down so she could be eye level with Gabe. "Your brother is a good man. We all make mistakes, but only good men make things right. Max made things right. And I respect him for it."

"Me too," Gabe said.

The first bell rang and Gabe went rigid. "I'm going to be late!"

"Run," Jess told him. "On the sidewalk. I can see you all the way. I'll bring your backpack later."

Gabe tolerated a quick kiss, and then he was off, racing down the sidewalk. Jess watched him go but snagged Max by the wrist when he began to move past her.

"I've got eyes in the back of my head," she said, parroting a phrase that she had used on her boys since they were toddlers. "You can't get away with anything." It wasn't true, of course. They got away with so much. There were so many secret places and hidden havens inside her boys. That scared her. But it also awed her. Max was his own person, his own universe of hopes and dreams and fears and secrets. And maybe that wasn't such a terrifying thing after all.

Max didn't pull away from her grip, so Jess chanced it. At first, when she wrapped her arms around him, he didn't move. But then she could feel his hands on her back. He hugged her hard for just a moment. It was enough.

"I love you," she said. "I'm proud of you."

Max pulled away and gave her a look that made her heart twist inside her chest. It was somehow sad and dignified and wistful all at once. "That's what Dad always used to say."

"He was so brave," Jess said, tucking the phone between her cheek and shoulder. She stuffed a thick stack of papers that she had to mark inside of her messenger bag and then zipped it shut. She'd be up for hours grading them tonight, but it didn't matter. Jess didn't sleep much anyway. "You would have been so proud of him, Dad."

"I *am* proud of him," Henry said. But it came out a little too fast. They both knew that Henry had been devastated when his grandson was caught red-handed. Quite literally.

"Well, I just wanted you to know that it's done." Jess slipped the strap of the bag crisscross over her chest and grabbed the phone in hand. "Look, I gotta go. The boys will be waiting for me."

"Will we see you this weekend?"

"I don't know. We haven't really thought

that far."

"Anna and I would love to see you and the boys. Maybe lunch after church on Sunday? Anna has a sweet potato chili recipe that she'd love to try out on you."

Jess rolled her eyes. As if the boys would touch sweet potato chili with a ten-foot pole. They were more the meat and white mashed potato sort. "We'll see, okay?"

"Fine. Just let me know by tomorrow."

Sweet potato chili and awkward conversations with her father notwithstanding, Jess was in a more buoyant mood than she had been in months. Well, maybe buoyant was overstating it, she decided, but the veil had lifted. If only a bit. Though it wasn't hope that blossomed beneath her breastbone. It was resolve. If Max could do hard things, if he could stand out in the freezing cold day after day and hold up beneath the scrutiny of almost the entire community, she could surely face one of her greatest fears: Caitlyn Wilson.

Jess hadn't liked Cate from the start. When Auburn Family Medicine hired the perky new transplant in town, everything in Jess had recoiled in distrust. Cate was young and lovely, a svelte redhead with striking green eyes and an adorable sprinkling of freckles across her perfect ski-slope nose.

Worst of all, she was as kindhearted as she was pretty, and her abandonment at the hands of one of Auburn's own (a thirty-something dentist who inconceivably found someone younger and sexier than Cate and ran away with her to Fort Lauderdale) cemented her as one of the most desirable — and tragic — girls around. "Men love messed-up girls," Meredith said, her lips puckered in shrewd disapproval. "Ergo, she's irresistible."

That's exactly what Jess was afraid of. Because without any warning at all, the enticing Cate Wilson had been hired as her husband's nurse. She hadn't been his choice — the board of directors took care of all the hiring and firing — but Jess wished that he would have protested a little more vehemently. Surely he could have done *something.*

"I have to run an errand this afternoon," Jess told the boys over after-school snacks. Max was grazing on anything and everything he could find in the cupboard. A handful of chips followed by a Chewy Chips Ahoy! cookie and then, blessedly, a few almonds.

"There's a pear on the counter," Jess said helpfully. "And some apples in the fridge."

"Where are you going?" Gabe asked.

Before she could answer, he said: "I want to come."

"Not this time, buddy."

"I'm not babysitting," Max said.

Clearly his newfound maturity was short-lived. Jess sighed. "Yes, Max, you are. I won't be gone long. Where do you have to be?"

"I'm going to the basketball game with some guys."

That made Jess pause. Max? Her Max going to a basketball game? He wasn't unpopular, not by any stretch, but lately he had been a bit of a loner. Ice cream at the drive-in after his last football game (they had lost, though Max scored the only touchdown for Auburn) was one of the last times Jess remembered him doing anything socially. That was a week or so before Evan's death. Max had a solid reason for being a hermit, but she was quietly thrilled to hear that maybe his self-enforced exile was ending.

"That's great," Jess said. "I'll be back in plenty of time to drive you to the game."

"Trey is picking me up."

"Okay." Jess wanted to ask if Trey's parents were going along or if his older brother would be taking the boys to the game, but she bit her tongue. That conversation could wait. "I just need you to hold down the fort here for an hour or so. Don't let Gabe watch TV the entire time I'm gone and don't ignore him."

"Yeah!" Gabe cut in. "Don't ignore me!"

"What am I supposed to do with him?" Max threw up his hands.

Jess shot him a hard look. "Be nice. Play LEGO or jump on the trampoline or —"

"Let's play hide-and-seek!" Gabe shouted.

"Sure. Hide-and-seek."

Max turned his eyes to the ceiling and groaned.

"I'm serious. Be nice."

Jess left the boys in the living room with a kiss blown in each of their general directions. Max was on the couch texting someone (Trey?), while Gabe riffled through the game cabinet trying to find something they were both interested in. Candy Land, Uno, and Monopoly had all been suggested and rejected by the time she shut the door. She said a little prayer that they would survive the hour without her.

It had been a very long time since Jess had darkened the doorstep of Auburn Family Medicine. There was no reason for her to stop by after she and Evan separated, and if the boys needed to be seen, Evan had usually taken them himself. Jess tapped her fingers against the steering wheel as she drove across town, giving herself a pep talk and trying to believe that she was doing the right thing.

Evan had liked Caitlyn. And at first, Jess had believed him when he said that their relationship was strictly professional. Later, he told her that they were "just friends." That the reason they were laughing when she stopped in to bring him lunch at work was because they had come to the same conclusion on a tricky patient. They were compatible. A good team. It was when Evan started to get secretive that Jess began to wonder if maybe there was more to their relationship than her husband was willing to let on.

Jess had never confronted Cate. She'd never dared to. And she didn't really want to now. This was about information. If anyone knew anything about Evan's relationship with Gabe's birth mother, it would be Cate. Evan worked too hard to have close friends, and both Meredith and Todd had taken Jess's side in the separation. Not that Evan had ever been tight with the Bailey family. He seemed to tolerate them more than he liked them.

Auburn Family Medicine was a community health center that provided services on a sliding scale so that anyone could receive care. Many of Evan's patients did not have insurance, and though it meant he worked for less than he would have at a for-profit clinic, neither Evan nor Jessica had cared. She had always been proud of her husband, his tender heart, his pursuit of justice. And Jess had been proud of the little clinic that felt just like family in the heart of Auburn, Iowa.

But now, standing in front of the door with the familiar silver plaque, she felt like she was entering a lions' den.

The bell chimed when Jess finally gathered the courage to step inside. Beth was behind the desk, and though she had her headset on and was squinting at her computer screen, she looked up when Jess walked through the door. Her eyes widened in surprise.

Jess had decided not to call beforehand, not to make an appointment or announce her visit. She didn't want to alert Cate to the fact that she was coming and give her an opportunity to work on her story. Jess wanted the unvarnished truth, and she believed that she would see it in Cate's eyes if she could only catch her off guard.

There were only a handful of people in the waiting room. An elderly woman was waiting with a man who Jess presumed was her son, and there was a young mother with a feverish toddler. He was limp in her lap, eyes half-closed, and her worry was an almost tangible thing. Jess wanted to re-assure her that her boy looked worse than he was. Those high fevers were scary, but rarely serious.

"Hi, Jessica," Beth called softly when her phone conversation ended. She rose out of her chair to extend a hand to Jess, but was tethered by her headset cord. She ended up half-bent with her arm outstretched. Jess hurried over and took it.

"It's good to see you," Jess said, and she meant it. They had hugged at Evan's funeral but hadn't seen each other since. The office sent a huge bouquet of flowers and a gift certificate to the grocery store. Jess hadn't sent a thank-you. But not because she didn't like the staff at Auburn Family. She just couldn't muster the energy it took to comb back over those gifts and condolences, those heartbreaking reminders that nothing would ever be the same.

"Good to see you too," Beth said. "I've been hoping you'd stop by."

"Oh?" Jess hadn't expected that.

"Yes. I've left you a few messages on your answering machine . . . ?" Beth looked uncomfortable, and she sat back down so that her head didn't have to be at an angle.

Jess thought of her home phone and the red, blinking light that she had been ignoring for weeks. She didn't have it in her to press play and listen to all the things that required her attention. She figured if anyone really needed her, they'd call her back. Obviously Beth had. Multiple times.

"Right," Jess said, faking recollection. "Sorry I haven't returned your call."

"No worries. I know it's been a difficult time." Beth glanced behind Jess, looking maybe for the boys. Her eyes flicked back to Jessica. "Would you like some help with the boxes? I'm sure there's someone who can give you a hand."

Boxes. Of course. Jess hadn't thought of her husband's office, of all the relics he had collected over the years. Framed photos of the family, knickknacks from the boys, a carved wooden elephant that he had been given on a medical mission trip to India over a decade ago. Jess closed her eyes for just a second and pictured his office — a little small, a bit disorganized — and a wave of sorrow washed over her. Never again would she sit in the straight-backed chair across from his desk and walk his Cross pen through her fingers. She had loved the cool, silver barrel and the way it felt against her skin. She had loved watching Evan push his glasses up on the top of his head and sit back with a heavy sigh.

"I'll be fine," she said, grateful that the words came out flat and even. "Are they in his office?"

Beth nodded. "Maybe . . . ?" But she stopped. Nodded. "Go ahead. Just head back there. Let me know if you need anything at all."

Jess hadn't expected to be let in quite so easily, but she was grateful that she wouldn't have to bully anyone to get her way. Cate didn't have an office, but the triage room where the nurses gathered was right next to Evan's. Jess could collect his things and hopefully snag a few minutes with Cate at the same time.

The hallway that led to Evan's office was lined with examination rooms. They were neatly numbered one through six and every door was closed. Jess could hear muffled conversations throughout the hallway, but no one was immediately visible. The triage room was empty.

Jess paused with her hand on the door to Evan's office. It had been several months since she had been here, and she took a shaky breath to steady herself. She realized in that moment that she hadn't believed their separation would be permanent. She had assumed that she would walk through this door again, carrying the pretzel bun and cold brisket sandwich that he loved from The Humble Bean, and smile as she saw his tired wave.

A swell of nausea rolled over her and Jess pushed open the door, afraid that whatever was in her stomach (tea and a bran muffin) was about to come back out. She grabbed the trash can and sank into the nearest chair, her chest heaving as she squeezed her eyes shut against the onslaught of memories. Of dreams that were breathing their last.

"Excuse me."

Jess's head snapped up. Cate was leaning into the room, a stethoscope over her shoulders and her dark blue scrubs setting off her bright eyes.

"Oh!" Cate visibly jerked back, her lips parted in surprise. "Jessica. I'm so sorry. I didn't realize it was you. The door was open and I thought a patient had taken a wrong turn . . ." She swallowed hard. Stood her ground. "I'm really sorry."

Jess wasn't sure if she was apologizing for barging in on her private moment or if she was sorry about something else entirely. Maybe both. "It's fine, Cate," Jess said. She put the garbage can down and stood. She was only shaking a little.

"Well . . ." Cate hooked a thumb over her shoulder. "I should go. Take as much time as you need."

"No." Jess waved Cate inside and then stepped behind her and closed the door. "I'd like to talk to you."

Cate looked around as if there might be another way out of the office. "I don't really have time right now. I'm with patients."

"A few minutes won't hurt."

"The clinic closes soon." Cate backed away and fumbled for the door handle behind her. As if Jess were unstable, dangerous somehow.

"We're going to talk," Jess said, crossing her arms.

Cate glanced at the delicate watch on her wrist and stifled a sigh. "After work," she said. "I get off in half an hour. We could meet at O'Malleys."

Jess hadn't pegged Cate as the type to hang out at the Irish pub, but she wasn't the only one who could use a drink. Jess's blood pressure was through the roof — her vision was blurred at the edges, the world glazed in starburst patterns. "Okay," Jess said. "I'll be there."

Cate nodded, her lips pursed together in a

pretty little bow. Jess couldn't help but hate her.

When Cate slipped out the door and closed it quietly behind her, Jess was left to contemplate the empty room, the sad boxes that sat piled in the center of an empty desk. The walls had been stripped of Evan's medical license and the wedding photo that he had hung there (Jess hoped that he had left it up even after he moved out, but she would never know). Everything looked vacant. Hollow somehow.

Jess walked slowly over to the desk and lifted the flap on the first box. There was a leather cup filled with pencils, a stack of notebooks, and the wooden elephant. Nothing much. Jess slid her hands around the box and lifted it off the desk, but when she moved to place it on the floor, the bottom gave out.

There was a mighty crash as the elephant hit the edge of the desk and careened to the carpet, and then a sound like rain as dozens of pencils scattered. Jess put a hand to her racing heart, grateful that the elephant had missed her foot and hoping the noise wouldn't send people running to her aid. No one came.

Jess sunk to her knees and surveyed the damage. The elephant had a deep scratch in his side, but nothing a little wood filler couldn't fix. Other than that, he was unharmed. The notebooks had fallen half-open, pages creasing and bent against the floor, and Jess picked them up carefully, smoothing out the paper as she went. They were empty for the most part. A few notes scribbled near the beginning. To-do lists and groceries. Jess learned her husband had an affinity for frozen lasagna.

The pencils were everywhere. Jess had to crawl on her hands and knees, gathering them from under the desk and beneath the chairs. One had made it all the way to the window. When she had a fistful, Jess hobbled back to the leather cup and dropped them all inside. But something didn't sound right. The pencils made a tinny, metallic click that was totally incongruent with the felt-lined bottom of the cup. She pulled them back out and tipped the cup so that she could see all the way to the bottom.

There, taped to the base, was a key.

Woman in Eagle Ridge
Women's Prison Died by Suicide
July 16, 2018

An Eagle Ridge inmate died on Thursday, approximately an hour after she was discovered unresponsive in her cell. The Scott County Coroner's office has identified the woman as twenty-five-year-old LaShonna Tate and ruled her death a suicide. Tate was serving a sixteen-month sentence for accessory to felony embezzlement.

Guards found her unresponsive in her cell around 7:00 a.m. during morning roll call. CPR was performed while they waited for an ambulance to take her to a local hospital. She was pronounced dead shortly after arrival.

The incident is being investigated according to protocol. According to Warden Stafford: "We do everything in our power to ensure the safety and well-being of those in our care. Unfortunately, incidents like these are traumatic for all involved. Our thoughts and prayers are with Ms. Tate's family."

Chapter 14

Lisa V.B.
41, mixed race, HS diploma
Curly gray hair, looks older than she is.
  Wears clothes several sizes too big.
Mother knows.
BURG, 34m, 14m pp

O'Malleys Pub was new, but it had been designed to seem old. Jess had never been inside before. The rectangular building looked like a converted warehouse, with tall, narrow windows that stretched nearly all the way to the sidewalk, and neat black awnings printed with the distinctive green logo of an entwining *O* and *M*. Inside, it was warm and dark. A huge fireplace flanked the back wall, and two worn leather couches studded with brass rivets were angled in front of it. Jess was drawn to the cozy arrangement, but it was too open — not nearly secluded enough for the things she wanted to say.

"How many?" A hostess materialized near Jess's elbow, linen menus tucked under her arm.

"Two," Jess said. "But just for drinks."

"It's Friday afternoon. This is the just-for-drinks crowd," the hostess said with a grin. "Want to belly up to the bar?"

"Do you have anything a bit more private?"

"Sure," she said, already heading in the direction of a table. "Follow me."

Near the back of the restaurant there were booths with paneled partitions that reached toward the ceiling and thick curtains hanging from brass hooks. "These are for show," the hostess said, tugging the red brocade fabric. "But I hope this is private enough?"

Suddenly Jess felt silly for making such a request. As if she were having an illicit tryst instead of meeting another woman for conversation. Okay, there was more to her meeting than that, but still. She had nothing to be ashamed of.

"It's fine," she said, scooting into the far side of the booth so that she could see the door. When the hostess left, she glanced around and realized that, although there were several people in the pub (it was early Friday evening, after all), there was no one that she immediately recognized. It was hardly a crime to meet with her late husband's coworker, but Jess wasn't in the mood to see anyone she knew. She couldn't stomach the thought of small talk, the inevitable pitying stares.

Jess slid her phone out of her purse and texted Max. *Home soon. Everything okay?*

He didn't reply immediately, but that wasn't unusual. Jess put her phone facedown on the table in front of her and read through the menu for lack of something better to do.

"Anything look good?"

Jess looked up, surprised to see Cate unwrapping a long, plaid scarf as she stood over the table. Jess had hoped to catch her walking in.

"I finished a few minutes early," Cate said, sensing Jess's question. "I have —" She paused, then pursed her lips together for a moment before she continued. "I have a date tonight. I can't stay long."

A date? Jess wasn't sure what to make of that. She decided to respond to Cate's question instead of prying into her love life. "I think the potato and sausage soup looks good," Jess said. "But I'm not eating anything."

"Me either." Cate lowered herself onto the edge of the bench opposite Jessica. She had left her coat on, but it was unzipped. A clear sign that she was here, but only for a minute or two. "A drink?"

They had to order something, so when the waitress came, Cate ordered a dirty martini with an extra olive. Jess asked for the same. She wasn't really into mixed drinks, but she didn't want to seem like a prude by ordering a mineral water, and the wine list was beyond overwhelming. Jess wondered if they looked like old friends meeting for a quick interlude between obligations, so in sync they ordered the same cocktail. The only thing missing between them was the natural chemistry of good friends, elbows on the table as they leaned in, easy laughter.

When the waitress left, Jess felt a surge of adrenaline like a struck match. It licked through her chest and raced down every vein, making her fingertips tingle. She realized she was scared to death.

But before Jess could gather her thoughts to utter a single word, Cate heaved a huge sigh. It came from somewhere deep inside and snagged in her throat. "I'm sorry," she said, tears welling in her eyes. O'Malleys was so dimly lit they seemed navy, bottomless. "I'm just so sorry about Evan."

Jess hadn't expected this. Or maybe she

had. If Cate had been Evan's lover, even for a season, it made sense that she would be devastated by his death. Jess felt herself icing over, her shoulders drawing back as she prepared for a fight.

"Thank you for your condolences," Jess said coolly.

"Look." Cate laid her hands palm down on the table between them and leaned forward. A tear spilled off her bottom lashes and disappeared down her cheek. "I know that you hate me and I know why. But you have to believe me that nothing ever happened between Evan and me. He was like a father figure to me."

Father figure? He was less than ten years her senior.

"Or an uncle, a big brother," Cate said, reading Jess's expression and shaking her head as if it didn't matter. "We were close, okay? We got along. Is that such a crime?"

"He was very secretive when it came to you," Jess said, leaning back, farther away from Cate's desperate attempts to make her understand. She didn't know what to believe. "It seemed like there was always something going on between the two of you. I saw the looks you exchanged. I know you texted each other all the time."

"It was innocent," Cate insisted, but

something in her face changed. She pulled back and laced her fingers together on the table between them. Took a deep breath. "Okay, it wasn't exactly innocent, but it's not what you think."

Jess saw red and was horrified to feel her eyes prick with tears. She knew it. She *knew* it. But no, she would not cry in front of this perfect woman.

"Don't," Cate said quickly. "Don't jump to conclusions. Hear me out."

"It's never okay to have secrets with another woman's husband," Jess hissed, her voice breaking to her great mortification. It was too late — she *was* crying. "Do you have any idea the pain you caused? The trouble you wreaked? I kicked Evan out of the house because of you."

Something in Cate's eyes flashed. She was a fighter, too. "Oh, that's rich. Don't you *dare* pin that on me."

"Two dirty martinis?" One of the bartenders had appeared at their booth, bearing a circular tray with their elegant drinks. Light from the chandelier above them danced across the distinctive, V-shaped glasses in a way that seemed almost indecent. Or at least far from suited for the heaviness between them, the tears on both their cheeks.

"Yes," Jess said, clearing her throat. "Thank you."

He set the martinis down and all but scurried away. Jess watched as Cate grabbed her drink and took two, three swallows in rapid succession. Then she set it down and plucked the diminutive sword from the edge of the glass, sliding an olive off with her teeth as if she were drawing strength from the cocktail. Jess wanted to do the same, but she settled for a tiny sip and was rewarded with a flame of alcohol that burned all the way down. It felt good.

"We weren't having an affair," Cate said, picking up the conversation as if they had never been interrupted. She shrugged out of her heavy coat and let it pool around her waist. Jess surmised the alcohol was making her hot, too. "I was never interested in Evan that way. But you know what, Jessica? *He* was never interested in *me* that way. I know what you think: pretty girl, single . . . But he only ever had eyes for one person and that was *you.*"

Jess didn't know what to say, so she didn't say anything at all.

"You were right, though; we did have a secret. And you might have known all about it, too, if you would have been just a little more willing to listen."

"What do you mean?" Jess whispered.

"I know how you felt, Jessica, and maybe that was a breach of trust on Evan's part." She realized what she just said and rolled her eyes. "Fine. It was. But he needed someone to talk to and you certainly weren't going to be it. So yes, he confided in me."

"About what?" Jess said, but she was scared to hear the answer.

"Gabe."

"What about Gabe?"

Cate ran her finger across the delicate rim of her glass, and then lifted it to her lips for another sip before she spoke again. "Evan was in contact with Gabe's birth mom."

"How long?"

"For years. From the beginning, I think."

Jess waited for the sting of betrayal, but she felt nothing. She knew this. Max had already torn the band-aid off that particular wound. What she wanted to know was *why*.

"Did he ever tell you why? Why would he go against my wishes?" Jess took a greedy, angry pull of her drink while she waited for Cate to answer.

In the end, Cate answered a question with a question. "Why wouldn't he?" she asked. "That woman gave birth to Gabe. What parent wouldn't want to know about their kid's birth mother?"

Me. I wouldn't, Jess thought. *If I had my way, I'd pretend she never existed at all.* Which, of course, was shallow and short-sighted, maybe even cruel. It certainly didn't conform to the hopeful outlook that they were encouraged to have during their home study and parenting classes. "This is a team effort," Meredith had told them. "Adoptive families are at their best when they are supportive of and integrated with birth families."

Jess had never wanted that. She wanted to be Gabe's mama, in body and heart and soul. She wasn't a jealous person, rarely selfish, but in this one thing she wanted it all. There was no room in her heart for Gabe's birth mother.

Evan had been a bit of a different story. "It makes sense to me," he said one night when they were lying in bed. The lights were out, the air in the room brittle because it was the middle of winter, but also because they were arguing. Jess was on her side, turned away from her husband.

"What makes sense?" she asked, taking the bait.

"Being involved with the birth mom. I mean, if I were an adopted child, I would want to know everything I could about my family of origin."

The term sounded strange coming from Evan. What did he know about families of origin?

"If you give something up, you've closed that particular chapter in your life, don't you think?" Jess tried to sound nonchalant, but her heart was thumping an unsteady rhythm. She already felt protective of her child-to-be.

"Well, this isn't a some*thing,* is it?" Evan rolled over and reached between them to put his hand on the rise of her hip. He rubbed his thumb along the edge of bone where it jutted out. "It's a some*one.* I'm not sure people are left behind as easily as an old couch or a bad habit."

Jess felt a flash of fury. "Thank you for enlightening me, Saint Chamberlain. I wasn't aware that people are more important than objects."

"Come on." Evan pulled her closer. "You know I didn't mean it that way. I don't want to fight."

But Jess *did* want to fight. She felt possessive and greedy. *Mine,* she wanted to say. *This child is all mine and has always been mine and will always be mine.* Of course, she knew that kind of thinking was antithetical to the very ethos of adoption. And Jess knew those barbed, angry, selfish thoughts were emotionally immature and maybe even deplorable. She hated herself a little for being so uncaring, so she curled tighter into herself and ignored her husband's advances.

Evan let it go. But when they heard that the mother who had chosen them to parent their child wanted a closed adoption, Jessica had silently sung the "Hallelujah Chorus." Clearly Gabe was meant to be theirs.

"Is that what he was hiding from me?" Jess asked now, more to herself than to Cate. Obviously Evan had let the conversation drop at the time, but he had silently, secretly pursued it on his own.

"I think so," Cate said. Her drink was gone and she looked longingly at the bar, seemingly contemplating another. But instead of flagging down a waiter, she pulled on her coat and stuck her arms through the sleeves. "I'd better get going. But yes, that's what I came to tell you: Evan was in contact with Gabe's birth mom. He even met her a couple times."

"Do you know her name? Where she lives?"

Cate stopped with her hands on the zipper of her coat. "That's the other thing. She died. Gabe's birth mom, I mean. I'm not entirely sure how, but Evan was really shaken up about it. I mean, *really* upset."

"Why?" The question was out before Jess could curb herself. She sounded downright nasty, even in her own ears. "I mean, of course he was upset. But did you ask him why it affected him so much?"

"Look, I don't know. But I can tell you that Evan kept a file on her. I never read the papers or saw what was inside, but I know that's what he was doing. He took patient notes the old-fashioned way, scribbling his thoughts down on a piece of paper instead of using the Dictaphone that the other doctors liked. It drove the secretaries crazy, but he liked to do things his own way."

Jess knew.

"But sometimes I'd catch him taking different notes. They were handwritten, too, scrawled on a yellow legal pad. He always flipped the notepad upside down when I caught him writing in that particular notebook."

"Who packed up his office?" Jess asked, suddenly thinking of the boxes in her car.

"I did." Cate ducked her head sheepishly and finished zipping up her coat. She stood and took the scarf that she had hung over the back of the booth. Winding it around her neck, she said defensively, "Beth called and called you. Finally she asked me if I would just box up his things."

"It's fine," Jess said. "I don't care. But is the notebook there? Did you find his notes?"

Cate shook her head. "No. He didn't keep them in the notebook anyway. He always tore out the pages and put them in an accordion file. I didn't find that, either."

"So you think the letters from Gabe's birth mom are in there?"

"I don't know," Cate admitted. "I guess so. Hang on . . ." She paused and thrust one hand deep into the pocket of her coat. Taking out a business card, she handed it across the table to Jess. "I almost forgot."

"What's this?" Jess accepted the card, fingering one bent corner as she watched Cate.

"I found it under Evan's desk when I was cleaning out his office. I meant to stick it in one of the boxes but I forgot. It's been in the pocket of my scrubs for weeks."

Jess glanced at the front. "James Rosenburg" was written in gold foil, and beneath that "Attorney at Law." She had never heard of James Rosenburg. He wasn't local; at least, she didn't think he was. Why would Evan need a lawyer?

"I would have just thrown it away," Cate said, "but Evan wrote on the back. I thought it might mean something to you."

Cate parted with a soft good-bye and her hand raised as if in blessing. Or maybe she was warding Jessica off, warning her to keep her distance now. Either way, Jess didn't really care.

She flipped over the business card. A phone number, an address. At the very bottom, Evan's careful handwriting in blue pen: *Leave it alone.*

Leave what alone? Jess couldn't even begin to guess. All the same, she slid the card into her pocket beside the key that she had tucked there. She hadn't really even had a chance to think about the key, to wonder why Evan had taped it to the bottom of his pencil holder. Maybe it had something to do with the accordion file. Maybe James Rosenburg was involved.

It wasn't like Evan to be secretive, but clearly he had been keeping things from her. Jess needed that accordion file. She didn't understand why her husband would go to such lengths to conceal a few handwritten notes about Gabe's birth mom, but Jess was desperate to find out.

She finished her drink and threw a twenty on the table. Cate hadn't paid, though Jess figured picking up her martini was the least that she owed the nurse after years of quietly loathing her.

It wasn't until she was putting on her coat that Jess realized her quick errand had turned into an entire afternoon away. She snagged her phone off the table and glanced at the time. It was after six o'clock. Even more disturbing was the string of texts that she had missed from Max.

Fine

Where r u?

Trey is picking me up in 15

I'm leaving g home alone!!!!!

Fine — we r taking him

Jess wasn't the cussing type, but she swore a blue streak in her head as she hurried out to her car. Max was going to be furious with her, and they had just reclaimed some ground. She'd make it up to him some way. Somehow. And she'd take Gabe out for supper. Just the two of them. It would be great.

One drink wasn't enough to put Jess over the legal limit, but she felt a little woozy hopping behind the wheel all the same. She wasn't buzzed, but she was a bit of an emotional wreck, and her conversation with

Cate was playing in her mind on repeat. She scoured the words for nuance, for hidden meanings that she had missed the first time around. Against her better judgment, she believed Cate. Jess just wished that she would have listened sooner.

There was no time for regret as Jess rushed down back streets in the direction of Auburn High. The boys' and girls' varsity basketball teams played a Friday night doubleheader, and she knew the gym would be packed. It wouldn't be easy to find Max and Gabe, but she could text them when she got to the parking lot. Maybe even have Max walk Gabe out so she wouldn't have to go into the gym at all. Jess had never been a fan of big crowds, and the fishbowl quality of her life these days only made her want to avoid people even more.

When Jess arrived at Auburn High, the parking lot was completely full. People had even lined the sidewalk and pretended the end of each row had an extra space, by parking as if the painted lines didn't mean anything at all. Jess had no choice but to crawl down a residential street, hoping for an open spot. She was over a block away before she found one. Jess parallel parked — a little crookedly — and grabbed her phone out of her pocket.

I'm here, she texted Max. *Meet me at the door?*

No response.

Jess zipped her coat all the way to her chin and even flipped up the faux fur–lined hood against the cold. She didn't wait for Max to reply. Better to find her boys as quickly as she could, and then take Gabe home. Max loved his brother, but his patience wasn't interminable.

The cold air nipped at Jess's cheeks and her exposed hands, and she realized with a start that the alcohol had dulled her senses a little more than she had initially wanted to admit. It was sobering, the cold air, and the understanding that she had been a negligent mother. Well, maybe "negligent" was a bit harsh.

Jess could hear the squeak of sneakers and the rhythmic beat of a basketball being dribbled down the court long before she was ensconced in the hot gym. The girl at the ticket table recognized her and waved her through, and Jess was grateful that she didn't have to dig in her purse for her faculty card.

The lights of the gym were startlingly bright after the subdued mood lighting of O'Malleys and the inky night outside. Jess blinked at the sudden onslaught of harsh, fluorescent bulbs and the screams of hundreds of adolescents. By the way the crowd was on their feet shouting, it was apparent Auburn had just scored.

"Hi, Jess."

Jessica turned to see one of her coworkers give her a half smile. Luke Tucker was a math teacher, a twentysomething new recruit whom all the female (and a few of the male) students had a crush on. He wasn't traditionally handsome, but he was confident, and there was something about the way he slid both hands in the back pockets of his skinny jeans. He was sexy. Everyone thought so. Luke was about the last person that Jess wanted to run into.

"Hi, Luke," she said, squinting at the crowd across from where she stood. She hadn't spotted Max or Gabe yet.

"Looking for your boys?" Luke said. "I'm on duty. I've been here since the start and saw them come in a while ago. I thought they were with you."

"I'm picking them up," Jess said. "Well, I'm picking Gabe up. Max came with a friend."

"I haven't seen them for a while," Luke admitted. He gave her a conspiratorial wink. "Gotta admit, though, I'm feeling a little jealous."

"Excuse me?"

He smiled crookedly and then said in a whisper: "I could really go for a drink right about now."

Jess was mortified. How could he smell liquor on her? She'd had a single drink.

"Oh," she said. "After the game, I suppose."

Luke nodded and then pointed across the gym. "I see Max. In the student section, right below the scoreboard about halfway down."

Jess followed his directions and sure enough, there was Max tucked in the very middle of a crowd of teenagers. They were watching the game, but something about the way Max stood at the center of it all — bearing the weight of one boy's arm slung across his shoulders and inclining his head to listen as another boy shouted in his ear — betrayed his sudden star status. But Max didn't seem to be enjoying himself. His mouth was a thin, tight line, his jaw set. As Jessica watched, he attempted a smile for the classmate who had been regaling him with a story, but it was flat and insincere. He looked miserable.

But even more concerning was the fact that Gabe was nowhere to be seen.

"Thanks," Jess said, preparing to cross the

gym. She would wait until the action was at the other end of the court and pray that the entire gymnasium didn't witness her searching desperately for her son. "If Gabe comes this way, would you hang on to him until I come back?"

"Sure thing," Luke said. "He's probably playing with the little kids in the balcony."

Jess doubted it. Gabe didn't like big crowds and he certainly didn't like groups of screaming children. If he wasn't in the gym, he was somewhere quiet. She just didn't know where.

There was a trio of teenage girls waiting to cross, and when the players ran to the opposite end of the basketball court, Jess joined them hurrying over the polished floor. The girls melted into the sea of people, but Jess stood at the corner of the bleachers, trying to get Max's attention. His gaze was elsewhere, anywhere and everywhere but on Jess. Finally, someone noticed her. The message was passed, telephone-like, up through the rows of cheering kids until someone finally tugged Max's sleeve and he turned to see her waving at him.

Max shrugged. *What?*

Jess plucked her phone out of her pocket and waited until he did the same. Then she texted him:

I'm sorry. Where's Gabe?

idk

But you took him along, right?

hes here somewhere

He stuck the phone back in his pocket, clearly dismissing her. *That's it,* Jess thought. *He's grounded.* But as much as she wanted to blame him, she knew that this was just as much her fault as it was his. Okay, maybe it was all her fault.

There was a long hallway behind the gym where the locker rooms and PE offices gave off the faint odor of sweaty sneakers and new rubber balls. It was off-limits during games, but Jess pushed through the double doors anyway, hoping that maybe Gabe had found a little peace and quiet in the long, empty corridor. He was nowhere to be seen. Next, she climbed the stairs to the balcony, a forgotten corner of the school that had been used for storage and was later converted into a weight room for the sports teams. Nowadays it was a vast sweep of empty, dusty space that kids used for games of tag or soccer when they could nab a kick ball from the PE storage room. Jess wasn't surprised that Gabe wasn't there, either. The sound of children screaming in delight was deafening.

The bathrooms? It wasn't like Gabe to hide out in a public restroom. His nose was hypersensitive and he particularly hated any scent that was artificial or chemical. Evan had once told Jess that the blue disk in the urinal set Gabe off. Evidently, he hated it so much that he braved touching it just so that he could drop it in the garbage can. Evan had made him wash his hands three times.

Where, then? Jess could feel herself twisting tighter and tighter, a coiled spring that would explode into action if only she knew where to go. Where was her boy?

Jess was standing beside the bleachers, one hand on a metal bar as she studied the crowd, when she heard a sound that didn't match the cacophony around her. It was a whimper, an exhale, a noise so fragile she held her breath as she waited to hear it again.

There. It was below her, beside her. It was beneath the bleachers.

The area beneath the bleachers was also off-limits because the crisscrossing metal supports were dangerously mazelike. Adults could hardly fit through, and kids often got stuck as they rummaged beneath the benches for lost coins and dropped candy. The school had taken to roping the area off with an orange, plastic chain and threatening detentions for anyone caught in the belly of the metal beast. But someone was under there.

Jess crouched down and squinted into the darkness, trying to make sense of the shadows and corners. Everything was angled and sharp, but near the back wall she could just make out a shape that did not fit among the brittle bones of the bleachers. A soft lump rose and fell, and guilt bathed Jess in the hot glow of shame.

"Gabe?" she said, half crawling, half walking toward the shape. "Gabe?" Jess didn't dare to shout, but a whisper would be drowned out by the clamor of the basketball game. Clearly whoever was crouched in the shadows couldn't hear her, so she kept going. Jess stepped in something sticky and it glued her foot to the floor for a moment, but she pressed forward, ducking beneath and between the supports until she was close enough to call again.

"Gabriel, honey, it's Mommy."

He looked up from where his head had been resting on his knees. In the slanted light from above she could see that his cheeks were glistening. He had been crying.

"Oh, honey." Jess stepped over the final metal bar that separated them and gathered her son into her arms as best she could.

"It's loud," he said, hiccupping around a sob. "It hurts my ears."

"I know, baby. I'm so sorry."

"Where were you?"

But what could she say? "I'm sorry," Jess said again. "I'm so, so sorry. Let's just get you home, okay, bug?"

Gabe had a much easier time navigating the underbelly of the bleachers, but he refused to let go of her hand. They wove through the girders together, taking much more time than if they would have traveled alone. But even though Gabe trembled every time the structure shook with cheers, he held her fingers so tightly Jess began to lose feeling in the tips.

The only way out of the gym was to cross beneath the basketball hoop in front of the entire crowd. This time Jess didn't wait for the game play to divert to the opposite side of the court. Instead, she scooped Gabe up in her arms, letting his long legs wrap around her waist and his head tuck tight against her shoulder. She walked out in front of what felt like the entire community, their eyes burning holes in the back of her bowed head. All the way to the car Jess could feel the *click-click-click* of Gabe's tongue on the roof of his mouth, the frenetic tremble of his hands where they were laced tight around her neck.

July 24, 2018

LaShonna is dead.

Honestly, I can't get my head around it. We were talking just a couple of weeks ago, about the baby and her birth plan and what to do next. I thought I had convinced her to talk to her mother. Place the baby in temporary custody until her release. I've known since the moment that I read LaShonna's first letter that letting him go was much harder than she ever imagined it would be. It took me a while to persuade her to try, but I thought that we were almost there. The last time she called, she told me that her mother was coming to visit. She was going to ask her to keep the baby. Fourteen months. That's all it would take.

LaShonna stopped calling in the middle of June. And no one would give me any information because I'm not family.

Today I typed her name in a search engine, hoping to find the name of a friend or relative that I could track down. Her former employer, even. Instead, I found her obituary.

It doesn't feel real. LaShonna is gone. And I don't know what happened to her baby.

CHAPTER 15

Faye D.
30, unknown, beauty school
Chin-length, curly black hair, green eyes.
  Scar across the bridge of her nose.
Best friend knows.
DWLR/DWI, 16m, 34w

By the time her father called on Sunday morning, Gabe had mostly forgiven Jessica. They were lounging in bed together, Gabe propped up on pillows and watching PBS Kids on the iPad, while Jess flipped through a magazine. It was a summer edition, something that she had picked up for the pool but never bothered to thumb through. Now the recipes for fresh fruit granitas and barbecue chicken seemed almost offensive, bright and happy, Kodachrome color when the world was dark and gray. Jess's eyes glazed over as she absently turned the pages.

When the phone rang, she nearly jumped out of her skin. And when she saw her father's name appear on the screen, she almost didn't answer.

"It's Grandpa!" Gabe said, eyeing her phone. He put down the iPad to reach for it.

"I've got it, honey." Jess palmed her phone and then tossed back the covers and sat up. Sticking her bare feet into slippers, she padded into the bathroom. "Good morning," she said, after sliding the little phone icon to answer.

"Hi, Jessica. It's Dad."

"Yeah, hi Dad."

"Anna and I didn't hear from you yesterday, so we went ahead and planned on you coming for lunch. I'm assuming that still works?"

Jess had never said that it *did* work, but this was typical Henry. She glanced at the clock on the wall in her en suite — 10:37. How could it be midmorning already? Clearly Henry and Anna were just out of church and on their way home. It was too late to politely tell them lunch didn't work after all.

"Sure, Dad." Jess grabbed a clean towel from the linen closet and draped it over the hook by the shower. She could quickly wash her hair at the very least. Show up looking like she took care of herself. Jess had already started the day at a deficit — Henry and Anna knew that she and the boys had not been in church that morning. Impiety was a strike against her parenting, even if Henry and Anna would never dare to directly confront her about it. "What time would you like us to come?" Jess found herself asking. "Can I bring anything?"

"Come by anytime before noon. You don't have to bring anything at all."

Jess would bring a bottle of wine. That always went over well. Saying a quick goodbye, Jess tossed her phone on the bathroom counter and hollered at Gabe. "Go tell Max that we're going to Grandpa and Anna's house for lunch! Tell him he can hop in the shower as soon as I'm done."

There was an indistinct reply from the bedroom, but she heard a muffled thud as Gabe's feet hit the floor. Then he was off running, no doubt to jump on Max and infuriate him with a rude awakening. But at least he loved his grandpa and was excited to see him.

Jess showered quickly and then wrapped a towel around herself as she smoothed moisturizer on her cheeks. A bit of foundation and a dab of lipstick were in order, and maybe some mascara to wake up her tired eyes. When the phone rang again, Jess answered the call without looking at who it was.

"We'll be there soon, Dad. I'm just getting out of the shower and —"

"Hello?" A voice that was decidedly not her father's interrupted her train of thought.

Jess yanked the phone away from her ear and looked at the caller ID. Deputy Mullen.

"I'm so sorry," Jess said, suddenly breathless. "I thought you were someone else."

"No worries," the deputy assured her, but there was no humor in his voice. He got right down to business. "I'm sorry to bother you on a Sunday, but there's been a development that you need to know about."

"Development?" Jess sank to the closed lid of the toilet and leaned with her elbow against the bathroom counter. She was cold in nothing but a towel and stifled a shiver. "What do you mean? I thought . . ." She didn't finish.

"You know how Evan was found without any identification? Well, it was discovered this morning."

"What do you mean?"

"We have his wallet and phone. And a file that he had been keeping notes in."

Jess's heart stalled for a second and then pounded painfully back to life. Something that tasted a lot like fear turned her tongue sour. "I don't understand. How?"

"We got a call from the manager at the Motor Inn last night. A guest was trying to get into the room safe but it was locked. Apparently it's been locked for weeks, because when they finally got it open, Evan's cell phone, wallet, and a key chain were inside."

Jess could hardly breathe.

"The maid who cleaned the room either never realized that it was locked or didn't care. Nobody noticed until last night."

"Didn't he check out?"

"Apparently not. He prepaid so his absence didn't raise any red flags." Mullen anticipated her next question. "There was a toothbrush on the counter and some clothes on the bed. He clearly wasn't planning on staying long, and the maid who cleaned out his room didn't recall anything that unusual. When we interviewed her she said she's seen far stranger things than an abandoned toothbrush and a pair of jeans hanging off the bed."

"The Motor Inn?" Jess said dumbly.

"It's a motel just outside of town," Mullen said helpfully. "He must have been staying there."

"Why?"

"That's the million-dollar question, isn't

it? I'm afraid I don't know. We were hoping you could shed some light on the situation."

Jess thought of her suspicions that someone had been in her house. The book in Gabe's backpack. Her growing file that cataloged every scrap of information she could collect on the people who made her skin prickle. James Rosenburg had been added to that list, and after Gabe fell asleep the night before, she had learned that he was a family lawyer near the Twin Cities. Had Evan been considering divorce? Jess had every intention of calling the Rosenburg firm on Monday to find out.

But a dog-eared copy of *To Kill a Mockingbird* and Cody De Jager's DUI conviction and a tenuous connection to a lawyer nearly two hundred miles away made Jessica only feel paranoid. Like a conspiracy theorist. Surely Deputy Mullen and his team were making real headway on Evan's case. Instead of sharing any of the information she had gathered, Jess said, "I don't know what to tell you. I have no idea why he would be staying in a motel in Minnesota."

"I thought you might say that." He exhaled slowly. "What about his phone? Forensics is investigating, but it's password protected. Do you happen to know what it is?"

Jess could picture the screen of Evan's iPhone. The family photo that he had used as wallpaper. It had been taken a few years ago when Gabe was still a chubby toddler and Max wasn't so angsty. Max's adult teeth had just grown in and his grin was too big for his face. Bright and beautiful and so filled with joy it was almost painful to see. He was on the cusp of all that was to come and he didn't know that the world was about to wipe the smile right off his sweet face. Was the picture still there? Jess didn't know whether to hope that it was or that Evan had changed it to something more mundane. Either way, her heart broke a little when she said: "EJMG1234. The first letters of all our names."

"Thank you," Deputy Mullen said. "We'll try that. Would you like me to mail you Evan's wallet and the file? Oh, and the keys. Forensics is looking at his phone, but his personal effects are yours now."

"No." Jess was seized with sudden purpose. She glanced at the clock and stood up quickly, hurrying into her bedroom to grab clothes. Gathering underwear, bra, shirt, pants, she said: "I would like to come and get them."

"It's a three-hour drive." Mullen sounded nonplussed. "It's Sunday."

"I know."

"It's not an emergency."

It is to me, Jess thought, and the deputy must have read her mind because he said: "Tell you what. I'll meet you halfway."

It was an offer she couldn't refuse, and almost as soon as she had hung up, Jess's phone pinged with an incoming text. Deputy Mullen had sent her the address of a café halfway between Auburn and Elmwood Park, the small town where Evan's wallet had been found. Google Maps told her it would take just under an hour and a half to drive. Mullen had been generous.

"Max, Gabe!" Jess shouted, hopping into her jeans. "Put your shoes on. We're leaving in five!"

Gabe stuck his head in her room. He was wearing a rumpled Minnesota Vikings T-shirt and a pair of gray sweatpants with holes in the knees. His hair was flattened to his head and sticking up on one side, too, but Jess decided to ignore it all. Gabe was six. He was allowed to look disheveled.

"Time to go," she said.

"You're still wet."

"Just my hair, bug. I'll put it in a ponytail. Is Max up?"

"He's in the kitchen," Gabe said, tilting his head to look at her sideways. "Are you

301

happy, Mommy?"

Jess rushed back to the bathroom and began to drag a brush through her hair. "That's a funny question," she called, but Gabe had followed her and was now standing in the bathroom doorway. "Why do you ask?"

"You're all . . . buzzy," he finally said.

"Do you mean excited?"

Gabe shrugged, his soft shoulders hovering for a moment around his ears.

"I'm going to meet a friend," Jess improvised. "I guess I am a little buzzy."

"I like it when you're happy," Gabe said, and came to wrap his arms around her waist. He buried his face in her tummy and sighed. Jess let one hand fall to his crown. She ruffled his bed head and promised herself that she would try to be happier for him. Cheerful, at least. Didn't he deserve that?

Max was showered and waiting in the car when Jess finally shouldered her purse and stepped into the garage. Her coat was in her arms and she stuffed it in the backseat while she buckled in.

"Why aren't you wearing your coat?" Gabe asked. "It's cold."

"I'm dropping you off at Grandpa and Anna's," Jess said, backing out of the garage.

"I have a bit of a drive and I didn't want to wear my coat the whole way."

"I thought we were having lunch," Max said. He was looking at his phone, but Jess had a small portion of his attention.

"I have to run an errand."

"On Sunday?"

Jess didn't say anything. The less they knew, the better. "I'll be back soon. You guys will have fun."

Henry and Anna had a shuffleboard table in the basement, a gleaming expanse of honey-colored wood that Gabe was completely enamored with. He loved to take the flat disks and whoosh them fast as lightning down the polished surface. It made Henry cringe a little (the shuffleboard had been a project that he and Anna worked on for the entire winter of their first year of marriage), but he didn't stop Gabe or reprimand him at all. Jess knew that Gabe would stay busy with the board until Henry plied him with games or Anna decided to bake with him. And Max would divide his focus between whatever football game was being televised and his Snapchat account. They'd be fine while she was gone for a couple of hours.

The only person she had to convince was her father.

"Let me go with you," he said when Jessica dropped off the boys. She pulled Henry into the entryway of his heritage home in downtown Auburn. There was a wraparound porch and a long sunroom that ran the entire length of the house. It was cold, but Jess didn't want the boys to hear where she was going.

"No," she told her father firmly. "I'm doing this on my own. I won't be gone long."

"Anna is perfectly capable of watching the boys for the afternoon."

"I know that, Dad." Jess put both of her hands on her father's arm and squeezed. "I love you, and I love your help, but I need to do this on my own."

Something in her look must have convinced him, because Henry pressed a hard breath between his lips and nodded once. "Fine. But call me if anything comes up. And I mean *anything.*"

"Of course."

Jess was already half gone, her fingers on the door handle. "I'll be back before supper. This is nothing, really. I just want to have Evan's wallet."

She drove in silence for over an hour, listening to the sound of her wheels whirring along the old highway. The sun was low in the sky behind her, washing the world in a pale, diluted light that shimmered feebly.

It was cold, bitterly so, and even though Jess had the heater turned on high, frosty air seeped through the windows, the doors, the floor vents. The dashboard thermostat proclaimed it was seventy-four in the quiet cab of her car, but the skin on the back of Jess's neck still prickled with goose bumps.

Maybe she was afraid. The landscape around her was well suited for tragic daydreams, crashes and heartbreak and little disasters like an affair, an illness, an end. The whole earth was brown from where she sat, dark fields and dead grass and beige skies. An occasional gnarled tree with bent limbs and arthritic joints. Every few miles Jess passed another car or two. The driver lifted a finger or a few in a halfhearted, habitual wave.

Evan had loved road trips. The long expanse of highway, the hum of the wind and the tires. When Jess's head became heavy and drifted to the curve of her seat, Evan had brushed his knuckles against her cheek and given her a smile that made her feel known. Maybe it was the way their breath mingled in the space between them, the understanding that for a few hours at least they were alone in the world, held together in this small space where they could stop working and racing and striving and just *be.*

Jess blinked hard for a second, remember-ing. They had been good in those moments. Those minutes that seemed to stretch out beyond the confines of time. When the obligations of their lives and the needs of other people and the pressures of a job that Evan loved so dearly weren't clamoring for his attention, they had been at peace.

By the time Jess pulled into the outskirts of Elmwood Park, she was shaking for real, her entire body trembling though she had turned the heat up as far as it would go. She slowed down past the Motor Inn, an uninspiring, L-shaped compound with maybe twenty rooms all facing an empty parking lot. Jess tried to picture Evan stop-ping in front of one of the blue doors, its paint faded to watered-down Kool-Aid and peeling in furred little curls. Number 4? Number 7? She wondered where he had stayed, which room had been the last place he laid his head. But that thought only made her suddenly fit to sob, so she yanked herself up short and kept on driving.

The diner didn't have a name, at least, not that Jess could see, but a neon sign blinked HOT COFFEE and a handful of cars proclaimed it open. There was no police cruiser in the parking lot, but Jess didn't know what Deputy Mullen would be driving anyway. Any one of the sedans in the parking lot could be his. She didn't know whether to hope that she had beat him there or not. Pressing her hands to her face, Jess took a deep breath and turned off her car. Then she grabbed her coat off the backseat and threw it around her shoulders. She ducked her head against the wind and hurried to the café entrance.

A smattering of people populated the red booths, and Jess was greeted by the scent of pancakes and beef gravy. Clearly this was an all-day breakfast café, but the chalkboard near the entrance proclaimed the lunch special to be roast and mashed potatoes. The clash of odors turned her stomach just a bit, but before Jess even had time to wrinkle her nose, she spotted the man she had come for. Deputy Mullen was in a booth near the back, raising his hand in greeting. He had seen her come in.

"Thanks for coming," he said as Jess approached the table. He rose to shake her hand, but there was an awkward moment when they both seemed to wonder if a hug was more appropriate. Jess still had her hand out when the deputy reached around her and patted her back firmly, twice.

"Thanks for meeting me." She sank onto

the padded bench and scooted to the middle. He sat opposite from her and circled his hands around his mug, though he made no move to pick it up. Jess realized his coffee was mostly gone and no longer steaming. Deputy Mullen had been here awhile.

"Would you like a cup of coffee? Something to eat? I ordered a meat loaf sandwich," he said. "It's good here."

"I'm not hungry," Jess admitted. "Maybe a Coke."

"They only have Pepsi," he said apologetically.

It didn't matter to Jess. She wasn't here for the food or the small talk. All she wanted was a hit of caffeine and her hands on that file.

Deputy Mullen waited until he had a plate of food in front of him and Jess had her Pepsi. It didn't take long, though the minutes felt endless to Jessica. How were the boys? Fine. Was she working again? Yes. Boy, it was getting cold. Sure was. Finally, after he forked a bite of the piping-hot meat loaf and swallowed it seemingly without chewing, Deputy Mullen said: "I'm sure you're wondering about Evan's things."

Jess forced herself to take a sip of her drink. It was flat. "Did the password work?"

"No. He must have changed it. But we'll

keep working on it."

She nodded.

Deputy Mullen seemed to size her up, and Jess sat a little straighter, trying to look capable of handling whatever he had to say to her. Eventually, he sighed and said, "I'm afraid I don't have much to tell you. They kept his clothes in the lost and found for a week or so and then donated them to Goodwill. Other than that, the room was clean. There's really no use dusting for fingerprints or anything after all this time. Eleven people have stayed in that room since Evan."

"Do you normally dust for fingerprints in the case of an open-and-shut hunting accident?" Jess was surprised by the edge in her voice.

Apparently, so was Deputy Mullen. He gave her a searching look. "No," he said. "We don't. Is there anything that you'd like to tell me, Jessica? Has something come up since the last time we talked?"

Lots of things, but nothing concrete. Nothing that Jess could offer up as evidence of some crime. She felt suspicious and maybe even a little delusional. Clearly her husband had been keeping secrets from her, but to imagine that they had anything to do with his death seemed downright absurd with Mullen sitting across from her. He was the professional. She was a grieving widow with an overactive imagination.

"It's just hard," Jess said eventually, because she had to say something. Her voice cracked just a bit and she was mortified by how close her emotions were to the surface.

"I know." Mullen reached across the table and patted Jess's hand. She didn't even realize that she had been picking at the corner of a napkin until the deputy stopped her nervous motion with the weight of his warm fingers. "This is completely normal, Jessica. Death is hard, even when you're expecting it. But this. There's no textbook for this."

Jess nodded once and carefully extracted her hand from his loose grip. She knotted her fingers in her lap. "I'm fine. We're all going to be just fine."

Deputy Mullen watched her as he wiped his mouth with a napkin. Clearly he didn't believe her. Tossing his napkin over his plate, he pushed his sandwich aside half-eaten and reached for a beat-up attaché. "It's not much," he said. "I don't want you to get your hopes up." He worked a stiff buckle loose and then peered in the depths of the bag. A moment later he held out a worn, brown leather wallet and a simple file folder.

Jess reached for them even as she felt a wave of disappointment. Cate had described an accordion folder, not a flat, colorless rectangle. What could it possibly contain? It was so pinched it seemed as if there wasn't a single piece of paper inside.

"There's a couple hundred dollars in the wallet," Deputy Mullen told her. "From the sale of his Jeep, we're guessing. Driver's license, a credit card, some receipts."

Jess rubbed her thumb over the soft fold of the slim wallet. Evan had always been a bit of a minimalist. A single credit card. His library card. Receipts carefully folded in half and then in half again and tucked in the corner of the pocket where he kept his cash neatly arranged in order of denomination. Ones in the front. Fifties in the back. Flipping the wallet open, Jess let her finger fan the stack of bills. There were more than a couple hundreds.

But Jess wasn't all that interested in the wallet. She tucked it carefully in her purse and then picked up the file. "You don't need this?" she asked, tipping it toward Deputy Mullen.

"We've photographed the contents, but we don't believe it's relevant to the investigation. Looks like notes on some of his patients."

Jess laid the file flat on the table in front of her and opened it with more than a little trepidation. She didn't know what she was hoping for or secretly dreading, but somehow it felt significant that she was finally holding a piece of Evan. Maybe even something that he had written recently. That held a clue to what had happened in the final weeks and months of his life.

But the file was not at all what Jessica was expecting. Just as she feared, there wasn't a single sheet of paper inside, just a rainbow of Post-it Notes stuck in careful rows on both sides of the open folder. They were arranged by color, and a quick count of the columns told Jess there were twenty-five perfect squares in all. Six columns and four rows with one lonely Post-it Note all by itself at the bottom. Eight yellow ones, eleven blue ones, five purple ones, and a single green one. They were all covered in Evan's handwriting.

"What is this?" Jess asked.

"We thought you'd be able to tell us."

Jess glanced up and realized that Deputy Mullen was studying her intently. "Is there something you're not telling me?" she asked.

"Is there something *you're* not telling *me*?"

Jess felt herself blanch. All the blood in

her cheeks drained to her toes and she felt suddenly light-headed. "No," she managed. "But I have no idea what this is."

"Names," Mullen said helpfully. He leaned across the table and stuck his finger on the first one. "Mariah K.," he said, reading upside down.

"I can see that. What do they mean?"

He sat back and shrugged. "Your husband was a doctor. Maybe he was doing some sort of study."

"On what?"

"You tell me," Deputy Mullen said. "They're all women. No last names, save an initial. There is a brief description of each woman and then a few words about their family and friends."

"What's this?" Jess squinted at the last line on the first Post-it Note, a collection of letters that comprised some sort of acronym.

"That I can tell you. Or at least guess." Deputy Mullen leaned back and crossed his arms. "Those are crime charge codes. Abbreviations."

"Excuse me?" Jess was trying to follow, but what he was saying just didn't make sense.

"What's the first one?" Mullen waved his hand as if to say: *Lay it on me.*

Jess squinted at the Post-it Note. It was

yellow, the very first square in a grid that was as neat and orderly as Evan himself. But put together, the scraps of paper were beyond mystifying. They were indecipherable. Jess took a deep breath, then put her finger beneath the letters in question and read: "Capital M-A-N slash D-E-L followed by a *C* and an *S.*"

"Sometimes different departments use different codes, but it's clear that those abbreviations refer to the manufacture and delivery of a controlled substance."

Jess's eyes shot to his. "You're kidding me."

"It's pretty standard. This shorthand is used on background checks, arrest records, warrants — you name it." Mullen seemed to be studying her just a bit too intently. "Do those letters mean something to you?"

"No. I mean, I don't think so." Jess hurriedly scanned the rest of them. "I'd have to look at them for a while, I guess, but nothing pops immediately."

He nodded. "I think they're pretty clear. Look, there's a yellow one near the end of that batch and two purple ones that all say P-R-O-S-T. Take a guess."

"Prostitution," Jess said, barely believing that she was having such an incomprehensible conversation.

"Bingo."

Jess deflated against the padded bench. "I don't understand," she said. "What does this mean?"

"I don't know." Mullen put his elbows on the table and templed his fingers. "But we plan to find out. Hopefully Evan's phone will point us in the right direction."

"You wanted to find out if I knew anything," Jess said as the reason for Deputy Mullen's eagerness suddenly clicked. He wasn't being nice meeting her halfway; he was hoping to glean some information.

He tapped his fingertips together. "It occurred to me. It's not why I met you, Jessica, but I'm glad I did. It's good to see you."

She realized she was biting her bottom lip and forced herself to stop. She sat up straight and pulled the file toward her. "This is mine?"

Mullen nodded.

"Thank you," Jess said. "For his wallet. For this." Jess tapped the edge of the folder on the tabletop, then gathered up her purse and coat and scooted out of the booth.

"Don't forget the keys." Deputy Mullen handed her a key chain filled with keys. "If you think of anything at all, please let me know."

"I will," Jess said, sticking one arm and then the other in the sleeves of her coat. She was grateful to have something to do so she didn't have to watch him watching her. But just at the moment she was ready to leave, Jess found that her feet stuck to the floor. She paused. Gathered up the courage and asked: "Do you still think Evan's death was an accident?"

Deputy Mullen looked away from her, out the filmy windows of the greasy diner, and furrowed his brow. It was a familiar expression, Jess could tell from the deep wrinkles that appeared on his forehead, between his eyes. After a moment he gave his head a little shake. "I don't know," he said truthfully. "I just don't know."

Conversation with Larissa Tate
(July 27, 2018)

LARISSA TATE: HELLO?

EVAN: HELLO, MS. TATE. YOU DON'T KNOW ME, BUT —

MS. TATE: I DON'T TALK TO TELE-MARKETERS.

EVAN: WAIT! I'M NOT A TELEMAR-

KETER. MY NAME IS EVAN CHAMBERLAIN. I WAS A FRIEND OF YOUR DAUGHTER.

MS. TATE: LASHONNA IS DEAD.

EVAN: I KNOW. AND I'M SO VERY SORRY FOR YOUR LOSS.

MS. TATE: DO YOU WORK FOR THAT LAW OFFICE?

EVAN: NO. I'M A FAMILY PRACTITIONER. I'M SO SORRY TO BOTHER YOU, BUT LASHONNA'S DEATH WAS SO UNEXPECTED, AND I JUST HAVE TO KNOW: DID SHE SPEAK WITH YOU BEFORE HER DEATH?

MS. TATE: I'M NOT SURE HOW THAT'S ANY OF YOUR BUSINESS.

EVAN: YOU'RE RIGHT. IT'S NOT. I JUST . . . I CAN'T SLEEP. MS. TATE, WHAT HAPPENED TO THE BABY?

MS. TATE: I HAVE NO IDEA WHAT YOU'RE TALKING ABOUT. THERE WAS NEVER ANY BABY.

CHAPTER 16

Kate L.
27, Caucasian, GED
Anorexically skinny, mousy-brown hair,
*   startlingly blue eyes.*
Brother involved.
ARS, 52m, 1yr 7m pp

Halfway home, Jess pulled onto a gravel road and parked in a field driveway. She had good reception, so she dug a pen out of her purse and found a directory of common criminal abbreviations on the web. Deputy Mullen was right. They were easy enough to decipher. A young woman named Kate (whom Evan described as anorexically skinny with mousy-brown hair and startlingly blue eyes) had been convicted of arson. Jessica assumed she had been given a fifty-two-month sentence, but she couldn't figure out the rest of the numbers. Did they signify how much time this Kate L. had already served? Jess just didn't know.

By the time she was done, Jess had unveiled charges of burglary (BURG), fraud (FRD), criminal possession of dangerous drugs (CPDD), homicide (HOM), and even DUI. Cody De Jager had gotten off with just a few months on his DUI conviction, but a woman named Ariana hadn't been as lucky. Maybe that was because she had also been carrying a concealed weapon (CW).

Jess stared at her scribbled notes, the strange collection of crimes and bizarre notations her husband had made. They were all women. And they were all criminals. Did Evan know them? Were they in his care somehow? Maybe that was the unifying factor — Evan had taken on a research project or something. But why hadn't he ever said anything to her about it?

Because they hadn't been together anymore. The thought made Jess's heart sink. Silence enveloped their home weeks and months before the official separation. The stillness became a fog, thick and viscous, impenetrable. Sometimes Jess would open her mouth to say something and just as quickly shut it. She became changeable as air, flowing around the rock that was her husband. And if he missed her, Jess couldn't tell. Evan was so busy, distracted. Wrapped up in something that she didn't understand

and he didn't explain. Maybe he had been all wrapped up in *them*.

Jess would give anything — *anything* — for the chance to sit in this car with Evan one more time. To fold her hand in his and study the laugh lines at the corners of his warm eyes. When had he stopped looking at her? *Really* looking at her? When had the words slowed to a trickle? Jess wished that she would have tried harder, that she would have found a way to reach her husband before the love between them had dried up altogether.

Jess sobbed in the car before tucking all her notes away and finishing the long drive home. When she arrived at her father's house, the boys were watching a movie with Anna.

"Star Wars," Henry told her. "The first one. Or, I mean, the new one."

"The seventh?" Jess guessed, hoping her father couldn't tell that she had been crying. If he noticed, he seemed willing to pretend he didn't.

Henry shrugged. "Sure."

"It's a little dark for Gabe, don't you think?" Jess took a few steps toward the living room where she could hear the strains of the classic *Star Wars* music cueing up a battle scene.

Henry tugged her sleeve to stop her. "It's fine. We fast-forwarded through the opening and Anna has her finger on the pause button. Max is happy. Gabe is happy. Everyone wins."

Jess was about to protest but found she just didn't have it in her. Nearly three hours in the car, plus the knowledge that Evan had been keeping something from her — something big, something she couldn't even begin to understand — made her feel heavy and slow. Unnaturally tired. She let her father lead her away from the living room and into the kitchen, where he pulled out a chair for her and motioned that she should sit down.

"Coffee?" Henry asked, but he didn't wait for an answer. He opened the cupboard above the sink and took down a silver tin. It was a little late in the day for Jess to have caffeine, but she didn't care. She doubted she'd be able to sleep tonight anyway.

In minutes the kitchen filled with the aroma of freshly brewed coffee, and Jess gratefully accepted the mug Henry offered her. He put the sugar dish in the center of the table and then sat down opposite his daughter.

"How'd it go?" he asked.

"Fine," Jess said, the word a sigh that left

her chest hollow. "It was fine, Dad. I have his wallet."

"Phone?"

"Forensics wants to look at it before they turn it over, but it's locked."

"Don't you know the password?"

Jess blew the steam off the surface of her coffee. "I used to. It didn't work, though. He must have changed it. Deputy Mullen is emailing me a questionnaire that might help."

Henry raised an eyebrow.

"Evan's first car and pet names and favorite color. Anything that might provide a clue about his password."

Henry reached for the sugar spoon and measured a small amount. Adding it to his coffee he said, "Maybe it doesn't matter one way or the other. What could they possibly find?"

A lot. Jess almost told him. She almost opened her mouth and explained about all the things that didn't add up in her husband's ostensibly straightforward accident case. But at that moment there was a whoop from the living room and Gabe came careening around the corner.

"Mom!" he shouted, surprised to see her. He hurried over and gave her a squeeze and then launched into an elaborate explanation of the movie and Kylo Ren and the Force. He took a step back and stretched his right arm out toward Jess, twisting his hand back and forth as he stared at her with a ferocity that made her bite back a smile.

"What are you doing?"

"Using the Force," he said, his gaze so serious he caused a deep line to form between his eyebrows.

"To accomplish what?"

Gabe tilted his head as if it should be obvious. "To make you do whatever I want."

"She already does whatever you want," Max said, coming into the kitchen. He was carrying an oversized bowl in his hands with a few handfuls of popcorn bouncing around in the bottom.

Jess chose to ignore his barb and said instead, "I guess you two don't need supper tonight."

"Meredith is bringing subs." Max handed Jess the bowl when she reached for it and turned to lean against the counter.

"What do you mean?" Jess was suddenly ravenous and tossed a few buttery kernels in her mouth. "How do you know that?"

"She texted me. Said she couldn't get ahold of you."

Jess felt her nose wrinkle in disbelief. She pulled her purse off the floor and rummaged through it for her phone. Sure enough, there was a string of texts and a couple of missed calls from Meredith. Jess belatedly remembered that she had put it on silent during her conversation with Deputy Mullen because she didn't want to be disturbed. And her phone wouldn't beep with alerts while she was driving. Even if it had, Jess had been too preoccupied to worry about much of anything besides her husband's final days and weeks.

"Sorry," Jess said, but she wasn't sure who she was apologizing to. Meredith? Honestly, Jess was starting to feel a little smothered. She loved her friend, but Meredith was being a bit overbearing. Before she could censor herself, Jess muttered, "We really don't need her to bring supper."

"That's what I told her," Max agreed. "She wouldn't take no for an answer."

Anna drifted into the kitchen, wearing a blanket around her shoulders and a whimsical half smile. "That was so fun!" she said, tickling Gabe with a tassel from what Jess realized was a caftan, not a blanket. "I think we should have a weekly movie night. Popcorn and candy and pajamas!"

"Yes!" Gabe shouted, batting at the tassel like a kitten. Clearly Anna and her youngest had bonded while Jessica was gone.

"That sounds nice," Jess said, hoping that she sounded as noncommittal as she felt. "But we should really get going. Thank you so much for having them Dad, Anna." Jess took one last sip of her cooling coffee and then pushed back her chair.

"Stay," Anna said. "We can order a pizza or —"

"Meredith is bringing supper," Jess said. "We really need to get home."

"Next time." Anna's smile didn't waver, and when Henry stood to put his arm around her, she leaned into him contentedly. "We would love to see you more often. You're always welcome here."

Jess wished she could be as enthusiastic about her stepmother as Anna seemed to be about them. But she just didn't have the emotional bandwidth to handle another complicated relationship. *Later,* she told herself as she gave Anna a one-armed hug. *I'll be a good daughter to her someday.*

The folder was tucked under the driver's seat and Jess was acutely aware of it all the way home. She was dying for the chance to study it further. To look for connections between the women or maybe, if she was lucky, Cody De Jager or James Rosenburg or Jake Holmes. Anthony Bartels. No one would escape her scrutiny.

But first she had to get past Meredith. Her friend's car was already in the driveway when Jess pulled up.

"Auntie Mer!" Gabe shrieked, ever enthusiastic. He launched himself from the car before Jess even had a chance to put it in park. When Jess glanced at Max and he rolled his eyes, she felt kinship bloom beneath her breastbone. It felt good to be united with Max in something, even if it was something less than cordial.

By the time Jess had the car off and was climbing out of the driver's side, Gabe and Meredith were coming into the garage. Gabe was clutching a Tupperware container to his chest, and Meredith had a paper bag in each arm.

"Supper!" Meredith sang, leaning in so that Jess could give her an awkward hug around the bulky parcels.

"Thank you," Jess said in spite of herself. "You really didn't have to do this."

"Sure I did," Meredith enthused. "When the mood strikes, I'd better make the most of it. You know from personal experience that I'm not the most thoughtful best friend in the world."

It was true. Meredith was a bit singular in her attention — and it was usually focused on herself. Well, that wasn't entirely true.

She wasn't selfish, just zeroed in on her job, her family, her hobbies. Jess didn't blame her. It was so easy to be wrapped up in the day-to-day. But ever since Evan's death, Meredith had stepped up her game. She was concerned, involved, present.

"Let me take one of those." Jess eased a bag out of Meredith's arms and chastised herself for being so uncharitable. She was lucky to have Meredith on her side, especially because she suspected Mer's famous buttermilk brownies — her weakness — were in the Tupperware container that Gabe was carrying.

"Todd made sandwiches," Meredith said once they were in the kitchen and unloading the bags. "Turkey and swiss on pretzel buns. And there are potato chips and French onion dip, and carrots and celery."

"And brownies!" Gabe announced, peering into the Tupperware container with barely contained glee.

"I'll take one of those." Max snagged a brownie before Jess could stop him. He took a big bite and said around the gooey confection in his mouth: "The sweet potato chili was barely edible."

Jess turned to hide a smile.

"Well, have a sandwich, too," Meredith said, slapping the counter to get Max's attention. "And don't forget your vegetables."

"Thanks." Jess put her hand on Meredith's back and gave a little rub. "This was really nice of you. I didn't realize how tired I was until now, but I'm going to have a bite to eat, put Gabe to bed, and then take a hot bath."

Meredith's eyes clouded for just a second. "Sounds great, Jess. But I was wondering if I could talk to you for a minute first."

Jess felt a prickle of concern. Meredith wasn't typically the serious sort, but all of a sudden Jessica wondered if her friend had brought supper over for a reason other than compassion. "Okay," she said a little over-brightly. "Would you like to have supper with us?"

"Actually . . ." Meredith looked around the kitchen, her gaze alighting first on Max as he finished the last bite of his brownie and then on Gabe where he sat at the table trying unsuccessfully to open the foil bag of potato chips. "I was hoping we could talk alone."

Jess stalked across the kitchen and took the bag from Gabe. Opening it in one swift motion she handed it back to him and said, "Tonight's not great for me. I haven't seen the boys all day and —"

She realized her mistake the moment the

words were out of her mouth.

"Oh?" Meredith asked. "Where were you today?"

Jess couldn't explain it, but she was gripped with a need to keep her meeting with Deputy Mullen a secret. Maybe Meredith was being too nosy, maybe she just needed to have something in her life that was hers and hers alone. Either way, she gave her hand a casual wave. "I had to run some errands. The boys stayed with Henry and Anna."

"I'm glad to hear that," Meredith said with a tight-lipped smile. Then she visibly softened, took a step toward Jess. "I know you're tired. Just a couple of minutes, okay?"

Jess left the boys with instructions to pour a glass of milk and eat at least a handful of veggies each. She doubted if they would obey her, but at least she had left them with a motherly edict.

Since the kitchen, dining room, and living room all flowed into one, there were few places in the Chamberlain house to go for privacy. So Jess led Meredith to the spare bedroom that they used as an office at the front of the house. It was untidy and poorly organized, a dumping ground for all the things that didn't seem to have a home. There were a few boxes of Christmas decorations stacked in the corner, and a printer on the desk that had been out of ink for at least a year. Jess hadn't been in the office in ages and set to self-consciously straightening up as Meredith shut the door behind them.

"Don't," Meredith said, waving her hands in front of her. "Seriously. I don't care. You've seen my house."

It was true. Meredith wasn't the world's best housekeeper.

"But you can't even sit down," Jess complained, lifting a stack of books off one of the chairs. She cast around for a place to put them and ended up setting them on the floor behind the desk. "There you go."

"So formal," Meredith teased, but Jess could tell that her heart wasn't in it.

"What?" A premonition rippled down Jess's spine like a chill. Meredith was really upset about something. "What in the world is going on?"

"Come and sit," Meredith said, sinking into one of the wingback chairs in front of the darkened window. The shades were drawn, but even if they had been open, the night was black outside. It was a thick and moonless night, heavy with clouds that swept in late and low against the wintry air.

"I don't want to sit."

Meredith sighed. "Please, Jess. Just indulge me."

Jess didn't say that she was always indulging her, though she wanted to. It just wasn't in her nature to put up a fuss. So she crossed the room with more than a little trepidation and perched on the end of the seat like she'd been told. "Say it," Jess whispered, crossing her arms over her chest protectively. "Whatever you came here to say, just say it."

"I received a phone call yesterday," Meredith began, then stalled out. She squeezed her eyes shut for just a second and tried again. "Someone called me with concerns about how things are going in Evan's absence."

Disbelief and fury tingled across Jess's skin. She opened her mouth to speak but couldn't. When Meredith started to talk again, Jess put up her hand to stop her. A moment or two passed in utter silence and then Jess managed to croak: "What is that supposed to mean? Who called you?"

"Don't make this harder than it already is," Meredith begged.

"Someone is concerned about me?" Jess's voice was shrill even in her own ears. "This house? My *kids*?"

Meredith ducked her chin down a notch.

Yes.

"I can't believe this. I can't believe you." Jess wanted to scream, to kick Meredith out of her house. To run away where prying eyes couldn't sift and measure her every action and inaction. She was seething, her blood rolling in a low boil that threatened to spill up and over.

Meredith looked miserable. "I'm a mandatory reporter," she said quietly. "You know that. Do you think it was fun for me to field a phone call about my best friend? What was I supposed to do?"

"Defend me." Jess bit the words off her tongue.

"I did, believe me."

"Did you *report* me?"

"No." Meredith had the good sense to look affronted. "But people are starting to wonder . . ."

"Wonder what?" Jess threw herself out of the chair and paced the room, her pulse high and hot, stinging in her cheeks. "I just lost my husband, Meredith. Who called you?"

"You know I can't tell you that."

"What did they say?" Jess was aware that she was almost shouting. If she didn't cool it a bit, Gabe would come running. She took a deep, shuddering breath and asked again, quieter: "What did they say about me?"

Meredith squirmed. It was so uncharacteristic Jess almost laughed. But there was nothing funny about their conversation. "I don't know what to tell you," Meredith said. "You have a six-year-old at home and there have been a couple of instances lately where it seems you may have forgotten that he needs your time and attention."

"Are you kidding me?" Jess hissed. "Gabe has my full attention."

"Always?" Meredith asked the question hesitantly, but she held Jess's livid gaze. "You've been a little busy lately."

"What are you saying?"

"And Max is clearly going through a rough patch . . ."

"That's my fault?" Jess threw herself down on the chair and leaned forward with elbows on knees so that her legs skimmed against Meredith's. "My boys just lost their father. We are going through one of the most difficult things a family could possibly face. I can't believe you're sitting here judging me!"

Meredith reached out and took Jess's hands in her own. She pinched just a little too hard, her thumbs digging into the fine bones of Jess's wrists. "I'm not judging you, Jess. And I'm not accusing you of anything.

I'm trying to be your friend. The fact that I'm even here — that I'm telling you this — is probably unethical. A breach of confidentiality at least. But because I love you I wanted you to know. People are concerned."

People. More than one? Jess was so horrified she could hardly breathe. "I can't believe it."

"Look, it's going to be okay. I just think you need to lie low for a while, you know? Stay home, keep your boys close."

Jess bristled and yanked away from Meredith's anxious grip. "What do you mean? Are you suggesting I hide?"

"Of course not," Meredith said. "But if Child Protective Services gets involved, there's not much I can do."

"Why did they call you?"

Meredith lifted a shoulder. "I'm your friend. I'm a social worker. I guess they saw me as a first step. Consider it a small grace."

"Grace?" Jess choked.

"Look, Jess, I'm trying to help you *and* do my job. I don't think you fully appreciate the position I'm in." She looked like she might cry, but Jess was unmoved. Of all the times for Mer to roll over and play dead. Jess needed an advocate. A fierce warrior friend. And Meredith was exactly the sort to rise to the occasion, but for some reason she wasn't up to the task this time. Jess could see it in the slump of her shoulders, the sad, desperate look in her eyes. Meredith wanted to be forgiven, but Jess needed her to take up a sword.

"Thank you for supper," Jessica said, dismissing her friend. "And thank you for telling me. But if anyone else decides to burden you with their opinions about my ability to parent my children, you can send them directly to me."

"Jess, I —"

"I'd like you to go now." Jess opened the door so that the sounds from the rest of the house filtered into the office. A laugh track from a television show and the clatter of dishes in the sink. Max as he said something indistinguishable to Gabe.

"Mom?" Gabe yelled from the kitchen, preternaturally aware that his mother was in earshot. "May I have a brownie now?"

"Sure, honey," Jess called back. She was grateful that there was only the slightest quiver in her voice.

Meredith stood a little unsteadily and took a few steps toward Jessica. "I'm sorry," she said. "I didn't mean to hurt you. I just wanted you to know . . ."

When she trailed off, Jessica didn't fill in the silence or make any move to comfort her friend. She knew that she was being rather horrible, hard-hearted and condemning, but she had never felt so attacked in her entire life. Auburn was a small community, but the fact that people were willing to gossip about a recent widow — and make their concerns known to a social worker — was beyond the pale. Jess loved her kids more than her own life, and she had spent the last thirteen years proving exactly that. Every decision she had made since the moment Max was born was made with his best interests at heart. How dare they judge her. How dare Meredith do anything other than defend her tooth and nail.

"Okay," Meredith said, setting her shoulders. She seemed in that moment to come to a conclusion, and it wasn't a charitable one. She gave Jessica one last, hard look, and then swept out of the room with an air of superiority. "Bye, boys!" she called, her words cheerful and bright, as artificial as her attempt at normalcy.

"Bye, Auntie Mer!" Gabe called. As Jess followed Meredith through the living room, she could see that Gabe's face was smeared with chocolate, his mouth ringed in frosting and a little brown dab on the tip of his nose. She felt sure that Meredith was clocking even that and made a point to head straight to the sink, where she started rinsing a washcloth to clean him up.

They said stiff good-byes over the heads of the boys while Meredith slipped on her coat and grabbed her purse. Then she was gone, the door shut just a tad harder than necessary, but excusable since the wind was howling outside. It had come from nowhere, this sudden, frigid gale that lashed the trees and made the house groan. It was exactly the sort of night that Evan had loved, and if he were with them, Jess knew that he would have set a log in the fireplace and hauled out the fat fleece blanket that they kept in a cedar chest beneath the bay window.

But he wasn't here. And he wasn't ever coming back. And Jess didn't know how to start a fire or conjure the same kind of magic that her husband could pull from thin air. Apparently she didn't even know how to take care of her own kids.

"You okay, Mom?" Max asked, putting the uneaten sandwiches in the refrigerator. She hadn't told him to do it, but that small victory was eclipsed by the fury that was blossoming in her chest.

"Fine," she said unconvincingly. "Everything is going to be just fine."

River Han
New Message Request from Evan
  Chamberlain
August 7, 2018

Dear Ms. Han,
My name is Evan Chamberlain and I'm
a family practitioner in Auburn, Iowa. I
saw your comment on the Eagle Ridge
Women's Prison Facebook page and
decided to reach out. It seems you have
been recently released from Eagle Ridge,
and I was wondering if you had some
information on a former inmate there.
Her name was LaShonna Tate. She was
a friend of mine, and her suicide was a
terrible blow. Because I am not family
(and do not know her mother), I'm unable to learn anything about her death
and the events that preceded it. Specifically, what happened to her child?
LaShonna was due at the beginning of
July, and the last time we spoke she
shared that she wanted to parent. Now
she's gone and I don't know what happened to the child. I know this is an
enormous ask from a total stranger, but
if you knew LaShonna, and if you know
what happened to her baby, I would be
so grateful for any information you have

to offer.

Gratefully,
Evan

Evan Chamberlain
New Message from River Han
August 7, 2018

I knew LaShonna. We weren't close or anything, but I knew who she was. Her suicide was hard on everyone.

I can tell you that LaShonna had her baby near the end of June. I don't remember when exactly, but it was a girl. She came back the next day and wouldn't talk to anyone. For what it's worth, I heard that she gave the baby up for adoption.

Having a baby in prison is a special kind of hell. My boy was born two years, one month, and seventeen days ago, and I still think about him every day.

CHAPTER 17

River H.
22, Asian, 2 years of college
Strikingly beautiful. Long hair, brown eyes,
  petite.
Disowned.
ABD, 68m, 2yr 1m pp

Rain lashed against the windows for hours that night, but sometime near two o'clock the wind stopped so abruptly the sudden silence woke Jess. She crept from her bed and pulled back the curtain to survey the street from her second-story window. The scene was still, but shivering with droplets that hung suspended from every branch and eave and dead blade of grass. It would have been lovely except for the sky — it was as black and ominous as the sable pools of water that had collected on her driveway and sidewalk. Even the streetlamps were no match for the darkness; they flickered and gleamed dully, the borders of their lukewarm cast indistinct and feeble.

As Jessica watched, the rain turned to sleet. It fell like tiny shards of glass and filled the air with the sound of distant applause, a thousand hands clapping for what would surely be a winter wonderland. A world of ice and indefinable beauty. It didn't seem beautiful to Jess. It seemed deadly.

Jess had been dreaming. No, not a dream, a nightmare, and she remembered it in ribbons that seemed to float just outside her vision. When she thought she caught a glimpse, it was gone. But the feeling remained, the sense that something, some*one,* was just behind her, reaching.

"Mom?"

Jess turned from the window, surprised at both the noise and Gabe's presence in her room. He had started out in his own bed that night, and when she had finally flicked off her lamp only a couple of hours before, both he and Max had been sleeping peacefully in their own rooms. When had he snuck into her bed?

"Mom, what are you doing?" Gabe called again, his voice muffled from sleep and the blankets that he had pulled up over half his face.

"Hey, buddy," Jess said, dropping the curtain and tiptoeing over to where he lay cocooned in her sheets. She straightened the tangle of fabric around him and kissed the top of his head. "Go back to sleep. Mommy was just looking outside."

"Is it snowing?" he asked, yawning.

Jess could hear the note of hope in his question, even though Gabe was barely awake. "No," she said, smoothing his hair. "Shhh." She crawled back into bed and was grateful when Gabe wiggled over to her and tucked himself tight against her side. But for a heartbeat or two, Jess held herself perfectly still, uncertain if Meredith would consider her six-year-old son too old to share a bed with his mommy. Jess hadn't been given a handbook, a list of dos and don'ts when it came to parenting a child from a trauma-based background.

It was so hard for Jessica to admit that her son carried that label. In fact, for years she had refused to admit that the boy she had raised from infancy could be anything but wholly attached. Entirely hers. Jess didn't want to believe that there had been some primal wound, an injury inflicted when the bond between Gabe and his biological mother had been severed. But as Gabriel grew, Evan had begun to revisit the books they had read during their home study. He started talking about how a sense of loss had etched itself deep in their boy's soul. Gabe's anxiety, emotional insecurities, and behavioral problems weren't an indicator of ADHD or Asperger's. They were the result of loss. Their Gabe, who had only known love from the day he was born, still bore an intrinsic wound. A separation that would forever change him.

There was no cure. No magic fix. But there was an ever-growing list of books Jess should read and seminars she should attend. New philosophies emerging about the stress-shaped brain and the connected child and parenting theory. Reactive attachment disorder. Forget consequences — love and logic was the way to go. And if Jess wanted to really work to repair the deep hurt Gabe would obviously spend the rest of his life enduring, she would invest in a full neurological workup at one of the few clinics in the country that worked with adoptive families, and then undergo the subsequent neuropsychological and behavioral therapy. The Chamberlains needed family counseling; Gabe an attachment specialist. Also weighted blankets, a dye- and sugar-free diet, and some framed photos of his birth family in places of honor throughout the house.

It was all so overwhelming.

And devastating. Jess felt like such a failure. Shame was a brick on her chest, a weight that was slowly but surely crushing her. But none of this was about her. It was about Gabe. What he needed. Her son was a child who had to live with the consequences of other people's choices. A little boy whose nighttime anxieties had only increased with the loss of his father. Jess loved him so much it ached.

Deciding she didn't care one bit about whether or not it was developmentally appropriate, Jess curled her arm around her son and pulled him close. She tried to sleep.

A muffled shout yanked Jess awake only hours later. Gabe was spread-eagled across Evan's side of the bed, still sleeping, and Jess sat straight up, trying to get her bearings. Her heart was pounding in her throat, her mouth sticky and tasting impossibly like lead. Blood, she realized as her tongue began to throb. She touched her cheek with trembling fingers and realized she had bitten her tongue. In her dream or because of a scream in her house, Jess didn't know.

A scream. Jess threw her feet over the side of the bed and raced toward her room door. The house was eerily calm, the hallway milky with gray light from the high windows at the peak of the domed wall. The sky looked strange, flat and close somehow.

"Max?" Jess said quietly, hurrying toward his room.

His door burst open. "No school!" he whooped, thrusting his phone at her.

"What?" Max's grin didn't make sense, his bed head and the sparkle in his eyes. Hadn't he just been screaming?

"It's canceled," he said, and Jess couldn't tell if he was ignoring her distress or oblivious to it.

School. Belatedly, Jess felt the pieces click into place. "A snow day?" she asked, squinting at the screen Max held before her. She would have chastised him for having his phone in the bedroom, but she was distracted by the automated text message from the Auburn School District: *Due to blizzard conditions, there will be no school at any of the Auburn campuses today.*

"What's going on?" Gabe came out of her bedroom rubbing his eyes and trailing a ratty blanket. He still slept with his baby blanket, and because Max had only recently given up his, he didn't tease his little brother about it.

"No school!" Max said, scooping Gabe up roughly and spinning him around. "It's been canceled because of a blizzard."

"A blizzard?" Gabe wriggled out of his

brother's arms and pounded down the steps. Max followed eagerly, the years melting off him at the prospect of a perfectly unplanned day. Even Jess couldn't stop herself from smiling as she trailed behind them both. She watched as the boys flung open the curtains in front of the big bay window and revealed a scene that took her breath away. Sometime in the early morning hours it had indeed begun to snow, and the world was a swirling storm of white. The flakes fell so thick and heavy it was hard to see past the end of the Chamberlains' driveway, and because the world was so monochromatic, it was impossible to tell just how deep the snow was. Very deep, Jess suspected, because the front steps of their house were little more than a giant, slanting drift.

"It's snowing!" the boys shouted, jumping up and down. No matter that they had both seen the text message. This was undeniable proof only inches away from their noses.

"And there's ice beneath that," Jess said, remembering the rain, the sleet. It was a snowstorm of epic proportions, the kind of blizzard that would not be easily overcome. She didn't say it to Max and Gabe, but she doubted that there would be school tomorrow, either. It would take some time to dig out from under this avalanche. And it was still coming down.

"I didn't know there was snow in the forecast," Jess said absently as she wandered toward the kitchen. Hot chocolate was in order. And cinnamon rolls, if she had yeast. She'd have to proof it first, of course. She couldn't remember the last time she had baked bread — or anything, for that matter.

Gabe had been praying for a snow day since school started at the end of August. She didn't blame him. Jess could clearly remember the magic of an unexpected snow day, and it was reflected in the hoots that were still coming from the living room. There was something special about the earth swathed in white, fresh and new and gleaming like a gift on Christmas morning.

When she was a child, Jess's mother had made cinnamon rolls from scratch on snow days and let Jess stay in her pajamas all day long. They played Scrabble and 7-Up 7-Down, a game that was usually reserved for the adults in her life. Jess felt a pang of loneliness and wished for a moment that she could remember the scent of her mother's skin. Betsy had worn drugstore perfume and lotion scented like raspberries and cream, but she had always carried an undertone of something warm and baking. Jess couldn't recall it and it made her heavy with loss.

"Let's do a puzzle!" Gabe said, running into the kitchen and throwing himself at Jessica. He nearly bowled her over with his enthusiasm.

"Watch a movie," Max said, following just a few steps behind.

"Both." Jess smiled. "We can do both. But first: breakfast. Cinnamon rolls?"

Her suggestion was met with enthusiasm, but when the little foil packet of yeast refused to bubble, Jess had to come up with a plan B. They settled on pumpkin-spice pancakes and hot chocolate with a dollop of whipped cream and a few stale rainbow sprinkles on top. It felt ridiculously decadent to Jessica, like something out of a storybook instead of her real, painfully messy life. It was crazy how a blizzard could turn back the clock — they laughed and joked as easily as they had in the months and years before Evan left. If it felt like something was missing, they pretended otherwise. Even Max was like the boy Jess remembered. Funny, bright, and sarcastic, but not in a hurtful way.

It was close to noon when Jess realized she was still wearing her pajamas and crawled out from underneath the pile of blankets on the couch to go find something to wear.

"No!" Gabe shrieked, launching himself at her.

Jess grinned, evading his grasp so that he flopped back down on the pillows. "I'm going to brush my teeth, not run off to join the circus."

Gabe giggled, but Max wasn't as amused. Their morning had been an absolutely unexpected delight, but the snow showed no signs of abating and already the house was starting to feel small.

"Nobody can get out," Max said, leaning over the back of the couch. His eyes were trained on his telephone. "All the roads are still closed."

He had been hoping to spend the afternoon at the gym, or at the very least to be able to make it to Trey's house.

"The storm of a century," Jess said, trying to make a joke. But it sounded threatening, not funny.

Upstairs, Jess grabbed her phone off the nightstand and checked for messages. Nothing from Meredith (she couldn't decide if she was hoping for an apology or if she was still too upset to accept it), but her father had texted and called.

No voice mail, but his messages became

increasingly urgent as the morning went on.

What a storm!

Electricity is out in part of town. Do you have power?

Everyone okay?

I'm coming over.

Jess quickly called her father. "Hey," she said when he picked up. Henry wasn't one for small talk, so she didn't bother. "I didn't realize the power was out."

"It's only a couple of blocks. A transformer blew," he said. "Anna and I are fine; how about you?"

"It's warm and well lit here."

"Good. Stay put. I'm going to try and dig out later."

"Don't bother, Dad." Jess pulled open her curtains and draped them behind the decorative hooks beside the window. Snow was piling up on the window ledge, blocking the feeble light of the furious day. "It's still going strong. The plows haven't even attempted a pass of our street."

"I don't think they're out at all yet."

"Then what makes you think you'll be

able to dig out?" Jess laughed a little. "Stay put. Seriously. We're fine."

"Do you know how to build a fire?"

"If I need to, I'll google it on my phone," Jess said. "It can't be that hard."

Her father wasn't the outdoorsy type. And he wasn't particularly hands-on, either. Henry could paint a wall or hang a picture, but he had never taught Jessica how to change the tire on her car (the Lancasters had a AAA membership for that) and she could not recall a single time in her entire childhood when they went hiking or camping. She barely knew how to roast a marshmallow much less build a fire without burning her house down.

Evan had been different. His dad was an avid camper and Evan had grown up crisscrossing the US in a hatchback Toyota Corolla with a three-man tent in the back. Just enough room for Bradford and Helen, with Evan tucked snug between them. One of Jessica's favorite pictures of her husband had been snapped in an unidentified campground with three happy faces poking out of the faded red tent. Evan was ten, maybe eleven, with longish hair in a sleepy tangle and skinny arms thrown around the shoulders of his parents. As if the roles were reversed. As if he were the father and they the children. Even at that age his smile was measured, mature.

If Evan were home, he'd have a fire roaring by now.

But Jess couldn't think about that. She told Henry, "If the electricity goes, we could always turn on the oven and open the door. It's gas." She could hear her father sputtering on the other end of the line. Clearly he hadn't registered the note of sarcasm in her voice. "I'm joking," she said quickly. "Trying to be funny."

"I don't find that very funny."

They hung up shortly after Jess convinced her father to wait for the plows, and she took a few minutes to put her room in order. Bed made, yesterday's clothes in the hamper. The manila folder from Deputy Mullen was on her nightstand and Jess flipped it open for just a minute and skimmed the notes she had written on a piece of lined paper tucked inside.

She had spent a couple of hours propped up in bed the night before trying to make sense of Evan's strange notes. First, she researched the crimes. He had categorized everything from felony embezzlement to counterfeit trademark — Jess wasn't even entirely sure what that meant. But as far as Jess could tell, there was no rhyme or reason to the convictions, nothing that tied them all together. The women were of varying ages and backgrounds, and they represented different races and interests.

Then there were the tenuous connections that Jessica had tried to make between the women on Evan's Post-it Notes and her own imperfect list. One of the women had the initials DJ, and Jess had drawn a line between her and Cody De Jager with a question mark. Maybe they were related? It was an almost ludicrous stretch, but it was all she had. And another had a surname that started with an H. Worthy of another line. Of course, Anthony Bartels and James Rosenburg were tied together by the thin thread of perceivable association: one was a social worker, the other a family lawyer. There was overlap there. Perhaps they shared a case or two. Maybe they worked with one or more of these women. Jess intended to find out.

The links were flimsy at best, pathetic at worst. Jess was convinced that her amateur sleuthing leaned far toward the pathetic side of the spectrum, but it had given her a sense of purpose all the same. Deputy Mullen and his team could keep investigating, and Jess would do her part. If she actually stumbled upon something significant, she'd share it.

But for now her hobby was becoming a secret obsession that was one of the only things keeping her sane. Or messing with her already fragile mental and emotional well-being. It was a toss-up.

Shaking her head as if to dislodge those errant, pesky thoughts, Jess walked over to the small desk in her room and slipped the folder in the top middle drawer. It felt wrong somehow to have it out when the boys were home. She couldn't stand the thought of them knowing that their father had kept secrets from them. That he had a folder filled with the names of strange women who had committed some pretty heinous acts.

"We're looking into it," Deputy Mullen had told her when she pressed him about the file in the diner. "But there's no reason to believe these notes are related to his death."

"They were hidden in a motel safe," Jess said, quirking an eyebrow in disbelief. "Clearly he was trying to keep them a secret."

"The safe also contained his phone, wallet, and keys. Was he hiding them? Look, Jessica. I've said it before: the simplest answer is often the right answer. There's just no evidence that the file had anything to do with what happened to Evan." Mullen raised his hands as if in surrender. Or maybe he was warding her off. "If something surfaces, we'll follow the lead wherever it takes us."

"But until then . . ."

"See if you can figure anything out. Like I said, my guess would be Evan was doing some sort of a medical study."

Jess had already scribbled notes to call Dr. Murphy and Dr. Sanderson, Evan's partners at Auburn Family Medicine — not that she needed to be prompted. The file was just about the only thing she could think about.

Her hand was still on the desk drawer and her thoughts a million miles away when Max came storming into her room.

"Where is it?" he demanded.

"Excuse me?" Jess spun, an easy smile on her face because the glow of their quiet morning lingered. But Max was not smiling.

"I said: Where is it?"

Jess took a step toward him, but he matched her movement by sliding back an equal distance. She almost laughed — he was still wearing his pajama pants and a rumpled T-shirt that said Allergic to Mornings — but she checked herself. Her son was clearly not in a laughing mood.

"I'm sorry, hon. I honestly don't know what you're talking about."

"My journal," he spat, crossing his arms high over his chest. His upper arms were filling out, the muscles defined in a way they hadn't been before. When had that happened?

Jess squeezed her eyes shut for a second. "I didn't even know you had a journal."

"Yes you did! I got it from Carter. Remember?"

It had been a long time, but Jess did remember. Over a year ago, when the tension in their house had become so thick and viscous it was hard to walk upright, she and Evan had decided that Max needed to talk to someone. Carter Mayfair specialized in youth therapy and shared the same office as their couples' counselor. They set up a few appointments so that Max could see Carter at the same time that they met with Eleanor. Couples counseling proved to be ineffectual, but against all odds Max had liked Carter. No one was more surprised about it than Max.

"He gave me a journal to write stuff in before bed." Max was pacing now.

Jess recalled the journal, and she also remembered that Max had downplayed it.

"It's not like I'm going to use it," he said after the final appointment, when Carter gave it to him. It was a parting gift of sorts, and Max looked skeptical when Carter clapped him on the back and leaned in to whisper one last thing. Max tried to appear disinterested, but Jess noticed that he ran his thumb over the leather cover, flipping the magnetic clasp that held it shut open and closed. Max liked it, whether he would admit it or not. And apparently, he had used it.

"Honey, I haven't seen that journal since you took it home. I thought you threw it away or gave it to someone else or something."

"I wrote in it!" Max was practically hyperventilating. "Like, all the time."

"Okay." Jess reached a hand out to soothe him, but he batted it away. "Hey, we'll find it. We'll figure it out."

"It's *gone.* I bet Gabe . . ." Max flung himself out the door and flew down the stairs. Jess followed hot on his heels.

"Give it back!" Max shouted. "You're such a baby. Give me back my book!"

Gabe was half-folded over the back of the couch, one leg on either side like an overgrown cat. He looked up slowly, eyes dazed from *Madagascar 2* and the bleary winter light that seeped through the windows. He squinted at Max. "What?" he said, and then slipped off the couch and crumpled to the floor.

Jess dashed to put herself between her sons. Gabe was giggling uncontrollably, pleased with himself and the silly act of falling off the couch. Max was irate, fists clenched as he glared at his brother in accusation.

"Cool it," Jess said, looking up at Max from where she crouched on the floor. She lifted Gabe by his arms but he was all floppy, his limbs like Jell-O. She left him where he was but took his chin in her hand and forced him to look at her. "Gabe, did you take Max's book? I'm being very serious right now. I need the truth."

Gabe snorted a little and shook his head. "I can't read!"

"You're learning," Jess told him, using even this unlikely opportunity to encourage him. His teacher had said positive reinforcement was necessary if they ever wanted him to progress. She snuck a quick glance at Max and watched as he rolled his eyes. Turning back to Gabe, she pressed him. "I need you to think really hard. Did you go into Max's room and take his book?"

"I'm not allowed in Max's room."

"That hasn't stopped you before." Max lunged at his little brother and poked him hard in the side with his foot. "It's black and has a lot of writing in it. What did you do with it?"

Gabe scrambled up, holding his ribs where Max had jabbed him. His features clouded. He shouted: "I don't have your book!"

Jess sighed. "Max, enough with the accusations. I don't have your book. Gabe doesn't have your book. Did you take it somewhere? Leave it at school, maybe?"

"I would never take it to school." He ran both of his hands through his hair and cupped the back of his neck. Jess could see that his jaw was clenched so tightly his teeth had to be aching.

"Okay, let's figure this out," she said. "Where did you have it last?"

Max turned abruptly on his heel and took the stairs two at a time. Because she didn't know what else to do, Jess followed. Not about to be left behind, Gabe raced after her.

"It was right here," Max said when Jess stopped in the door of his room. He indicated his box spring, a flat expanse of pale blue fabric pulled taut over a wooden frame. He had thrown off the mattress. It was crooked on the floor, the sheets and blankets half ripped off. Clearly he had been upset to find his journal missing. "This is where I kept it."

"Have you checked under the bed?"

He shot her a livid glance.

"Okay. How about behind the night-stand?" Jess moved deeper into the room as Max shook his head. "Desk? Closet?" She reached for a pile of clothes on the floor and shifted it to the side. Nothing. "Your backpack?"

"I've looked everywhere," Max said. "It's gone."

All at once the fight seemed to leak out of him. It left him weary, the corners of his mouth so low Jess worried that he was going to cry. He sank to the box spring and seemed to wilt there, his shoulders slumping forward and head hanging so that his hair covered his face.

"Hey," Jess said softly. She sat beside him and chanced a touch. He tolerated the weight of her hand on his back and she felt a rush of affection. And concern. "It has to be around here somewhere."

He didn't move.

"It must be pretty important to you." Jess rubbed her hand in a slow circle.

"It's full," he admitted, his voice barely a

whisper. "I've written on almost every page."

Jess was shocked that Max had kept a journal, but she kept her surprise to herself. She was thrilled that he had found a way to express himself, to deal with all the things that had happened. And she was suddenly very angry that it was gone.

"When did you realize it was missing?" she asked, standing abruptly.

"Ten minutes ago."

"When's the last time you saw it?" Jess approached Max's desk and, when he didn't object, began opening drawers and scanning the contents. Mostly junk. Old papers, ballpoint pens missing their caps, a ball of sorts made of duct tape and pages ripped from a magazine. *Sports Illustrated,* she guessed.

"I don't know. A couple of weeks ago?"

"That long?"

"Yeah. I've been locking my door during the day, but I guess I should have started doing that sooner." His words were venomous, bitter.

Jess froze for a heartbeat and then turned to face him. "What's that supposed to mean?"

Max scowled at her. "I know what you did. After you went through my stuff I started locking my door."

"What in the world are you talking about?" Jess said, exasperated. "Say what you mean, Max. I've had more than enough of your games."

"I mean that you didn't do a very good job of sneaking around. I know that you were in my room. I knew it the second I stepped into it. You left stuff out of place — you might think my room is a disaster, but *I* know where everything goes." Even though Max was angry, he didn't shout. He was resigned, resentful. But he stayed on the box spring and pulled his legs crisscross beneath him.

Jess studied him for a minute, hands on her hips and heart in her throat. Then something clicked into place. She crossed the space between them and sank to her knees in front of her son. "When was I in your room, Max? Think about it. When did this happen?"

He shrugged. "I don't know. A couple weeks ago."

"Think."

After a few seconds Max said, "The day we all got sick. You were downstairs with Gabe and my room was all messed up. I knew it was you. Who else would it be?"

Jess's mind whirled back to that night. A

crooked picture, a tented curtain. The feeling that nothing was quite as it should be. That someone had been in their house. Max had felt it too.

"What was in your journal, Max?" She hardly dared to voice the question, but really, what could it be? He was thirteen years old. Surely nothing of consequence existed in his personal diary.

"I don't know," he said. "Stuff."

"About school?"

He tilted his head to give her a furtive glance. Just as quickly as his eyes met hers they skidded away to his hands, his lap. "Dad," Max said eventually. "I wrote a lot about Dad."

October 10, 2017

Carter says that anxiety needs a place to go. That if it doesn't come out, it will rattle around inside looking for an escape. When it comes out sideways its ugly, he said. Like what I said. Then he listed drugs + sex + delinquincy (his word). He made his hands all crazy and said it would come out like an alien baby and there'd be blood everywhere. He was trying to be cool, but i said I don't watch alien movies and I don't know what your talking about. But anyway i'm not sleeping. Last year I made a list of all the swear words I could think of and then I burned it in the backyard. Maybe I'll do that again.

What I'm mad about:

1. G is a baby and mom lets him do anything he wants
2. D+M fight when they think I'm asleep (even if i was, i'm not deaf)
3. school sucks + I kinda like Elsie F but she like Maddox P
4. sometimes i wish i had a birth mom and dad like G — I'd find them and maybe live with them if they were cool and had $$
5. D has a secret

— Max

CHAPTER 18

Catrin W.
30, African American, working on GED
Shoulder-length weave, rainbow-painted
  fingernails, athletic build.
No one knows.
ADW, 49m, 7m pp

It was after suppertime when the plow finally made it down the Chamberlains' road. By then the snow had stopped and the storm clouds had moved on, leaving behind wispy strands of cirrus that spanned the starry sky. As the moon rose, the long streaks of clouds slashed across its pale face, scarring the evening with a reminder of the violence that had come before.

And it had been violent. In the afternoon, the weight of the snow and ice had become too much for several of the tree limbs. They bowed and splintered, yearning toward the ground until they screamed and cracked and crashed down. The sugar maple in the

Chamberlains' front yard lost a branch that was almost the thickness of Jessica's waist, and when it snapped free, the sound ricocheted like a gunshot and ended in a boom that made Gabe scream.

The snow was sixteen inches deep according to the news, but when the street was finally clear, it was piled on the curbs at least three feet high. Meadow Drive looked like a tunnel, a sparkling, surreal tunnel, and beneath the snow the concrete was black with a thick lacquer of ice.

Mere minutes after the plows drove out of sight, the twin beams of headlights drew everyone to the window as a truck pulled up in front of the Chamberlains' house.

"Grandpa!" Gabe shouted, running for the door. "It's Grandpa!"

Henry Lancaster didn't own a truck, but his neighbor had allowed him to borrow his in order to dig Jessica out. "There's a plow blade on the front," he said in greeting when Jessica met him in the garage. "You can't exactly use a shovel for this."

Jess was already pulling on her North Face snow pants, her plush mittens, and heavy boots. Being a mother of boys necessitated such accoutrements. There were sledding hills to enjoy and snowmen to make, plus the occasional pond skating adventure or

366

wintry hike. All the same, Jess didn't wander out into the snow all that often, and as she pulled her balaclava over her head, she was met with the faint scent of exhaust. Snowmobiling. The last time she had worn snow gear was when Todd had taken pity on the Chamberlain boys and appeared in their backyard on his snowmobile. It was near the end of March and Evan had just moved out. A late-in-the-season dump of snow had blanketed the world in white, and they had all taken turns riding behind Todd on the snowmobile, accelerating across wide stretches of flat fields and thrilling at the lash of snow in their faces. It was one of the first times the boys had laughed after Evan left.

The memory stuck like a broken zipper, but Jess yanked herself past it and pulled down the fabric in front of her mouth to offer her dad a faint smile. "Thanks for coming. You're right: I don't think we could have dug out on our own."

Evan had always done the shoveling, and because he genuinely enjoyed it, he insisted that they didn't need a snowblower. But Jessica was grateful for the bulky machine that she helped her father lift down from the back of the truck. He gave her a quick lesson and then used the truck to clear the worst of the snow. Jess only feared for her landscaping a couple of times — as far as she knew, Henry had never used a plow blade attached to a pickup truck before.

The moon was high and casting diamonds on the snow when Henry and Jess stopped to survey their handiwork. Gabe had thrown on his snow gear, too, and was tearing up the fresh expanse of white on the front yard. With the truck and the snowblower silenced, Jess could hear his shrieks of delight as he threw up the soft, wet snow and thrust handfuls of it in his mouth. She could remember the taste of snow herself, the light, cold whisper of frost and nothingness on her tongue.

Henry was grinning. "What a storm!"

Jess didn't say anything.

"Hey, why so glum?" He elbowed her, their puffy arms whisking off each other in a lisp of water-resistant fabric.

"I guess I'm not as charmed as you are by the destruction."

There was definitely destruction. Branches littered the snow, sinking to hidden depths in places and reaching heavenward in others, knobby fingers stretched in supplication. Some trees seemed to melt, long limbs curling down like something from a fantastical Dr. Seuss story.

"It'll be a nightmare to clean up," Jess said. "In the spring, when everything melts. And I'm not sure my cherry blossom will survive."

It was true. The lovely little tree near the sidewalk looked like it was weeping. Or mourning, maybe, the burden it carried simply too great to bear.

"We'll plant a new one," Henry said with conviction. "A trio if you'd like. A fresh start sounds pretty perfect right now, wouldn't you say?"

Jess could feel him looking at her sideways, waiting for her to respond. She knew he wanted nothing more than for her to leave this pain behind and walk into a future that held all the possibility she believed she forfeited when Evan walked out the door. But she wasn't ready to move on just yet.

"Did Evan ever confide in you?" Jess asked carefully. She kept her attention trained on Gabe. He was climbing over the fallen limb, crawling between the narrow branches and clearly enjoying some adventurous fantasy.

"What do you mean?" Henry sounded just as cautious.

"After we were separated." Jess turned to her father quickly and reassured him. "Evan was a part of our lives for twenty years, Dad.

I wouldn't be upset if you stayed in touch while we were separated. In fact, I'd be disappointed if you didn't."

Henry searched his daughter's eyes for moment and then nodded almost imperceptibly. "Yeah," he admitted. "We had lunch a couple of times. He loved you, Jessica. He wanted to work it out."

"I know." Jess paused, then pressed on. "Can you tell me what you talked about?"

Henry sucked in a breath. "Wow, Jess, I don't know. I can't say that our conversations were all that memorable. Typical stuff. Day-to-day."

"He never talked to you about a project he was working on? Maybe a study of some sort?"

"I don't think so." Henry was silent for a few moments while he seemed to comb his memories. "Want to explain what this is about? Does it have something to do with your meeting with Deputy Mullen?"

Jess wasn't ready to talk about it. "Just a hunch." She shrugged, but it was difficult to do in her bulky winter coat. "I want to know everything about his final months. We weren't together, but I always thought that we'd find a way to work it out."

"Me too, honey."

Jess was surprised to see that her father's

eyes had misted over. Or maybe it was just the gleam of moonlight on the snow. "How about a cup of coffee?" she said.

"Too late for caffeine." Henry shook his head. "But if you have an herbal tea, I won't say no. My fingers are frozen."

At the mention of cold, Jess realized that her hands and feet were numb. And her nose. She had pulled her balaclava beneath her chin to talk with her dad, and now her lips were parched and dry, her chin so stiff she was slurring her words.

"Gabe!" Jess called. "Time to come in!"

"No!" he shouted back. "I'm not done yet!"

Since she hadn't allowed him to play outside during the storm, she left him with strict instructions to stay in the front yard and come as soon as he was called. "I'm making hot chocolate," she said. "And when I knock on the window, I want you to come running."

"Pinky swear!" Gabe agreed, but he was already turning away to continue building what appeared to be the wall of a fort around the fallen limb.

"Where's Max? Didn't he want to enjoy the snow?" Henry asked when they were ensconced in the warm kitchen, blowing their pink noses and warming their fingers beneath a stream of tepid water.

Jess flinched as feeling trickled back into her frozen hands. "He's in his room. Max is having a bit of a rough day."

"Oh?"

Jess wasn't sure what to say. She landed on: "He lost something. He's pretty upset about it."

"Anything I can do to help?"

"Not this time, Dad."

The teakettle whistled, and Jess lifted it from the burner and brought it to the table where her dad had taken a seat. He looked tired, older than he had only yesterday. His eyes were hooded, the lines in his still-handsome face pronounced in the slanting light. But it was late and they had worked hard. His weariness was easily excusable, even if Jess knew that it was more than just exertion. Before he drove over, Henry had dug himself out, and though they used the truck and the snowblower, the sidewalks and edges had to be done by hand with a shovel. Jess was tired too.

They sat in silence for a few minutes, pouring hot water and sinking the fragrant tea bags with their spoons. Jess had chosen a peppermint tea, and just the steam of it soothed her throat and warmed the prickling skin of her cheeks.

"I thought of something," her dad said, chancing a sip of his tea. It was too hot and he put it back down. "Something about Evan, I mean."

Jess felt herself go very still. Her father had spent so much of his life keeping other people's secrets that it was all but impossible to pry information from him. Even mundane things that most people would never consider sensitive or gossipy, Henry would refuse to divulge. Better safe than sorry was his motto. Or maybe, loose lips sink ships. Both.

"He asked me once about the legal side of adoption."

Jess exhaled. "We had a lot of questions when we adopted."

"No, this was recent. Late this summer, maybe?" Henry stared into his tea. "No, it was September, I think."

"Why was he asking about adoption this September?" Jess mused.

"He wanted to know if I had any experience with forced adoptions."

"What's a *forced* adoption?" Jess felt herself bristle a little. Adoption was such an integral, beautiful part of her life she didn't like associating negativity with it in any way. *Forced* certainly didn't sound positive.

"I didn't know myself and I told him as

much. I'm afraid I wasn't very helpful."

"Do you know why he was asking about it?"

Henry shook his head. "But I looked it up later. Apparently some agencies use unethical practices to separate birth mothers and fathers from their children."

"That's ridiculous." Jess took a long pull from her scalding tea and burned her tongue. She wouldn't be able to taste for a couple of days, but she didn't care. It drove her crazy when people didn't understand something that was so near and dear to her heart.

"I'm not offering personal commentary on it, Jess. I'm just telling you what I discovered."

"Well, it can't be true."

Henry gave her the same look that he used to give her when she was a kid and being stubbornly pigheaded. "Just because you don't want to believe it doesn't mean it's not true."

"Why would Evan want to know about that?" Jess said, ignoring her father's pointed stare. "It can't have anything to do with Gabe." The second his name passed her lips, Jess remembered that he was still digging in the snow.

Apparently Henry thought the same thing

because they pushed away from the table in unison, their conversation forgotten. Jess hurried over to the front door and threw it open, letting in an icy drift of snow that spread over the hardwood and immediately began to melt. It took a moment for her eyes to adjust to the darkness outside. "Gabe?" she called. "Gabe! It's time to come in!"

There was a flurry of activity by the fallen limb and Gabe poked his head out from behind a wall of white. His stocking cap was furred with ice and she could see even at a distance that his cheeks were crimson.

"Just a few more minutes!" he whined.

"Absolutely not." Jess crossed her arms over her chest and stomped her feet against the chill. "I'm watching you until you're in the garage."

"I'll meet him there and help him with his gear," Henry said at her shoulder.

"Grandpa's waiting for you," Jess said, relaying the message, and watched as Gabe hung his head dramatically and clomped off in the direction of the garage door. It was a task because the snow came up to his thighs, and in no time he was giggling as he wrestled his way toward the driveway and the door that his grandfather had flung open to welcome him.

Jess waited until Gabe was in his grandpa's arms, and then she bent down to try and push the snow that had fallen inside back out the door. They had shoveled off the steps, but apparently they hadn't gotten close enough to the door. By the time Jess was done, there was a puddle of icy water on the floor and her hands were once again numb from cold.

Henry and Gabe were making a ruckus in the garage, banging out Gabe's boots and hooting about something apparently hilarious, so Jess took the opportunity to check on Max. The door to his room was closed, but when she knocked, no one answered.

"Max?" Jess tried the handle. It wasn't locked, so she called again and eased it open. The lights were on, but Max was nowhere to be seen.

The bathroom was across the hall, but the door was ajar and the room was dark. "Max?" Jess raised her voice a little, peeking her head in each of the rooms in the upstairs hallway. Gabe's room, the spare room, even her own bedroom and bathroom were dark and empty. Standing at the top of the stairs, Jess shouted: "Max? Where are you?"

Henry and Gabe were on their knees in front of the dark fireplace. Henry looked over his shoulder as Jess came down the stairs. "I thought Max was in his bedroom," he said, then turned his attention back to the task at hand. He set a preformed fire log onto the metal grate and picked up a box of matches. "We're going to cheat, Jess. All you have to do is light the corner and then throw a couple logs on top . . ."

But Jessica wasn't paying attention. A quick check of the office proved that it was also empty. As were the kitchen, screened-in porch, and the main floor bathroom. Their basement was unfinished, a huge expanse of concrete and two-by-fours that they had framed but never drywalled. The Chamberlains had always planned to complete the basement, but they had never gotten around to it. Jess yanked open the door and heard her voice echo in the emptiness. Max wasn't there, either.

"He's gone," Jess said more to herself than to her father and son.

"Who's gone?" Gabe asked, scrambling up and running over to comfort her.

"Max."

"He can't be gone," Henry said. "Where would he go?"

Jess gave Gabe a squeeze and then eased herself out of his embrace. "I don't know.

But we better find him. It's freezing out there."

Her heart began to thrum a frantic rhythm, a clip that made her fingers tingle with something other than cold. She was worried, but Jess was also angry. It was just like Max to pull something like this, to disappear without saying a word, on the night of the worst storm to sweep through Northwest Iowa in twenty years. When she got her hands on him, she didn't know whether she would hug him or ground him. Both, she decided. But first she had to find him.

"I'll hop in the truck," Henry said, patting his pockets for the keys he had stashed there. "Gabriel, why don't you ride along with me?"

"Wait," Jess called as she searched the kitchen for her phone. Where had she left it? Maybe Max had been considerate — maybe he sent her a text or left a message on her voice mail. Jess finally discovered her phone on the counter beside the refrigerator, but there was nothing from Max. And when Jess dialed his number, he didn't answer. She muttered a curse under her breath.

"We'll find him," Henry said. "He couldn't have gotten far. You said he was upset about something. Maybe he just went for a walk."

"He could have told us!"

"He's thirteen," Henry reminded her. "His brain isn't functioning at full capacity."

Jess didn't remember her father being so understanding when she was a teenager. She had been strong willed and foolish, too, but she hadn't given her parents nearly as much trouble as Max gave her. She wondered sometimes if it was all her fault. If she was as terrible a mother as she sometimes believed herself to be. God help her, being a mom wasn't for the faint of heart.

"Keep your cell phone on you," Henry said, zipping up his damp coat. There were snowflakes still glistening on the shoulders, and as Jess watched, he shivered. Whether it was from the cold or concern for his grandson, Jess couldn't tell. "I'll call if I find him. What will you do?"

"Search the neighborhood. Stay close to home. Maybe he just wanted to enjoy the snow."

Jess laced up her boots as her dad and Gabe hopped in the truck and took off slowly down the road. She could tell that Henry had his headlights on high beam, and Gabe's face was pressed to the window, hunting for a sign of his big brother in the winter wonderland that had descended on their neighborhood.

Her father was right — Max couldn't have gotten far. And yet, she was so desperate to have him safe and sound, to know where he was, that she found herself choking on angry sobs. Max must have snuck out when they were all busy clearing the driveway. The snowblower threw a wall of powdery snow ten feet into the air and created a ghostly cloud that had obstructed Jess's view. Never mind the sound. The scrape of the plow and Gabe's happy screams only added to the chaos. Jess could imagine Max slipping on his boots and fading into the night. But why? And where?

Before she took off, Jess made sure that Max's coat and boots were indeed gone. They were. But as far as she could tell, nothing else was missing. So he was on foot, or, she hoped he was.

The Chamberlains' garage had a back door that was half-hidden behind a long work bench that ran the length of the garage, and Jess had paid it no mind when she passed in and out on her way to clear snow. The door opened onto a small, square patio that tucked against the side of the screened-in porch, and during the summer the grill lived here. It was the easiest way to access the backyard, and as Jess approached the entrance, she could see that the door was wedged open a couple of inches. A small avalanche of snow that had tumbled onto the concrete made it impossible for the door to shut completely. It was obvious that someone had used the door, and recently.

Jess's heart was in her throat when she flicked on the floodlight that splashed across the backyard in a sudden harsh glare. It illuminated exactly what she expected to see: a furrow in the snow. A path that led over the patio, past the swing set, and off into the darkness. Away.

Evan Chamberlain
RE: Question for you
To: Henry Lancaster

Hi, Henry.
Thanks for meeting me for lunch last week. It was good to see you.

Wondering if you could answer a couple of questions for me. What do you know about the issue of so-called forced adoptions? I have a couple of legal inquiries that I'd like to run past you if you're open to it.

Thanks,
Evan

Henry Lancaster
RE: Question for you
To: Evan Chamberlain
CC: Robert Wales

Evan,
I'm afraid your question is beyond my purview. I'm not even familiar with the term you mentioned. However, I'm cc-ing a good friend and colleague, Robert Wales, in this conversation. Robert has some experience with adoption law and may be able to answer your questions.

All best,
Henry

Evan Chamberlain
RE: Question for you
To: Robert Wales

Hello, Robert.
I hope it's not presumptuous of me to email you out of the blue. I'm Henry's son-in-law and have just a few questions about the issue of forced adoptions.

Specifically, what are the legal rights of a birth mother who may have been coerced into giving her child up for adoption? I'm sure you can understand the nature of my question is personal, and if you need more clarification I'm not sure I can offer it at this time. Either way, thank you for your time and consideration.

Best,
Evan

Robert Wales
RE: Question for you
To: Evan Chamberlain

Hello, Evan.
The short answer to your question is this: a birth mother who has signed away her child has no legal rights to that child. Of course, the moral and ethical implications of what you are insinuating is much more complicated than an email exchange can accurately account for. I would be happy to meet you for coffee to continue this discussion if you wish.

Regards,
Robert

CHAPTER 19

Kateri O.
19, Native American, HS diploma
Nearly bald, tattooed scalp. Looks much
  younger than she is. Lonely.
Mother knows. Father says he'll kill her.
CPDD/CW, 52m, 4m 1w

Jess trudged through the snow, following Max's footprints to the edge of the Chamberlains' yard. Their property backed onto a small copse of trees and a gulley that trickled with water in the spring but was otherwise dry and treacherous. In the fall, leaves gathered in the trough and disguised the indentation in the earth, and Jess had wrapped her boys' ankles on numerous occasions after they raced brazenly through the grove and twisted them. Beyond the trees, cornfields stretched as far as the eye could see. Though their neighborhood was the picture of suburbia, the Chamberlains lived on the very outskirts of town, and Jess dragged herself through the deep snow with a growing sense of urgency. There was nothing out there but wind and snow and a sweep of endless sky. Did Max have a death wish?

Her son's footprints were two slim trenches, and Jess dragged her own boots through the uncertain path he had carved. Even though Max had paved the way, it was still tough going, a workout that made Jess hot beneath her heavy coat in spite of the freezing temperature. In minutes she was the unique combination of sweaty and cold, and panic-stricken on top of it all.

If her phone was ringing in her pocket, Jess would never hear it, but she was glad she had taken it with her all the same. She would stop at some point, maybe near the leaning fence that marked the edge of a farmer's field, and remove her gloves so she could check in with her dad. A part of her wondered if she should let him know that she found Max's trail, but they both knew that he was on foot. Jess had no doubt that her dad was circling the neighborhood, making his orbit wider and wider as he searched for his missing grandson. And that circuit would lead him to the gravel road and out of town. Max would hit the road eventually. He had to.

The world was brittle and bright at times, but when a strand of wispy clouds crossed the moon, the night fell into long shadows. Jess hesitated for just a moment at the line of trees, but Max had plunged inside and so did she. Weaving through gnarled branches and fallen logs, Jess stumbled down the short ravine and nearly got stuck at the bottom. The snow was almost up to her waist here, and she had to use an ice-slick sapling to pull herself up and out. She was heaving by the time she cleared the grove, but Jess stumbled forward at an unexpectedly swift pace until she abruptly realized that Max's trail had ended.

Jess stopped, gasping, and whipped around to see if she had missed something in her pursuit. But there was no way. The snow was fresh and unmarked, Max's carved escape route the only blemish in the otherwise unworldly white. Jess moaned, surprising herself with the sound. It was thin, agonized, and for some reason it made her think of Evan. He had been alone on a night like this, and it was enough to make her weep.

But Jess couldn't think about Evan. Her Max was everything right now, and thirteen-year-old boys didn't disappear into thin air.

"Max?" Jess tried to shout, her voice reedy

and weak beneath a universe of cold. "Max, are you here?" Her words were swallowed by the night.

Jess choked on a sob and thrust her hand into her mouth so she could clamp down on her mitten. She bit her fingers so hard that she yelped, but the pain also brought her to her senses. Max's footprints were gone, but as she stood there on the verge of hysteria, she realized that though there were no longer runnels where his boots had hewn through the snow, the landscape was not the same.

Yanking off her mitten with her teeth and letting it fall to the ground, Jess fumbled in her pocket for her cell phone. Her fingers were stiff, but she managed to locate the little icon that turned on her flashlight. In seconds, she had a narrow beam of bright light trained on the field before her.

At the place where Max's footprints vanished, there was a smooth line in the snow. Beyond that, there was a thick band that had stamped a uniform pattern and then another smooth, straight line. The entire flat track sat above the snow in a way that Max's erratic progress simply couldn't. It was as if whatever had made the mark was suspended.

A snowmobile. Max had been picked up

by a snowmobile.

The flashlight beam on her telephone didn't reach very far, but Jess could see that the snowmobile tracks ran east to west. Or west to east. Back into town or leading away from it, she didn't know. But there was only one person Jessica knew who owned a snowmobile.

Jess texted her father two words: *home now*

No caps, no punctuation, but it was the best she could do, given the circumstances. She would have called from the edge of the field, but she was trembling from head to toe and was afraid that she'd drop her phone in the snow and lose it beneath the frigid carpet. So she let her dad and Gabe know where she was headed and started back the way she had come, hoping and praying that her hunch was right.

"Did you find him?" Henry asked, hurrying into the garage at almost the same moment that Jess stumbled through the back door. Gabe was in his arms, his cheek folded against his grandpa's broad shoulder.

She shook her head, dislodging errant flakes that had shaken loose from tree branches and alighted in her hair. They landed on her nose, her eyelashes, and didn't melt. "No," Jess said. "But I think I know where he is."

They didn't bother taking off their gear but huddled in the mudroom while Jess dialed the number. The tension was palpable between them, hope and fear pressed side by side as Jess put the phone on speaker and held it so that everyone could hear. It rang twice before Meredith picked up.

"Hey, Jessica!" she said. "What do you think of this snow?"

It was as if they had never fought, but Jess could hardly remember that they had argued anyway. Everything paled in comparison to this. "Is Max with you?"

"No . . ."

Gabe whimpered and Jess tightened her grip on the phone. "He's gone, Mer. We can't find him and —"

"Wait a second," Meredith interrupted. "Jess, hang on. I think you may have misunderstood me. Max isn't with me *right now,* but I know where he is. He's with Todd."

"Thank God," Henry breathed.

Jess couldn't speak at all.

"Do you mean to tell me that you didn't know?" Meredith's voice cracked.

"No." Henry reached out and gently took the phone from Jessica. She had started shaking but put her arms out for Gabe so that she and her father could switch tasks. Gabe went willingly to his mother, wrapping his legs around Jess's waist and nuzzling his nose in her neck. She held him so tight she feared he'd pop.

"He left without a word," Henry said. He had switched the speaker phone off and stepped out of his boots so that he could finish the conversation in the warmth of the living room. As Jess followed mindlessly in his wake, she heard him continue: "No, no note. Nothing. Jessica is pretty shaken up."

Jess sank to the couch with Gabe still curled around her. He was uncharacteristically quiet, the tension of the last half hour pulling him taut as a cable. Sometimes he exploded in shouts and screams and bursts of frantic, nervous energy. And sometimes he tunneled in, becoming almost catatonic as his little mind shut out all stimulus. This reaction made Jess uneasy, but it was easier to cope with than the whirling dervish that Gabe sometimes transformed into.

"They're bringing Max home," Henry said, dropping onto the couch beside Jess. He set her phone on the coffee table in front of them and then laid his head back against the cushion. Rubbing his eyes with the heels of his hands, he sighed.

"Thank you," Jess managed. She wanted to say, *For helping with the driveway and for helping me look for Max,* but words felt like altogether too much work.

"You have nothing to thank me for." Henry gave her knee a warm squeeze.

He was smiling, but Jess could tell her father was exhausted. "We're fine, Dad. You should head home. I'm sure Roy would like to have his truck back."

"Are you sure?"

"Positive."

He gave her a skeptical look but leaned in to give Gabe a kiss on the cheek. Pushing himself up from the couch, he said, "Meredith is bringing Max over as soon as he and Todd get back from snowmobiling. It shouldn't be long."

"Was it Todd's idea or Max's?" Jess asked.

"Max's," her dad admitted after a heartbeat. "Apparently he texted Todd, asking for a ride. Todd and Meredith assumed you knew and approved."

Jess nodded once.

"It'll get better," he told her. "Don't be too hard on him. He's not thinking clearly."

"I know."

After a moment Henry added: "He's not trying to hurt you."

But that was hard for Jessica to believe.

When her father was gone, Jess stood up carefully and carried Gabe upstairs. He was deadweight in her arms, exhausted and emotionally drained, and she didn't even try to put him in his own bed. Instead, she carried him into her room and deposited him on Evan's side of what was now her ridiculously oversized king bed. Gabe would end up there anyway.

"Are you mad at Max?" Gabe asked as she pulled off his jeans and switched them out for the plaid pajama pants that he had left crumpled on her floor. Normally he'd fuss and insist on the football pants, but he was tired and his skin was still clammy to the touch. He didn't complain.

"Yes," Jess said. Lying wouldn't do her any good. Gabe struggled in some areas, but spotting a falsehood was not one of them. He seemed to know her inside and out.

"Why?"

"Why do you think?"

"Because he ran away."

Jess sighed. "Max didn't run away. But he left without telling me where he was going."

"He always does that." Gabe put up his arms to let Jess pull his sweatshirt over his head. She patted the pillow and, when he settled in, pulled the comforter up to his chin.

"Tonight was different," Jess said. "It's dark and cold. We just had a big storm. Do you think it was smart of Max to disappear like that?"

Gabe shook his head gravely, dark eyes fixed on her. "It wasn't very nice, either."

"No, it was really rather awful."

"I'm sorry," Gabe said. He sat up and wrapped his arms around her neck, squeezing her close.

"Thanks, buddy."

Jess stayed with him for a few minutes, rubbing soft circles on his bare back until he went completely still. Gabe wasn't asleep, not quite, but close enough. She kissed his temple, inhaling his sweet little boy scent, and snuck out of the room on tiptoe. On the landing, Jess realized that she had forgotten to make him brush his teeth or even go to the bathroom. But she couldn't force herself to care.

The house seemed unnaturally still after the drama of earlier. There were blankets strewn all over the floor and half hanging off the couch. Max and Gabe had left plates on the end tables, mugs with an inch or two of sludgy hot cocoa on the mantel. Evidence of their snow day littered the entire living room, but at least one thing was as it should be: the fire log that Henry had started in the fireplace was crackling merrily. The cheerful orange flames didn't match her mood, but Jess was grateful for the warmth. She opened the glass doors and cautiously added two split logs. Almost immediately the frayed edges of wood began to glow.

Jess had the house set in order by the time a car pulled into her driveway. She could hear the slam of doors, and after a few seconds the creak of the garage door opening. Neither Max nor Meredith said a word as they slipped off their shoes and came into the living room.

Jess was leaning against the dining room table, watching them as they entered her space. Max had his hands stuffed in the deep pockets of his gray joggers, and he refused to look at her. But he walked right past her on his way to the stairs, and paused long enough to give her a tepid, one-armed hug.

"Sorry," he muttered.

"We'll talk later," she said. "Go get ready for bed."

He didn't argue, even though it was just nine o'clock and bedtime was one of his favorite quarrels.

When Max was out of earshot, Jess turned her attention to Meredith. Her friend stood there, hair pulled back in a messy ponytail and eyes tired behind her glasses. They were slipping down her nose, but Meredith didn't try to right them or wipe the look of abject regret off her face.

"I am so sorry," Meredith finally said. "I can't even begin to tell you how sorry I am."

"It's not your fault." But Jess didn't make a move to welcome Meredith in or ease her discomfort in any way.

"I should have asked," Meredith said. "I should have checked with you."

"Things aren't always as cut-and-dry as they seem, are they?" Jess stared until Meredith gave a heavy sigh.

"You're right." Meredith took a few steps toward her. "Life is messy."

Jess's arms were crossed over her chest, but when Meredith reached out, she let her friend hug her.

"I'm sorry," Meredith said again. "About tonight and about not defending you the way I should have. You're an excellent mom. The best. I know that, and I should have shut down anyone who tried to say otherwise."

"Yes, you should have." Jess pulled away and headed toward the kitchen. She was still angry and needed some time to cool down, but she was grateful that Meredith was willing to apologize. It was a start. "Would you like a drink?" Her kids were both home safe and sound, and although she had to work in the morning she knew a glass of wine would help her find sleep. Hopefully.

"I can't," Meredith said, but she followed Jess into the kitchen anyway. "I have to get home. But you should definitely have one. No, have two."

There was a bottle of red uncorked on the counter. Jess snagged a wineglass from the cupboard and poured herself a tiny amount. A few sips couldn't hurt. Leaning against the sink she took a sip and hung her head, rotating it slowly from side to side in an effort to work out the kinks.

"I'm getting you a massage for Christmas," Meredith said.

"I'd prefer a beach vacation."

"Maui." Meredith closed her eyes, a smile playing on her lips.

"Santorini."

"How about Bora-Bora?" Meredith laughed a little. "Can I come?"

"I'm not going alone." Jess took a swig. "But I highly doubt a tropical beach is in my future."

"Hey, someday." Meredith looked concerned. "This is a stage, okay? A season. I've got your back. You'll get through this."

Jess wasn't so sure. But if there was anything that she had learned in the last couple of days, it was that she couldn't continue letting life happen to her. Jess knew what she had to do, but she wasn't sure if she wanted Meredith to be a part of it or not.

"Do you have plans for Thanksgiving?" Meredith asked when the silence became strained.

Jess was glad that she was looking at the floor instead of at Meredith. Surely the surprise on her face said it all. She had forgotten about Thanksgiving entirely. But it was this week, of course. In just a couple of days.

"My dad and Anna are serving a meal at the nursing home," Jess said, composing herself. "They've done that for a few years now. Evan and I always had a little celebration with just the four of us." And Bradford. Evan picked up his father and doted on him in the most tender way. Jess remembered wishing that he would shower her with that sort of affection. But none of that mattered now.

"Come to our house!" Meredith touched Jess's shoulder to make her look up. "We'd love to have you. Seriously. It's just going to be us and Todd's sister's family. They have two kids in college."

Jess was already shaking her head. "No thanks."

"I insist." Meredith was already heading toward the door, clearly determined not to take no for an answer. Jess knew that it was her way of apologizing, of doing penance for the pain she had caused.

"Fine." Jess wouldn't win and there was no point in trying. "What do you want me to bring?"

"Absolutely nothing. A healthy appetite and your gorgeous kids." If she was laying it on a bit thick, Meredith didn't seem to notice. She was obviously utterly taken with the thought of making up for her shortcomings with something as tangible as a feast.

"Okay," Jess said, lifting her wine to her lips yet again. It was gone and she set her empty glass on the dining room table a little self-consciously. "Thanks for bringing Max home."

Meredith tiptoed over the carpet in her shoes and pulled Jess into a quick hug. "Thank you for forgiving me."

Jess smiled, but she hadn't done any such thing. Not yet. And whether or not she found it in her heart to forgive Meredith at all depended on how her friend responded to Jess's plan.

"I'm going to need your help," Jess said. The demand was out of the blue, a gauntlet thrown in the midst of what had somehow become a cheerful reunion. Jess knew she was messing that up, but she didn't care. "I know you think I'm crazy, but there's more to Evan's death than meets the eyes." She studied Meredith, waiting for a reaction that didn't come.

"Okay." Meredith's expression looked deliberately blank.

Jess wasn't sure what to make of it, but she pressed on. "He was keeping a file. I'm going to find it."

Meredith nodded; there was a hitch in the movement. A hint of skepticism. All the same, she said, "Of course. Whatever it takes."

StolenAtBirth.com
Home Page

The truth about adoption is far more complicated than people imagine. While the Baby Scoop Era of the '50s, '60s, and '70s is considered to be behind us, the fact remains that adoption is a flawed system and a for-profit industry. As such, it becomes evident that, like any commodity, demand informs production. This creates a dynamic in which the transfer of parental rights can be assigned a price tag. To assume that all adoption is the result of a benevolent desire to protect children from foster care, institutionalization, or abuse is naive at best and deliberately ignorant at worst. It is important that we shed light on unethical and inhumane practices so that we can make positive changes for the benefit of all parties involved in adoption.

Coercion is the simplest, most extensive tool used in forced adoptions. Shady practices and misleading information can result in the separation of children from their birth parents — even when giving up the child for adoption is not the birth parents' first choice. Some birth parents do not have the financial means to battle adoption agencies in the courts of law. Others do not have the resources to overcome the insurmountable pressure to give up or revoke their parental rights. They are taken advantage of, fed false information, and pitted against one another as the industry seeks to line their pockets and feed the adoption machine.

Cultural views of adoption further under-gird the narrative that "unwanted" children are rescued from the gutter and placed in loving homes. And while many adoptive families may have no idea about the dark underside of adoption, they willingly accept that adoption is always in the best interest of a child.

We must advocate for birth parents, provide the necessary counseling, support, and information so that they are empowered to make well-informed choices. We seek truth in difficult circumstances and fight for children to remain within their families of origin whenever possible. We believe in reunification and the sovereignty of birth parents as they make decisions that will impact their children and themselves for generations to come. We seek truth and justice and whole, healthy families.

CHAPTER 20

Angel P.
27, African American, HS diploma
Chin-length natural hair (twists), morbidly
*   obese. Kind, maternal, beloved.*
Friend knows.
CWIK, 49m, 2y pp

School the next day was a free-for-all. The buses ran late because of the snow and ice, and kids filtered into school high on excitement and the promise of a short week.

"Only a day and a half!" Dayton Cummings, one of Jess's favorite seniors, said when he threw his backpack down on his desk before first period. "That's just over ten hours of school. I don't even know why we bothered this week."

Jess gave him a rueful smile, but she felt the same way. She would have happily abandoned her lesson plans and strict schedule for the freedom of more time to research.

After Meredith had left the night before, Jess had gone upstairs to do more internet stalking. Max had been in his room when she checked on him, and for once he didn't pull away when she cupped his face and kissed his forehead. He wasn't quite contrite, but he clearly felt bad for causing such a fuss. "You scared me," she said. "Please don't ever do anything like that again." He nodded, and she caught a whiff of his freshly washed hair. Cedar and sage and essence of Max. His nod wasn't an apology, but it was a good place to start. It was easy for Jess to forgive him, if only because she was so grateful for the way he let her hold him close for just a moment.

Gabe was already curled up in her bed, exhausted from playing in the snow and staying up past his bedtime. Jess kissed him, too, then pulled the blankets up to his chin and sat beside him with her laptop on her thighs as she clicked every possible tab on the James Rosenburg Law website. She knew that family law was mostly divorce related, but she couldn't believe that Evan had been looking into legal action without at least talking to her. He was distracted, not heartless. Besides, the website proclaimed that Rosenburg Law specialized in matters of domestic violence, juvenile

403

delinquency, and child abuse.

Jess had shut her computer with a quiet *click*. Child abuse. What was she supposed to do with that?

Leave it alone. The three words on the back of the business card were unmistakably Evan's handwriting. Had he left a message for her? Jess just didn't know. But no matter Evan's intent, the note didn't deter her. Jess's life had always been dedicated to her boys, but they needed her now in a way that she never could have anticipated. She would fight for them.

Jess slid the laptop onto her bedside stand and curled herself around Gabe, kissing the warm nape of his neck. He didn't stir, so she held him tight, whispering prayers of protection over the sweet son in her arms and the one down the hall, too.

Now, surrounded by energetic teenagers and struggling to follow an obsolete lesson plan, Jess realized what her next step had to be. She had to take the keys Deputy Mullen had given her and go through Evan's town house. It was the last thing she wanted to do, but she knew that the file she sought was most likely hidden there. Or sitting right out in the open. What reason did he have to hide anything in his own home? Surely Evan's computer was there, too, and though it would be password protected like his phone, Jess felt certain she could crack the code. She just hadn't been able to muster up the courage until now. Evan's town house was a graveyard, a monument to their failed relationship, the horrifying truth that she would never have a chance to make everything right again. Jess just couldn't bring herself to face it until now. *Tomorrow,* she told herself.

Today, Jess had another path to take. And it led her straight to Luke Tucker.

All through the first few periods of the morning, Jess taught with a measure of her focus on Luke. She rehearsed what she would say and how she would say it. His imagined responses were varied and entirely unpredictable. Jess had no idea how Luke saw her. A pathetic middle-aged woman who had just lost her husband? A nonissue? A coworker he respected? Jess doubted very much that the final possibility was true. But by the time she found him in the teachers' lounge during lunch, it didn't really matter. She was ready.

The offices at Auburn High had been redesigned in the last couple of years, and the teachers' lounge was a haven. Jess didn't usually frequent the bright, relaxing space, but when she had a reason to darken the door, she was struck by how incongruent the room was with her preconceived ideas of what a public school faculty lounge should look like. There was a plethora of windows and soothing colors on the wall. The tables were all rustic wood in a high, glossy varnish, and the chairs were curved and comfortable. An industrial-sized stainless steel refrigerator hummed in one corner, and several overstuffed armchairs were curled around low, round tables.

Luke Tucker was ensconced in one of the overstuffed chairs, cupping a mug of what Jess assumed was soup. He dipped his spoon in and blew across the steamy surface as he chatted with Vincent Porter, one of the history teachers.

"Mind if I join you?" Jess asked, walking over. Her own boldness was a shock, as electric and thrilling as a dare, and she wavered just a little as she claimed the chair opposite them.

"Of course not!" Luke was the first to speak and he welcomed her warmly, even though his gaze registered something close to shock that the staff loner had deigned to join them. But he smiled just the same.

"Good to see you," Vincent said, moving a stack of books that he had apparently dumped in the middle of the table. "It's been a while, Jessica."

What could she say? They all knew why she had been gone, and they could guess why she now avoided her coworkers like the plague. But here she was, sitting across from a pair of them and attempting a self-deprecating smile. "The kids are crazy today," she said by way of explanation. "I had to escape."

This made perfect sense, and the two men sat back laughing. "Tell me about it." Luke shook his head. "Today is a complete write-off. And why they're making us come back tomorrow is beyond me. We won't accomplish a single thing."

"You sound like every student who entered my classroom today." Vincent took a bite of his wrap and a dollop of what looked like ranch dressing oozed out the end and plopped on the paper plate he was holding. Jess was reminded of why she often spent her lunch breaks alone.

They talked about workload and the upcoming Thanksgiving break with a bit of school gossip thrown in. It seemed the teachers were just as checked out as the students were — no one much wanted to be at Auburn High for the few required hours this week. Jess mostly listened and bided her time.

When Luke stood up and stretched, Jess casually picked up her own wrappers and mug. "I'm giving a pop quiz," Luke said with a bit of a glint in his eye. "I'd better go polish my armor."

"You're going to need it!" Vincent laughed. As an afterthought he added, "It was nice to see you, Jessica. I hope you have a happy Thanksgiving."

"Thanks," Jess said, though she had barely said two words since she sat down. She wasn't much up for conversation. "Happy Thanksgiving to you, too." Then she took off in the direction that Luke had gone, reaching the sink only seconds after he left it and quickly rinsing her mug. She tossed the wrapper of her granola bar in the garbage can and hurried after her trendy coworker. If another teacher tried to catch her eye, Jess plowed on determinedly, and no one attempted to stop her.

"Luke!" Jess called. "Wait up." He was already halfway down the hallway, his long legs making short work of the distance to his room. His classroom in the math and science hall was on the opposite side of the building from Jess's, so there was really no way for her to casually bump into him alone. She had no choice but to follow him. To make a point of the conversation that she both wanted to have and dreaded. Jess had never been good at confrontation, and by the time she caught up with Luke, she was as winded as if she had run a race. Her heart beat high and fast in her throat and she could feel her cheeks flaming.

"You okay, Jessica?" His gaze washed over her and he reached out a hand, concerned.

But Jess took a step back. "I'm fine. I need to talk to you."

"Okay," Luke said. "How about my room?"

The hallway was mostly empty, the majority of the kids no doubt clustered in the lunchroom or watching the intramural volleyball game championship that was supposed to happen yesterday. It wasn't a big deal, but there was much hoopla surrounding the event anyway, and Jess was grateful that there were only two kids sitting at the very end of the long hallway. They were cross-legged on the floor, textbooks spread across their laps. They didn't pay an ounce of attention to Jess and Luke.

"It won't take long," Jess said, straightening her shoulders.

"Sure." Luke glanced at the students, then shifted a little so that his back was to them. He crossed his arms over his chest in a motion that seemed wary, and that only added fuel to Jess's fire.

"I can't believe you did that," she said without preamble. The depth of her own anger surprised her. Her voice trembled just a bit, but Jess found that she *was* able to do this, to confront someone. And it felt good. "The next time you have a problem with me, you can talk to me about it. Okay?"

Luke's eyebrows knit together and his arms seemed to drop from their protective posture of their own accord. One side of his mouth curved up a bit as he said, "Excuse me? I have no idea what you're talking about."

"I know it was you." Jess barely stopped herself from rolling her eyes. "How dare you judge me. You're not a parent. You don't know." The moment the words were out of her mouth, Jessica realized that she didn't really know anything about Luke Tucker at all. Maybe he was a parent. Suddenly she could picture him with a petite wife, the sort of woman who would wear boho dresses and leggings with sparkly TOMS. Their baby would use only cloth diapers and have long hair that required everyone who met him to wonder if he was a boy or a girl.

"I'm not sure how my parental status is relevant," Luke said. No mention of a wife or child. "But I still have no idea what you're talking about. And I'm not a fan of being accused of something I can't even defend myself from."

He turned on his heel and walked the short distance to his classroom without a backward glance.

Jess felt a surge of fury. How dare he walk away from her. She rushed after him, but his classroom appeared to be empty. She spun to find Luke standing behind her with his hand on the door. He shut it softly.

"I thought we might like to continue this conversation in private," he said. "The last thing we need is to be grist for the school gossip mill." Luke leaned against the door and stuck his hands in the front pockets of his black jeans. He arched one eyebrow at her, but his expression was warm, inviting. "Can you please explain to me what you're so upset about?"

Luke left her off-balance somehow. He was too nice, too understanding in the face of her obvious anger. His kindness took the wind out of her sails almost immediately. Jess sagged a bit, pulling the sleeves of her sweater down over her palms in an act of comfort, of self-defense.

"You called Meredith," she said with less vim than only a few moments ago.

"Meredith who?"

"Bailey," Jess said. All at once she saw herself through his eyes. She did indeed look crazy. "Meredith Bailey is Jayden's mom. She volunteers here sometimes. I thought you knew her. I thought . . ."

"Hey." Luke flashed her a grin. "Sounds like a misunderstanding. No worries. What did you think I told Jayden's mom?"

"Forget it." Jess put her face in her hands and took a deep breath. "I'm so sorry. I just made a complete fool of myself, and I think I'm going to slink off into oblivion now."

She tried to move past him, but Luke stopped her with a hand on her arm. He touched her lightly, momentarily, and then just as quickly as she registered the weight of his fingers they were gone. "Are you okay?" Luke asked.

"I'm fine," Jess said quickly. Too quickly, but Luke didn't press her.

"For what it's worth, I'm really sorry about everything," he said. "I can't imagine how hard all of this has been for you."

Luke was wearing a tie and Jess found herself staring at the uneven knot because she couldn't bring herself to look at his face. The tie was crooked a bit, and not quite tight enough. She wanted to reach out and straighten it, pull the dark blue fabric taut and fix the sagging triangle. But that was, of course, utterly ridiculous. She surprised herself by speaking to his chest: "I thought you reported me for leaving my kids at the basketball game. And for picking up Gabe after I'd had a drink."

His laugh was rich and unexpected. "Are you kidding me?" he said. "I used to be a lifeguard, and parents would drop their kids off at the pool for hours at a time. I think Gabe was just fine with his big brother for a few minutes."

"I thought so too." Jess looked up and found him staring at her, a smile playing at his lips. "But I had been drinking."

"Last I checked, you were a grown-up," Luke said. "You're allowed to have an alcoholic beverage."

Jess wouldn't have been surprised if he winked at her. But she didn't care. She felt validated, normal for the first time in a long time.

"Look, I'm sorry I teased you. But I swear, I didn't mean anything by it. And I'm no narc." Luke tugged at the end of his tie, making it even more lopsided. He pressed his lips together for a moment, thoughtful. "Do you mind if I ask what exactly it is you thought I told her?"

Jess paused for a moment, but Luke was

disconcertingly easy to confide in. "That I was an unfit mother." The words were off her tongue before Jess could fully consider the consequences.

Luke stared. "That's insane."

Jess shrugged. "It's okay. Meredith understands."

"No, Jessica. That's crazy. I can't believe someone would do that." Luke pushed away from the door and put his hands on his hips. His eyes had clouded over, his expression hardened.

"I'll figure it out," Jess assured him. "I think I'm making too much of it."

Luke quirked an eyebrow at her. "Meredith Bailey is a social worker, isn't she? I thought she worked for the child advocacy center."

"She's an independent home study provider and adoption facilitator," Jess said.

"A mandatory reporter." Luke nodded. "That's malicious. To seek out a social worker like that? It's cold."

Jess agreed, and that's exactly why she had sought Luke out in the first place. "Do you think someone is trying to . . ." She couldn't finish the thought.

Luke studied her for a moment, obviously struggling to strike the right balance. He didn't want to ignite an already incendiary situation, but whoever called Meredith had made a bold move. "I don't know," he said eventually. "But I'd want to figure out who reported you and why."

"I'm sorry I accused you," Jess said.

"I would have done the same thing."

The school bell shrieked overhead, announcing the end of lunch and the five-minute window for students to gather their books and make their way to class. Jess winced a little — at the sound or at the implications of yet another unanswered question, she wasn't sure herself. But she gave Luke a wan smile.

He seemed to want to say more, but thinking better of it, he reached for the door. Swinging it open for her, he said: "I know this sounds a bit nuts, but let me know if there's anything I can do to help. I mean it."

Jess believed that he did. But she doubted she'd be calling up Luke Tucker anytime soon. "Thanks."

"I hope the rest of your day looks up," he said. "And I hope you figure out who the informant is."

Jess laughed, but it was dry and short-lived. "I think I've proven my deductive powers are feeble at best."

"It's a pretty serious accusation. I think

I'd keep hunting if I were you."

Jess lifted a shoulder, hoping to appear nonchalant. But a chill tickled the nape of her neck. Luke didn't realize the power of his words, the way her skin rippled with something akin to horror at the realization that this was, indeed, a hunt. She just didn't know if she was the hunter or the hunted.

Lost Mamas Message Board

A place for birth moms who've lost a child through coercion, intimidation, manipulation, or worse. We advocate and fight for one another and VENT.

THERIVERWILD: HEY, HAVE ANY OF YOU BEEN CONTACTED BY SOME GUY NAMED EVAN CHAMBERLAIN? HE'S A DOCTOR — I LOOKED HIM UP, HE'S LEGIT. HE WAS ASKING QUESTIONS ABOUT A GIRL WHO COMMITTED SUICIDE AT EAGLE RIDGE. @VIV87, DO YOU REMEMBER LASHONNA TATE?

VIV87: @THERIVERWILD U NUTS. I'M NOT TALKING TO NO ONE. HOW DID HE FIND U?

THERIVERWILD: @VIV87 EAGLE RIDGE FB PAGE. I LEFT A COMMENT ON A PIC.

VIV87: @THERIVERWILD STALKER.

MARIAH(NOTCAREY): @VIV87 NOBODY SAID YOU HAD TO TALK. @THERIVERWILD WHAT'S HIS ANGLE? ARE YOU TALKING?

THERIVERWILD: @MARIAH(NOTCAREY) YEAH, A LITTLE. HE WANTS TO KNOW WHAT HAPPENED TO HER BABY. SAYS LASHONNA TOLD HIM SHE WAS GOING TO PARENT, BUT THE NEXT THING HE KNEW SHE WAS GONE. I DIDN'T TELL HIM THIS, BUT SHE WAS MESSED UP WHEN SHE CAME BACK. HUNG HERSELF WITH A SHEET.

LISALYNN: @THERIVERWILD AND THE BABY?

THERIVERWILD: @LISALYNN INITIUM NOVUM.

BBG: OF COURSE.

THERIVERWILD: @BBG SO DO I TELL HIM ABOUT LOST MAMAS?

BBG: @THERIVERWILD ISN'T THAT THE POINT OF ALL THIS? RAISING AWARENESS AND EXPOSING THE CORRUPTION AND FINDING OUR BABIES? HELL YEAH, YOU TELL HIM.

Chapter 21

Elizabeth N.
33, Caucasian, 6th grade ed.
Spiked hair, dyed purple at the tips. Active,
  restless, ADHD?
Boyfriend knows.
PROST, 78m, 11m pp

"I need to see Dr. Sanderson today." Jess clutched the telephone to her ear and turned away from her students. She had assigned them ten minutes of silent reading, a story that she had picked almost at random only seconds before they walked through her classroom door. *The Story of an Hour,* which was an odd choice to say the least. Even as she instructed them to turn to the page in their textbooks where they would find it, she felt a prick of conscience. A dead husband, a grieving wife. Freedom was something she hadn't considered in any of this. Jess wanted answers. She wanted the truth.

"I'm sorry, Mrs. Chamberlain, but Dr. Sanderson doesn't have any available appointments today."

Jess could hear another phone line ringing in the background. She had no doubt that the clinic was booked solid today. Overbooked if she knew anything about the way Auburn Family Medicine ran their practice. It was hard for people who cared so much about their patients to turn anyone away. Especially so close to a major holiday.

"What time does the clinic close tonight?" Jess asked, trying another tactic.

"There are no appointments scheduled after four forty-five."

Of course, Jess knew what that meant: after the backlog of a busy day, the final few appointments that had been scheduled for late afternoon would finally trickle into the examination rooms well after five o'clock. And the clinic staff might make it to their cars by six. If they were lucky.

"Thank you," Jess said.

"Would you like to make an appointment for tomorrow? There are only a couple left."

"No thanks." Jess was already pulling the phone away from her ear. "Happy Thanksgiving," she said in the last second before she clicked off her phone.

"You feeling okay, Mrs. Chamberlain?"

one of Jess's students whispered from the row closest to her desk. "Because you should go home if you're sick."

"I'm fine, Kaden." Jess stuck her cell phone in the top drawer of her desk and grabbed the textbook that her students were currently reading out of.

"We don't want to get sick," someone else chimed in. "I mean, if you need to go home, we can handle things here."

A few chuckles lit up the room. Jess could feel their energy — it was thick and charged, sparking between the desks and the twenty-some teenagers with their auras of Axe body spray and candy-scented lotion. The whole room seemed like it would spontaneously combust on the weight of a single word.

"I'm beyond fine," Jess assured them. "Healthy as a horse."

"Who says horses are healthy?"

And just like that, the tenuous silence evaporated. Books were slammed closed as her students erupted in laughter. It didn't take much.

It was obvious that no one was capable of having a meaningful discussion, so Jess separated them into groups and had them work on alternate endings to the short story. They groaned, but it was imaginative busy-work. Only Jess was captivated by the prospect of rewriting the ending of a story gone horribly awry.

When school was over, Jess picked up her boys earlier than normal and headed into town.

"Where are we going?" Gabe wondered, the prospect of an outing delighting him.

"Home," Max said. "I have homework."

"Really?" Jess gave her son a sidelong glance. "Who assigned homework when there's only half a day tomorrow?"

Max said something unintelligible and began dragging his finger through the steam that was collecting on the passenger-side window. Usually that drove Jess crazy — she couldn't stand fingerprints on her windows — but she held her tongue. She had to choose her battles and this was not going to be one of them.

"I have to make a quick stop before we go home," Jess said, directing her answer toward the backseat and Gabe. "It won't take long — I promise."

"Just drop us off," Max complained.

"I'm not leaving you alone."

Max shot her a furtive glance beneath a fringe of blond hair that Jess realized was getting too long. But she was far more concerned with the look in his eyes. Knowing? Guilty? She couldn't quite decide, but he didn't press her any more about dropping them off before attending to her errand. *Later,* Jess told herself. *I'll deal with him later.*

The afternoon sun was blinding, glinting off the snow like cold steel. It glared, hard and unmoving as Jess navigated the ice-packed streets. Even wearing sunglasses she had to squint, but the brightness was misleading. It was so cold that a crust had formed over the newly fallen snow, a crisp layer of frost that snapped when she drove over a section that the snowplows hadn't fully cleared. The crunch beneath her tires was unsettlingly violent.

Jess turned into the Bomgaars parking lot and pulled up to a squat little Coffee Hut that was situated near the entrance. When the ice-fishing cabin turned coffee drive-through first appeared in Auburn, Jess had scoffed at it. But the Coffee Hut had good coffee and even better hot chocolate. It was mildly peppermint flavored and topped with an extravagant swirl of whipped cream. She hoped it would appease her boys.

By the time she dragged them into Promise Adoption, Gabe was humming happily, a creamy mustache smeared across his upper lip. Max wasn't as mollified, but he followed willingly enough, his hot cocoa in one hand and a math textbook in the other.

"You can wait here," Jess said, motioning to the plush seats. Someone had put up Christmas decorations since the last time she was here, and a skinny artificial tree with white lights and silver decorations twinkled coolly in the corner. Max flopped down in the nearest chair with no regard to where it was or which direction it was facing. Gabe found the kid's table almost immediately and set to work on the puzzle that remained exactly as it had been when she saw it weeks ago.

"I'll be back in a few minutes," Jess said, dropping a kiss on the top of his head. He smelled of the coconut oil she had smoothed in that morning. "Don't tip this over." She tapped the lid of his drink gently and gave him a warning look.

"I won't." But his words were rote; he wasn't paying attention to her.

"And, Max?" When he looked up, Jess continued: "Keep an eye on your brother."

He nodded once. Good enough.

Though Samantha had undoubtedly watched the entire exchange, when Jessica approached the tall receptionist's desk, Samantha greeted her as though she had just walked in the door. "Hello, Mrs. Chamberlain."

Jess wasn't quite sure where to stand. The desk was more of a counter, really, curved and long and recently festooned with an artificial garland that was twined with sparkly ribbon and tiny clear-glass baubles. It was impossible to get close, so Jess hovered nearby. "Thanks for squeezing me in on short notice," she said.

"I have just a bit of paperwork for you to sign before I take you back to see Anthony." Samantha pushed her dark hair behind her ear and held out a clipboard.

"Thank you." Jess accepted it graciously, but the lovely receptionist wasn't nearly as warm as she had been the first time Jessica came in. Samantha pulled up the corners of her mouth in the likeness of a smile, obviously leery of the woman who had breezed into her office demanding answers not so long ago. Good thing Jess had made an appointment this time.

She took the clipboard to the nearest chair because the decorations made it impossible to get close enough to write on the counter. Samantha had implied that there was an assortment of paperwork, but when Jess took a look at what she had been given, she found it was just a single sheet. In fact, it was a sheet that she recognized.

When she and Evan had adopted Gabe,

they had signed a consent to communication form — which was actually a consent to noncommunication, or communication through an intermediary. Promise Adoption held their papers and acted as a post office of sorts, but the only way their sealed papers could be released was through a court injunction. Jess wasn't sure what she was signing now, but a quick scan of the two short paragraphs told her all she needed to know. Just as she asked, Anthony was petitioning to open the file and reverse the communication consent form they had agreed to over six years ago. All he needed was her signature proclaiming that this was what she wanted, too.

Jess glanced over at Gabe, pen poised in her hand. The tears that sprang to her eyes were hot and sudden, an overflow of the love and anger and despair and hope that were fierce and full in her chest. He was as much a part of her as her own breath, but she knew that strangers would never peg him as her son. Dark haired and brown eyed, he looked absolutely nothing like her. And their differences were more than skin deep.

"Love wins," Jess told herself. She wanted to believe it. She wanted to trust that this was only a part of their story. A bump in the road that would fade in the rearview with time and perspective. But she wasn't so sure.

Jessica signed the paper anyway.

Samantha led her back to Anthony's office, clipboard in hand. "Anthony," she said cheerfully, rapping on the door. "Your four o'clock is here."

With more grace than Samantha had mustered, Anthony rose from behind his desk and came to give Jessica a hug. She tried not to stiffen in his unwanted embrace. "It's good to see you again," Anthony said, taking the clipboard from Samantha and wordlessly dismissing her. "What about all this snow?"

Jess wasn't in the mood for small talk, but she let him have his way as he sorted and re-sorted papers at his desk and chatted about the weather and the snow that had blanketed Auburn in white. Anthony's kids were ecstatic about an unexpected day off school, and Jess was tempted to ask him if they were biological or adopted. The distinction had never mattered to her before — her kids were her kids — but she wondered if Anthony Bartels "got it" or if this was just a job.

"Well," he finally said, heaving a sigh and placing both of his hands palm down on a nondescript manila file. "After we talked a few weeks ago, I looked more deeply into your case."

Jess tried to nod, but her head just gave a jerky bob.

"The paper you signed was a request to open Gabe's file. It's hard to tell what the judge will do, especially if only one party is petitioning for a reversal. But I did some digging and there is more information that I can share with you."

"Thank you," Jess whispered. She didn't want to be as affected as she was, but it was hard not to feel like a piece of the puzzle was hovering just outside her grasp. Or rather, on the desk in front of Anthony. And she hadn't decided if she could trust him or not.

"Your noncommunication clause was not legally binding," he said. "It was just a good-faith agreement between two parties who wanted the same thing. There was no contention and no reason to make it legal or official. As I understand it, you were both — adoptive family and birth family — open to dialogue at some later point."

Jess didn't really remember that part of the adoption process, but then, Evan had handled most of the details. She was in charge of preparing their home and family for a new addition, and Evan handled the paperwork. He was a task-oriented perfectionist who actually enjoyed those sorts of things. Jess had bought a crib set with little trains and read every book she could get her hands on about bonding and attachment and parenting a child from a "hard place." She wondered what else she had missed.

"So," Anthony said, opening the file. "Turns out I can share some things with you."

"What sorts of things?"

"Our log." He lifted a sheet from the folder and handed it across the desk to Jess. "We record every time a document is added or removed from a communication file. The record includes time, date, and the person who added it or removed it."

Jess looked at the paper in her hand. It wasn't a very long record. Just six entries in all, seemingly dated in pairs. June mostly. A couple in July. The same name was listed after every memo.

"Our former secretary," Anthony said, anticipating her question.

"But you don't have the letters?" Jess already knew what he would say, but she had to ask anyway.

Anthony shook his head. "We don't make copies."

"Okay."

"There's more." Anthony took the next sheet of paper. "In the state of Iowa a birth mother can sign a consent form authorizing the state to provide the child with her name, last known address, and last known telephone number should the child request that information when he or she reaches an age of majority. We don't have a copy of the form, of course, but our records indicate that Gabriel's birth mom signed it."

"I don't understand. Gabe's not eighteen."

"Yes, but this will help all the same. It proves that Gabe's birth mother was open to contact, that she wanted her information to be available."

Jess realized she was biting her bottom lip and stopped. It was warm and swollen where she had been worrying it. "Is there anything else?"

"Only this." Anthony held up a standard-sized envelope. There was a stamp in the corner that was smudged with the faint blue lines of a cancellation mark and a pair of addresses that were too small for Jessica to read. "Promise Adoption owes you an apology," Anthony said. He ground his jaw and a tendon popped near his ear. Above his beard, his cheeks were as smooth as a child's. "As far as I can recall, this has never happened before."

"What's never happened before?" Jess's stomach twisted in anticipation.

"Apparently we lost a letter. Samantha found this when she was pulling your file. It's kind of amazing that she discovered it at all. She was wearing a bracelet and it slipped off and dropped into the filing cabinet. If she hadn't gone fishing for her bracelet, she would never have found the letter."

Jess's heart stuttered. "Is it from her?"

Anthony shrugged, but held out the letter for her to take. "We don't open the letters, Jessica. We just deliver them. I'm sorry that this one is being delivered so late." He pushed back from the desk and gave Jess a thin-lipped smile. "Maybe this is a good thing?"

Jess wasn't sure what to say.

"I'm going to give you a few minutes." Anthony clasped her shoulder for a second before he left the office. It was fortifying and apologetic and maybe a little pitying, but all Jessica felt was confused. He shut the door quietly behind him and she found herself alone with a letter clutched in her hands.

Jessica turned it over and studied it from every angle, running her fingers along the edges and smoothing her thumb over the address that was neatly printed in the upper left-hand corner. There was no name over the house number and street, but it had originated from St. Paul. That was something. Jess held the thought carefully: Gabe's birth mom had lived in St. Paul. It was the first thing she learned about her.

In some ways, Jess knew that sliding her finger beneath the seal was the beginning of the end. She could never again pretend to not know. She could no longer be disconnected from the woman who had given her a son. But in other ways it was an open door, a fresh start. Truth, after years of pretending that everything was as it should be when it wasn't.

Opening the letter was a declaration. A commitment.

Jess worked her thumb into a gap near the corner and ripped.

April 13, 2017

Dear Gabriel Allen,
Happy birthday to you! You're five years old today, buddy. I can hardly believe it. Of course, you won't read this letter

until you're eighteen (if you even read it at all), but know that today I am celebrating you. Chocolate cake (my favorite — maybe it's yours too?) and five red candles. When I blew them out, I made a wish for you. Don't even ask: it's a secret. ;-)

I have a confession to make: I saw you yesterday. I promised myself a long time ago that I would never bother you, that I would let you make the choice someday about whether or not you want to be a part of my life. But it's been a hard promise to keep. Your mama doesn't want me around, and honey, I don't blame her. She doesn't know me. She doesn't trust me. And yet, I've always secretly hoped that one day she would realize that there's room for both. That we both love you. Two mamas doesn't sound so bad, does it?

I have to tell you something. I went to your house. Yes, I know where you live, and no, I'm not going to tell you how I know. It's a long story (but I promise I'm not a weirdo and I wasn't stalking you). I just wanted to see you. Maybe even say hi. I thought that I could ring the doorbell and ask for directions or something. You don't know who I am. She doesn't know who I am. It would be so easy to tell a little white lie and see your face.

But when I pulled down your street, I saw you. I'm sure you don't remember this, but it was really warm yesterday. Warm for April, anyway, and though there were still patches of snow on the front lawn, you were riding your bike in a T-shirt. Your bike is red (that's why I bought red candles!) and it doesn't have training wheels — or any pedals, for that matter. You were pushing yourself along, running, really, and laughing like the world was filled with everything good. I pulled over and watched you for a while. It was hard to tell at a distance, but it looks to me like you got your grandpa Andrew's nose. And your coloring is all mine. You're golden, Gabriel.

I wanted to step out of the car, but just as I grabbed the door handle your big brother came outside. He's handsome, kiddo. Tall and blond and kind of like a boy in a music video I used to love. He saw you on your bike and got this wild little smile on his face. When he started chasing you, you screamed and went as fast as you could. But he caught you anyway and grabbed you beneath the arms so he could spin you round and round. The bike fell, but you didn't care. You were both giggling so hard. And then he put you down and rubbed his knuckles against your hair just like a brother should.

He loves you. I hope you know that. I'm sure you fight — if you're like my brothers, you fight all the time. But you can't fake the way he looked at you. The way his hand fell so easy against your dark head. It was pretty amazing to see.

Your mama came outside right after that. She had car keys in one hand and shin guards in the other. I think it's amazing that you play soccer. Guess what, buddy? Me too. I guess that's something you got from me. You went running and grabbed those shin guards so fast! She smoothed your hair and gave you a quick kiss and then you were all in the car, backing out of the driveway. Your mama waved to me in the rearview mirror and I waved back.

You have such a beautiful life, Gabriel. It makes me really proud that I was strong enough to let you go. And now when I think about you, I can picture you in that place, surrounded by love, a part of a family.

Your mama is beautiful, too. She fights for you. I can see it in her. It's in the way she touches you, the way she moves. She deserves every ounce of your love. But if there's something I've learned, it's that love comes in a limitless supply. I hope yours spills up and all over everyone around you. And I hope you can save just a little bit of it for me.

Love, your birth mom,
LaShonna

CHAPTER 22

Heather J.
39, mixed race, GED
Tall, thin, shoulder-length dreads.
  Antagonistic, paranoid.
Everyone knows.
CSCS, 41m, 13m pp

Jessica was grateful that the bathroom at Promise Adoption Agency was down the hallway and far from the front reception area. Her boys didn't have to see her tear-stained face or wonder at her bloodshot eyes. She had been wearing makeup, but it was a smudged mess, and rather than trying to fix it, she washed her face in the bathroom sink with pink industrial hand soap.

The cold water was fortifying, the antiseptic soap sharp and abrasive. It grounded her, and by the time Jess left the bathroom she had more or less collected herself. Eyedrops, mascara, and a dab of rose-colored lipstick had returned her to a semblance of normalcy, and she had effectively walled off the letter in her heart. For now. It was tucked in her purse, a time bomb disguised as a plain white envelope. Jess had much to process, but as with everything lately, it felt like now was not the time. She had been kicking the can of her fraught emotions down the road for longer than she could remember. It was only a matter of time before she burst.

"Is there anything I can do?" Anthony asked when she paused in his office on her way out.

"I'm fine." Jess tried out a smile. It stuck, but it didn't come close to reaching her eyes. "I just have a lot of things to think about."

He nodded in understanding. "I'll file this tomorrow." He held up the papers that Jessica assumed requested their adoption records to be unsealed. "I have to be honest with you, though: it's going to take a while. I'm pretty sure the court is closed tomorrow, and then there's the holiday . . ."

"It's not a problem," Jess assured him, waving her hand to dismiss his concern. "No rush."

Anthony paused for a moment, clearly wanting to say something else, though Jess's body language did not invite further intrusion. He probed anyway. "Would you like to talk about what's in the letter?"

"No." Jess turned to go, but something made her pause. What did she have to lose? "Does Promise ever work with James Rosenburg Law?"

"James Rosenburg," Anthony repeated. He looked confused, but Jess couldn't tell if it was because he truly had no idea what she was talking about or if he was trying to stall. "No, I don't think I've ever heard of him."

Jess spun on her heel. "Please call me when you hear something."

"I'm not done yet!" Gabe half shouted when she walked into the reception area. The puzzle didn't look much different than it had when Jess had left him at the little picnic table, but he had moved several pieces around.

"It's okay, bug." Jess crouched down beside him and wrapped her arms around his solid frame. She nuzzled her nose into the nape of his neck and pressed her lips to his warm skin. But he was already wriggling out of her embrace.

"I have to finish it. I only have ten pieces left."

There were far more than ten pieces left to fit into the puzzle, and as Jess studied it she realized that Gabe had forced a couple of mismatched pieces into the wrong spots. One cardboard corner was bent and frayed.

"We'll start a puzzle at home." Jess tried to soothe him by rubbing soft circles on his back. "We have lots in the closet. We can do it together over Thanksgiving break."

"I want to do *this* puzzle!"

"He's been like this since you left," Max said from behind a *People* magazine.

"You could have helped him." Jess pushed herself up and reached for Gabe's hand. "Come on, buddy."

"I did." Max tossed the magazine on the table in front of him. It slipped right off the smooth surface and landed facedown on the floor. Max didn't pick it up. "He wouldn't let me touch a single piece."

Gabe was crying now, whimpering something about puzzles and pieces fitting together. He did this from time to time, became fixated on something that he couldn't do. But he couldn't have a meltdown. Not here. The evidence against her would be too compelling if Jess had to manhandle her bawling son out the door of the adoption agency. Gabe had lost it in public places before. Jess had been forced to grab onto whatever flailing limb she could catch and pin a smile to her face while she tried to safely, carefully remove her wild child from a triggering situation. People didn't understand. She worried that Anthony Bartels would certainly not understand.

"Here," Jess said, fishing in her purse and coming up with a fun-size candy bar. More sugar, but if it calmed him down, it was worth it.

Gabe took the candy, momentarily placated, and Jess snagged him by the hand and led him to the door. "It was a difficult puzzle," Jess muttered to herself, fishing in her coat pocket for her car keys. "There were too many pieces."

Max caught her eye, and she was surprised to see him give a single, fierce nod of agreement. She forgot sometimes that in spite of all his angst, he loved Gabe, too.

"I have one more quick stop," Jess said when everyone was buckled into the car. Gabe was still mewling a bit, but his mood hadn't swung into a full-blown tantrum, and for that she was eternally grateful. His mouth was smeared in chocolate and he didn't seem to register her announcement, but Max did.

"No," Max said definitively. "Drop me off at home if you have to, but I'm not sitting in another waiting room for half an hour. I have a test tomorrow."

"What?" Jess flicked on her blinker and merged into oncoming traffic. Auburn was hardly a metropolis, but the window between after school and after work was always busy. She wanted to give Max her full attention, but she was focused on the road. Jess managed: "That doesn't make sense. Who would schedule a test for the half day before Thanksgiving break?"

"Mr. Wallis."

"Science?"

Max drummed his fingers on the console between them. "Yes, science. I have to study."

"It'll just be a couple of minutes, Max."

"That's what you always say."

Jess could feel frustration coming off her son in waves. It was heady, laced with oak and resin and just a hint of sweat. He had PE today, Jess could tell. He refused to shower afterward and she didn't blame him. She remembered all too well the gauntlet that had been the girls locker room during her adolescence.

"I promise," Jess said, softening. "Mere minutes. You can stay in the car. We'll leave it running."

But catching Dr. Sanderson after work was easier said than done. The parking lot of Auburn Family Medicine was crammed with cars — so much so that there wasn't a single parking spot available. Jess circled through the lot and back onto the road so that she could go around the block and try the back entrance where the employees parked.

"Why are we at Daddy's work?" Gabe asked from the backseat. His voice caught on the word "Daddy," but Jess wasn't sure if it was because of emotion or because his vocal cords were weary from whining.

"I have to talk to Dr. Sanderson for a minute." Jess turned down the back alley and drove to the spot that had been marked for her husband. The sign denoting Dr. Evan Chamberlain's space had not yet been removed, and it was conspicuously empty in a parking lot that was so crowded there was an SUV with two tires straddling the curb.

"But why?"

Jess pulled into her husband's space and put the car in park. Draping one arm over the backseat she gave her youngest a small smile. "I'll be back in a minute," she said, avoiding his question. Jess could feel the fragility of the moment, the fine strands of emotion that corded her heart at the thought of the letter secreted away in her purse, and the understanding that this was incomprehensible to her children. An awful, wicked situation that left them tender. Vulnerable. "I'll be so quick," Jess promised, hoping it was true. "You won't even know that I'm gone."

Jess couldn't slip in the back door even if she wanted to — the clinic was locked tight as a drum because of the fastidiously monitored cabinet that was filled with prescriptions. So she hurried around the side of the building, pulling her coat close and tucking her chin beneath the fringe of faux fur that lined her hood.

The waiting room was packed to the gills, overflowing with people in various stages of distress. Even though Jess had spent nearly twenty years with a family practitioner for a husband, she was surprised by the crowd of people, the need that filled the room with a quiet desperation.

It was a bad time. Though there was little that Jess wanted more in that moment than to interrogate Peter Sanderson, it was obvious that her timing was way off. Digging in her purse, Jess came up with an old receipt and a ballpoint pen that was missing its cap. Making her palm into a table of sorts, Jess scribbled a quick note.

Beth was behind the receptionist's desk

again, and she looked up at Jessica with a frazzled expression that she tried to mask behind a fake smile. Jess wasn't buying it, and she wasn't going to take a second more of her time than necessary.

"Hey, Beth. Sorry to bother you on such a busy afternoon. I have a note for Dr. Sanderson," Jess said, holding out the folded receipt. "Could you please make sure that he gets it?"

Beth took the paper reluctantly, but Jess knew that it was the only hope she had of getting in touch with Peter soon. Beth wouldn't give out his cell phone number. Not even to Jess. And though Jessica could call the clinic directly and leave a voice mail on his private line, with the waiting room backed up as much as it was, she doubted he'd listen to it before Thanksgiving. Jess couldn't stand the thought of waiting any longer. She felt like events had wound themselves around her, whirling tighter and tighter until she had no choice but to spin free or snap.

"I'll try." The red light on Beth's headset started to flash and she put up one finger as if to ward Jessica off.

"Please," Jess said. "It's important."

Beth nodded, but she was already saying hello to whoever was on the line. Jess stayed put, watching until Beth took a tack out of the cork board beside her and pinned the note at the very center. She glanced back at Jessica as if to say: *There.*

Jess nodded and gave her a little wave, but Beth had already turned away.

Gabe was calm as they drove home, so Jessica took a quick detour and grabbed a rotisserie chicken from The Food Court. She had a bagged salad in the fridge and a couple of potatoes sprouting in the pantry. It wouldn't be hard to make up a few mashed potatoes. Jess felt nearly frantic with energy — capable of whipping them herself.

"I'm hungry now," Gabe complained as they stomped off their feet in the entryway and hung their coats on hooks. Max was already on his way to his room, science book tucked under one arm.

"We'll have supper in half an hour. You can wait that long." Jess carried the plastic container into the kitchen and set it in the oven to stay warm. Then she went riffling through the pantry for the potatoes she was sure were there. Emerging with the sagging mesh bag in hand, she asked, "Want to be my helper?"

Gabe shrugged. "What do I have to do?"

"Peel potatoes. It's easy."

They washed their hands at the kitchen sink and then Jess showed him how to run the peeler down one side of the soft, brown potato. A flat strip fell, revealing the cool, white flesh beneath. It was a magic of sorts, and Gabe thought so, too. He bit his bottom lip as he took the potato from her and began to pare off little snips of skin.

"I'm not good at this," he complained after a few minutes.

"You're great at it." Jess glanced into the sink at the pile of peels and then took the potato from Gabe. It was dusted brown from his now-dirty fingers, but she ran it beneath a thin stream of water and it emerged nearly unblemished. "See? Good job."

Gabe wasn't as convinced, but he grabbed another potato and began the process again while Jess cubed the one in her hand into a small pot. She couldn't stop herself from stealing peeks at her son. The edge of the sink hit him square in the chest so his arms were curled up and over. It looked uncomfortable, but he didn't complain. He just set his jaw and focused on what he was doing, oblivious to everything but the task at hand.

It was so encouraging to see him so engaged. Jess loved it when Gabe found his rhythm, when the neurons that kept him sparking like an explosive calmed down enough just to let him *be.* He was a wonder to behold.

What had she looked like? The thought snuck up on Jessica so suddenly she had to put her hands on the counter to steady herself. It wasn't something she had ever considered before. Gabe's birth mom was a black spot in her personal history, a bit of trouble that Jess would rather forget. But here she was imagining her. With Gabe's neat, little nose. A head full of his soft curls. Skin that was at once brown sugar and candlelight, infused with warmth from within. Jess had no doubt that she was singularly lovely. The kind of woman who required a second glance.

Jess wished for one startling moment that she had known her.

Of course, they had her complete medical history. Several pages of diagnoses and diseases, things like hypertension and breast cancer on the maternal side. But after glancing at those clinical, impersonal sheets Jess had tucked them away and barely given them a second thought. Gabriel was her son — *her* son — and somehow all of those dispassionate facts and figures seemed completely detached from who he really was. None of that mattered. None of it was him.

But as she stared at Gabe carefully peeling another potato, Jess felt for just a moment that she was looking at a complete stranger. What secrets lurked beneath his skin? What preferences and proclivities? He passionately loved dill pickles, and Jess could hardly stand the smell. When they ordered hamburgers at McDonald's, he grabbed hers before she took a single bite and plucked off the pickles for her. And Gabe liked to sing. In the shower and in the car. While he was playing with his LEGO, and sometimes especially when it was irritating his brother. Jess couldn't carry a tune in a bucket.

"What's wrong?" Gabe asked.

Jess looked up quickly, feeling like she had been caught in the act. Of doing what? Wishing that things had been different? That *she* had been different? She had been young and hurting and ignorant. The world looked very different from where she now stood.

"Nothing's wrong." Jess forced a smile and reached for the potato that he was holding out for her. "Thanks so much for helping me."

He picked up another potato, humming

as he laid the peeler against the skin and began to laboriously flick off little shavings.

It flashed through her heart so fast Jess wondered if she had thought it at all.

I wish you had known her.

And then: *I'm sorry. I'm so very sorry.*

September 29, 2018

Dad's townhouse is kind of a shithole. I mean, it's new and all, but I hate it here. So does G. It doesn't help that Dads a total psycho these days. He's always on his computer or writing things down and stuffing them in this old file folder. I have one like it for school, but it's plastic and see-thru so I can find what I need. Ds is brown and dark and he's always dumping everything out and rearranging it and talking to himself. But don't try to help! He'll freak out. Yesterday I found a business card on the table for some law office. James Rosenburg. And Dad yanked it out of my hand. Leave it alone! he said. And that's funny because he had written those exact words on the back of the card.

I thought M+D might get back together but now I don't know. I think JR is a divorce lawyer. G asks me when we're all going to live together again so I lie and say soon. But I don't think so. Ds not interested in us anymore. Not really. I was trying to help G with an assignment today and D lost it. He felt bad afterward, I could tell. So he told me some stuff about Gs birth mom and told me not to tell M. Its kinda weird. Her name was LaShona, but Dad said she died. I guess that's sad, but I didn't know her. D didn't know her either. Not really. But I'm pretty sure he's trying to help her. I just don't know why.

M says D is a helper by nature. Duh. As if we don't all know. D doesn't have any decorations in the apartment, but theres a picture in the living room that says: "You have not lived today until you have done something for someone who can never repay you." Maybe thats why he forgets sometimes to do things for us.

— *Max*

451

CHAPTER 23

Vivian H.
24, mixed race, working on GED
Dark hair dyed blond, roots showing. Small
  as a child. Looks 12.
No one knows.
MANSL/DEL CS, 30m, 17m pp

Dr. Sanderson called after Gabe was asleep. Jess was curled up on the couch in the living room, wrapped chin to toes in a fleece blanket and shivering anyway. The TV was on, a rerun of *Fixer Upper* blinking in the background, but Jess wasn't watching it. Her eyes were glazed over, her mind elsewhere. When the phone rang, she nearly jumped out of her skin.

"Hi, Jessica. It's Peter Sanderson."

Jess sat up, the blanket slipping off her shoulders as she clutched her cell to her ear. "Hello." Her voice was thin, unused. "Thank you so much for calling me back."

"Of course, Jess. Anything for you." He

went quiet for a moment, and if Jess was right, he was swallowing down some black emotion. She was reminded once again that she wasn't the only one who missed Evan. "How are you doing?"

"We're okay." Jess reached for the remote control and turned off the TV. The house was enveloped in a sudden stillness that seemed to crackle like ice forming. "It's hard."

"I know. I mean, I don't know. But I'm sorry."

"Thanks for calling," Jess cut in, rescuing him from having to say more. He was obviously struggling. No one seemed to know how to talk to her anymore.

Peter cleared his throat. "Your note said it was an emergency?" There was a hint of worry in his tone. Jess realized that he'd likely hop in his car and drive right over if she asked him to. Her request was much less complicated.

"I probably shouldn't have said it was an emergency," Jess admitted. "But I really wanted you to call me back. I have some questions for you."

"Anything."

Jess reached for the folder that she had placed on the coffee table. Her notes were there, each musing circled or underlined, and every page crisscrossed with arrows. A map to everywhere and absolutely nowhere. Jess was out of her element, but she dove right in, pretending that she already knew much more than she did. "I was hoping that you could fill me in on Evan's research project."

"Research project?"

"Yes. He was conducting a research project on female inmates."

"Inmates?" Peter truly sounded shocked. It wasn't the response that Jess had been hoping for. She was grasping at straws, trusting that one or two of her hunches would turn out to be on track. Or, at least not completely harebrained. It seemed she wasn't going to be so lucky. Peter grunted softly. "I honestly have no idea what you're talking about. I didn't realize that Evan was doing any sort of research project."

How could she be at a dead end already? "I would think that would be a difficult thing to keep secret," Jess mused more to herself than to Peter.

"Agreed. Though . . ." He stopped, and Jess felt her heart stutter.

"Yes?"

"Well, he was gone from time to time. I mean, we all take time off, but Evan was really particular about, well, everything. He didn't miss work unless he was on his death bed."

His choice of words was thoughtless, and Peter's little gasp told Jessica that he knew it. But she wasn't offended. Instead, her mind was racing. She knew exactly how much vacation Evan had used. Jess kept their books and it was a detail she had meticulously recorded. Other than scheduled vacation days, Evan had taken exactly three days off for pneumonia in the last two years — at least, pre-separation. The only way she had convinced him to stay home was by appealing to his common sense. "You're going to get your patients sick," she said. And he had finally agreed.

"When was he gone?" Jess asked Peter, writing **ABSENT** in bold on the top of a clean sheet of paper.

"I don't know exactly. A handful of times. The reason it seemed strange to me was because it was so last-minute. Evan was supposed to come into work, and when he didn't, Dr. Murphy and I had to pick up the slack." Peter seemed to hear himself say the words and he rushed to explain. "Not that we minded or anything. It was fine. It was just surprising that he was gone."

"Of course. Do you know how many times this happened? One or two? More?"

"I'd say half a dozen times. I wondered if he was home with Max or Gabe or something, but he never gave us an explanation. He was just gone."

"And you don't know where he went or what he was doing?"

"No. And then, of course, he was gone the entire week before he died."

Jess had written "6+?" on her paper and she circled it a few times in frustration. "Was he secretive? Did he seem different somehow?"

Peter sighed. "I don't know, Jess. Sometimes it's tempting to look back and try to find meaning in every detail. More often than not, it's just not there."

But Jess wasn't buying it. Not this time. Under normal circumstances she tended to agree with Deputy Mullen: the simplest answer was the right answer. Jess liked straight lines and smooth edges and things that could be neatly categorized and filed away in their proper place. Her careful containment strategies seemed naive and ineffectual now. And she was just starting to understand that maybe she had been approaching this wrong from the start. Jess hadn't been skeptical enough. She hadn't asked enough questions or fought for answers when her inquiries couldn't be satisfactorily addressed. She wasn't about to make that mistake again.

"Do you remember Cody De Jager?"

Peter made a sound in the back of his throat. "I can't discuss Evan's patients with you."

"So he was still seeing Evan?"

"Jess —"

"Look, I'm not going to make anything of it; I just want to know if he's still in Auburn. I haven't seen him in a really long time."

"As far as I know, he's still around," Peter said reluctantly.

"And cleaned up?"

"On again, off again. You know how it is. You don't think he has anything to do with . . ." Peter trailed off. "Wait. I don't want to know. What are you doing, Jess?"

"Just trying to get my head around everything," she said, standing up. The blanket fell away and pooled at her feet. In its absence she was suddenly cold. She marched into the kitchen, fighting a full-body tremble, and spread her folder out on the counter. Pawing through her junk drawer, she changed course. "Evan had to have gone somewhere, right? Maybe that's when he conducted his interviews. He left work and —"

"Look, Jessica. I'm a bit out of my depth

here," Peter cut in. "If you have questions, I think you should direct them to the authorities. I was just Evan's friend."

Jess emerged from the depths of the drawer triumphant, crowded key chain in hand. She was barely listening to Peter anymore. "You're right," she said distractedly. "I'm sorry. I shouldn't have bothered you."

"No bother. I'm always here for you. And Jess? I might be overstepping my bounds here, but may I ask you a question?"

"Sure." Jess tucked her finger through the key ring and palmed the keys so they wouldn't jangle. Abandoning her notebook, she hurried through the house, grabbing her coat off the chair where she had thrown it and tossing pillows in search of her purse.

"Are you seeing someone?" Peter paused for a moment. "I mean, a counselor? Therapist? Pastor? Do you have someone you can talk to?"

Jess stopped, one arm through her coat. "What?" She hadn't heard him. Or hadn't been paying attention. She spied her purse half hidden beneath the coffee table and snatched it up.

"It's my professional opinion that you need someone to talk to, Jess. Mental and emotional health is equally as important as physical health. If not more so. You've just experienced an incredible loss. I hope you're working through it with someone who can help."

It wasn't the first time that Jess had been told she needed counseling. And while she wasn't averse to the idea, she hadn't gotten around to setting up any appointments. "Thank you," she said, adjusting the phone so she could stick her other arm in the coat sleeve. "I'm not. But I will be."

"I'm glad to hear that. And Jess?"

"Yeah?"

"We're praying for you, Leslie and I. And I mean that very sincerely."

"Thanks, Peter."

There was a lump in her throat when she hung up, but Jess didn't have time to fall apart now. Taking the stairs two at a time, she rushed to Max's room and rapped lightly on the door with her knuckles.

"It's open," came the muffled reply.

"Hey." Jess stuck her head in, zipping up her coat with one quick snip. "I have to run out for a minute."

"Now?" Max looked up from the science textbook he had splayed open on his bed. A notebook rested on his knee and one hand clutched a black, felt-tipped pen. His favorite.

Jess felt a rush of affection for her prickly, brilliant son. "Yes, now. I won't be long."

"Where are you going?"

"Forgot something at school," Jess lied. "Gabe is asleep in my bed. Just comfort him if he wakes up, okay? Tell him I'll be home soon."

"Fine." Max's attention was already back on his textbook.

"I'll leave your door open so you can hear him if he gets up."

"Sure."

Evan's keys were heavy and unfamiliar in Jess's coat pocket as she pulled out of the driveway. Her key chain held exactly four keys: car, house, school, classroom. But his had always been a cacophony of jangling silver, each toothy wedge of metal biting back a little secret. Jess really had no idea why he needed so many keys, and she certainly didn't know what they were all for. But she was about to find out.

It took her four tries to find the key to the front door of his town house. It had a golden cast and seemed unnaturally bright. New. Jess hated it for a moment, detested this small, inanimate object that signified the distance between them, the steps he had taken to set up a life apart from her. But before she could be sucked under by regret,

Jess turned the handle and stepped over the threshold into Evan's apartment.

She had never been here before. In the driveway, yes, but not inside the town house where Evan had spent the last several months of his life. It was cold and stale and empty, skinny with loss. Lonely. Jess fumbled against the wall by the door, patting the wall in search of a switch and the promise of light.

When she finally found it, the pale wash of color didn't offer the respite she was hoping for. Jess was standing on a small square of tile just inside the front door. There was a bare hook on the wall beside her and a plastic tray for shoes that cradled a pair of lace-up work boots. The laces were frayed, the black soles rimmed white with salt from winters past. For some reason, the thought that they would never be used again, that Evan would never lace them up to head out and shovel the driveway in the blue predawn of a December morning, made Jess suddenly, furiously nauseous.

She lurched onto the carpet, trying to decipher where the bathroom would be in a two-story town house with a cookie-cutter layout. A narrow staircase rose into the darkness to her left, and to her right there was a cramped living room that opened

461

onto a galley kitchen. No sign of a bath-room, so Jess stumbled past a threadbare couch into the kitchen, where she stood heaving over the sink, fingers curled around the rim of the cold, stainless steel bowl.

This was why she hadn't come before. This was why she had avoided Evan's apart-ment like the plague, knowing that she could put it off because his lease was paid up through the year. Someday, she had told herself, believing that someday might never come. Maybe she could have a crew come in and clean everything out so that she didn't have to face it. Maybe her father would offer to do it for her. But now that she was here, she knew that could never happen. The space was hers to excavate.

The apartment was sad, but it bore traces of Evan like scars. A mug he loved had been turned upside down on the drying rack. It was a camper's mug, tin with a handle, green flecked with white. He had bought it for himself at an outdoors store, a hopeful purchase more than a practical one, because he wasn't afforded many opportunities to camp. How many years had Evan sipped coffee out of that mug? And draped over the back of one of the chairs huddled around a small round table was his favorite sweatshirt. It was thick and oatmeal colored, emblazoned with a Patagonia label on the chest, right above where his heart would be.

This place didn't smell like him, it didn't hold his essence, but there were hints of him everywhere, and when Jess's stomach finally stopped convulsing, she found herself wanting to touch everything. Maybe if she ran her fingers over the places he had been, the things he had touched, she'd find fragments of him still hiding. Waiting for her.

But that was foolishness.

Jess had come for a reason. She stuffed her feelings down deep and began to systematically search the small apartment. It had been too painful for her to come before, but now she pushed through those barbed emotions and forced herself into every room, every closet, every nook and cranny.

On the main floor there was a kitchen, living room, spare bedroom, and bathroom. Everything was neat and impersonal, secondhand or bought without regard for color or pattern or theme from the home goods section at Target. A striped comforter fought with curtains in a faded plaid, and the lone pillow on the narrow twin bed was tucked in a peach-colored pillowcase. Clearance rack finds, no doubt. Evan had always been frugal.

Jess assumed that the bedroom on the

main floor was for the boys when they spent the weekend. In the top drawer of the dresser she found a handful of extra clothes. Boxers and socks, a pair of pajama pants with emojis that were obviously for Gabe. If Jess knew her sons, Gabe slept in the bedroom (or with Evan) and Max took the couch. He had always been able to sleep anywhere, anytime. Still, the thought of her boys curled up wherever they could find room, nestled under dusty afghans or on sagging mattresses, made her heart constrict.

The bathroom was equally vacant. Beneath the sink was a stack of extra toilet paper rolls and a bottle of toilet bowl cleaner. Nothing more.

A thrill of urgency gripped Jessica, and she hurried up the shadowed staircase. It was even colder upstairs — if that was possible — and smaller than she imagined it would be. A tiny landing offered Jess two options: a door to the right and another to her left. A second bathroom was behind the door on the left, and that meant Evan's bedroom was the only room yet to explore in the dismal apartment. Jess found the light switch and illuminated a scene that closely resembled everything she had already observed.

The bed was topped with a comforter in an indistinct brown. Taupe or tan or beige. Jessica could never tell the difference and she was certain Evan couldn't either. But it was made, corners pulled tight and the hem an even foot above the floor. Under the window stood an old nightstand, thick with varnish and boasting turned legs that screamed 1980s. One lamp, one empty glass on a coaster, one dog-eared paperback. And against one wall there was a closet with bi-fold doors that were cracked open just an inch.

Jess started there, pulling back the hollow core doors to reveal a closet that smelled and looked exactly the same as it had for their entire married life. Evan arranged his shirts by color so that his wardrobe was a lopsided rainbow — it leaned heavily toward neutrals, with just a handful of primary colors thrown in. And the scent was pure Evan, the same cologne he had been wearing for years — sandalwood and cool water. Jess choked back a gasp, barely resisting the urge to bury her face in his polos and dress shirts, to inhale what little remained of her husband.

But Jess was also starting to feel a familiar disappointment. Evan's apartment was so organized and impersonal that there was simply no room for mystery. This was not a place where a riddle could be solved, and there wasn't even the barest hint of what Evan had been up to — why he had been absent at work and taking notes on female convicts and disappearing into the Minnesota wild on dark autumn nights. None of the things that Jessica had discovered made sense against the backdrop of his so-called home. No, this wasn't a home. This was a place to exist.

Jess swiped her palm against the carefully aligned shirts, mussing the fabric and scattering the hangers so that they were no longer a perfect inch apart. The shout of metal on metal was startling, and Jess fell back a little. But as she did, she realized that there was something crammed on the floor of the closet. Crouching down, she reached into the depths of the gloom and pulled out a gym bag.

As long as Jessica had known Evan, he was not the gym-going type. He ran occasionally, but mostly he went on long walks with her and cut the lawn with a push mower and chased his boys. He worked long hours on his feet and ate healthy and didn't smoke. At different times (usually January of each new year) they both claimed that they needed to put themselves first and get in shape, but besides halfhearted bursts of passion between the constant hum and press of a frantic day-to-day life, they never managed to carve out the time.

But when Jessica pulled back the zipper, there was a pair of new tennis shoes, gym shorts, and a couple of mesh-fabric T-shirts. Even soap on a rope in a container so it wouldn't make his clothes slimy, as well as a travel-sized shampoo. Evan was going to the gym. Regularly, it seemed. And according to the plastic card attached to the carabiner on the strap of the Adidas bag, he was a member at Eclipse Fitness. Below his printed name Jess read: OPEN 24 HOURS FOR ANYTIME WELLNESS.

A quick glance at her watch told Jessica it was past ten. But Max was home with Gabe, and if she remembered correctly, Eclipse was only a couple of miles away. A detour on the way home wouldn't hurt anything.

And maybe, just maybe, Evan had chosen to hide his secrets somewhere a little farther from home. Like in a nondescript gym locker.

River Han
New Message from Evan Chamberlain
October 12, 2018

River,
Thank you so much for the information you have provided and the time you have taken to talk to me. I am so grateful. I also appreciate the introduction to Francesca.

I have done as you requested. The name on the ID is Sam Nelson. Please tell Francesca I will be there next Friday. It seems unnecessarily clandestine to me, but you can tell her I promise that this conversation will be off the record.

Gratefully,
Evan

Evan Chamberlain
New Message from River Han
October 13, 2018

She'll be ready.

River

CHAPTER 24

Ariana G.

20, Caucasian, 2-year degree (secretarial)

Natural redhead, chin-length. Freckles,
* unnaturally blue eyes.*

Ex-boyfriend knows.

DUI/CW, 49m, 2yr pp

Jessica had never been to a twenty-four-hour gym before. But Eclipse Fitness was welcoming enough. The entire front of the building was bright with windows, and behind the frosted glass exercise machines were lined up like sentinels. They were empty now, or almost. A towel was thrown over a rowing machine near the end of one row, and at the back of the well-lit facility Jess could just make out a burly figure lifting weights. He seemed to be alone. But Jess wasn't about to be deterred.

The front door was locked, and there was no one behind the reception desk. Thankfully, Jessica had grabbed the carabiner with

Evan's tag, and when she held it beneath the magnetic pad near the door, it blinked green. The door clicked open.

Inside, Eclipse Fitness smelled exactly like Jess expected it to: of rubber and dryer sheets and old sweat. Music was blaring from speakers that dotted the ceiling, a playlist that was curated to stimulate and inspire if the throbbing, rhythmic bass line was any indication. The man at the back of the wide-open space didn't even glance up when Jess let in a draft of cold air. He probably appreciated it, considering the dark patch of damp that was spreading across the front of his tank top.

Jess shouldered her purse, grateful that no one was going to pepper her with questions but uncertain about where to start. From her vantage point near the door, there was no bank of lockers, no place at all, really, to hide. She wandered down the first row of equipment, away from the free weights and the mat where the lifter still huffed and puffed. She walked past the room where classes were held, toward the men's and women's locker rooms, and — jackpot! — two walls full of lockers.

They were just large enough to hold a duffel bag, a towel, an extra pair of shoes. Definitely big enough to hold a file. Jess realized she was holding her breath.

"Can I help you with something?"

Jess spun on her heel, surprised by the sound, and even more shocked when she saw the weight lifter standing behind her. He had draped a towel around his neck and he was using it to wipe his forehead as he studied her with narrowed eyes. Or maybe he was just exhausted, lids half-mast because he had pushed himself to the very brink.

"A locker," Jess said, summoning a fragile half smile. The man was wearing short shorts and a gray tank top that was black in all the places where he had sweat through. Jess wasn't short — five foot seven and then some in her winter boots — but he towered over her as if she were a child. "My husband is a member here and I'm looking for his locker."

Jess bit the inside of her lip as she waited to see how he would respond. It was late and she was painfully aware that they were alone — that the hallway where they stood was not visible from the parking lot or the street where any passerby could watch people working out as if they were animals behind glass in a zoo.

But the man shrugged and ambled past her on his way to the men's locker room.

"Good luck," he said. "I hope you know which one it is."

"Is there anyone here?" Jess called after him. "I mean, an employee?"

"Sometimes," he said over his shoulder. "Not always. Depends on the night." He pointed to a corner as he disappeared into the locker room, and Jess was left to follow the invisible line his finger had drawn. A camera was mounted near the ceiling. Of course. When she looked around, she realized they were everywhere.

Maybe the cameras should have given her pause, but Jess didn't care. She wasn't doing anything illegal. At least, she didn't think she was. Alone again in the hallway, Jess exhaled and hurried to the nearest bank of lockers. They were all numbered with three digits and fitted with a four-digit combination lock. Turning a slow circle, Jess realized there were dozens of them. Hundreds? How would she ever know which one was Evan's?

No doubt they were just assigned when a new member joined, but as Jessica walked with her knuckles trailing down one row, she discovered that several of the locks weren't latched.

What would Evan choose? Max's birth month and day? 5/24. Jess walked past the 200s, 300s, and 400s until she found the grid of lockers marked with a 5 as their first digit. Locker 524 was unlocked and empty. Dead end.

Gabe's birthdate was 4/13, but when Jess found locker 413, it was locked tight. She tried several different combinations (important dates and their house number and even 1234), but nothing worked.

It was impossible. Slumping against the metal wall, Jess knew the likelihood of finding the right locker and then thumbing in the right combination was next to none. There were countless possibilities, and she couldn't begin to channel the frame of mind Evan had been in when he picked the locker and set the combo. She would have to wait, come back tomorrow, and hope that Eclipse kept a comprehensive master list. Jess would have to explain that Evan wasn't coming back.

But as she pulled the zipper of her coat closed and palmed Evan's key card, she caught a glimpse of the back. Beneath a black line and a barcode there was the address of Eclipse Fitness. 555 Travers Lane, Auburn, Iowa.

555.

Could it be so simple? Or could Evan have known that when he walked into those woods in Minnesota there was a possibility he would never come back out? Jess thought of the book, the scrap of paper, the number scrawled in Evan's hand. It was their home phone number, and although she had assumed it was the map that led Deputy Mullen to her, maybe it was meant to chart something different altogether.

555-440-3686

The 555 was taken care of by virtue of the address, so Jess made her way to locker 440 — the next series of numbers in their phone number. It was eye-level, in the very middle of the wall. Nothing set it apart from the dull, dented doors around it, and the lock was the same black cylinder as all the others.

Jess held the lock in her fingers and tried to tamp down the emotion that ghosted up in her chest. It was hope or fear or anticipation, she couldn't tell. Maybe all of them. Maybe love, because she suddenly felt closer to Evan than she had in a very, very long time. If she was right, if she knew this, then she still knew him — even though she had spent the last several months of her life convinced that they had grown irrevocably apart. Perhaps the distance between them wasn't as great a void as she had believed it to be.

Jess turned each dial carefully, deliberately.

They clicked slowly beneath her fingers until the final number ticked into place: 3686.

The little silver loop snapped up and swung open.

Evan's backpack was nestled on Jessica's lap, wedged between the steering wheel and her puffy winter coat. It was crazy, she knew, but she couldn't stand the thought of putting it on the seat beside her. It had to remain in her possession, touching some part of her body, or she feared it might evaporate into thin air. Surely this was a dream. For a minute or so, as Jessica drove down darkened streets on her way home, she was fully convinced that she was sleeping in her bed, Gabe curled up beside her. She wanted answers so desperately that it only made sense she had fabricated an alternate reality in her subconscious. A reality where she wasn't paranoid and out of touch, where someone *had* broken into her house and Evan *was* involved in something she didn't understand — and maybe his death wasn't an accident after all.

What was wrong with her? Why couldn't she leave well enough alone, grieve her husband's loss, and try to get on with her life?

Because she was right. And the backpack proved it.

It was the only thing in the locker, a worn, navy canvas pack that Evan had carried for years. White threads crisscrossed the straps where her husband had, on several occasions, attached identification tags before he flew with it. He had a bad habit of ripping off the paper but leaving the tiny loops intact. Jess knew the bag was his the second she laid eyes on it.

In the hallway at Eclipse, she had quickly unzipped the main pocket. A brown accordion folder was inside. That was all Jessica needed to know.

The clock on her dashboard glowed 11:00 as Jess pulled into her driveway. It was later than she hoped to be, but there was nothing to be done for it. She was home now. Though the lights in the garage were on and the door to the house was cracked open. Jess didn't remember turning the lights on (the bulb over the garage door opener was enough) and she certainly didn't recall leaving the door open. She was a stickler for closed doors, especially when it was cold, and was forever chastising the boys for leaving them unlatched. *People do unusual things when they're stressed,* Jess decided. And in a hurry, uncertain, maybe a little obsessed.

She kicked off her shoes, let her coat fall to the floor, and slid the strap of Evan's backpack over one shoulder. Even in her own home she wouldn't let it out of her sight. The pack was light enough, easy to carry. Jess could take it with her to check on the boys — and then she would spread everything out on the kitchen table. Start to make sense of the last few months of her husband's life.

Deputy Mullen. He came to mind unbidden, but Jess knew the second she pictured his weathered face that she would have to call him. Just not quite yet.

The lights in Max's room were off, and Jess squinted in the darkness to try to make out his shape in the bed. A pile of blankets and books and a couple of pillows created a tangled landscape that made Jess roll her eyes. How could he sleep like that? But when she tiptoed to the edge of the bed and gently patted her hand against the various lumps, she found his leg rather easily. He was under there, head buried beneath a pillow and his science textbook digging into what she assumed was his hip. Max was out cold.

Jess's bedroom was equally dark, but her eyes had somewhat adjusted to the dimness, and the moonlight reflecting off all the snow bathed her bed in a wan glow. It was empty.

Comforter thrown back, white sheets exposed to the cool night air, no Gabe.

Jess felt the backpack slip from her shoulder. It hit the floor at the same moment her heart seemed to plummet to her feet. She could feel the fall, and it almost took her to her knees.

The bathroom. He had to be in the bathroom.

Jess rushed across the bedroom and flung the door to her en suite open. It was filled with shadows and decidedly empty — she knew that Gabe wasn't there even before she whipped back the shower curtain and poked her head inside the linen closet. "Gabe?" she whispered. And then, because it was ridiculous to try and hush her alarm, Jess shouted: "Gabe? Gabe!"

Turning on every light in her bedroom, Jess threw back her covers, looked in her closet, and dropped to the carpet to rummage under the bed. Nothing. Then she was up and running down the hall to his bedroom, still yelling his name. But Gabe's bedroom was as desolate and hollow as her own. His *PAW Patrol* comforter lay flat against his mattress, leaving no room for a stuffed animal beneath its smooth surface

— never mind a little boy. He wasn't in his closet, toy chest, or hiding in his curtains.

"What are you doing?" Max bumped into the doorframe of Gabe's room and leaned there, rubbing his eyes as he stifled a yawn.

"Where's Gabe?" Jess asked, her voice splintering on his name.

"In your bed."

Max turned, ostensibly to climb back into his own bed because his mother was being mental, but Jess caught him by the shoulders and twisted him around to face her. His hair was sticking up all over his head, his cheek already lined from the creases in his pillow. Max had always slept like the dead.

"He's not there," Jess said. "He's not in my bed. Where is he, Max?" She wanted to shake him a little, wake him up, but she restrained herself.

Her son's gaze sharpened as he caught a whiff of her panic. It was contagious. "He's got to be around here somewhere." But Max didn't sound convinced. Jess had been shouting his name, and Gabe hadn't emerged from wherever he was hiding. Their house wasn't that big, and from where they stood on the landing above the main floor, it would be easy to hear Jess's shouts. If he was in the kitchen or curled up on the couch in the living room, Gabe should have come running by now.

"Gabe!" Max's voice split the silence of the empty house, and Jess felt her self-control shudder. She was seconds away from losing it completely, from running through the house like a banshee or maybe crumpling to the floor in a sobbing puddle. She hadn't left the garage light on or the door open. Jess knew it.

Gabe was gone.

Max was already down the stairs and Jessica followed on legs like wet cement, heavy and soft and not nearly stable enough to support her frame, no matter how slight. She clung to the banister with two hands, and stayed standing by virtue of willpower and little more.

"He's not in the kitchen," Max said, racing back to her. "Not the pantry or the porch."

Jess felt a waft of cold air then, the breath of winter that Max had let into the house when he wrenched open the door to the porch and scanned the icy space. A tremor began at her center and rippled out until her hands were shaking. She clasped them together to stop the hysterical motion.

"Think," Jess said more to herself than to Max. "Where would he go?"

"What if . . ." But Max didn't finish. They

couldn't imagine the what-ifs or they might never summon the courage to go on.

"I'm calling the cops." Jess stumbled toward the kitchen, desperate for the telephone and the promise of help. She had never dialed 911 before, but the thought of doing so now was such a comfort she couldn't stop a moan from escaping her lips. How could Jess explain this? How could she help them understand that she was only gone for a little while, that Max was old enough to babysit, that this wasn't her fault? But it was. It was all her fault and she knew it.

It took Jessica three tries to press the on button on the handset, her fingers were vibrating so badly. She managed to key in the nine, but just as she was about to complete the call, Max shouted from the living room.

"Mom!" There was something about the way he said her name that made Jessica come running, phone still clutched in a death grip.

There, standing in his football pajama pants tucked into his winter boots, was Gabe. Jess sagged to the ground, knees hitting the hardwood with a sickening smack as she stretched out her arms. In an instant, Gabe was in them. But not before Jessica noticed the tear stains on his cheeks, the coat zipped up to his chin, a John Deere stocking cap that she didn't recognize crammed onto his head.

"Where were you?" Jess wanted to cry. She wanted to hold him at arm's length and make sure there wasn't a single scratch on him, not a hair out of place. And then she would demand to know where he had been. Why he had left the house on a snowy night in November. Where he had gone. Jess wanted to ground him from ever leaving the house again. At least until he was sixteen. Maybe twenty. But she couldn't say or do anything at all other than cling to him for dear life.

After a few moments he wiggled, pushing away from her so that he could look her in the eye. "Where were *you*?" Gabe asked.

Jess laughed, but it turned into a sob.

"We thought there must be some sort of mistake."

The sound of an unfamiliar voice snatched Jess's attention from her son. Standing in the entryway, just behind a very confused-looking Max, were her neighbors Harlan and Betty Henderson. Or Mr. Henderson and Betty, as Gabe liked to call them. They were retired farmers, well into their eighties but happy to garden the little plot they had cultivated in their backyard. Gabe had a deep and abiding love for Mr. Henderson, and had learned to prune the leaves from a tomato plant and when to pick green beans for peak flavor and tenderness by apprenticing under the older gentleman's watchful, wrinkled hand. The breast pocket of Mr. Henderson's shirt always held a couple of chocolates for Gabe, and their sweet, intergenerational friendship had been a source of great joy for Jessica over the years.

Now, her elderly neighbors looked concerned, and Jess realized that standing just behind the diminutive Betty was a police officer in uniform.

Jess pushed herself up, leaving one hand on Gabe's shoulder as she did so. "What happened?" she asked, swiping the heel of her hand across her cheek.

"You were gone," Gabe said at the same time that Mr. Henderson said, "I told her not to call the police."

Betty gave her husband a dark look, but it was diminished by the pink sleeping cap that she had forgotten to take off. She was dressed in a long, old-fashioned nightgown with a hem of eyelet lace, winter boots, and a Mack jacket that was so soft and worn it looked like it had been one of Mr. Henderson's favorites — forty years ago.

"Mrs. Chamberlain?" The cop stepped forward, hands on hips. He didn't offer to shake her hand or even introduce himself.

"Yes." Jessica rubbed a slow circle on Gabe's back. He tucked himself against her, snaking both arms around her waist as if to stake his claim. Or to stop her from ever leaving again. "I'm so sorry. I stepped out for a minute and Gabe must have woken up . . ."

"He came to our house," Mr. Henderson confirmed. "He said no one was home, but I knew that couldn't be true."

"It is true!" Gabe huffed. "Mom was gone and Max was gone and even the car was gone." He stuck out his chin, defiant. "I'm supposed to go to Mr. Henderson's and Betty's house."

"If there's a *fire.*" Max rolled his eyes. "Or an emergency."

"It *was* an emergency! You left me!"

"I was here," Max said. "In my room, sleeping. Like you were supposed to be."

"I looked for you!" Gabe shrieked.

"Not good enough."

"You did the right thing," Betty cut in, making a move toward Gabe. She seemed to think better of it and stopped, wringing her hands inside of her knit mittens instead. "You are always welcome at our house, Gabriel. I'm just glad this was all a misunder-standing."

Mr. Henderson and Betty accepted Gabe's enthusiastic good-bye hugs, deflected Jessica's thank-yous, and then slipped out the door to return to their own beds.

"I have just a few questions for you," the police officer said, lingering. He was impos-ing by virtue of his starched uniform and the gun holster at his hip, and Jess could feel Gabe stiffen beside her. This was so stressful for him, the sort of event that could send her son spinning off his axis for days at a time. Never mind that the officer had a kind face. The patch on his shoulder said Tunis, and Jess half expected there to be a pin underneath that proclaimed this his first year of service. He looked impossibly young, with a sprinkling of acne around his jawline and a red bump on his neck where it looked like he had nicked himself shaving. But Gabe didn't see any of those things. He saw the tall, intimidating frame, his thick billy club, radio, and gun.

"Of course." Jessica forced a tight-lipped smile. She squeezed Gabe's shoulder and gave him what she hoped was a fortifying look. "Boys, why don't you head upstairs? I'll be there in a minute."

Max crossed his arms and headed toward

the staircase, but when he reached the bottom, he waited for Gabe to catch up. As Jessica watched, her oldest unfurled his long arms and swept Gabe up into them, tossing his little brother over his shoulder like a sack of potatoes. It was "you scared me" and "I'm glad you're okay" and "I love you" all wrapped up in a little rough-housing. Gabe giggled all the way up the stairs, his anxiety at the presence of Officer Tunis forgotten. Jess had to swallow hard.

"I am so sorry," she said when the boys were gone. She held out her hands in apology, supplication. "Betty was right. This was all just a misunderstanding."

Officer Tunis had taken a notebook out of his pocket and he flipped it open, pen poised above the paper as he regarded Jessica gravely. He didn't crack a smile or do anything at all to ease her discomfort. "I'm a little fuzzy on the details," he said. "Was Gabriel home alone?"

"No!" Jess said. "Of course not. Max, my other son, was here. He's almost fourteen." She hoped the officer didn't ask when exactly Max's birthday was. The truth was, he had only recently turned thirteen.

"But Gabe said he couldn't find Max?"

"He was sleeping. He was buried under his blankets and he's impossible to wake

486

up . . . Gabe must have been confused. He must have panicked." Jess realized she was babbling, but she didn't care. Gabe was safe — that's all that mattered. She wanted Officer Tunis and his questions to disappear.

"And where were you tonight, Mrs. Chamberlain?"

"Eclipse Fitness," Jess said, surprised. She wasn't sure she wanted to tell him everything, but it was the truth. She didn't say any more.

"And has this ever happened before?"

"Excuse me?"

"Has Gabriel been left home alone?"

"He wasn't," Jess said, crossing her arms over her chest to stop them from shaking. "That's not what happened. And no. Never."

Officer Tunis nodded once then scribbled something in his notebook. Jess wanted to snatch it away from him and read what he had written about her. About her family. "Okay, then," he said, oblivious to or intentionally ignoring her distress. "I'd like your cell phone number in case I have any further questions."

Jess repeated it and he copied it down carefully, then snapped his notebook shut and slid it back into his pocket.

"Do you have to file a report?" Jess asked.

He nodded.

"What does that mean?"

"We have to record everything, ma'am."

"But —" Jess didn't finish. Instead, she stuck out her hand. Better to get him out of her house. Out of her life. "Thanks for your help. It was nice to meet you."

Officer Tunis shook her hand, but he didn't seem to think that meeting Jessica was very nice at all. Before he turned to let himself out the door, he gave Jess one last, lingering look. And he didn't appear to like what he saw.

CONVERSATION WITH FRANCESCA HOFFMAN
(October 19, 2018)

FRANCESCA HOFFMAN: IT'S SIMPLE, REALLY. THEIR JOB IS TO CONVINCE ANY PREGNANT IN- MATE TO GIVE HER BABY UP FOR ADOPTION.

EVAN: WHO'S "THEY"?

FRANCESCA: I HAVE SOME GUESSES, BUT I COULDN'T TELL YOU FOR SURE.

EVAN: HOW IS INFORMATION PASSED?

FRANCESCA: A BUSINESS CARD. INITIUM NOVUM ON ONE SIDE, PHONE NUMBER ON THE OTHER.

EVAN: IT'S A WHISPER NETWORK.

FRANCESCA: SURE.

EVAN: BUT WHY DO IT?

FRANCESCA: EMPLOYEES GET PAID BY REFERRALS.

EVAN: EMPLOYEES? HOW DOES THAT WORK?

FRANCESCA: MONEY IS DEPOSITED IN A BANK ACCOUNT. IT'S A NEST EGG FOR RELEASE. EVERYONE WANTS TO GET OUT, BUT IT'S HARDER THAN YOU'D THINK. ON THE OUTSIDE, I MEAN. MONEY HELPS.

EVAN: WHAT ABOUT THE BIRTH MOTHERS?

FRANCESCA: THEY'RE PAID, TOO. FIVE THOUSAND DOLLARS FREE AND CLEAR.

EVAN: ARE YOU SURE?

FRANCESCA: I DON'T KNOW. I'M NOT OUT, AM I?

CHAPTER 25

Francesca DJ
32, Latina, GED
Shoulder-length dark hair, blond tips. Heart
  tattoo on cheek.
No one knows.
MUR1, Life, 2yr 4m pp

Jessica slept fitfully, dozing when Gabe was in her arms and waking with a gasp when he wasn't. The warmth and weight of his limbs was soporific, and as long as she could feel his touch somewhere — fingers on her arm, leg thrown casually over hers, forehead to forehead on the pillow — she was okay. But then he'd roll away and Jess would feel his absence like a loss. In the morning, she was up well before her alarm clock, head cradled in her arm as she watched Gabe sleep.

His birth mother was right. Gabe was golden. Bronze cheeks and smooth, high forehead and eyes that sparkled nonstop.

Some people lit up when they smiled or laughed, but not Gabe. He was lit up all the time, shining from somewhere deep within, from some source that was as mysterious to Jessica as God himself. She reached out and brushed the plane of his cheekbone with her knuckles, so softly she was sure it wouldn't wake him, but the moment her skin grazed his face Gabe opened his eyes.

"Do we have school today?" he asked, as if he had been awake for much longer than a second or two.

Jess smiled. "Yes. Half a day. It'll be over in no time."

"And then Thanksgiving?"

"Well, that's tomorrow, but yes, we have Thanksgiving break."

Gabe whooped and did a frantic little dance that made the sheets billow around them. So Jess made a tent out of the blankets and let him burrow deep toward the foot of the bed. He was a diver, an explorer, a fox in its den. He was safe and contained and close enough to touch. Jess wished she could keep him that way for longer than a few minutes in the morning. She was no stranger to the effects of the passage of time. How quickly Max had distanced himself from her. He had gone from her little lap-sitting booklover to an independent teenager in the blink of an eye. And as much as Jess wanted to hold him near, keep him safe, she knew that Max — and Gabe — were stepping slowly but surely away from her every single day.

In the tranquil light of a new morning, a fresh start, it was tempting to just call in sick. Jess longed to skip school, but she knew that was impossible. It was cruel to even imagine. "How about a bath?" she said instead, hoping to lure Gabe out of bed. "We have time for bubbles."

Gabe untangled himself and practically fell to the floor in his hurry to hop in the tub.

While Gabe splashed contentedly, Jess got ready for the day. It was only a half day, so a few sprays of dry shampoo and a messy bun fit the bill. As she stuck bobby pins in to secure the knot, she heard the shower turn on in Max's bathroom. He was up too, and somehow the comforting sounds of her house in the morning were galvanizing. They could do this thing, survive one more day before relaxing into a break that would give them time to collect themselves. Jess felt like the bits of her life were scattered over the horizon, detritus in the aftermath of an explosion that left no corner untouched. They had some gathering to do.

Some mending. Jess hoped Evan's notes would help her make some sense out of it all.

In the drama of the night before, Jess had all but forgotten Evan's backpack. When she finally climbed the stairs well after midnight, Gabe was lying wide-eyed in her bed with the lights still on. She practically tripped over the pack, but her focus was on her son. Jess nudged it to the side with her foot and promised herself that she'd get to it later.

This afternoon. Tonight. The weekend. Evan had been gone for almost five weeks, but in many ways it felt like much longer than that. Jess felt like a stranger in her own life and she longed for a bit of stability. A firm foundation on which she could stand and begin to rebuild her world. She was ready for answers. For the chance to step beyond the fog of grief and confusion that made everything feel so uncertain.

Jess was grateful that her youngest loved baths because his post-bath routine was one of his least favorite activities. Though she loved massaging the lotion into his lean, taffy limbs, he shifted and complained and sometimes escaped her ministrations before she could finish. But today he stood quietly.

"I was scared," he said suddenly.

"What?" Jessica's eyes flicked to his. They

were big and brown and just a touch sad.

"When I woke up last night. I thought you left me."

"Oh, honey." Jess pulled him close, ignoring the cream that had not yet been absorbed into his skin. It would leave streaks on her shirt, but she didn't care. "Baby, I am so, so sorry. I would never leave you."

"Daddy left."

Those two words tore at Jessica's heart, shredding what was left of it. "That was different," she managed. "Daddy didn't leave you on purpose. He couldn't help it."

"What if you can't help it?"

What if? Wasn't that exactly what Jess feared most? What if she couldn't protect her sons? The thought twisted in her mind, making her irrational. She'd bite and claw and kick and steal for her kids. Move heaven and earth. Commit murder if she had to. She'd *stay.* Whatever it took.

"I'm not going anywhere," Jess said, holding him at arm's length so he could see the truth written all over her face.

"Promise?"

"I promise."

But that wasn't good enough for Gabe. "Pinky swear?" he asked, holding out his skinny little pinky.

Jess wrapped his tiny finger in her own

and squeezed tight. "Pinky swear," she said, sealing a covenant in her own flesh and blood.

Blessedly, school was a whirlwind of teenagers and bells and noise and the traditional Thanksgiving assembly, which included the band and orchestra and a cleverly written but poorly executed skit about gratitude. The morning passed in a blur. Jess wasn't sure she had ever been so thankful to turn off the light and close the door to her classroom when it was all over. Her emotion was fitting, she supposed, for the holiday, but it felt like much more than a short break from school. It felt like a new beginning.

Which was why she wasn't alarmed when she pulled into her driveway and saw Meredith's car parked there. Jess waved to her friend, who sat in the driver's seat as she watched them pull up. The car was still on, a cloud of exhaust pouring out of the tailpipe like a lit cigarette. Jess's smile tilted just a bit when she realized that there was someone with Meredith. A man whose face was turned away from the passenger-side window. But from what she could see of the back of his head, he didn't look like Todd.

"Why is Auntie Mer here?" Gabe asked,

pressing both his hands against the window as he stared. The glass was filthy with his fingerprints. "And who's with her?"

"I don't know." Jess put the car in park and turned it off. She had texted Meredith earlier, written three short words followed by a nondescript period. *I found it.* Mer knew exactly what she was talking about. Maybe she wanted to help Jess sift through Evan's file, try to put the pieces of the puzzle together. But Jess couldn't say that to her boys. "Maybe she wants to talk to me about our Thanksgiving plans tomorrow."

"We're going to Todd and Meredith's?" Max pulled up his nose, and Jess was surprised by his obvious reluctance.

"What do you mean?" Jess yanked her door open, continuing the conversation with her eldest over the hood of the car. "You love the Bailey family."

Max shrugged and he opened the back door for Gabe. The little boy scrambled out and raced toward the house, eager for a lunch of "anything goes" like Jess had promised on the way home. But Max didn't follow his brother. He stood next to the car, waiting for Meredith and her mystery guest to appear around the corner of the garage. They could hear her engine stop and then a single car door slam shut.

"Hey, Mer." Jess smiled when Meredith walked around the corner. "Good timing. Would you like a cup of tea or something?"

But the set of Meredith's face made the world feel suddenly unstable. She acknowledged Max's presence with an indecipherable look and a curt nod, then turned her attention to Jess. "We need to talk," she said. "In private."

Jess felt goose bumps prickle her skin. "Max," she said, "why don't you go help your brother with lunch?"

"He can make himself a peanut butter sandwich." Max folded his arms across his chest and glared at Meredith.

Where was this animosity coming from? But Jess didn't have the luxury of wondering right now. She needed obedience. "Go," she said sternly. "Now."

Max turned his glower on Jess, but she held his gaze and in the end he gave in. Stalking from the garage, he shot Meredith one last black look and slammed the door to the house behind him.

"Sorry," Jess said. "I don't know what that was all about."

But Meredith didn't seem to have registered Max's rude outburst. She took a few steps toward Jess and stopped. One more step and then she checked herself and thrust her hands deep into the pockets of her wrap coat. Meredith sighed hard through her nose, lips puckered and turned down at the edges as if she was trying not to cry. "I've never had to do this to a friend before."

"What?" Jess sank back, her heart crumbling to pieces in her chest. It skipped a beat. Two. "What are you talking about? What's going on?"

Suddenly Jess caught sight of the man who had been in the car with Meredith. He had slipped quietly from the vehicle and was standing in the shadows just outside the garage door. He wasn't wearing his uniform, but Jess immediately recognized his baby face. It was Officer Tunis.

"What are you doing here?" Jess's voice squeaked. She hated herself a little for being so transparent, so clearly moved. What did she have to be afraid of? But even as she berated herself, she realized that Meredith was talking.

". . . not for long," she was saying. "We'll get this all straightened out in no time."

"Wait. We'll get what straightened out?"

"Custody," Meredith said, and the word landed at Jessica's feet like a bomb.

"Custody? Of my kids? What are you talking about, Meredith?"

Jess watched as her friend cupped her face

in her hands for a moment. Her shoulders shook like she was sobbing. But when she looked up again, Meredith's gaze was almost cold. She walked quickly to where Jessica was standing and took her by the shoulders. "You have to trust me," Meredith said. "How long have we been friends? Years. It's been years and years. You're like a sister to me. I hate having to do this, but I have no choice."

"You always have a choice," Jess whispered, shrugging off Meredith's heavy hands.

"It's my job, Jessica. What would you have me do? Would you rather have someone else standing here? Someone who thinks you're a terrible, neglectful parent and that your kids are better off without you?"

"Do you think that?" Jess could hardly utter the words.

"Of course not. But I don't get to decide. You want the official spiel?" Meredith clamped her mouth shut, her jaw working as she wrestled with herself. "Fine. Someone called the hotline. You're being investigated for neglecting your children. I'm supposed to interview them each separately right now, make them take off their clothes so that I can inspect their bodies for bruises or cuts or burns."

A sob escaped Jessica's lips, but Meredith kept going.

"It's my job to look in your cabinets and determine whether or not you have nutritious food in your home. I'll walk through your house in search of unsafe living conditions, for filth or rats or bugs."

Jess gasped for air, sucking in the cold afternoon so that it chilled her to the bone. She could feel herself go numb from the inside out, a hollow, terrible feeling that cemented her to the ground where she stood. She was petrified, frozen in time by shock and hurt and horror that was too great to bear. "No," she said, but the word was formless and empty, a futile cry.

"I'm not going to do those things," Meredith said softly, leaning toward Jessica so that Officer Tunis would not hear. "I pulled some strings. I'm not going to make your boys take off their clothes for me."

Jess whimpered.

"But I have to walk through and do a home inspection. Everything has to be documented. You understand that, don't you?"

No, Jess did not understand. She didn't understand anything anymore, including how her heart could possibly keep beating inside of her chest. This was a nightmare. It was worse than a nightmare.

"And instead of assigning Max and Gabe to a Safe Families home in the area," Meredith continued, "I've been given clearance to place them with your dad and Anna."

When her legs started to give, Meredith wrapped her arms around Jessica's waist and frog-walked her over to the low bench where the boys sometimes sat to pull on their boots. Jess fell on it, knocking her head against the wall so hard that she had to drop her forehead in her hands to stop the world from spinning. But maybe it was careening anyway, detonating like a charge so that when the dust settled there would be nothing left. A void.

"You can't do this," Jess said into her palms. Even she didn't know who she was talking to. Meredith, Officer Tunis.

"I wish I didn't have to," Meredith said. She crouched down and took Jessica's hands in her own. "Look at me. Come on, Jess. Look at me."

Jessica somehow managed to force her eyes to meet Meredith's gaze. There were a few dots of mascara on her friend's cheeks, evidence that Meredith had been rubbing her eyes recently. Crying? Jess hoped so. She hoped that her life and her family were worth a few of Meredith's tears. More than that. Jess hoped that this was killing her best friend, that she felt as gutted as Jessica did. *Fight for me,* she wanted to say. And wasn't that what she had been aching for all along? For someone to fight for her, to come kicking and screaming, soul bared and heart in hand, ready to battle. But maybe Jessica would have to fight for herself.

"Do it," Jess bit the words. "Get it over with."

"Listen to me — we'll work it out." Meredith squeezed her hands, tried to give her a slight smile.

Jess wanted to slap her.

"I promise. They'll be back in no time."

But Jess barely heard her. She had made a promise to Gabe and she wasn't about to break it. Her boys could go to her father's house. But in a day, maybe two, she'd have them back. She would do anything it took. Anything.

Dear Jessica,
I feel like Hansel, leaving crumbs all along the way. It's ridiculous, I know.

I'm overreacting. But I know too much to believe this is as innocent as it looks, and I don't want to leave you without an explanation.

Love makes a family, and sometimes love tears a family apart.

I'm so sorry I let it tear apart ours.

CHAPTER 26

It was a nightmare. A slow-motion tragedy that played out in tears and disbelief, followed by fury and then absolute mayhem. Jess stayed in the garage while Meredith went into the house to talk to the boys. It was Jessica's decision: she knew that everything raw and real in her would revolt if she saw her sons' reactions to Meredith's grim news. Jess didn't trust herself. What would she do? Throw things or scream like a madwoman or barricade them all in a bedroom and refuse to ever come out? She would make everything a hundred times worse. And they would never let her get away with it. Meredith hadn't brought Officer Tunis along because they were friends.

The policeman stood with his back against the garage wall and scuffed the floor with his foot. The toe of his shoe made a half-moon pattern in the dust on the smooth concrete, and he took care to get the arc of the curved line just right. He didn't want to be there, Jess could tell. He snuck her the occasional sympathetic glance, but it made her skin crawl to think that he pitied her. So she ignored him, or tried to, and wrung her hands together in her lap. Jess hadn't moved from the bench — she didn't trust her legs to support her — so she did the only thing she could think to do: she prayed while a storm was raging inside her heart and inside her house. It was less a prayer than a guttural cry, a groan, a sob, a lament.

The shouts were audible even with the garage door closed. A thump, two, and then the sound of running feet. Each sound tore through Jessica as easily as a bullet and left her spent and bleeding.

On her fingers, Jess cataloged the people who she suspected of making the call that would rip her children from her. Cara Tisdale. Jake Holmes. Mr. Henderson and Betty. Who else had seen or heard or suspected something they deemed irresponsible? Cody De Jager. Caitlyn Wilson. Anthony Bartels. Officer Tunis. A gym full of people as she carried a crying Gabe out. Jess had run out of fingers, and Meredith had once told her that all it took was a single accusation. Just one. Once Child Protective Services was involved, there was protocol that had to be followed. An investigation. Possibly drug testing, a mental health evaluation, interviews with neighbors and friends, teachers and relatives who may have witnessed something incriminating. They would sink their teeth into her past, eager to lay bare the bones of her every mistake and misstep. It all counted — and it would all count against her.

When the door to the garage finally opened and Meredith stepped out, it was to wave at Officer Tunis in surrender. His hands were jammed deep in the pockets of his coat and he gave her a hunch-shouldered shrug as if to say, "Who, me?"

"I'm going to need your help," Meredith said.

He hesitated for a moment, and in those spare seconds Jessica pulled herself to her feet. "I'll do it," she said, staggering toward the door.

"No, I don't think that's a good idea." Meredith shook her head, her expression unreadable. Was there sorrow there? Regret? Jess sure hoped so. But she wasn't about to let Meredith stop her either way.

Jess didn't slow down when she reached the place where Meredith stood with her arms spread wide across the doorframe. It looked as if she would block her, refuse to let Jess pass, but when it became clear that Jessica would run her down to get through, Meredith sighed and fell back.

"Please don't make this harder than it already is," Meredith said.

Jess didn't acknowledge her.

The house seemed so different Jess had to blink to get her bearings. How could a few minutes change her life so irrevocably? But she already knew that the entire world could be transformed in the span of a second. Nothing would ever be the same. Even if she got her boys back tomorrow, nothing could erase the fact that today they had been taken away. She couldn't stop it. She couldn't protect them.

"Mommy?" Gabe was curled up on the couch, knees pulled tight to his chest and enveloped completely by Max's long arms. Both boys looked stricken, and Gabe's eyes were puffy and red from crying. Max had been crying, too; Jess could see it in the flush of his damp cheeks.

Jess crossed the space between them and sunk to her knees in front of the couch. The boys untangled themselves and knotted their arms and legs around Jess so she didn't know where she stopped and they began. Someone's fingers kneaded her back desperately, and though the pinch was painful, Jess welcomed it. They were so solid, so real, so immediately in her arms. Gabe's neck was salty where she kissed it and Max was sharp with the scent of cheap deodorant spray and the acrid tang of fear. He seemed to be a small, frightened little boy instead of the almost-man he was.

"Meredith is going to take you to Grandpa and Anna's house," Jess whispered against Max's hair. She kissed his head where she could reach it. The curve of his ear, his jaw. He didn't pull away.

"Why?"

"Because. Just for a little while."

"How long?" Gabe squeezed her extra hard, lacing his fingers together around her neck as if he could permanently attach himself to her. As if clinging tightly could stop Meredith and Officer Tunis from taking him away.

"I don't know, bug. Not long, okay?"

"But you promised."

Jess felt all the air leave her in a panicked squeak. She was spiraling, dread pulling her under by centrifugal force. Surely she would drown.

"It's a mistake," Max said. He pulled back a little but kept one hand on Jessica's shoulder and the other arm wrapped tight around Gabe. "This is all just a misunderstanding."

"Max is right." Jess fixed her eldest with a look of such love and wonder his eyes filled and his lip quivered. She dug deep and somehow managed to give him a small, brave smile. "We'll get this figured out in no time, okay? And in the meantime, you get to spend Thanksgiving with Grandpa."

"And Anna," Gabe added.

"Yes, and Anna. She makes the best pumpkin pie, remember?"

It was pumpkin pie made from a can of puree and generic frozen crust, but Anna topped it with a swirl of homemade cinnamon whipped cream. Gabe loved it, and his expression brightened a little at the thought. It was devastating to see him smile in spite of his swollen nose and bloodshot eyes. Jess pressed a quick, hard kiss to his forehead and stood before she lost her resolve.

"They're ready," Jess told Meredith.

Meredith was standing in the living room, watching Jessica say her good-byes. Something in Jess severed at the sight of her best friend watching her writhe in pain, and when Meredith moved in for a hug, Jessica stepped away.

"Not now," Jess said. What she meant was: "Not ever again." She knew it was part of Meredith's job. That her friend was trying to spare her the indignity of having a stranger come into her house and tear her life to shreds. Jess's mind skittered to the thought of a stranger taking her children into their bedrooms and inspecting their bodies for injuries that she allegedly may have inflicted. When Jess had smoothed lotion on Gabe's dewy skin just that morning, she had run her fingers over shallow cuts on his skinny legs, a couple bruises, and a dark, black thumbprint on his hip. Who knew where or how children amassed their many minor wounds? Running and jumping and losing track of the corners of tables and doorways and walls. Jess had never once lifted a hand in anger toward her children. She hardly believed in time-outs, never mind spankings. But she knew what each mark would look like to someone searching for evidence of wrongdoing.

Maybe Meredith deserved a thank-you for sparing Jessica from all that. But Jess couldn't bring herself to do it. She couldn't even look at Meredith.

Jess gave her boys one last, crushing hug. First Gabe, who clung to her and then decided he would ask Grandpa to take them out for supper. After all, it was almost like Friday since they didn't have school in the morning.

Max's emotions were a little more complicated. "I hate her," he whispered into Jessica's neck.

She shushed him, cradling the back of his head. "She's just doing her job."

Max started to say something but seemed to think better of it.

"Text me anytime," Jess murmured. "Call me. Day or night. I'll answer it. I promise."

Max took a shuddering breath, squeezed Jess one last time, and then left without a backward glance. He took Gabe by the hand and the two of them disappeared into the garage.

"Get out," Jess whispered, staring at the spot where her boys had been only seconds before.

"Jess?" Meredith took a tentative step toward her.

"I said get out."

Out of the corner of her eye, Jess could see Meredith hang her head. Then she sighed heavily and walked slowly to the door. When she shut it behind her, it barely clicked. The house was shrouded in silence. It wasn't until Jess saw Meredith's car drive past the front window that she let herself go. She was a marionette whose strings had been cut, a body who exhaled its soul. Her scream was enough to splinter glass.

■ ■ ■ ■

Jess refused to answer her phone. It rang and rang, sometimes with barely a pause between cycles, so she turned off the ringer. Her father texted instead.

I want to come over but have been advised to keep my distance. At least for today. I'm so sorry, honey.

Jess didn't respond. She didn't want to see anyone anyway.

We'll work this out, I promise.

A few minutes later her phone vibrated again: *I've talked to a lawyer.*

She thought: *You are a lawyer.*

Henry read her mind. *We need someone who's not related. I called the best. We're meeting on Friday.*

Friday? But it was only Wednesday afternoon. Jess couldn't stand the thought of not seeing her boys for two days. Then a horrifying realization gripped her. Jess wasn't sure if she was even *allowed* to see Max and Gabe. The earth gave way and she was falling again, sobbing again.

Jess had so many questions, and she knew that Meredith could answer them, but there was no way she was calling up her former best friend to chat about the fact that the formidable Mrs. Bailey had just forcibly removed her sons. She seethed with anger instead. Considered how justified she would be in smashing Meredith's face in, then cried until she felt wrung out and dehydrated. Tried to ignore her father's texts.

At some point she grabbed her phone and googled "how to get my kids back." She regretted it almost immediately.

Be honest with yourself, was the first piece of advice. Jess was supposed to get real, evaluate what went wrong, and set up a plan to ensure that the same mistakes would never be made again. *My husband died,* Jess wanted to shout. *In a horrific, unexpected way, and I'm not convinced it was an accident. My life has been a giant extenuating circumstance . . .* But there was no one to listen, and the rest of the steps were equally baffling and unspeakable. *Acquire legal counsel, request a psychological evaluation, be patient and compliant.* Jess didn't want to do any of those things. But the final imperative made her heart turn to stone in her chest: *Don't give anyone a reason to think you're unfit to parent.* What did that even mean? She just wanted her kids back.

But curling up the edges of her shock and grief was the specter of shame. Was Jess a bad mother? Had she neglected her children? There was hardly a day that went by that she wasn't racked with guilt over some parental blunder. She yelled when she should whisper and disciplined when what her boys really needed was her time and attention. Maybe she deserved this. And maybe her boys deserved a better life than she could provide for them. The thought made her physically sick.

By the time the sun had dipped below the edge of the horizon and the living room was bathed in an eerie purple light, Jess was hollow as a shell. She was broken, empty. And when someone knocked softly on her door, she didn't get up to answer it or even move from where she was cowering on the couch.

"Jess?" Meredith's voice preceded her presence and Jessica felt herself recoil.

"Go away," she croaked, her voice hoarse from disuse and weeping.

"No." Meredith appeared in the doorway to the mudroom. She leaned against the jamb and slipped off her shoes. Instead of coming any closer, though, she lingered in the entryway. Just the fact that she was hesitating caused Jess to look up. Meredith usually moved with purpose, with intent. She had little room for regret, and even in this terrible thing Jess expected her to be firm. Justified. But Meredith looked anything but sure of the role she had played in breaking Jessica's heart. Her hair was tangled, the part crooked and drawn at an unflattering angle for her face. And she was wearing a thick sweatshirt several sizes too big. It made her seem lumpy and heavier than she was — a look that Meredith would never usually step out of the house in. She didn't look like herself. And she wasn't acting like herself, either.

"I don't want you here." Jess glared, pretending that seeing Meredith so disheveled didn't prick her. She didn't want to love her, but their friendship wasn't going to be so easily discarded. "I can't talk to you right now."

"I didn't have a choice." Meredith spread out her arms in supplication or surrender, Jessica couldn't tell. "You don't understand. And I can't explain it to you. But you have to believe that I was trying to protect you. All I've ever tried to do is protect you."

Jess almost rolled her eyes at the melodrama. As if this were some cosmic battle between good and evil. As though Meredith alone held the keys to all that was fair and right, Jessica's would-be savior in tortoiseshell glasses and turquoise fingernail polish.

Meredith gave her a long, sad look, then seemed to decide something. She ignored

Jess's protests as she marched past her into the kitchen.

"What the hell do you think you're doing?" Jess cried. But she didn't have the energy to follow Meredith or try to kick her out of the house. Jess's legs were twisted beneath her, tingling and heavy with lack of circulation. She felt anchored to the couch, bound by anguish and the hopeless understanding that her reasons for living were just outside of her reach.

A few minutes later, Meredith appeared with two glasses. Tennessee Honey, by the look of the golden molasses shine. Wordlessly, Meredith handed one glass to Jessica and brought the other to her lips. She drank it quickly, finishing it with a bit of a grimace and a harsh exhale.

Jess thought for just a second that she shouldn't be drinking, but grief evaporated that fragile sentiment. Tipping the glass, she swallowed the shot Meredith had given her. It was bitter when it should have been sweet, but Jess decided that anything mixed with misery would be.

Meredith reached for her empty glass and took them both back into the kitchen. Jess could hear the water running and the snap of the dish towel as Meredith cleaned the glasses. A cupboard door opened and closed. Then a few long, quiet minutes passed before Meredith finally came back into the living room. She sat on the edge of the chair next to the couch.

"I'm sorry," she said simply. "I never wanted it to be this way. I never meant to hurt you."

"Is that supposed to make me feel better?"

Meredith held her gaze. "I know it doesn't. But I also need you to know that I'm only doing what I have to do."

"You could have fought for me."

"Believe me, I did. Sometimes we have to do hard things, Jessica. Things that other people might not understand."

"You're supposed to be my best friend." Jess was horrified when her voice came out a whimper. It was pathetic, laced with self-pity. But she couldn't help it. Jess brushed fresh tears from her eyes, disappointed to discover that she hadn't, in fact, cried every last drop, and furious that she was wasting what was left on Meredith.

"I tried," Meredith said. "I really did."

"I want you to go."

Meredith nodded and took a deep breath. She used her thumb to smooth away a tear that had left a trail down her own cheek. So she did have feelings. This *did* affect her.

But Meredith shattered the delicate moment by asking: "Where is it, Jess?"

"Where is what?"

"Evan's file."

In the terror of the afternoon, Jess had forgotten all about Evan's file. It had been overshadowed by her suddenly much bigger, much more devastating problem. "I don't know, Mer." Jess heard herself call Meredith by her nickname. It was fingernails on a chalkboard, a sudden, painful screech. She tried again, but her words felt slow and thick in her mouth. "Why do you care?"

Meredith clapped her hands on her knees and stood up. "I'll find it, Jessica. You might as well just tell me where it is."

"They're mine," Jess said, but she wasn't sure anymore if she was talking about Evan's papers or her boys. "You can't take them away from me."

Meredith disappeared from her line of sight, and Jessica unwound her legs to follow. They were unusually dense, dull and unresponsive though she kept telling herself: *Go!* When her feet finally flopped to the floor, Jess was engulfed in a wave of nausea. The room spun, blurring at the edges until she squeezed her eyes shut and leaned forward on her bent arms, forehead in her clammy hands.

When was the last time she had eaten? Jess couldn't recall. And she remembered now why she shouldn't have had that drink. Her doctor had said Xanax and alcohol should never mix. How much was in the glass Meredith had given her? Jess couldn't remember, and she also couldn't remember if she had taken her antianxiety meds that morning or not.

It was impossible to know how much time had passed when Meredith came back into the living room. Jess's head felt too big for her neck, but she tipped up her chin to catch a glimpse of her former friend. Meredith seemed cool and collected, unaffected by the alcohol that they had consumed together. She checked the watch on her wrist, then righted the navy backpack that was slipping off one shoulder. The backpack felt important somehow, but Jess couldn't think of why.

"What are you doing?" The words didn't sound right in Jess's ears, and they didn't feel right, either. They were too big, too complicated, so fuzzy with uncertainty they stuck like burrs to her tongue.

"You're so sad, Jess." Meredith spoke softly, her expression one of pure sorrow.

Jess nodded, unable to speak. She was sad.

So sad. She wanted to lay her head down and go to sleep. Perhaps when she woke up, this would all be a bad dream, a nightmare posing as reality that she could shed as easily as her pajamas. Jess would roll over and Evan would be there, watching her. He'd touch her face. And down the hallway, her boys would be waking up. Opening their eyes in a home where they were safe and loved. Together.

But Meredith wasn't going to let Jess sleep. She was sliding her hands under Jessica's arms. Crouching in a weight lifter's stance, Meredith took a deep breath. Then she heaved Jessica to her feet and slung one of Jess's arms around her shoulders.

"Where are we going?" Jess tried to mumble. It came out jumbled and wrong, and Meredith didn't answer.

They were a few agonized steps away from the couch when Jess's phone buzzed against the coffee table. Somewhere in the back of her mind she felt a compulsion to answer, a need to break free from Meredith's powerful embrace and grab her phone, but her limbs refused to comply. They shuffled along in the direction of the door, ignoring the muted hum. She didn't want to go, but Jess's leaden legs stomped their slow progress obediently.

"Come on," Meredith said, heaving Jessica over the lip of the door and down the single step into the garage. Jess's feet were heavy, but they complied.

Jess wanted to say, "Where are we going?" but the question floated just out of reach. She lunged for it, and felt the ground swim up to meet her as Meredith spat out a curse.

"Stop it!" Meredith almost fell but managed to right them both. She yanked Jess close and propelled her the remaining distance. Gasping a little, she propped Jess against the car and wrenched open the driver's-side door. "Here we go," she said.

Somehow this was comforting to Jess. Someone else had taken control and she didn't have to worry about it anymore. Jess wasn't even sure what it was. But if Jess listened closely, she could almost make out the sound of someone screaming. *No. No, no, no . . .* She closed her eyes and tried to still herself but was interrupted by Meredith wrapping both arms around her middle and picking her up. Jess was only a few inches off the ground, but her limbs flopped like a rag doll, and it took Meredith three tries to get her into the driver's seat.

The task accomplished, Meredith sighed heavily and lifted Jess's legs one at a time until they were also in the car. Then she reached over and turned the ignition. The car revved to life.

"I wish you wouldn't have done this," Meredith said. She took Jessica by the chin and looked deep into her eyes. Tears were streaming down her cheeks, but Jess couldn't imagine why. "I wish you could understand that the needs of the many outweigh the needs of the few."

Well that was interesting, wasn't it? Jess knew she should be focusing on something else, but she recognized that line. That sentiment. She had taught it before. In the far reaches of her conscious she dug and came up with names like winter bulbs. Shakespeare, Thoreau, Poe. She discarded them all. Austen? No. When it finally landed in her palm, real and solid and true, she smiled a little: Dickens. Jess tried to say it, to tell Meredith that she knew what she was talking about.

But Meredith wasn't paying attention to her anymore. As Jess watched, her friend lowered the driver's-side window a couple of inches and then shut the car door. She let herself out of the garage without a backward glance.

BEFORE

"Hop in," Meredith said. "I can take you somewhere."

Getting in the car with her was the last thing Evan wanted to do, but a quick glance over his shoulder at the ruined LeSabre assured him he had no choice. She wouldn't leave him anyway. Not now.

Evan heaved a sigh and yanked the door open, climbing into the passenger seat with a sense of dread. He didn't realize until he was halfway into the vehicle that there was another person in the car. A man was in the backseat, his face in the shadows. "Who's this?" Evan asked, his hand still on the door and one foot firmly planted on the gravel road. He could still run. Slam the door and sprint to the cover of the trees. But that was ridiculous.

"A friend," Meredith said noncommittally. "Don't you have a bag or something? Do you need to get anything from your car?"

The question was innocent, but her intent was far from it. She was pretending, but there was no reason to.

Evan gave her a long look. Meredith's face was tinted blue from the dashboard lights, but she was still lovely. Hair shiny, lipstick in place. Her mouth was the red of a rose about to turn, but maybe it was just a trick of the shadows and his own grim imagination. She was almost regal in her wrap coat, and the creamy wool drawn sharp against the line of her jaw gave her a queenly bearing. Meredith certainly considered herself above the law.

"I don't have anything with me," Evan said, holding up his empty hands. "And just so you know, Jessica has no idea what's going on."

"Get in the car, Evan." The man in the backseat had a voice like warm honey, rich and syrupy. "You're bleeding. You need help."

"I know who you are," Evan said. He felt brazen, suddenly indomitable. He had put the pieces of the puzzle together, and here was his final proof. *James Rosenburg.*

The man leaned forward and offered his hand over the backseat. He was wearing a gold Rolex and his skin was unnaturally tan for a cold October night. "You should have been a detective, Dr. Chamberlain."

Evan shook his hand reluctantly, but it was an entirely ordinary handshake. If he had been expecting James to crush the fine bones of his hand like some cartoon villain, he was disappointed. In truth, James's smile seemed genuine, his concern sincere. "Shut the door," James said, sitting back.

What choice did he have? Besides, now that he was half-seated, Evan wasn't sure that he could stand up again. His head was throbbing, his hand trembling just a little where it rested on the handle. Evan slid the rest of the way into the passenger seat and closed the door behind him. "Clearly you've been following me," he said, pulling the seat belt over his chest and struggling to find the buckle. He found he couldn't focus on two things at once — the seat belt and the predicament he was in — so he held his tongue until the belt finally clicked. Finally. "Maybe you can answer a few questions I still have."

"Oh?" Meredith put the car in drive and pulled away. She flicked her eyes in his direction as if a mere glance could help her discern the truth from lies. A small smile played at the corner of her mouth. "I'm not sure what you're talking about."

Evan ignored her. "Francesca told me how

it works."

Meredith turned to stone beside him. She held her shoulders straight, her chin slightly lifted as she crawled down the gravel road. Pebbles pinged the underside of the car, but she gave no indication that this bothered her. Only her hands on the steering wheel and the way they were pinched white told Evan that he had struck a nerve.

"The business card. The promise of money. Five thousand dollars, Mer. I think a court would consider that a bribe." Evan watched her closely, waiting for a reaction that never came.

Instead of exploding, Meredith gave him a pitying look. "Adoptive parents are allowed to pay for the medical, legal, and counseling expenses of the birth mother. You did."

"Through the agency," Evan said. "The legal way. Is that where you come in?" He swiveled in his seat and glared at James. The strange man was cloaked in shadow, but Evan could make out the hard line of his jaw, the spread of his broad shoulders. Maybe he played football in high school. Or maybe he was just big boned. Either way, he cut an intimidating silhouette. Evan had no doubt it did him many favors in court — although he seemed harmless enough, he looked threatening.

"Here," James said, ignoring Evan's question and handing him a wad of tissue from somewhere in the recess of the backseat. "You're still bleeding."

Evan took the tissue and pressed it to his forehead. Almost immediately it was wet, but when he tried to pull it away, a thin layer stuck to his skin. He blinked hard, trying to clear his head, to get his bearings. It didn't help. He felt tired, confused, and he found himself staring at the lump of bloody paper in his palm. For a moment he didn't know what to do with it, but then he rolled down the window and threw it out. The blast of cold air was invigorating.

"The money," he said, more to himself than to Meredith and the mysterious James. "Those women — they did it for the money." He was losing what little composure he had. What Meredith and James were doing was unbelievable. Sick and twisted and a perversion of a system that he had believed in heart and soul. "A private account? A lump-sum deposit? From what I can tell, it's a Class C felony. And just the tip of the iceberg."

Evan wasn't sure how far they had come, but when Meredith swung her car down a field driveway and lumbered off into the woods, he realized that they were really and truly in the middle of nowhere. There were no more headlights, no distant glow of the farmsteads that dotted the Minnesota landscape. It was so dark Evan could feel the weight of the night press down on them. Meredith put the car in park and swiveled to face him.

"What do you think you know, Evan?" It was James, from the backseat, and he was talking so quietly Evan should've turned around. But he couldn't. His head hurt too much and he was afraid he might throw up again. But he knew the answer to the question. Everything. *I know everything.*

Evan didn't have anything to lose. It wasn't like Meredith was going to kill him for what he had discovered, dump his body, and go on as if nothing had ever happened. Meredith was cunning, but she wasn't a sociopath. She had a heart. Larger than most, actually. He had seen it at work many times over the years. Meredith cared deeply about the birth moms she worked with, the kids, the families. She loved his wife, his children. She was passionate and tenacious and loyal. And clearly appallingly misguided. Evan hated what this would do to her. To her family.

And James was in a suit, for heaven's sake.

Evan couldn't turn around, but now that he thought about it, he knew that the man was wearing a dark suit coat with a pale shirt beneath. A tie. He had glasses and hair that was blond or white or gray. James Rosenburg was a lawyer. A professional, a mere man, just like Evan.

"Leave it alone," Evan said, and wasn't aware that he had said it aloud until James laughed.

"Leave what alone?"

"That's what your secretary told me when I called your office. I said I had some questions about a woman named River Han and the son she gave up for adoption."

"Good advice. How did you find me?"

"They're putting it all together," Evan said quietly. "The women you've used. Francesca filled in the missing pieces."

Surely Meredith and James already knew that. How else had *they* found *him*? Eagle Ridge Women's Prison was hours from quaint Auburn, Iowa, and it was ludicrous to believe that the two of them had just randomly happened upon him on a gravel road in south central Minnesota. They had been following him. And wasn't that exactly what he had been afraid of all along? That this thing was bigger than he could imagine. That there were powerful forces at work.

It's why he dyed his hair and wore strange clothes and sold his car. Evan wanted to step out of his own skin, to shed himself and any connection that might link his family to everything he was learning. Clearly his efforts were in vain.

Evan realized that Meredith and James had probably talked to Francesca before he did. When he started investigating, he had realized that his path would converge with whoever was pulling the strings behind this unethical operation, but he hadn't believed it would be his wife's best friend until the moment she rolled down her car window. He had his suspicions, but he had hoped they were unfounded.

"Tell me." Meredith sounded as if someone had a belt around her throat, but her face was calm and impassive.

"I know you've been buying babies."

She blew a hard breath through her nose and jerked away from him. "You couldn't be more wrong."

But Evan kept going. "So far I've found twenty-five women spread over four states. They all tell the same story. A pregnancy, a prison sentence. What's a convict supposed to do with a baby? But then one day someone catches her alone. The whisper network tests the waters, and if she's open to the possibility, she's given a business card. Name on one side, number on the other. Simple. Unobtrusive."

Meredith stared out the windshield and refused to acknowledge his words. So Evan kept going. "Initium Novum. I had to look it up. Latin for 'New Beginning.' " He laughed a little in spite of himself, but it made him instantly nauseous. He pressed a hand to his stomach. "I have to give you credit for that. It's clever, concise. A bit mysterious. I'm sure it made those moms feel like they were doing something noble."

"They were." James sounded unreasonably calm. Evan's blood was starting to boil in his veins, throb in his temples and forehead and fingertips. "What they did was honorable. It was right. What do you think happens to babies whose mothers are in prison?"

Evan ignored him. "What you've been doing is coercion, Mer. It's buying and selling human beings."

"That's not true!" She screamed the words, her sudden outburst fragmenting the quiet of the night. "Have you seen what I've seen? Have you removed a child from a home where he has been neglected? Abused? There are people in this world who treat kids like animals, Evan. Worse. I know you know that."

"I do," he conceded. He reached for Meredith, touched her arm gently. "And it defies explanation. It makes me crazy. I feel like I could kill anyone who would hurt a child with my bare hands."

"So you understand." James leaned forward, catching Evan's gaze. "I represented a little boy who was chained, Evan. Chained up like a dog. A girl who was sold by her father. She was four."

Evan's stomach lurched and it had nothing to do with the car accident and his pounding head.

"We're saving these kids, Evan." Meredith reached for his hand and held it. "You get that, right?"

For a moment, Evan wasn't sure what he believed. He thought of Gabe, shackles on his little wrists, maybe a purpling bruise on his perfect cheek. Bile rose in the back of his throat and he had to cough it down. But as he swallowed, Evan thought of LaShonna. Pretty, earnest girl with love in her eyes. She wasn't the sort of monster they were portraying. LaShonna broke the mold. Maybe they all did.

"No," he said, almost against his own will.

"Some people aren't fit to parent," James

said. "I'd say convicts are at the top of the list."

"It's not your choice to make," Evan managed. "LaShonna hung herself because she lost her baby."

"I didn't know she was Gabe's birth mom." Meredith reached for Evan's hand and squeezed it too hard. "I swear, if I would have known, things would have been different."

Evan yanked away. "But what about the other women? What about their kids? What about the questions they'll have as they grow, and the families that could have been a part of their lives?"

"They're better off," Meredith insisted. "You get that, right? We're giving them a stable, loving family. No drug abuse or domestic violence or pedophiles. No unsecured guns in the home or sketchy boyfriends or mean drunks." Meredith's chest was heaving, her cheeks flushed with color.

What had she seen? Evan could only begin to imagine. He had treated cigarette burns on a toddler and set the broken radius of a boy who was equal parts terrified and angry when he insisted he had fallen down the stairs. Once, Evan had witnessed a three-month-old with retinal hemorrhaging. Shaken baby syndrome. It made him so upset he punched the concrete wall of the hospital where he had been working and fractured his own hand. But Meredith was a social worker. She saw this sort of abuse — and things Evan was sure he couldn't even begin to imagine — day in and day out. How did that affect a person? Evan wasn't surprised that she wanted to *do* something about it. Something that stepped beyond the carefully drawn laws, the rules that meant everyone was innocent until proven guilty. In the time it took to determine culpability, a child's life could be forever changed. Or snuffed out.

"I get it. I really do. But you don't know that those kids are better off being placed with an adoptive family."

"I do," she said, her eyes flashing as they caught the light blinking from the dashboard.

Evan put his forehead in his hand, forgetting for a second that it was sticky with blood. He pulled his palm away, slick and warm again, and wiped it on his pants. It was a lose-lose situation and he knew it. Maybe Meredith and James were right. Maybe making these mothers an offer they couldn't refuse was the right thing to do. He thought of his son, of the little boy who, if he had stayed with his birth mother, would have been shuffled to relatives or foster care during her incarceration. No father, no stability. A ward of the state when his mother hung herself with a sheet. What would Gabe's life have been if he weren't their boy? It made his heart ache.

And yet. Meredith and James were trying to play God.

"I can't let you keep doing this," Evan said. "It ends tonight."

Meredith was quiet for a long moment, and when Evan looked up, she was staring out the windshield into the black night. "Get out," she said softly.

"Excuse me?"

"I said: get out."

Evan grunted. "You're kidding, right? I have no idea where we are."

"You heard the lady," James said. "You have legs. You can walk."

"This is insane."

"Get out now!" Meredith shouted, hitting the steering wheel with each syllable.

"Okay." Evan put up his hands. "Okay." He found the door handle and wrenched it open. Tendrils of cold air licked his hands, his face. Fine. He could walk.

For the first time in hours he regretted leaving everything behind in his motel room. He had carefully reviewed the visitor information for the women's prison and knew that he couldn't take much inside. What he did take was subject to inspection. And since he wasn't about to let an officer thumb through his file or scroll through his phone, he left the Motor Inn with nothing but a fake ID in his back pocket. The name, Sam Nelson (an unremarkable, place-filler of a name), matched the one Francesca had written on her approved-visitors list. After he used it, he threw it in the Dumpster behind a gas station on the edge of town. His name — his real name — wasn't linked to any of this. But it soon would be.

Evan stepped out of Meredith's car empty-handed. But before he cut himself off from her and James completely, he leaned in and said, "We'll work this out, okay?"

She didn't respond, so Evan eased the door shut. It sealed with a muted thud and he was left standing in the cold.

Evan looked at the sky, searching for the moon and some indication of which direction he was facing. But clouds had blown in heavy and low, bursting with moisture that laced the air with the scent of coming rain. He would have to just start walking, hope he hit a road or a farmhouse eventually.

It was a lonely feeling, setting off in the dark. But all at once Evan remembered that he wasn't entirely alone. Tucked in his pocket was a scrap of paper. A number that identified the coordinates home.

Max had scribbled the phone number on a piece of paper for Gabe one weekend when the boys were staying at his town house. Evan's bachelor pad was bare bones, not exactly the kind of place where you could easily find a notepad. It wasn't Max's fault that he grabbed the only thing he could find. But when Evan had realized what it was — what Max had used — he lost it.

"Do you have any idea what this is?" He waved the paper in front of Max's nose. It bore the page number and a portion of the title, a procession of digits in Max's messy hand. It was just a fragment of the story that Evan hoped to someday share with his youngest son.

"A corner of a page," Max scoffed. "So what? Gabe is supposed to have his phone number memorized by Monday, so I wrote it down for him. What's the big deal?"

Evan didn't mean to explain, but suddenly it was tumbling out. Not all of it, just the bits about LaShonna. About who she was and why she mattered. And the thing was, Max understood. He got it. It meant something to him, too.

"Write the number down on a different piece of paper," Evan told Max. "Look in the recycle bin." He intended to tape it back into the book, to mend what had been broken. But instead, he ended up tucking the book in Gabe's backpack for later and keeping the torn piece. He carried it around, a talisman of sorts. A reminder of where he was from and the assurance that his family was just a phone call away. He didn't even remember when he started using the numbers as his own personal code. A promise that things would be the way they once had been. Better.

Touching the scrap of paper in his pocket, Evan imagined finding his way back to his motel room. Calling Jess. What would he say? He wasn't sure. But he suddenly longed to hear the sound of her voice, even if all she said to him was: "Hello."

When Meredith turned her headlights on, Evan was bathed in a sudden spotlight. He raised his hand to shield his eyes from the unexpected glare. Maybe she had an attack of conscience. A change of heart.

But he never had the chance to turn around.

CHAPTER 27

"Real courage is when you know you're licked before you begin, but you begin anyway and see it through no matter what."
— Atticus Finch,
To Kill a Mockingbird

When Jess woke, her throat was dry and scratchy, aching. Something was in her mouth, her nose. She tried to open her eyes, but they felt glued shut. Raising her hand took every ounce of her concentration, and as she did so, something began to beep. It sounded angry, insistent.

And then there was a voice. "She's awake!"

The sound of feet pounding the floor, a shuffle, an alarm that rang long and was silenced.

"Jessica," someone said. "Jessica, can you hear me?"

She could feel someone leaning over her, the presence of a body close enough to touch. But Jess was swimming away again, adrift on a current that was warm and hypnotic. Comforting. Someone was calling her name. They were too far away, so distant from where she was floating. Jess gave herself over to the pull of gravity, but for just an instant a barb of worry lodged itself in her chest. There was something she had to do — she just couldn't remember what it was. Someone needed her? It didn't matter. Jess wiggled herself free of the small, sharp hook and let herself go. She slept.

Evan was there.

And Jessica was twenty-one years old again, slim and lovely and fit from long runs and deep sleep and the gorgeous flush of youth. It was the night she first laid eyes on Evan; Jess knew it because she could feel the promise of him shimmering beneath her skin.

Her senior year of college she took a job as a waitress at the country club, and on weekends she wore a short black skirt and a white blouse and carried trays of hors d'oeuvres between men in perfectly tailored suits and women in dresses she could only dream of wearing. The women ignored her.

The men smiled, taking a caviar and crème fraîche tartlet with a wink. But not Evan.

He was out of place in a sea of black, tall and unkempt with a mop of hair in desperate need of a trim. He needed a shave, too, but none of that occurred to Jess. It was impossible not to love him just a bit because he seemed so wholly unconcerned with the desperate posturing happening all around him.

Jess balanced her tray and wandered toward the entrance where a banner had been hung announcing that the event was a fund-raiser for the children's hospital. She had worked everything from PTA meetings to wine-and-canvas nights for stay-at-home moms, and the truth was they all felt the same. But in a room filled with social climbers, Evan stood out. Jess watched him as she wove between clusters of beautiful people, fascinated by his casual disdain. By his chinos and polo shirt, his shoes that were scuffed, the laces frayed at the ends.

There was a gentleman in a motorized wheelchair and an expensive suit, and Evan spent the entire evening at his side, cultivating a friendship that would later sustain him through the rest of med school and his residency until his best friend would pass away at the painfully unfair age of twenty-eight.

Of course, Jess couldn't know any of those things when she offered Evan and Raymond a thin slice of baguette spread with pink pepper goat cheese. Raymond accepted, Evan declined. But Raymond looked at Jess knowingly, at the way her gaze lingered on Evan just a heartbeat too long, and grinned.

On their first date, Evan saw a woman slip on the ice in a parking lot they were driving past. He turned the car around and found her on her knees, blood spilling down her temples and onto the frozen ground where it coagulated almost immediately. They waited with her — Jess holding her hand and Evan pressing a dusty car blanket against the back of her head — until the ambulance came.

There was the neighbor boy who lived next door to their first apartment. Evan fed him prepackaged fruit cups and cheese sticks and chocolate milk in individual-sized serving boxes that didn't need to be refrigerated — all foods that he and Jessica never ate, but that he started to keep in their pantry when he realized that Alonso was always, *always* hungry.

Cody De Jager was skin and bones and brown fingernails, and he broke Evan's heart in two. Jess had resisted their unlikely friendship, but Evan saw something in that broken boy that no one else could see. "He's a lost cause," Jess argued. "He needs another chance," Evan insisted. In the end, they were both right. Cody was a little boy trapped in a man's body, a wounded soul who simply couldn't get past the hurt of a childhood that loomed tragic and large as a mountain. But Evan had taken him by the hand anyway, had made him believe, if only for a while, that he was worth the fight.

Evan looked at them all and saw things that no one else could see.

"You never saw me," Jess whispered. She didn't know she was crying until a tear slipped right off her chin.

"Oh, Jess."

Evan's hands were warm when they cupped her face, and Jess wondered at how she could feel him. He was gone — she knew that. Evan Chamberlain had died, and maybe she had too? Somehow it didn't matter, because she was here and she could feel him and it was enough. Their life together was a breath of wind, a hint on her skin, and Jess found that she could remember everything. *Everything.* First kiss. Wedding day. Max's birth. Evan had laughed and cried and dropped the video camera on the floor and shattered it. There was no footage of those first minutes when Max lay wailing on Jess's bare chest. But it didn't matter. She knew it all by heart.

And here he was.

Evan ran his thumb over her lips. He said, "I always saw you."

"No you didn't."

"You just didn't need me the way that they did."

She closed her eyes. "You're wrong."

"No. You're the strong one, Jessica Chamberlain. You always have been."

"I'm not."

"You're the strongest person I've ever known."

She was there.

Jessica couldn't see her face, and every time she reached out to catch the edge of her coat, the woman was gone again. Folded into the shadows of this place where Jess found herself sifting memories like sand. But Jess knew who she was.

LaShonna Tate. Gabriel's birth mom.

If her name had been a wound, it was healing now. A scar that would always remind Jessica of what she had been given — and what Gabe had lost. Because even before Evan died, Gabe's life had been marked by deep loss. Jessica knew that now. She could still feel the moment Max's warm, writhing body had been placed on her chest. The curl of his fist like a chrysalis about to unfold, the pink flush of his translucent skin. He was a part of her, fresh from her own body, a fragment of her soul that fell to earth and was now blinking, unseeing, at the familiar sound of her voice. It was supernatural, miraculous somehow. But LaShonna's arms had been the first to cradle Gabe. Her voice. The scent of her warm skin against his. She was a part of him.

It was something that Gabe couldn't understand right now, but Jess saw it engraved in the palms of her sweet son's hands. He was two people, caught between what might have been and what would be. And Jess hadn't given him space to live in that reality. To hold in tension the truth that he had two mothers, and they both were worthy of his love.

"I'm sorry," Jess called around the corner, running now. Stumbling. "I didn't know."

No answer.

"I was selfish," she cried.

LaShonna was silent.

"It can't be undone," Jess whispered. "But I love him."

I know.

"He needs me."

And if it was a dream or a hallucination or something entirely mystical, Jess believed she heard someone say: *Go.*

Three days.

Jessica lingered in a coma for three days, though Henry and Anna told Gabriel that Mommy was very tired and needed a good, long rest. When he visited, he crawled into the hospital bed with her and traced the line of the IV as it snaked up her arm. Gabe kissed her cheek when no one was looking.

"Wake up," he whispered.

And one day, Jess did.

Afterward, when she was sitting up in bed, propped on pillows and surrounded by balloons and bouquets of flowers and stacks of books and magazines and cutouts of newspaper articles that mentioned her by name, Henry told her everything. He explained in fits and starts between Jessica's sudden, frequent naps that she had lost three full days of her life. And while she was sleeping, the world had changed.

"It's good to see you awake," Deputy Mullen said when he came to visit her. He refused to sit in the chair that turned into a bed, and leaned instead against the wall with his hands dug deep in his pockets. Jess didn't know him well, but she knew this was his stance, as much a part of him as the slightly bulbous nose on his face. It was comforting somehow, to have him nearby doing exactly what he was supposed to do.

"It's good to be awake." Jess tried out a smile, the muscles in her face still tingling from a cocktail of medications and disuse. It worked. Mullen smiled back.

"They gave me the full rundown. Xanax, whiskey, carbon monoxide poisoning . . . What were you trying to do? Kill yourself?"

Jess felt her smile fade.

"Sorry, too soon." Mullen heaved a sigh and pulled a stool from the corner of the hospital room, rolling it close to the bed. He perched on the padded seat and reached for Jess's hand where it lay on top of the starched, white sheet. "I'm sorry I let this happen."

"It's not your fault," Jess protested, but he shushed her with a quick shake of his head.

"I should have listened to you. We should have pushed harder. Seized Evan's computer, gone through his town house, anything. Everything."

"You were following protocol. I didn't even know what he was up to." Jess wiggled her fingers a little inside of the warm paw of his hand, but Mullen held on tighter.

"We should have looked into the Minnesota connection more. Eagle Ridge was less than sixty miles from Elmwood Park. When we discovered Evan's file with all those convictions, we should have pressed it more."

"You told me you looked into Eagle Ridge," Jess said.

"We did. But there were so many inconsistencies. We didn't dig hard enough." Mullen passed a hand over his jaw and sighed. "I failed you."

"Don't be ridiculous."

"That's where he was, you know. Eagle Ridge, I mean. That night, before he died."

Jess both wanted to know and didn't. She wasn't sure how much she could take. In the end she asked, "What do you mean?"

"He was interviewing an inmate. Trying to figure out the truth behind Initium Novum."

Jess's head ached. It felt too heavy for her neck, but she didn't want to lie back against the pillow and stop Mullen from talking. It happened all the time these days. She drifted off midconversation and woke up in an empty room. "I'm not sure I understand," she said, forcing herself to focus.

"Communication between Meredith and

the inmates she was working with was done primarily through word of mouth. A not-so-sophisticated whisper network." Mullen's eyes narrowed as Jess blinked along, but he kept talking. "When Evan made plans to visit Eagle Ridge, they leaked. That's how Meredith knew he was going there."

"It doesn't seem real," Jess said.

"We're still conducting interviews and will be for a long time. No one wants to talk about it." Deputy Mullen squeezed her hand one last time and let go. "He's really a hero, you know. Without him, I'm not sure we would have ever realized what was happening."

Jess knew, but she was still trying to get her head around exactly what that meant. She knew the facts. At least some of them — the ones she could remember and piece together from her conversations with her father and now Deputy Mullen. Jess had been scratching at the surface, uncovering the truth one tenacious scrape at a time. But the whole picture was still a little blurry.

Meredith quit Promise Adoption because she couldn't stomach watching another birth mother change her mind at the last minute and decide to parent her baby. It had happened one too many times amid circumstances that Meredith knew would be devastating for the child — and she had spent the early part of her social work career intervening in situations that had gone horribly wrong. She had witnessed altogether too many hurt kids. Too many *dead* kids. When one of the potential birth moms that Meredith was working with was sent to prison, she realized that she might be able to do something about an epidemic of child neglect, abuse, and endangerment.

Her relationship with James Rosenburg was entirely an accident. He was presenting a clear-cut child abuse case in a hearing, and Meredith was called in as an expert witness. The case was dismissed after a long day of testimony, and they both watched as a little girl was released into the custody of a father they knew would someday kill her. They ended up in a nearby bar, drinking at first to numb the shock and then because they were so damn *angry*. Maybe the things they admitted wouldn't have been confessed in the light of day or without the aid of alcohol. But the perfect combination of vodka and fury revealed commonalities they couldn't have predicted, and they realized that maybe there was something they could *do*.

Five thousand dollars rolled nicely into adoption agency fees, and offering a gift to birth mothers who followed through with the adoption didn't seem like a bribe at all. It seemed just and fair, a small token of appreciation for making a choice that was best for all involved. Never mind that it was coercion. That it was its own form of human trafficking. Meredith had done everything in her power to ensure that the women who were given this choice really had no choice at all. And the adoptive families had absolutely no idea what was going on.

They weren't the only ones in the dark. Meredith didn't know that James was padding the books, charging the families more than he let on and pocketing the money himself. For Meredith, it was all about principles. For James, money played a starring role — at least, after he realized he could play the part of Robin Hood and benefit from it too. It was what caused him to step out of the back of Meredith's car and lift his shotgun to his shoulder. She knew that he had the gun on the floor by his feet, but she swore that it was for intimidation purposes only. To make Evan believe that they were serious.

It chilled Jessica to the bone. What they had done was more than just manipulative. It was calculating. Cold. Meredith's cunning in pressuring women at their weakest, most vulnerable moments was horrifying. And when Jess was alone, at night in the hospital when her kids were asleep at Grandpa and Anna's house and the nurses had left her to rest, she couldn't sleep. The trajectory of Meredith's life, the path that her decisions had set her on, had flung her so far out into space it was hard to reconcile the woman Jessica knew with the person who had crushed up a spoonful of Xanax and stirred it into a shot of whiskey for Jess to drink, and then put her best friend in a car to make it look like suicide.

It was insane.

But at the heart of Meredith's twisted logic was a desire to help and protect. To ensure that as many children as possible were given a chance at a beautiful life. A new beginning.

Heaven help her, but Jess got that.

That sort of love, that fierce, aggressive, relentless love was the same thing that she felt for her own kids. Hadn't she said as much? Jess would do anything — *anything* — for her boys.

"What's going to happen to her?" Jess didn't mean to speak out loud, but suddenly Deputy Mullen was patting her knee beneath the sheet.

"You will never have to see her again. I

guarantee it."

How could Jess begin to explain the way that made her feel? Safe and grateful and vindicated. But also betrayed. And so, so sad. What about Todd? What about Amanda and Jayden? Those sweet girls that Jess had watched grow from little girls into young women. Her heart ached at the pain they must be feeling. She knew that right now they probably hated her. Or at the very least, that they were very confused. In so much pain. But Jess hoped that someday she might be able to wrap her arms around them. To tell them that she loved them still.

"What about all those families? And the women . . ." Jess's father had sat with her one afternoon and explained that LaShonna Tate, Gabe's birth mom, had been among the women Meredith exploited. She'd been pushed into a corner, compelled by a mixture of need and guilt and intimidation to give up her second baby. It was strange to have a connection with this woman — her son's mysterious first mom — but Jess knew what it was like to lose a child. She could close her eyes and feel the ache of empty arms. Jess and LaShonna were bound together in a sisterhood of grief.

I wish I could have known her. The thought came unbidden, but Jess didn't shove it away. She embraced it, a hope that would never bloom.

"It's complicated," Deputy Mullen said. "Evan made it easy for us by keeping careful notes. And we finally deciphered those last letters and numbers. He was referring to gestation and, in some cases, how far each woman was postpartum."

Postpartum. Was it too late for them?

Mullen anticipated her question. "Many of the women we've contacted *wanted* to give their babies up for adoption. The money Meredith paid them was certainly a bonus, but they would have done it anyway."

"And the rest?"

"They can't have their kids back." Mullen rubbed the stubble on his jaw and gave Jess a melancholy smile. "That's not how it works."

Jess pinched her eyes shut, squeezing the bridge of her nose with her fingers. Her whole body was hot, the headache a raw, throbbing thing that made her feel flayed wide open. These sweats, the sudden pain, weren't uncommon these days. But she knew that this ache was closely linked to a broken heart and unshed tears, not the naloxone they had used to reverse the effects of the Xanax Meredith had given her.

"You need to rest. I should go," Deputy

Mullen said. But as he stood, there was a scuffle in the hallway and a crash as Jessica's hospital room door burst open.

"Mom!" Gabe came careening into the room followed by Max and, a moment later, Henry. Jess didn't have a chance to greet them as Gabe launched himself onto the foot of her bed. The ventilator was gone and the oxygen cannula, so the only thing Jess had to worry about was her IV. But she didn't care. She threw her arms around her baby, catheter and headache be damned.

Holding him was the sweetest thing in all the world, and Jess was overwhelmed that she was allowed to do it at all. When Meredith came and removed Max and Gabe from her custody, Jess had wondered if she'd ever see her boys again. But it turned out Meredith had been lying even about that. No one had called the child help hotline. From the very beginning, Meredith herself had planted doubts in Jessica's mind. She'd manipulated her fear and feelings of inadequacy, and when she believed that Jess posed a real threat, Meredith had lied to Officer Tunis and Henry and Jessica, too. She wasn't sure she could ever forgive Meredith for that.

"Hey, bug." Jess hated it that her voice was hoarse — especially because it seemed to bother Gabe that she didn't sound like herself. But she was getting stronger in every way, and today Gabe grinned when she spoke.

"You sound like you!"

"I do?"

"Better," Max said, putting one hand on his hip as he regarded her. "You should really do something with this, though." He waved his fingers in front of his face.

"Thanks a lot."

"It's the man of the hour," Deputy Mullen said, reaching for Max. For a moment it looked like they would shake hands, but then Mullen pulled Max in for a hug. "You're a hero."

"I wouldn't say that," Max demurred, but he couldn't hide the smile that tugged at the corner of his mouth.

Jess had heard the story a half dozen times, but she didn't think she would ever tire of it. She was alive because of her son. Because he was stubborn and tenacious and brave.

"I need to hear this straight from the horse's mouth," Mullen said. "Tell me how you knew your mom was in trouble."

Max lifted one shoulder, trying to appear nonchalant. But what he had done was remarkable. He had seen things no one else noticed. "When Meredith and that cop drove us to Grandpa and Anna's house, her purse was on the seat between them. It was open and I could see a book inside."

"How'd you know it was your journal?"

Max gave Mullen a withering look. A look that said: *How could I* not *know?*

"Wait," Jess cut in. "Why did Meredith want Max's journal?"

"We believe she was looking for any evidence that Evan might have left behind," Mullen explained. "James Rosenburg was named in Max's diary."

"It's not a diary," Max said, tugging the cuff of his sleeve.

"Definitely not a diary," Deputy Mullen confirmed. "Brilliant, actually, that you paid such close attention to detail. Names are important. Go on."

Max stalled for a moment but found his footing. "So I knew she had been in our house. She was the one who had taken my journal. And then when I tried to call mom and she didn't answer, I knew something was wrong. She always answers her phone when I call. She promised."

"He kept trying to tell me," Henry said, cupping his hand on Max's shoulder. "But I wouldn't listen. We were all upset. Gabe was crying."

"Was not!" Gabe called from his spot on the bed beside Jess.

Henry ignored him. "So Max snuck out and stole my car."

"I didn't steal it; I borrowed it."

But Henry was clearly bursting with pride. No justification necessary. And why shouldn't he be? Max wasn't fourteen, but that hadn't stopped Evan from taking him driving on gravel roads and in parking lots. He knew how to drive. And though Max was neither legal nor the best driver on the road, he pulled into the Chamberlains' driveway as the garage filled with exhaust. And as soon as he opened the door he knew. He dialed 911 from the house phone, and while he waited for the ambulance to arrive, he shut off the car and opened all the garage doors. Then he held Jessica's hand until they came and took her away.

The paramedics were so preoccupied with Jessica they left Max behind when they squealed off, sirens blaring. So Max found Jess's phone on the coffee table in the living room and made two calls. One to Henry, and the other to a contact he found in Jessica's address book: Deputy Mullen.

Meredith was a mess when they questioned her, and the backpack she had taken from the Chamberlains' house was still in the backseat of her car. Evan had laid everything out as meticulously as a medical chart, every scrap of evidence was carefully ordered and cross-referenced so that putting together the pieces was almost like reading a novel. And suddenly, his strange file with the color-coded Post-it Notes made sense. Through Facebook and private conversations and word of mouth, he had identified twenty-five women from four different prisons who had used Initium Novum to place their babies with adoptive families. He was building a case.

"You'd make a great detective someday," Deputy Mullen told Max. His mouth was quirked in a half smile, but his eyes were serious.

"I didn't do anything." Max shrugged. "I didn't figure anything out. I just thought that my mom might be in trouble."

"Don't diminish it," Mullen said, leveling a finger at him. Then he slapped his hand against his thigh. "I almost forgot!" He grabbed his coat off the end of the bed and patted the pockets until he found what he was looking for: a flat, silver box. He held it out for Jessica.

"What is this?" she asked, taking it from him. It was polished nickel, about the size of a postcard and an inch deep. When she shook it, it made a dull, knocking sound. Something was inside.

"It was in Evan's accordion file," Mullen told her. "There's a tiny padlock. We could break it open, but we thought we'd ask you first. I don't suppose you have the key?"

Jess shook her head, but as she did so an errant thought fell loose. "Yes," she said, surprising herself. "I think I do!"

Max fetched her purse, which had been hanging on a hook in the small hospital room closet. There, inside the zippered coin pocket of her wallet, Jess found the key.

"This is from Evan's office," she said, holding it up. "I didn't know what it was for, but maybe . . . ?" Jess let the sentence hang as she tried the key in the little padlock. It fit. A half turn and the lock popped open. Jess slid the cover back.

"What's inside?" Gabe asked, leaning into her lap as she shook out the contents on the bed.

There were five pictures in all, each one frayed at the corners and dotted with a tiny hole at the top. A tack, no doubt. Perhaps they had been attached to a bulletin board or stuck to a bedroom wall. Jess had no idea how Evan had gotten them, but when she saw them, she understood why he wanted to keep them safe.

She was lovely. Dark hair and big brown eyes. She had a dimple in one cheek when she smiled, and slightly uneven, very white teeth. The way her eyebrows arched and made her look perpetually happy was endearing. And so was the way she threw her head back when she laughed.

"Who is that?" Gabe asked, holding one photo close.

Jess brushed her lips against his forehead and closed her eyes. She had absolutely no doubt about who was in the pictures. The resemblance was impossible to miss. "That," she whispered against his soft skin, "is your birth mom."

AFTER

"You plan on stopping in Rapid City tonight, right?" Henry lifted the last suitcase into the trunk of the car and shut it firmly. "It's a long, boring ride from here to there. I think it's important that you stop and refresh."

"We already have a hotel booked." Jess laid a hand on her father's arm and stood on tiptoe to give him a kiss on the cheek. "We'll be fine." She didn't tell him that they also had a reservation in Gillette and another in Sheridan. Rapid City was six hours away, but they didn't want to be chained to a schedule. If the Wyoming border called to them, they had no reason to stop. The late June day stretched out before them, sunny and bright, and the road seemed to whisper a welcome.

"We're good, Grandpa. We've got two drivers." Max held up the car keys and gave them a happy jingle.

Henry looked alarmed. "You're not letting him drive first, are you?"

"He has his learner's permit," Anna reminded her husband before folding Jessica into a hug. "Max is a *great* driver." For Jess's ears only she said, "Be safe. Have fun. Keep us updated, or I may have to commit your father, okay?"

"Promise." Jess squeezed Anna, hoping that her stepmother could feel the affection in her embrace. "Can't guarantee we'll call every day, but Gabe will text emojis non-stop. You'll block my number before the end of the trip."

"Oh, I doubt that." Anna laughed.

"I'll send you the dancing grandmas GIF." Gabe circled his arms and wiggled his hips in a bad impression of an equally bad dance move.

"What's a GIF?"

"Grandma." He rolled his eyes but wrapped her in a hug all the same, smacking her cheek with a kiss when she offered it to him. "Love you."

"Love you too, buddy." As Jess watched, Anna cupped her grandson's face in her hands and blinked back a tear. But Gabe couldn't tolerate the affection long, and after a second he had slipped out of her reach and was climbing into the backseat of the car where his stuffed animals and *PAW Patrol* books beckoned.

"Twenty bucks says we don't make it to the South Dakota border before he asks: 'Are we there yet?' "

Jess batted away Max's outstretched hand. "I don't bet, but you'd go down if I did. I don't think he'll make it to the edge of town."

"I can't believe you're doing this," Henry said, throwing his arm around Max's shoulders. "What an adventure."

It was an adventure indeed. After the dust had settled and Meredith's trial was over, they all felt ready for a fresh start. Jess's first instinct was to reach out to Gabe's grandmother. Unfortunately, when Larissa Tate heard why Jess was calling, she hung up and refused to answer any subsequent calls. Jess was glad that she had chosen not to tell Gabe what she planned to do. Maybe someday Larissa would change her mind. Or when Gabe was older he'd have a stable enough foundation to understand that family isn't always determined by blood. It's born in tender moments, refined by fire, strengthened by the kind of love that knows no beginning or end.

Larissa Tate may have rejected Jessica's invitation, but Brian and Grace Munroe didn't. It wasn't as easy to locate them as Jess hoped it would be. Meredith's files on the children she placed through Initium Novum were spare at best. All the adoptions were closed, the families seemingly grateful for the no-strings-attached arrangement. But Deputy Mullen had fought hard for them. He worked with the personnel at Eagle Ridge to determine where LaShonna had given birth and when it had happened and who was there. It took months, but he found them.

"LaShonna's baby is their one and only. They seem like a really sweet couple," he said when he handed over their contact information to Jess. A telephone number, full names, and even an address. They lived in a little town in the heart of Idaho.

Jess could hardly speak. She was holding in her hand a ticket. A hope. A wish that beat fragile wings against her chest. What would they say? They were the last connection Jessica had to any of Gabe's blood relatives. She was both terrified that they would reject her advances and fearful that they wouldn't. This was an entirely brave new world for her.

When Jess finally summoned the courage to call, Grace Munroe listened in silence to her fumbling attempts at an explanation.

Even in her own ears the story sounded impossible. Insane. But when Jess was all done and finally waited with her breath lodged firmly in the back of her throat, it became apparent that Grace was crying. She just didn't know if they were horrified tears or happy tears until Grace exclaimed: "I can't believe Isabella has a brother!"

Jess bit back her own sob.

This was right. It's what Evan would have wanted. And LaShonna, too.

Isabella Lynne Munroe had brown eyes and brown curls and a button nose just like her big brother. She was about to celebrate her first birthday on July 2, and her entire family was going to be there to help her blow out the candles. It was hard for Jessica to believe. Not because it was happening, but because she didn't just allow it, she *longed* for it. A year ago she would have never understood how important it was to hold the ones she loved loosely. To accept that they were all a part of a tapestry much larger and more beautiful than she could have ever imagined. And the lives that intersected her own, that wove in the spaces between her and her children, were sacred. They needed one another. They were better together.

"I hope we like them," Max said as he

headed toward the driver's seat. "What if the Munroes are crazy people? Aren't there a lot of militias in Idaho?"

"They seem like wonderful people," Jess said.

"How would you know?"

"We're Facebook friends. Everybody knows that people are their truest selves on Facebook."

Even Henry laughed.

They pulled away with the windows down and Jess leaning out of the passenger side to wave as they disappeared around the corner. Max was in the driver's seat, hands on the wheel at the perfect ten and two, just like his grandfather. And his father, too. Jess studied her son's profile and felt a lump rise in her throat. Sometimes she missed Evan so much she felt like she couldn't breathe. But she could. The air was scented with the glossy tang of geraniums in bloom and rain that had fallen the night before. The sun was orange behind them, spilling light all along the way.

ACKNOWLEDGMENTS

Acknowledgments are always difficult to write, but after doing it eight times you'd think I'd have learned a thing or two. And yet here I sit, overwhelmed while I reflect on the creation of *You Were Always Mine.*

This book is the most personal thing I've ever penned. As a mother of children biological, adopted, and gone before I ever had a chance to hold them, I wanted to write a story that was both a compelling read and a compassionate, respectful, honest exploration of the many different sides of motherhood and adoption. I've been a mom for fifteen years, but will probably always find this topic to be fraught with deep emotions: love, fear, hope, inadequacy, longing, joy, loss, and so much more. As mothers (and as women who participate in the act of mothering by teaching, mentoring, befriending, and in many other ways impacting the lives of children) we are well versed in feelings of doubt and guilt, and it is my hope that this book whispers even a little inspiration: *Keep loving. Keep fighting. Keep doing the hard things that you know are good. Link arms, friends. Stand in the gap, fill the empty spaces. Rise up and fight for everyone's children, for those who are hurting and suffering and lost. They're all our kids and we all belong together.*

As I blaze my own path as a mother and an author, I have had so many people link arms with me, and I am beyond grateful to each and every one of them. Thanks to friend and fellow adoptive mom Nikolyn Kredit for planting the seed that grew into this story. Big bear hugs to Darcie Van Voorst, Juliana Else, Katrina Ten Napel, and Katie Nice, who keep me sane, offer the best advice, and make me laugh. Our social worker Heather Jackson made a bigger impact on our family than she'll ever know. And of course, the birth mothers and foster moms who are a part of our story are among the best and most beautiful people I know. Thank you for trusting us.

In the writing realm, I'm eternally grateful to my Tall Poppy sisters. Thanks for being such good friends and advocates. Danielle

Egan-Miller has been my faithful agent for nearly a decade now, and like fine wine our partnership only gets better with age. Editor Daniella Wexler and the entire team at Atria Books (Mirtha Pena, Kayley Hoffman, Bianca Salvant, and everyone else behind the scenes) have been amazing champions and cheerleaders. I'm so humbled to be supported by such a spectacular group of people.

I know I'm forgetting someone and it breaks my heart to do so, but be well assured of my gratitude and love. And please don't take it personally. I routinely call my children by the wrong name, so clearly my memory is not everything it should be.

As always and forever, all my love to my favorite people, Aaron, Joseph, Isaac, Judah, Eve, and Matthias, as well as Mom and Dad and Amber and Andrew, who are our support system and safety net. And our dear BC Baarts and Kampens. I adore you all. None of this is possible without you.

Finally, reader, I write for you. I hope in some small way you were entertained, maybe even moved, by this story. Thanks for reading and for broadening your perspective by climbing inside another person's skin and walking around in it. Don't ever stop expanding your capacity for compassion.

xoxo
— Nicole

ABOUT THE AUTHOR

Nicole Baart is the mother of five children from four different countries. The cofounder of a non-profit organization, One Body One Hope, she lives in a small town in Iowa. She is the author of eight previous novels, including *Little Broken Things* and *The Beautiful Daughters.* Learn more at Nicole Baart.com.